GOBBELINO LONDON & A COLLISION OF CATASTROPHES

GOBBELINO LONDON, PI
BOOK SEVEN

KIM M. WATT

For further information contact www.kmwatt.com

Cover design: Monika McFarland, www.ampersandbookcovers.com

Editor: Lynda Dietz, www.easyreaderediting.com

ISBN ePub: 978-1-7385854-4-1

ISBN Ingrams paperback: 978-1-7385854-6-5

ISBN KDP paperback: 978-1-7385854-5-8

First Edition July 2023

10 9 8 7 6 5 4 3 2 1

To Sylvie
Who believed in my stories
Even before I did.
And still does.

CONTENTS

LEEDS HAS TEETH

THERE COMES A TIME IN EVERY CAT'S LIFE WHEN ONE NEEDS TO take stock of where one is, and where one's road is leading. To meditate on times past and times yet to come, and to consider paths to be taken or not, dreams to be lived or shared or laid to rest.

Or so I've heard. Mostly people keep killing me off before I get to such a point, and since that seemed unlikely to change anytime soon, I figured I might as well get a jump on things in this life. If I had time, obviously, since right at that moment I was being forcibly removed from my body, thrust across a bone-chilling void, and deposited unceremoniously at the feet of a sorcerer.

Which was made only marginally less alarming by the fact I knew the sorcerer concerned.

"I'm done," I said.

Ms Jones looked at me, eyebrows raised.

"All this. Out-of-body experiences. Every Folk and their familiar trying to kill me. I resign."

She waited, although one corner of her mouth quirked up slightly.

"This was never in the job description," I pointed out.

She folded her long-fingered hands together, her elbows resting on her knees. She was sitting on a roughly hewn stone bench and wearing bright blue Doc Martens that were luminous against the dull grey floor. "I wasn't aware you had a job description," she said.

"Well, if I did, it wouldn't include this," I said, and pressed my claws experimentally into the flagstones beneath me. They didn't feel quite right. They *looked* alright, if a bit damp and grimy, and with dubious things growing in the cracks, but there seemed to be a strange give to them. Maybe they were actually some sort of sorcerer laminate flooring. It was hard to be sure of anything in the smoky, uncertain light of the sconces on the wall. "Where are we?"

"You tell me. It's your subconscious."

"It is not," I said. "You're the one dragged me out of my body."

She gave a little *maybe* sort of shrug. "I called you. I didn't *bring* you anywhere. You're just seeing what you expect to see, and so am I." She looked around, and while I wasn't a fan of the whole stone dungeon and squidgy floor vibe I had going on, I very much did not want to know what a sorcerer's subconscious meeting place looked like.

"So?" I said, before she could decide to share any details with me. "What is it?"

She turned her gaze back to me. Her eyes were dark and distant in the low light, but I'd seen them as pale and clear as spring frosts, and I don't think either were the truth of her. I could smell that truth, though, even in my own subconscious or wherever we were. Ancient and deep-rooted and vaguely feral. "You took your time leaving wherever you were," she said.

"Whitby," I said. "And not my fault. We tried to leave, but there were Black Dogs keeping us in, and then there was a whole thing with Reaper Leeds and the pirate captain and the Sea Witch, plus there was a kraken and this bloody mermaid who Callum still owes a favour to, and don't forget the damn parrot—"

She held up a hand. "Sorry I asked. I can't keep you here too long—"

"Why?" I asked. "Where are you? What's happening? We've—"

"Because at some point you won't be able to go back into your body," she said, which made all my questions about where our missing sorcerer had been hiding out – and what an ancient, powerful being had to hide from in the first place – suddenly very unimportant.

"Hurry up, then," I said, and she gave a very un-sorcerer-like snort.

"I need to know the situation in Leeds," she said. "And I need you to locate Malcolm."

"We already did that, then he ran off with a pack of weres."

"So go and find where he's run to. I need you to keep hold of him for me."

"*Why?*" I still couldn't understand why a creature who reeked of power, who could make reality dance and physics shudder, had such a thing for a balding, pot-bellied dentist with bad teeth.

"Because you I can find easily. Him, I currently can't. The weres must be keeping him hidden, and I'm not about to trek about chasing down every were pack in the north when you can just get on and finish the job you started."

I wrinkled my snout, but it didn't seem to be the time to argue. Not when I was at risk of becoming permanently disembodied. "Alright. But we've got our own things on, you know. Gerry's missing. And Gertrude's in trouble with Grim Reaper Yorkshire, so we need to check on her, and—"

"Why's she in trouble?" Ms Jones frowned at me. "And why was she in Whitby? She's Reaper Leeds, isn't she?"

"Mini-break. But at least *she* didn't lose her scythe—"

"Someone lost their scythe?"

"I'm trying to tell you, if you'd let me finish—"

The sorcerer got up abruptly. "No time. I'll be in touch. Find Malcolm."

I opened my mouth to say that a *little* help might be nice, maybe some sort of charmed wolf whistle or magical were muzzle or something, but it was too late. The terrible, bone-chilling grip of the void laid into my bones, and the dungeon was torn away from me, but not before I saw Ms Jones give the smallest grimace of pain, as if standing had hurt more than she'd expected.

But before I could wonder what secrets our friendly local sorcerer was hiding, I thudded back into my body with a stomach-churning crash. For one horrified moment I thought I was going to bounce straight back out again, that I'd already been away too long and my body had moved on without me. My paws didn't seem to fit right, and my ears were too cold, and I was being jostled so violently that losing my grip on my skin seemed entirely likely. I blinked around, trying to get the world to make sense, and realised I was being carted at a sprint across a frozen field of churned earth, clutched to Callum's chest by one of his hands while he flailed wildly for balance with the other.

A sharp, hungry *crack* rang out behind us, and Callum yelled, "*Don't shoot!*"

"*What?*" I squawked, and tried to twist in his grip so I could see what was going on. All I encountered were the bright eyes of Green Snake, staring at me with alarm. Or possibly disapproval, or delight, or who knew. Snakes don't give much away.

Another *crack* snapped behind us, and now I could hear

dogs barking. Callum hit a gate and scrambled over it onto a weed-strewn, rutted track sandwiched between drystone walls, half crushing me as he slipped on the rungs.

"Watch it!"

"You want to be dog dinner?" he managed, stumbling as he landed then taking off in a gangly, long-legged sprint as the clamour of the dogs reached the gate. I still couldn't see them past his flapping coat, but I decided I was better not to. There was a lot of snarling and *I will tear your throat out* barking going on that didn't sound like empty threats.

"*And stay out!*" a woman bellowed behind us, and punctuated it with another potshot from whatever firearm she was carting. Callum yelped and ducked, stumbled, managed a few more unsteady strides, then his borrowed wellies slipped on the frozen ground and he went down hard, rolling into a clumsy half-somersault. I threw myself clear, skittering over the hard ruts and coming to a stop next to a clump of nettles growing out of the base of the wall. I peered back down the lane and spotted a head topped with a soft, faded purple felt hat glaring over the gate at us. Multicoloured crocheted flowers decorated the hat, and under it all I could see was a red nose and an angry scowl. A couple of dogs had their heads through the rungs, and two more had their paws up on the top. Their barking went up a notch when they spotted me, but they didn't seem to be about to come after us.

"Bloody cat people," the woman hissed, and rested what looked an awful lot like a rifle on the top bar of the gate.

"We're going," Callum shouted, scrambling to his feet. He'd torn the knee of his jeans and his hands were grazed. "I just wanted to use your phone!"

"Likely story," she shouted back. "I know your type! Preying on defenceless old ladies!"

"I'd hate to see what she calls *un*-defenceless," I muttered.

"Our car's broken down," Callum called. He was backing

away up the track, so he obviously wasn't holding out much hope of being invited in for a cuppa. Which, as I recalled, had been one of the motivations for walking to the creepy farmhouse we'd spotted from the road as the reluctant February dawn had spread across the moors. We'd made it to the gate that led into the yard before Ms Jones had unceremoniously summoned me, so I'd evidently missed all the fun. "I've lost my phone, and it looks like snow."

"Oh, boo hoo," the woman shouted. "Go tell your sob story to someone who cares, and *get off my land!*" She punctuated that by swinging the gun in our direction, and Callum turned and bolted back up the track, wellies flopping wildly.

I decided I definitely needed to revisit the bit where I was rethinking my life choices, but it was going to have to wait. I sprinted after him.

OUR CAR WAS where we'd left it, pulled into a lay-by not far from the entrance to the farm track, but still far enough for cold paws and an out-of-body experience. We'd pulled into it last night when the engine had started making unhappy noises and even worse smells, and it had steadfastly refused to start ever since. Traffic had been non-existent, and our decrepit phone had no signal out here, even if we'd known a car doctor to call.

I scrambled to Callum's shoulder as we walked, coughing pointedly when he fished his cigarettes out of his pocket and paused to light one. Other than the murderous old lady's dilapidated house, dribbling smoke from one chimney and with a sagging, mossy roof as patchy as a shedding snake, there were no other buildings in sight. No cattle either, and no sheep, just the curling tails of old stone walls to divide the rocky fields. It was a scoured and disinterested landscape, snow coating the heather and spackling the black skeletons of stunted, wind-twisted trees, griming the tumbled rock and hard edges of the land. There was no colour anywhere I looked, the world turned two-tone under a low grey sky and the snow just making things starker rather than softening it. I couldn't even see any birds circling to pick our bones after we died of exposure.

All of which was either the fault of the weres, the mermaids, or the sorcerer. Or possibly the troll. I hadn't decided yet.

"What happened?" Callum asked me, once he'd sucked down a couple of lungfuls of smoke. "Was it Ms Jones?"

"As no one else seems inclined to drag me out of my skin, that's a good guess."

"And?"

"And she still wants her dentist," I said with a sigh.

"That's all she said?"

"Pretty much. She threw me back pretty quickly. But apparently she can't find him because the weres are hiding him, so we have to." I looked at Green Snake as he poked his head out of Callum's pocket to look at me. "So now we have to find Dental Dan as well as Gerry."

"His name's Malcolm. Or Walker. Not Dental Dan."

"He should be called Pain in My Tail."

Callum made a non-committal sound and unlocked the car so that he could pop the bonnet. It had been running perfectly when we left Whitby, but I had a feeling that was due to a little non-typical mechanical help from someone at the boarding house we'd stayed at. Evidently non-lasting help, too.

"I'm thinking about my life choices," I told Callum, jumping to the ground.

"Are you?" he asked, without much interest. He propped

the bonnet up, and poked around inside with more hope than expertise.

"I don't want to be a PI anymore."

He straightened up and looked at me. "Oh?"

"It's bad for my health. Stress levels. All that sort of thing." I inspected the soft black fur on my flanks, which was flecked with white dust. "I think I'm having an allergic reaction to it."

"That might be from the salt water."

"Also something I want to avoid in the future."

"It wasn't so bad."

"I'm flaky!"

"I wouldn't say flaky," Callum said, leaning against the front of the car and puffing smoke into the chill air. "A bit fickle, maybe."

I glared at him, and he grinned. The thin, keen wind rumpled his mess of copper-streaked hair and pinched my ears, and the winter sun was small and pale and ineffectual as it drifted across the edge of the sky.

"Have you fixed it yet?" I demanded.

"Would I have gone to get shot at if I could?"

"You're not even trying."

"Would you like a go?"

"Don't be a parsnip. I haven't got thumbs." I twitched my ears at him pointedly.

"If only that was the only thing you didn't have," he said, and I narrowed my eyes at him.

"Shall I point out who saved you from the kraken?"

"Green Snake?"

The snake in question bobbed his head, and I huffed. "Well, other than him."

"Gertrude?"

"I really am done," I said.

"Honestly, I'd like a change myself," he said, staring down the empty road. "It's been a *year*."

It had been a year. It had started with a simple enough job: find a stolen book. Only that had very quickly gone pumpkin-shaped – pumpkins with tentacles and teeth – when it turned out that the book was a Book of Power, the client was our sorcerer Ms Jones, and the thief was her very human Dental Dan ex-boyfriend, more technically known as Malcolm Walker. The book had tried to turn reality inside out, and I'd finally dumped it in the void that runs within all things, the Inbetween, which cats use to move from one place to another without bothering about annoying things like doors and walls and so on. That had almost got me monster munched, since the void is anything but empty, and had resulted in us being somewhat indebted to a very displeased Ms Jones, who had had a huge chunk of her power tied up in the book. Hence my being subjected to out-of-body experiences at alarmingly regular intervals.

Then there had been the outbreak of undeadness in Leeds, including Callum getting all *grrr, brainzzz* on us for a bit, which just took going undercover a bit too far. We'd fixed that with help from Ms Jones and Gertrude the reaper, as well as a couple of cats, one Watch, one not. The Watch being the cat council who keep the human and Folk worlds separated, and also the ones most likely to ensure I *did* get monster munched in the Inbetween, as they had it in for me for reasons I couldn't quite recall, and had already fed me to the beasts at least once. As it happened, though, Claudia of the lovely mismatched eyes might've been Watch, but she had a slightly more lenient attitude toward me than seemed to be typical.

We'd followed the zombie hunt up with a unicorn hunt in the pocket town of Dimly, which had ended in a pitched battle in an underground warehouse against Callum's sister and a bunch of goons, since it turned out he wasn't quite as clueless a human as he liked to pretend. He was a North, a human family that had run the north of the country with a mix of muscle, money, and magic for centuries. He just wasn't so keen on the whole thing. Unlike his sister.

Then more of Callum's past had come calling, in the form of his dead bestie who turned out not to be dead, and whose magician dad, with the help of some necromancers, had tried to pull an ancient god through from another realm to basically rule the world. Well, mostly the magician wanted his son back, but the necromancers definitely wanted to rule the world. And we'd kicked *that* in the teeth too, which should have earned us a bit of a break, but had instead landed us dealing with hairy bloody werewolves and trying to find Walker. We'd found him, but not Ms Jones, who was currently missing along with Claudia, and then we'd had to flee Leeds before things got really dicey.

I'm not sure what scale of *dicey* we were using anymore. Anything less than *imminent annihilation* was starting to seem pretty stress-free.

Anyhow, fleeing had got us to Whitby, which should have been a quiet little backwater to recoup in, but instead mermaids had stolen Gertrude's girlfriend; the drowned dead had stolen three other reapers *and* their scythes, which was unlikely to be a good thing; Callum had ended up indebted to a mermaid; a Sea Witch had got the hump and sicced a kraken on us, and I'd had to sort the whole lot out again. Well, with help. I'm exceptional, not super-cat.

And now we were meant to be on the way back to Leeds to look for a missing friend, but were instead sitting by the side of a narrow, empty road high in the North Yorkshire Moors while our old car collected little drifts of blown snow and we worked on our frostbite. I'd like to say I expected more from life, but it all felt pretty much situation normal.

"Try it again," I said to Callum. "Maybe it just needed a rest."

"For the whole night?" Callum looked dubiously at the engine, but ground his cigarette out in the snow and tucked the butt back into the pack before slamming the bonnet down. "And it can't exactly have overheated in this weather."

"Under-heated?" I suggested.

"Pretty sure that's not an issue for engines."

"Is for me," I said, jumping past him into the driver's seat then across to the passenger side. Callum swung in after me, tucking his long old coat around him. It still smelled faintly of seaweed, and I really wished we'd been able to leave it with the mermaid. He patted the dashboard encouragingly, pulled at a knob, pumped a couple of pedals, then tried the key again. The engine hiccoughed and gave the groan of a dying buffalo.

"Don't think it was rest it needed," he said.

"Call the AA?"

He gave me an amused look. "Gobs, we can barely keep fuel in it. How d'you think we can afford AA?"

"I thought it was like a charity thing. You know, meet in church basements then go and tow cars as penance or something."

He snorted. "Different AA. We need the Automobile Association, not the one you're thinking of. And the car AA definitely charges."

"Could we try the other one then? Since they tow cars anyway?"

"They don't have anything to do with cars."

"That's very misleading."

He started to say something, then shook his head and took a packet of cat treats from the open front of the glove-box. "Snack?"

"Obviously."

🐍

THE DYING of exposure outcome was starting to look more and more like a possibility, and despite the empty skies I was actively watching for circling vultures when a tractor appeared on the road, puffing and grumbling and jolting along the tarmac. It pulled in behind us in answer to Callum's enthusiastic waving, and the short, muscular woman who swung out looked at me, curled under Callum's spare jumper on the front seat with Green Snake just visible peering out of cover, then at Callum, shivering in his hoody and coat and a very bright striped scarf as he asked if we could get a lift to a bus stop or something. She grunted, pulled her wool hat tighter down over her ears, opened the car's bonnet, clattered around for a moment, then pointed at the driver's seat.

"I already tried," Callum started, turning the key, and the car bellowed into life with something like alarm, as if it had already resigned itself to a cold death and wasn't sure about being revived so unceremoniously.

The woman clattered something else, making the car rev and belch black smoke, then slammed the bonnet, nodded at Callum, nodded at me, and retreated into the enclosed cab of the tractor. A snatch of rousing opera drifted out as she opened the door, then was cut off as she closed it after her. A moment later she was rumbling away down the road again, not looking back.

Callum revved the engine cautiously, then wrestled the car into gear and pulled back out onto the empty road.

"Are there car magicians?" I asked, as the heater started to dribble marginally above-freezing air. "Because I think she was a car magician."

"Possibly," Callum agreed. He was hunched over the

wheel as if he suspected the engine might fail if he relaxed for an instant.

"Much better than the AA."

"Cheaper, too," he said.

"I still think we should have tried the church basement one. I mean, it'd be a challenge for them, right?"

"You're a challenge for anyone," he said, more to himself than to me, and I decided to take it as a compliment. My nose was still too cold for arguing.

The car kept going, although Callum was so anxious about it that we almost ran out of fuel before he finally stopped. Which wasn't *that* different from our usual situation, to be honest, but this time it was due to lack of confidence in the car restarting rather than our normal lack of funds. Being pirate ship crew in Whitby had been surprisingly lucrative by our standards – at least until the boat sank. Tips had been good and accommodation provided, and other than the mermaids and hungry kraken, it had been a good job. It was amazing how often the PI trade paid in gnome-made fungi drizzle scones or pixie-crafted carnivorous pens, none of which exactly paid the rent.

Callum rushed out of the garage and back to the car with a takeaway cup of tepid tea in one hand and a couple of promisingly greasy paper bags in the other. He wedged the cup between the seats, dumped the paper bags unceremoniously on top of Green Snake and myself, and grabbed the key, looking at me.

"At least we're at a garage," I said. "Seems like a good place to break down."

He gave a small nod, closed his eyes, and turned the key. The car grumbled into life with a few less coughs and splutters than usual, and we looked at each other.

"Car magician," I said, and we pulled back onto the road, seeking out the quieter routes down toward Leeds as the wide bleak expanses of the moors crumbled to tame fields and old stone towns, then to the scraped swathes of subdivisions and industrial estates and the endless sprawl of the cities, resolutely, furiously human.

I thought it would feel safer than the hostile expanse of moors and the press of the endless, hungry sea behind us, but it didn't.

There were too many things waiting for us in Leeds, and most of them had teeth.

2

A HERO'S RETURN

EVEN IF OUR APARTMENT HADN'T BEEN A LITTLE BIT WONKY since the Book of Power incident, with mysterious gaps that appeared in the walls and whistled into other dimensions for a night or so before they vanished again, the last time we'd been home something had tried to shove me straight into a void. I wasn't sure if it was the Inbetween, the same void the Watch keep trying to shove me into, or if it was a different void and someone else doing the shoving, but either way I wasn't keen for a repeat. Going back to the apartment seemed like a bad plan when there could still be a trap waiting for me. Plus our landlady would *definitely* be waiting, along with her large and expressionless sons. We hadn't exactly had time to give notice, and she wasn't the sort of person we could say, *sorry, something came up* to. Or we could, but then her large expressionless sons would express her displeasure for her.

But we weren't heading back to Leeds because it was home. We were heading back because, among other things, we had reason to believe that our friend Gerry was in trouble. Our last contact with the troll mayor of Dimly had been a weird phone call which someone else had evidently forced him to make, and before leaving Whitby we'd had a message we thought was from Poppy, one of his young troll charges. It had been as cryptic as a young troll with a shaky grasp of English (but still a better grasp than most trolls, who tend to consider *fight me* to be a complete conversation) could make it, so we weren't actually sure it was about Gerry. But he and Poppy were two of a very small handful of people who weren't actively trying to kill us (again, unusual for trolls), so we couldn't ignore it. Gerry had sent us to Whitby to keep us safe, and if he was in trouble then it was probably because of us.

Walking into Dimly, a magic-ridden pocket town nestled into the outskirts of Leeds like a particularly virulent boil, was a risky proposition at the best of times, and this was about three worlds removed from the best of times, given the aforementioned weres, magicians, and other hazards. So heading straight there to look for Gerry was occupying a similar spot to a return to our apartment on the list of bad options we had.

Callum poked our new phone as we stopped at a set of lights, Leeds growing up around us in a snarling mix of old, stained brick buildings and a rush of glossy regeneration, all resting uneasily next to each other along the half-smothered edges of the river Aire. It was a new phone as in we'd had to buy it to replace the one a kraken was presumably using to decorate its nest, which we'd bought to replace one a Black Dog had stolen after chasing us into the sea. Which encapsulated our Whitby experience, really, but anyhow – in all other senses the phone was ancient, and since we always had pay-as-you-go we no longer had our usual number. However, we did still have most of our contacts, since there's phone magic as well as car magic. Now Callum put it on speakerphone as we rolled on, the roads feeling broad yet crowded after Whitby, the press of buildings and people too cluttered and loud, the sky too low and claustrophobic.

"You've reached Gerry, mayor of Dimly," the phone told us. *"Please leave a message and I'll—"*

Callum cut it off with a sigh. "Still nothing."

"Have you left a message?" I asked. "Maybe he's not answering because it's a different number. Screening his calls or whatever." I don't think I really believed it, but I also didn't want to believe anyone could really threaten a full-size troll who looked like he was hewn out of Yorkstone, even one with a penchant for twinsets and nice hats. Certainly no more than I wanted to believe certain sorcerers actually needed to hide from anything.

"I don't want to," Callum said, fishing in his pocket. He came up with a piece of Whitby jet, black and dully glossy. He rolled it in his fingers as he drove, and I could smell the sea on it. "It could make things worse for him."

We were both silent for a moment. We had no way to contact Poppy, and even if we had, I don't think I'd have wanted to. The more she stayed out of this, the better. She might not be as eloquent as the mayor, but I trusted her more than I trusted pretty much anyone in this world. It was hard not to have faith in someone who believed so firmly in the goodness in all abandoned things.

"Emma?" I suggested finally. "Maybe Gertrude's back. And we did say we'd contact her as soon as we got to Leeds."

"True," Callum admitted. Emma was Gertrude the reaper's human partner, who had been kidnapped by the Sea Witch. We'd got her back, but Gertrude had been marched off by her boss for whatever the reaper equivalent of detention was, as punishment for going on a mini-break. Which seemed a bit harsh to me. It was only Whitby, after all.

Callum scrolled through the phone and hit another

number. It rang briefly, then someone picked it up with a bright, "Hello?"

"Emma?" Callum said.

"Yes, you've reached Dead Good Cafe," she said, in those same bright tones.

"Emma? It's Callum—"

"No," she said immediately.

"What?"

"You can't come here. I know I said to, but Gertrude's still not back, and no one will tell me when she will be, and I can't risk bringing any trouble here." There was a tightness in her voice, but no hesitation. "I'm sorry."

"That's fine," Callum said. "We understand. Are you okay, though?"

There was a pause that went on for just a moment too long, then she said, "I will be. Sorry." The phone clicked off. We stared at each other, and a car honked irritably. Callum sped back up so that he could rush to wait at the next set of lights.

"That seems bad," I said. "Gertrude still not back?"

"It's only been a day," he said.

"Still. I thought she was just going to get a stern talking to about not leaving Leeds or something." I shifted on the threadbare seat, whiskers twitching. "What d'you think's happened?"

"I hate to think," Callum said, tucking the jet away again and taking his cigarettes out instead. "That's reaper business. I doubt we could get in the middle of it even if we wanted to."

The hair on my back popped to attention just at the thought. And if reapers weren't enough, the Dead Good Cafe also served as a foster home for baby ghouls, which was something I was happy to stay as far from the middle of as possible. "Right. So there's no point worrying about her, but we also can't stay there. So where to next? We can't just drive around all day." Or what was left of the day – the early February night was already on the way in, hastened by heavy dull clouds that crushed the city ever closer around us.

Callum hesitated, shooting me a sideways glance. "There's—"

"I am *not* going to Magic Boy's palace. Even if he has got good chicken." His dodgy magician bestie might live in a house with more spare rooms than I had spare lives, but that didn't make it safe. *Nothing* about Ifan was safe.

"That's a high degree of resistance for you." Callum lit a cigarette and rolled the window down a little to let the smoke out. I wheezed anyway, just to make the point. "No apartment, no Dimly, no Gertrude, no Ifan. Who's left?"

"Pru?" Pru had been the other cat that had helped us deal with zombies, as well as a couple of other sticky situations. She was as fearless as she was hairless, and also pretty much my favourite cat of the moment.

"Her human doesn't know anything about Folk," Callum said. "We can't risk it."

"Not to stay. But what if we just asked Pru if she knew what was going on? If she'd heard about Gerry, or our apartment, or anything?"

Callum looked at me. "A reaper helped us, and now she's been hauled off by her authorities. A troll helped us and is now possibly missing. Claudia's Watch, but she helped us, and she's gone too. And Ms Jones. What d'you think might happen to Pru's human if we go anywhere near her?"

Neither of us spoke for a long moment, while Leeds rushed and roared around us, and my back twitched and rippled with the sense of returning to the lair of a vast and hungry beast. One that I couldn't even see, but knew was there. Waiting with the sort of patience that brings down empires.

"We've got nowhere," I said.

"Welcome home," Callum replied, as the light turned green and we rolled forward with the traffic, simply to be moving.

⁓

SINCE WE COULDN'T START by finding somewhere to stay, we went with the next best – or least worst – option. Starting our search for the dentist. Not that we *hadn't* been going to get started fairly smartly, since sorcerers aren't known for their patience or leniency, but it would've been nice to feel we had a wall to put our backs to first. That didn't seem to be happening, though, and the sooner we found the dentist, the sooner we could have a sorcerer to put our backs to instead. Or to put in front of us, more to the point. So we went to the last place we thought Walker might've been, and also the last place a cat wanted to go. A were bar.

Callum leaned through the open doorway, peering into the dimness and frowning at the neon signs and two-for-one drink posters that had replaced all the old metal and wood that had been going on the last time we'd been here.

I snuffled the door frame and looked up at him. "They're not here anymore," I hissed, keeping my voice low.

"Hello?" he called, ignoring me.

"I'm telling you – there's no weres in this place." It says a lot about just how few options we had that we'd voluntarily returned to Yasmin's bar, in the dark arches of the old industrial buildings in Bradford. When we'd been here before there had been the dank, savage whiff of wolf mixed in with bright lemon cleaning stuff and a curious, light scent that spoke of open fields and bright skies and the glory of fleet, fast paws. Now all I could smell was the dull stink of stale beer and bored desire and the acrid reek of exhausted, pointless rage, half concealed by bleach and fear. It smelled like every pub everywhere.

"We need to check," Callum muttered, then raised his voice as a man approached out of the shadowed reaches of the bar, wiping his hands on his jeans. "Hello?"

"Yeah?" the man said, examining Callum. "We're not hiring."

"I'm looking for Yasmin," Callum said. "She had this place about a month ago?"

"That's when I took it on." He crossed muscled, tattooed arms over his chest. He was wearing a black T-shirt with the name of the bar emblazoned across the front, and I could smell his hair gel from here. "Saved it, really. She was running some alcohol-free thing in here, like *that* was ever going to work. Women get some weird ideas."

Callum gave him what was probably supposed to be an all-guys-here grin, but which mostly looked like he had toothache. "Yeah, weird. D'you know where she is now?"

"Nah." The man gave Callum a curious look. "Trying to punch a bit above your weight there, aren't you?"

"I'm just a friend."

"Yeah, sure. Anyway, don't bother. I tried. Reckon she must be playing for the other side." He made a regretful noise. "What a waste."

"She would quite literally eat your face," I said, and the man looked around, puzzled.

"That your phone?"

"Yeah, sorry," Callum said, nudging me with a boot. "Got a contact number or anything?"

"No. I only met her a couple of times – she insisted everything go through the estate agent. Bloody pain, it was."

"Can't imagine why," I said, avoiding Callum's light kick. "Imagine depriving herself of such company."

The man blinked and glanced around again, as if sure he'd

heard something, but not sure what. Humans know cats don't talk, so obviously it wasn't me.

"Alright," Callum said. "Thanks anyway."

"Yeah, sure. You should come back Friday, though, mate. It's ladies' night – I do it right classy, you know, two for one on the bubbly and so on. Can't miss." He gave a broad, lazy grin, and I retched so hard I actually started throwing up a hairball. The man finally looked at me properly. "Is that yours?"

"Yeah. Think he's allergic to something," Callum said.

"Something," I agreed.

"More of a dog man, myself," the man said. "Bit girly, cats, aren't they?"

Callum shrugged. "Never thought about it."

"Well, they are. You want a dog. And a decent one, you know. None of these soppy little lapdogs, or some fluffy lab or something. I've got a pitty."

Callum made a non-committal sound, and I said, "Is it called 'A Lingering Sense of Self Doubt'?"

That bit he heard, but again – I was a cat, so it couldn't have been me that said it. Callum scowled at me, and the man scowled at Callum, then said something that was anatomically impossible and also startlingly intimate, and slammed the door in our faces. I finished throwing up my hairball, then looked at Callum.

"Don't you dare move it."

"No intentions of it," he said, tucking his hands into the pockets of his coat. "Come on, my girly little kitty."

"He meant you were girly, not me," I said, trotting after him. "Although, if you want to go with the caring for one's appearance stereotype, I am a better candidate."

"Other than the dandruff."

"That's an allergic reaction."

"If you say so."

YASMIN'S BAR – or, rather, the bar that had been Yasmin's and was now a bastion of fervent masculinity – was in the centre of Bradford, a city to the west of Leeds. Once there had probably been vast tracts of forest and farmland between them, but these days they had swollen and spread to form one amorphous beast, outskirts becoming suburbs crushed between the two. Dimly was out on this side of Leeds too, a rotting tooth sending waves of infection across the Folk world. I was almost certain I could feel it, hot and fevered, at the edge of my consciousness, and I wondered what was happening in there. What had happened to Gerry, and what was waiting for us when we, inevitably, had to return.

We'd parked in front of a strip of shops beyond the train station, and we walked back without talking, the streets crowded with shoppers and workers hurrying about the place with urgent purpose. It wasn't the sort of city where anyone would worry much about a human talking to a cat – most cities weren't, when you came down to it. Everyone's just a half step away from *difference,* and the only people who really worry about it are the ones who fear they've already taken that step. But with Dimly seeping its own breed of strangeness into the world, I couldn't shake the sense that we were more visible than usual. That we weren't passing under people's attention the way we usually did, and that there'd be others out here who were actively looking for us. Leaving Whitby had left us exposed, and away from its narrow streets and wild cliffs and ancient charms I could feel the attention of others scraping at my bones.

It was a relief when Callum let us back into the car, not just to get away from the wind but from that sense of being noticed. He seemed to feel it too, because he let out a slow breath and rolled his shoulders before he started the car. The engine turned over happily again, so whatever magic the farmer had worked was still holding.

"I was really hoping not to go back to life on the streets," I said. "Being a stray has its upsides, but I'd kind of got used to not having to fight the local tom for my dinner."

"We're not at that point yet," Callum said.

"Are you sure? I'm not seeing a lot of options here."

"There's one." He pulled out of the parking spot, and I could see the skin on his knuckles white with the force of his grip.

"Such as?"

He glanced at me sideways, then looked back at the road as he indicated to join the slow flow of traffic. "Ifan."

"Have you been at the paint thinners or something? *No.* Not the magician."

Callum didn't look at me. "Ifan will know what's going on with everything. With the weres, with Dimly, with Gerry – maybe even if there's any news on the necromancers. You know this."

"We also know he almost took us out with fireballs. *Twice.* And let's not forget that oh, yes, he also likes *playing* with the godsdamned necromancers."

"It's that or nothing, Gobs. We can't go back to our flat – it'll have been rented out by now anyway, and there's no one else we can go to. We can't risk trying Pru and putting her human in danger, or anyone else, for that matter."

I thought about it. "So by going to Ifan we could put him in danger?"

"It's possible."

"I do like that idea. But still no. I'm certain he wants to turn me into cat chum, since I'm a steadying influence on you."

"Is that what you are?" Callum took Green Snake out of

his pocket and set him on the dashboard, where he immediately draped himself over a heater vent. "What d'you think?"

Green Snake tilted his head, which was helpful.

"I vote we stay out here," I said. "Even a couple of nights in the car's better than sneaky bloody magicians."

Green Snake shuddered and curled in on himself.

"I vote Ifan's," Callum said. "We *know* he's devious, so we won't let our guard down. And I don't know about you, Gobs, but I feel a bit ..." He trailed off, hesitating, and I sighed.

"Exposed?"

"Yeah. Don't know if it's just being out of Whitby or what, but it's making me jumpy."

"Me too. And I don't think it's just being out of Whitby. I mean, that's part of it, but it feels like everyone here's looking for us. And there's too many people."

Green Snake looked from one to the other of us anxiously, then finally pointed his nose at Callum. I bared my teeth at him, but he ignored me. Trust the snake to pick the magician. At one point we'd lost the bloody reptile and he'd sneaked off with Ifan. He was literally in the dodgy turnip's pocket. So who knew what angle Green Snake was playing, since a head tilt couldn't tell us much.

"There's nowhere else," Callum said. "I don't trust him, but I don't *not* trust him either, if you see what I mean."

"No," I said. "But with any luck we can make things nice and dangerous for him."

"I like how you always look on the bright side."

"It's a talent."

Callum snorted and put the indicator on, pulling across a couple of lanes of traffic and heading toward the looming threat of the magician. At least it was in the opposite direction to Dimly. I almost thought I could feel the pocket town no matter where I turned now, like feeling the heat of a fire on my fur.

Which seemed like a bad development.

CATS DON'T HAVE any innate magic, as such. Sure, we can scratch a few charms into things, and we can *shift*, stepping into the Inbetween and back out again entirely. I say *we* in the general sense. In the specific sense, I couldn't because certain Watch cats had held me in there to be chewed by the beasts that roam endlessly through the void. It had been an unpleasant way to end my last life (maybe others as well, but I couldn't remember), and it also meant that if I put a paw in the Inbetween it was likely to be bitten off. The beasts follow my scent the way I follow the whiff of frying bacon. But all cats know magic when we sniff it, and as we headed north and east, away from Bradford and away from Dimly, I patrolled the car restlessly, jumping into the back seat to peer out the back window, crossing from one side to the other, returning to the front to sit down only to get up a moment later and start again.

"Gobs, stop," Callum said the second time I jumped across his lap to put my paws up on his window, scanning the road for … something. The sorcerer's heavy, muscular bike, perhaps, parting the rain with its hungry grumble. Or a pack of weres racing the cars toward us. Or tentacles or voids or something else entirely.

"I can't help it," I said. "I can feel something coming."

"I can't feel anything," he said, lighting a cigarette from the butt of a previous one.

"No, doesn't look like it."

He gave me a sideways look, but didn't put the new

cigarette out. "We're both on edge is all. Being back here, and not being able to get in touch with anyone."

"Speaking of that, why don't we call Magic Boy rather than go straight there?"

Callum blew smoke toward the gap in the window, which merely served to swirl it back around the car. "I was thinking surprise might be better than giving him time to prepare."

I stared at him. "So you're not entirely clueless."

"Evidently. Now stop climbing all over the bloody place before I get stopped for having an animal loose in the car."

"I hear jail cells are pretty warm," I said, going back to my seat. "All meals provided, too."

"Let's keep that as plan C."

"Aren't we already on about plan H?"

"We can circle back if needed."

I WAS LEANING PRETTY hard toward circling back when we pulled into a wide, tree-studded street on the north side of Leeds and puttered softly down it. It was lined with high walls and *not for you, commoner* gates, and the only cars we passed that weren't delivery vans looked like they cost the equivalent of a small town's annual budget.

"Are you sure we can't revisit the jail idea?"

"I'm not getting myself arrested just because you hate Ifan," Callum said, pulling up at a set of tall, solid metal gates with rust streaks marring the pale green paint. Definitely not up to neighbourhood code, that.

"I don't hate him. I simply object to how many times he's popped up in the middle of things that have almost got us killed. It's a pattern, you know?"

"Do you really want to end up at the RSPCA or something? Because they won't put you in a cell with me." He wound his window down and pushed the intercom.

"Not even just for the night? You could fake a drunk and disorderly and I'll be your emotional support animal."

"I'm not getting arrested," Callum said, more sharply than was required, and the gates blew open in front of us so hard that they smashed into the walls to either side. One popped off a hinge with a screech of torn metal, and the other rebounded, flying back to latch itself closed again. Beyond the open side I could see the potholed gravel drive curling up to the front of the house, and running down it a slim man in jeans and a T-shirt, his feet and the smooth dark skin of his forearms bare. He threw out a hand and the one intact gate opened again, a little more circumspectly this time.

"Last chance," I said. "Quick, before he blows our tyres out or something."

"I'm almost sure this is a better option than lurking about the streets of Leeds waiting for something to eat us," Callum said, watching Ifan stop mid-run and wave enthusiastically, beckoning us in.

"*Almost* seems risky," I said.

3

SAFE, ISH

CALLUM PULLED FORWARD THROUGH THE GATES, AND AS WE passed them a shiver ran over my spine. Somewhere on the edge of hearing I caught a small, faint *snap,* and suddenly the constant pressure of Dimly was gone, like a splinter that had been worming its way deeper into a paw and growing ever hotter had just up and vanished. The sense of being exposed, of being *noticeable,* went with it, and as the gates swung shut again in dutiful response to another of Ifan's waves (the one with the broken hinge leaning somewhat drunkenly against its partner and leaving a little gap at the bottom where they met), I took a breath that was suddenly easier than any since we'd left Whitby. Maybe even before.

And I did *not* like it.

"Callum!" Ifan grabbed the driver's side door and wrestled it open, looking for a moment as if he were about to fling himself in, then stepped back like a chauffeur instead and bent to look inside. "And Gobs. You're okay."

"Pretty much," Callum said. "Should I park?" He pointed through the windscreen at the gravel turning circle at the end of the drive, pocked with muddy potholes. The house stared blandly back at us through its two storeys of tall windows, the door lying open onto a dim-lit foyer full of shadows. The winter skeletons of ivy crawled over the walls, and a huge old Bentley rusted quietly near the garage. Nothing had changed, not even the mouldy, non-functioning fountain in the middle of the turning circle or the fluffy heads of dead weeds all over the gardens.

"Love what you've done with the place," I said to Ifan, and he flashed me a quick, easy grin.

"It's winter. Give me a couple of months with no one trying to fling me through summoning circles or needing interference run with weres and I'll have it looking croquet-ready."

"No one *needed*—" I started, and Callum tugged on the door pointedly.

"I'm going to park."

Ifan let the door go, and we rumbled up the drive with him jogging behind us, keeping to the grass in his bare feet. I hoped he got frostbite.

"*Needed?* He's acting like he saved us from weres!"

"He did say that he thought that's what he was doing."

"Absolute rotten bloody beetroot with worms in."

"Possibly," Callum said, parking with the nose of the car to the Bentley, so that there was still a clear route to the garage. "But did you feel it as we came in?"

"Obviously. He's strengthened the charms."

"And if even I can feel it, it's by a *lot*," Callum said. "We're safe as we can be in here."

"Sure. Until we want to get out."

Callum made a face that suggested he'd already thought of that but was trying to ignore it, and then Ifan was hauling his door open again. This time the magician leaned in and grabbed Callum's arm, pulling him out and straight into a hug. I jumped out onto the gravel, Green Snake slithering after me, as Callum patted the shorter man on the back a little awkwardly. "Um, hi," he said.

Ifan stepped back, one hand still on Callum's arm, grinned, and said, "Tea?"

"Oh God, *please.*"

The two men turned toward the house, Ifan slinging one arm over Callum's shoulders, and I looked at Green Snake.

"And just like that. One mention of tea and he's anyone's."

Green Snake tilted his head, presumably in agreement.

"Hey," Ifan called from the front door. "I just bought some fresh salmon this morning. Fancy it?"

"*Yes,*" I said, and bolted after them.

Look, we've all got our price.

THE HOUSE DIDN'T LOOK that much different inside, either. The freaky taxidermy army was still in residence in the foyer, hawks gliding on invisible strings above the stairs that curled up to the next floor, and slightly threadbare foxes and deer and rabbits were frozen along the walls as if interrupted in the middle of some secretive zombie forest dance. The biggest change was that the overstuffed living room we passed through on the way to the kitchen looked a little less overstuffed, with just a couple of big sofas left in it, and the stridently floral wallpaper had been painted over. An over-sized TV on one wall was playing the news on mute, and a fire rumbled in a log burner that had taken over from the open hearth.

Ifan led the way through to the kitchen, which was still all black and chrome and slick surfaces, and flicked the kettle on. Callum had picked Green Snake up when we came inside, and now he set him on top of the kitchen island. I jumped to one of the stools and looked around suspiciously.

A pizza box rested next to the back door, and an unwashed blender jug was sitting in the sink with green stuff smearing its sides. It could've been some arcane potion, but judging by the empty bag lying next to the chopping board, it was more likely a smoothie. Unless baby spinach was a popular ingredient in arcane potions. A smart speaker was playing something heavy on guitars in the corner, and the whole place gave off more of an *affluent bachelor* vibe than a *deadly magician* one.

"So," Ifan said, setting two mugs on the counter and getting the salmon from the fridge. "What d'you need? Because I'm going by the way we left things that you're not here for a social call." His tone was light, but there was tightness at the corners of his mouth, and smudged shadows under his eyes as he looked at Callum.

"You mean after you tried to blow us up?" I asked.

Ifan unwrapped the salmon. "I didn't try to blow you up."

"You did. At Muscles' *and* at the club."

"At the club I thought Callum was about to be eaten by angry weres. I may have overreacted a little." He topped up the mugs with boiling water, then went back to the salmon.

"And at Muscles'?"

"Gobs, leave it," Callum said. He'd peeled his old coat off and was looking for somewhere to hang it.

"There's a fire through there," I said to him.

"Do I suggest burning your coat?"

"Mine's *attached.* And it's glorious. And doesn't smell of fish."

"That was your coat?" Ifan said. "I didn't like to ask."

Callum scowled at us both. "It's not that bad."

"It is," Ifan and I said together, then he added, "You can have one of mine. I'm with Gobs on this one." He grinned at me, and I stared blankly back at him.

Callum muttered something under his breath and hung

the coat on the back of one of the stools. "It'll be fine once it dries."

"I've got spares," Ifan said. "And some boots, while we're at it. Why are you wearing *wellies?*" He peered down at Callum's feet. "With fish scales, no less."

"I borrowed them," Callum said. "A Black Dog ate mine."

"Of course it did." Ifan pushed a mug of tea toward him, then finished chopping the fish and set one bowl in front of me and another in front of Green Snake. He took a packet of biscuits from a cupboard, slid them to Callum, and finally sat down, examining us. "So tell me," he said. "Other than new shoes, what do you need? You must really be stuck if you've come here." He gave us a slightly uneven smile, cupping his mug in both hands.

"It's not like we had nowhere else," I said around a mouthful of salmon. I'd had one uncertain moment when I'd wondered if it were wise to accept food from magicians, but it was a bit late. We'd done it before. And besides, this was seriously fancy salmon. It had come all done up in paper, and not the chip shop sort, either.

"Eh," Callum said.

"We've got options," I insisted.

Ifan took a sip of tea. "Look, if it helps, you can't be much safer than here."

"Really?" I said. "Your bloody taxidermy tried to eat us, and that was even before the whole ancient gods being raised in the basement thing. It's not super safe, is it?"

"That was when it was Dad's," Ifan said. "It's mine now, and it's safe for you." He looked at Callum as he spoke. "I promise."

Callum glanced around as if checking for rogue taxidermy, then said, "So it's just you."

Ifan shrugged. "Far as I can tell, Dad's definitely gone. I've been looking, and there's no sign of him. That makes me the last of the Lewises, and the most powerful magician in the north." He said it almost regretfully, which jarred with the words. It was like someone saying, *so I suppose I've inherited the cat food factory* with a tear in their eye. "I should be able to offer some pretty solid help, if you'll take it."

I sat back on my haunches, licking my chops as I looked at Callum. He'd opened the packet of biscuits, and now he took one out, examining it like he'd never seen one before. To be fair, they looked as posh as the salmon, and had so many *no this* and *no that* labels emblazoned on the pack that I wondered they had anything left in them at all. Most of our biscuits were broken and mislabelled. Callum had bought a packet of *Ginjar Nobs* the other day that had been such a curious shade of luminous orange he'd thrown them out without trying them. He may well have never seen biscuits that looked as though they came with their own pedigree before.

He dunked one in his tea, took a bite, then said, "Nice."

"Yeah, they're not bad," Ifan said, taking one, and for a little while the kitchen was quiet but for the slurp of tea and the burble of the radio, which had moved on to something very stompy. I didn't mind it, but Green Snake keep peering at the speaker irritably. He seemed to have quite clear opinions on music, and they veered more toward pretty singing and elevator music, as far as I could tell.

Finally Callum folded his forearms on the island, his sleeves pushed up and his skin pale against the black marble. "So what's happening?" he asked.

"That's a pretty large question," Ifan said.

"Alright. What's happening in Dimly?"

"Still so large." He grinned as Callum made a frustrated noise. "Seriously. It's *Dimly*."

"Is Gerry alright?" I asked. "Have you heard anything?"

"I haven't heard that he's *not* alright," Ifan said. "But I've not been back to Dimly since the whole were thing."

"Well, this is useless," I said to Callum. "Thought you said he was our best source of information."

Callum ignored me and said, "Why haven't you been back?" He was watching Ifan steadily, and the magician looked away, rubbing one forearm as if he had cramp.

"I'm not entirely welcome."

"So they've got some sense, then," I said, but neither man looked at me. Green Snake did, though, and stuck his tongue out. I bared my teeth in return.

"Why aren't you welcome?" Callum asked, and Ifan *hmm*-ed.

"Ez is back up and running," he said. "And not on a small scale, either."

"Of course she is," Callum said with a sigh. Ez, his sister, the only other North left after the Watch had wiped out everyone else. Callum had been long gone by that point, turning his back on all of it, all the power and all the money, and she'd stepped into running the family business. She traded everything from American breakfast cereals and Japanese chocolates to enchanted hat pins and unicorn dust weapons, and everyone knew that if she didn't have it, she'd get it, whatever *it* might be. Some products were marginally legal in Folk or human worlds. Much of it was unknown in human worlds. And some of it was the sort of thing that shouldn't be traded by anyone, ever, because it could tear holes in the universe. But where there's demand, there's supply, and there's Ez.

"Gerry was meant to be reforming her or something," I said. "Had her on cleaning sewers and all sorts."

"I don't think that lasted long," Ifan said, taking another biscuit. "Ez is a tougher prospect than reforming wayward troll kids."

I opened my mouth to say that *nothing* could be harder than convincing trolls to not be trolls, but then remembered we were talking about Ez. I had another piece of salmon instead.

"Have you heard anything about them, then?" Callum asked. "Poppy and William?"

"Sort of. Apparently he sent them off, out of Leeds. Guess he was worried something might happen to them if things got too bad for him in Dimly. Bit weird, those two."

"They're modern trolls," I said. Which, as far as I could tell, involved dressing well, taking elocution lessons from Gerry, and having career paths – animal rescue for Poppy, and hospitality for William. All of which *was* weird, really, as trolls are best known for making a living smashing heads, and for finding words of more than two syllables unnecessary. But I wasn't having some sneaky magician insulting them. They were worth at least four of him, and not just in size.

"So Gerry's there on his own?" Callum asked. "When did you last see him?"

"Not for a bit," Ifan said. "Like I say, I haven't really been back to Dimly. I've still got some contacts, but not everyone's so keen to speak to me these days."

"Shocking," I observed, and he gave me a look that was mostly amused.

"I mean they won't speak to me because it's too dangerous, not because they don't like me."

"That's what you think."

Callum gave me an impatient glance, then looked back at Ifan. "Why?"

"Because Ez and I have some differences of opinion."

Callum nodded. "And no one wants to be on the wrong side of Ez."

"No one wants to be on the wrong side of a North." Ifan

tapped his fingers against his mug. "Last I heard Gerry was still mayor, even if he was clinging on by his favourite manicure. But I don't see how it can last. Ez is fully back in business, and Dimly's becoming known as the place to be again."

"Place to be for who?" I asked.

"Anyone who can make themselves useful. To Ez, that is."

"Muscle and smugglers?" Callum asked.

"Magicians and magic-workers, too," Ifan said. "When my contacts stopped talking to me I tried to sniff around a bit, but she's put the word out that I'm to be shown the door pretty quick if I turn up. Suppose she figures anything I find out will get back to you." He smiled slightly.

"Or she just doesn't like you," I said. "I mean, she's a devious bloody sewer-dweller, but she's not silly."

"I'd really forgotten how much I love your company," Ifan said, and I showed him my teeth.

"What about the weres?" Callum asked. "Have you had any contact with them?"

He hesitated, then said, "A little. Not in person."

"What does that mean?" I demanded.

"It means Yasmin calls me every now and then to ask if I've found out how to get Anton out of wolf form."

"He's still stuck?" Anton hadn't been able to change back to human form since the explosion at the were club, which I was still convinced Ifan was responsible for. "Are you even licensed to do magic?"

He gave me a half smile. "Are you licensed to stick your nose into everything?"

"I'm a *PI*," I snapped.

"Sort of," Callum said, and I growled at him, then looked back at Ifan.

"Fine. So you don't know where Yasmin is, then?"

"No. I don't even have a number. It's always withheld."

"You didn't *ask?*"

"Of course I asked. But I guess she'd rather I didn't have that info. You may have noticed she's a *little* protective of her pack."

"So she should be, with you around," I said. "What about necromancers?"

Ifan shrugged. "Haven't had contact with them since they tried to feed us to the Old One. For obvious reasons."

"Ms Jones? The sorcerer?"

"No desire to cross paths with her ever again. No idea."

I narrowed my eyes at him. "So, what – you've just been sitting here the whole time like a forgotten Halloween pumpkin, rotting away and knowing nothing about what's going on *anywhere?* My fishy breath, you have."

"I told you I've been trying. No one's talking."

"Then what's the use in us being here?" I demanded. "So far all we've got is stuff we could've figured out for ourselves with a couple of phone calls." Which, fine, we hadn't actually been able to make, but still. One expected more from the most powerful magician in the north.

Ifan sighed, looking down at his hands, then said, "Cal, you want another cuppa?"

Callum was resting his forearms on the island, rolling the piece of jet between his fingers. He didn't look like he was even listening to us, but he said, "Sure."

"Good. Because I need something stronger." Ifan put the kettle on, then took a bottle of whisky and a glass from the pantry and set them on the island, pouring himself a generous tot.

"This seems ominous," I said. "Is this where you tell us you're really sorry, but you've got some Old Ones out the back who're going to use our bones for biscuits?"

"Gobs," Callum said, tucking the jet into his jeans pocket. He came up with a pink seashell and frowned at it.

"What? He's given us *nothing* so far, and now he's hitting the bottle. It doesn't look great."

"Nothing other than a safe place," Callum said, putting the seashell back with the jet, and looked at Ifan. "I'm right, aren't I? The charms are heavier. We're hidden here."

"There's nothing can get through," Ifan said, taking sip of whisky. "The whole property is reinforced, the house doubly so. It's the safest place in ... well, anywhere."

"Why?" Callum asked. His voice was calm and level, but he'd interlaced his fingers on the worktop, and his knuckles were white.

Ifan didn't answer right away, just made Callum's tea, clattering about with the spoon and the milk. When he spoke it was with his back to us, and he said, "Because at some point Ez is going to come for me." He turned and looked at Callum. "She'll come for me, because if the most powerful magician in the north isn't standing with her, then she's going to expect that I'm standing against her." He pointed at the kitchen door, out to where the charms twisted around the walls and encircled the house, an unseen perimeter alive with power. "Whether Gerry's still there or not, Dimly is hers in everything except name. She's a North, so if she claims it, it's hers. And anyone who wants a piece of it's going to have to go through her. So if you want to find necromancers, I have a good idea where they'll be." He took another sip of whisky and added, "And at some point, she's going to make sure no one's left who can change that."

Callum didn't say anything for a long moment, then he said, "And *are* you standing against her?"

Ifan slid the mug of tea to him, some slopping over the rim on the worktop. "I don't want to stand for anything. I was never even that into being a magician. *I* wanted to hang out on a beach in Mustique and drink fruity rum drinks."

"Don't we all," I said, and even Green Snake looked quite

taken with the idea. It was probably closer to his natural habitat than Leeds.

Ifan looked at me and said, "Maybe you should."

"Why?" I asked, but I already knew. I could smell it in the quiet wash of grief that had deepened around Callum like a noonday shadow, see it in the set of the magician's face as he looked back at the only other North in the country.

"Because she'll come for me, too," Callum said, and threw a longing look at the whisky. Then he took another biscuit and added, "Gods know why. She beat me at *everything* when we were kids. I'm hardly a threat."

"Maybe she knows you better than that," Ifan said, and Callum's face twisted, like the biscuit had soured in his mouth.

"Do you have any custard?" I asked the magician. "I think this calls for custard."

CUSTARD WASN'T FORTHCOMING, but Ifan offered me some almond milk, which was terrible and I spluttered all over the glossy worktop in disgust.

"Callum, he's trying to poison me!"

"Can't imagine why," Callum said. He'd put his cigarettes on the counter, one already out of the packet and ready to be lit, but now he held his hand out to Ifan. "Give me your phone."

"Why?" Ifan asked, but handed it over anyway. It was as sleek and glossy as the kitchen.

"I'm trying Gerry again. We need to find out what's going on in there, and it's worth trying from another number." He pulled the number up on our tatty phone and tapped it into Ifan's, putting it on speakerphone. It only rang a couple of times before the message came on again.

"Hi, you've reached Gerry—"

Callum hung up, thought about it, then scrolled through our phone and tried Ms Jones' number from Ifan's phone. Still nothing, and he made a frustrated noise.

"How the hell are we meant to find out what's going on when we can't get hold of *anyone?*"

"Yeah, your magician's not much help," I said, and Ifan raised his glass to me. "If we want to get out, can we? Through the charms?"

The magician rolled his hands together, a quick smooth movement as if he were washing them, then spread his fingers with an ozone whiff of power to reveal a key. It was old steel, a little rusted at the edges, with a short, fat barrel and a slightly ornate head, and he slid it across the worktop to Callum. "That'll get you in and out," he said. "It'll get *anyone* in and out, though, so don't lose it."

"What're you thinking?" Callum asked me. "Who do we try?"

"Just wanted to make sure we had the option, is all," I said. "Make sure we're not locked in here for all eternity."

"I wouldn't inflict that even on myself," Ifan said, and I got up and stretched.

"Well. Since we've got a safe bed for the night, I'm sleeping."

"We need a plan," Callum started, and I jumped to the floor.

"We need sleep, *then* a plan to deal with your sister, find Gerry, find the dentist, and get Ms Jones. Which is too much for tonight. Is anything going to eat me?" I directed the question at Ifan.

"Probably not," he said. "I wouldn't go in the east wing upstairs, though. No one's been in there since my grandmother vanished, so either she'll be really hungry, or whatever ate her will."

"Magicians," I grumbled, and padded into the living room to sit and groom myself by the fire. We did need a plan. But I wasn't sure my plan was the same as Callum's. After all, he was the one Ez and her army were going to be coming for.

I was just one small black cat, and no one ever paid much attention to small black cats.

4

JUST STEPPING OUT, MAY BE SOME TIME

MAYBE THE WORLD AT LARGE DOESN'T PAY MUCH ATTENTION to small yet exceptionally well-formed black cats, but *someone* was paying attention when I took the key carefully from the bedside table in the guest room where Callum was sleeping, face down with his arms and legs flung wide. His stubble – which had grown past the limits of stubble and into the region of whiskers in the last few days – was finally gone, and he smelled of so much soap and shampoo that I was hardly likely to sleep anyway. The dried-seaweed-and-pipe-smoke whiff that had been hanging around since Whitby hadn't been great, but it was better than ginseng and wooden sandals, or whatever posh magicians used.

Green Snake slithered out from under the pillow and watched me jump to the floor with the key clasped firmly in my teeth. It smelled of old steel and old secrets, and it made my whiskers twitch.

"You're not coming," I said around it, and he pointed his nose at the key. "I'm going to bring it back."

He did the nose thing again.

"How the hell else am I going to get out?" Of course, I wasn't sure how the key was going to help either, as presumably it was for unlocking the gates as well as parting the charms, and locks are not in my admittedly extensive skillset.

Green Snake slipped off the bed and nosed the key, trying to take hold of it, and I stepped back.

"Keep your scaly little snout out of it," I hissed at him, and headed for the door. I'd insisted Callum leave it off the latch so that I could come and go without swinging off door handles, and also that a small window in the utility room was open for the purpose of late night garden visits. Ifan had been a bit huffy about that, since he reckoned it affected the house charms, but when I asked him which tub he preferred me to use as a toilet he'd come around to my way of thinking pretty quickly.

Now I prowled down the hall, smelling the whiff of magic and cologne drifting from the magician's room at the end of the hall and extending tendrils across the scuffed but still richly red and green carpet. There were threadbare patches here and there, and darker spots where old furniture had stood or questionable things had been spilled, but the intricate pattern of flowers and interlinked, curving vines was still clear. Magicians can afford fancy stuff that lasts forever, I suppose. Portraits lined the wood panelling of the walls above me, but I didn't pause to look at any of them. Looking at portraits in a magician's house was up there with poking their taxidermy when it came to bad ideas. And no, that's not a euphemism.

Green Snake wriggled along behind me, pausing now and then to stick his tongue out at a particularly tangled knot of pattern in the carpet (I'm not saying any of it was moving at the corner of my eye, but I was also carefully ignoring anything that *might* be moving at the corner of my eye), and we paused on the landing above the stairs. Stuffed birds hung in the wide atrium of the stairwell, and a mix of city and moonlight washed through the windows that looked over the front garden toward the gates. The landing we stood on curved under them, a broad walkway that swept across to what had to be the east wing. Instead of a matching hall to the one I'd just come out of, there was a heavy wooden door secured with three large bolts, hefty padlocks forced through the hasps. A dislocated sense of loss and rage drifted through the door to me, and I turned and trotted down the stairs, ignoring one of the taxidermied rabbits when it hopped unevenly across the foyer below, as if it were playing hopscotch on the marble tiles in the moonlight. It looked too small to do more than nibble on my tail, anyway. I hoped.

I did hesitate at the bottom of the stairs, though. Not because of the rabbit, but because of the door at the back of the big entrance hall. It was shut, but once it had led to the old magician's study, and below that into his evil mastermind laboratory-slash-place for summoning Old Ones. I didn't really fancy going down there to see what sort of redecoration might have occurred, but I also didn't trust Ifan. No matter what he said about being in the same canoe as Callum, I still suspected him of planning to roll it over and feed us all to the river monsters. Or to Ez, more to the point.

I skirted the rabbit, which was pirouetting with jerky grace in the light coming through the windows, and went to sniff around the study door. There were charms plastered all over it, and I wondered if it was unlocked, and if the key would let me through unnoticed. Maybe, but maybe it also wasn't worth risking just yet. Not when our options for safe places were so thin on the ground.

"Gobs." Even though Callum's voice was soft, I almost backflipped in fright. I spun to find him halfway down the stairs, leaning on the railing. He'd pulled a T-shirt and jeans on, but he was barefoot and his hair stuck out at bewildered angles. "What're you doing?"

There was no putting the key down subtly, so I just hoped he couldn't see that well in the shadowed foyer and spoke as clearly as I could with it still in my teeth. "I'm nocturnal. What d'you expect me to do – sit about and watch you sleep?"

Callum padded down the stairs, skirted the dancing rabbit, which had been joined by a weasel turning somersaults around the edges of the room, and joined me at the study door. He crouched down and took hold of the key. I resisted him for a moment, then let go with a sigh. He just looked at me, eyebrows raised.

"I thought I might try to find Tam," I said. "She's got no human to worry about, and I think she could probably take down Ez with a single bite, given the chance."

"Not out of the realms of possibility. But how were you going to find her? On foot?"

"No, I was going to call an Uber."

He smiled slightly, bouncing the key in his hand. "Do you even have any idea where to start looking?"

"I just thought, you know, sneak about, see what I can turn up."

"And never mind that things are a bit dicey at the mo."

"For you, not me," I said.

"Sure," he said. "That thing in the flat was nothing."

I shivered despite myself, chills curling up my spine and around my ears at the memory of the void gaping behind me, and *something* trying to pull me in, cold and implacable and unmoved. And it would have succeeded, except Callum, moving through a frozen world, had snatched me back. Had moved when nothing else could. "How did you do it?" I asked, the question dropping into the stillness of the house. I hadn't asked before, I'd let him keep his secrets, but now it felt that everything not shared was one more thing that could kill us. "How did you move when I couldn't? When Tam couldn't? How did you get us back?"

He sighed slightly. "I'm not sure."

"That's not an answer. And you never gave me a proper answer in Whitby. You just said your family was *mostly* a criminal dynasty. But it's more than that. So tell me what you really are."

"I don't know if I have a proper answer, Gobs."

"*Try.*"

He spread his fingers. "You know as much as I do. I'm a North. That's all."

I backed away from the rabbit as it waltzed a little too close, glass eyes glittering in the moonlight, then looked back at Callum. "So tell me what a North is. People keep saying you're *sort of* human. And Anton, when he sniffed you – what did he mean about *your sort?* What *is* your sort? Are you some kind of fae? You're not elf, you're too ..." I examined him. "Too you. And you're not sorcerers, or magicians. What the hell *are* the Norths?"

He wrinkled his nose. "Not great people, to be honest."

I growled. "I will bite you. I know we have an agreement, but excruciating circumstances and all."

"Extenuating."

"What?"

He looked at the key, then at the door to the magician's lair. "D'you reckon it'll get us in there?"

"Maybe. Or maybe it'll awaken the freaky taxidermy army again. Answer the question."

He rubbed his face with one hand, and even in the dim light I could see the shadows under his eyes. "Fine. We *are* the north, Gobs. We're human, but we're also the north. The land lends us her power." He shrugged. "It's why I couldn't leave, even though I left Dimly and my family."

I blinked at him. "The north … you're *guardians*. I didn't even know there were such things anymore." There had been plenty of them once, when humans had still made sacrifices to small local gods or god-like things, had swapped practical, often edible acts of worship for fair weather and good harvests.

Guardians had been those who spoke for the land, who were so tightly bound to it that they may well have been carved from it. The legends said they could raise floods to protect their borders, bring down storms to drive out those who would harm their territories. Without guardians, the land would crumble, bereft, and the opposite was true, too. The guardians suffered as their land suffered, which was why the steady assault of progress had rendered them all but powerless. No one worshipped them anymore, or gave them sacrifice, and the land was tamed by tarmac and steel rather than hands and hope. The power was gone, or slept so deep beneath the earth that it may as well be. Or so the stories went. But it was all so long ago that the stories had become tangled up with those of actual gods and old religions, and no one knew what was truth and what was the eternal embroidery of storytelling.

Callum seesawed his hand. "Custodians, more like. We're meant to protect the land, but what it really means is that as long as you can justify something in your head as being good for the north – good for the rivers, or the trees, or the people – and really believe it, you can tap into the land's power and use it. We don't have magic, as such. We're just conduits. And my family worked out how to convince themselves that anything *they* wanted was what the north wanted." He shrugged. "And so, multigenerational criminal empire."

I considered it. "Ez. If you believe she's *bad* for the north ..."

"In theory I could be a risk. But I don't use the land. Never have. I don't even know how to tap into it." He spread his hands. "I really am just human."

"Does Ez know that?"

He gave me a dimpled half smile. "She should."

He sounded about as optimistic about that outcome as I felt. "Could you not try and go all North on us?" I asked. "It seems like it'd be really handy."

He snorted. "We were all meant to be taught how to tap into it as kids, but I was always running away from the lessons, and finally Mum gave me a choice: learn it all, or learn nothing. I chose nothing." He gave an odd, tight little smile. "Bet you can imagine how popular that made me."

"Sounds kind of like being a cat that won't go with the Watch."

"Pretty much."

I watched him for a moment. As very much not-fun as being trapped in the Inbetween had been, at least I didn't really remember my own kind betraying me. Plus cats don't do the whole familial duty thing, so I just carried a general cat grudge rather than a specific one. But when it came to the tight human circles formed of blood and tradition, where family's held up as its own religion, its own *kind*, near enough ... well, being outcast from those who were meant to be your safety would leave wounds that ran deep, and they'd fester in terrible ways.

"Were the lessons so bad?" I asked.

"Yeah." He reached for his cigarettes, but he didn't have his coat, so he just cracked his knuckles instead, making both the rabbit and the weasel stop to stare at us. "The worst. You know, imagine this pig is destroying the land by digging all the endangered flowers up, and watch its head explode."

"Ew," I said.

"And they were just the warm-up." He didn't meet my eyes, and I heard him swallow, a hard flat sound in the silent hall. "So I quit. I never learned any of it, and so no, I'm not a North. Not in that sense. But I suppose I *could* be, in Ez's eyes." He sighed. "Anyhow, all I can think is that's how I grabbed you. I'm more anchored to the world than most people, I suppose."

I considered it for a moment, then said, "I'm slightly disappointed, to be honest."

"Oh?"

"Yeah. I mean if you'd been some sort of half-god or fae warrior, it would've been much cooler. And more useful."

"Sorry to disappoint." His mouth twitched at the corners as he looked at the study door again. "Do we try it?"

"Maybe not. You know, in case this actually is the safest place for us, we should probably aim to not get kicked out for snooping. But I am going looking for Tam."

"I'm coming with you, then."

"Well, why not. I hadn't even figured out how I was going to give Green Snake the slip yet."

"I'll get my boots." He ran lightly back up the stairs, and I watched him go, then looked at the snake.

"Be quieter next time," I said, and ran for the kitchen and the utility room beyond.

I DIDN'T HANG ABOUT. Callum might be a great gangly thing, but he's quicker than he looks, and the odds of him trusting me not to sneak off were pretty low. That doesn't speak to any level of distrust in our relationship, merely the fact that we've known each other for long enough now that some things are just understood. Such as the simple truth that cats don't take direction at all, never mind *well*.

So I slipped out the window and sprinted for the gate with my ears back and my tail high, frost crackling under my paws and the air cold as the moonlight on my snout. The faint diesel and concrete scent of the city drifted over the walls, but in here the ground was soaked in magic. It was older than Ifan, older than his dad, maybe older than his entire family. In some places power rises to the surface, and smart magic-workers build their homes where they can take advantage of it. It's much easier to fuel an empire when you're sitting on the well.

I was at the gate before I heard the front door open, and the crunch of gravel under Callum's borrowed boots. I looked back in time to see him sprinting after me, his coat flaring around him in the dim light, and Green Snake emerged from the grass not far behind me, looking peeved.

"Gobs!" Callum half shouted. "Wait!"

This was not the sneaky getaway I'd imagined, but if I could just get out and away, then ... then I wasn't sure. If I could shift, it'd be easy. All I'd have to do was get past the magician's charms and I could be sailing off across the Inbetween, tracking Tam through the scents she left behind. Since I couldn't, it was more likely to be a sprint to the nearest bins and hide out under them until Callum got sick of looking for me.

But I had to do *something*. I couldn't hang out here with the magician able to feed us whatever tale he wanted, presenting us his version of reality with a half smile and a slice of salmon on the side. For all we knew, Dimly was still firmly in Gerry's control, and the troll just had the hump with us for some reason and wasn't answering. Maybe we'd inadvertently insulted his favourite dress designer.

And I didn't want Callum coming with me. As much as I hated leaving him here with Ifan, I didn't think he'd wind up as a human sacrifice in the immediate future. The magician was as dodgy as a truck stop oyster, but he seemed to be keen on making sure Callum stayed safe at least for the moment, which indicated he wasn't going to turn him inside out in the next hour or so. But outside those gates, all bets were off. Or they were likely on, but not in Callum's favour.

So I dived for the gap left by the broken gates, unsure if I could get through without the key and hoping I wasn't going to be turned into a hamster. The charms set up a shiver in my bones and a dull, ugly ache in my teeth as I scrabbled my way through, the cold metal of the gate pressing me into the dirt beneath. For one moment I thought they wouldn't let me go, the magic clutching me greedily, but Ifan was obviously more worried about people getting in than cats getting out. I pushed harder, feeling like I was trying to break the skin on some old milk, then I was abruptly through and onto the moonlit street.

I dropped to my haunches, feeling suddenly, violently exposed, and peered both ways, knowing I needed to get moving before Callum caught up. Out here, though, with no bushes or parked cars to provide cover, I was starting to reconsider what had seemed like a really solid plan from the relative safety of the house. The street was empty at least, the low light turning the tarmac into a dull, dark river and the trees into skeletal figures frozen mid-dance by my appearance. The orange glow of the streetlights pushed the moonlight back, and a security light blared on over the gates of the house across the road. I squinted at it, spine prickling.

"Gobs," Callum called, and the gates rattled as he messed about with the key. "Gobs, get back here, you divot. We'll take the car. You're not getting far on foot, are you?"

He did have a point. It *would* be easier. But that meant

him being out here, and I couldn't have it. Not until we had a better idea what was going on. So I straightened up, trying to get the fur on my spine to settle, and padded off the pavement into the middle of the street, away from the shadow of the magician. I stopped there, where I could feel the city begin to establish its slow pull, deep and old as the house itself, thinking, *Tam.*

Not that I thought I could will her into being, or set up some mysterious Tam-signal in the cloudless sky or anything. But maybe if I thought about her hard enough I could get some inkling of where she was, even without being able to go into the Inbetween. It was a small hope, to be honest, but tracking is hardly an exact science.

I'd already decided I was just going to have to make myself scarce before Callum got the key to work and hope I came up with a plan later, when a wolf came out of the nearest alley at a flat sprint. Its head was low, teeth bared, but it didn't snarl or growl, simply charged me with its muscles rolling under its pelt, claws scoring the tarmac as it came. I yelped and broke for the safety of the nearest tree, and another wolf emerged from behind it, mouth wide with delight. I stopped hard, hindquarters bunching, and before I could recover the magician's gate swung open with a screech and a clang, rending the quiet of the night. The wolves stopped, turning toward the sound, and Callum shouted, "Gobs, *here!*"

The wolves started to pad toward him, their movements deliberate and filled with awful intent, and I lunged to intercept the closest, the one that had been behind the tree.

"Oi, Fido!" I yelled. "Pick on someone smaller than you! That's your deal anyway, isn't it?"

The wolf paused, looking at me with its lips drawn back from its teeth, and I tried desperately to see if it was one we knew. They all smell the bloody same.

"Yasmin?" I said hopefully, and the wolf snarled so loudly I stepped back. Well, it might have been a scuttle. "Guess not."

"Gobs, come here," Callum said. He stepped away from the gates and they immediately slammed shut, making him jump. The wolves stopped with matching growls.

"Oh, that's great," I said. "Well done."

He glanced at the gates, then back at the wolves, raising his hands in a *halt, who goes there* gesture that I doubted was going to do much at all.

"Great," I repeated. "I was fine till you turned up, you know!"

"Sure you were," he said. "*On foot.*"

"*Paw,*" I said, and the wolves exchanged glances, then started to prowl toward Callum again.

"Go for the wall," Callum said, not looking away from the wolves.

I was already running. Not for the wall, though. Instead I sprinted straight down the centre of the road, yelling as I went. *"Here wolfy wolf wolf! Run run run as fast as you can, you can't catch me I'm the— Hairballs!"*

A van burst out of the side street ahead of me with a screech of tyres, wobbling precariously on the edge of balance as it cornered. It slid almost to the opposite pavement before it recovered and barrelled toward me, engine screaming while the driver wrestled with the gears. I froze in the glare of the headlights, unsure which way to run given how the thing was swinging from side to side, and behind me Callum yelled my name.

The van barely swerved around me, the passenger's side bumper almost brushing my ears. I flinched, and the side door flew open.

"*Get in!*" someone shouted, and someone else leaned out of the door with an enormous gun in their hands. They pumped it furiously, then let loose a blast of water with a whoop. I could faintly smell garlic. A third person was firing a slingshot through the passenger window, hurling what looked a lot like salad potatoes at the wolves. I started to turn back, looking for Callum, but he was already sprinting toward me, the wolves in snarling pursuit. He snatched me up with one smoke-scented hand and lunged for the van, and we tumbled in together. The driver floored the accelerator, and we took off with a dramatic squeal of rubber on tarmac. The water-gunner fell backward into us, bounced off, and almost rolled out the door, but Callum grabbed them, and then everything was a tangle of limbs on the van floor.

There was one precarious moment as we roared off, side door still open, the wolves coming after us faster than the van could manage to pick up pace. One of them lunged, paws clawing at the door and teeth snapping far too close for comfort, then one of the passengers in the crowded back of the van bopped it on the snout with a half-full bottle of discount whisky. It lost its precarious grip with a yelp and fell away, rolling twice before I lost sight of it.

I scrabbled out from under Callum and jumped to an empty seat as he wrestled the door closed against the thundering momentum of the van. We'd managed to get up to some sort of creaking speed, and I braced myself against the swaying movement so I could peer back down the street. The magician's gates had opened again, and Ifan stood in the centre of them, bare-chested and shoeless, both hands up in a *what just happened* gesture as the wolves stared after us. Then we rounded a corner and he was out of sight before I could see if he was about to be eaten or hand out doggy treats.

I opened my mouth to point out to Callum that his buddy hadn't exactly seemed surprised by the wolves, and someone else spoke first.

"Right, chaps! Good work all round. Targets recovered. Any injuries to report?"

"Tristan?" Callum said.

"You have *got* to be kidding me," I muttered, and stared around at the van's grey-haired, grinning occupants.

We'd been rescued by the OAP army.

5

THE OAP ARMY RIDES AGAIN

THE VAN WAS LONG, WITH A BACK SEAT IN WORN FABRIC THAT spanned its width, and a big area behind it at the very back in which a motorised scooter was wedged. Callum was still on the floor, squeezed into a narrow aisle between the door and two smaller sets of seats. Both sets were occupied. Tristan was sitting bolt upright on the one in front of me, a big ginger tom with slightly scruffy fur, and a woman in a floral apron and woollen hat was in the one behind the driver's seat, a large sack of potatoes at her feet and a small knife in one hand. Another man was on the floor with Callum, still clutching the water cannon. He was shirtless under his military jacket despite the cold, the sagging skin of his belly distorting his tattoos and hiding some of the more graphic bits.

A woman leaned in from the front seats as we thundered down the road, screeching on the corners and treating stop signs and the centre line with equal disregard.

"Hello again," she said. "Callum and Gobbelino, isn't it?"

We hadn't seen Tristan's Old Age Pensioners' army since our showdown with the necromancers in the magician's house, and we hadn't expected to. They should've been playing lawn bowls in matching anoraks, not lurking around houses of power armed with potatoes and water guns.

"Ah, yeah," Callum said. "Colonel, wasn't it?"

"You can call me Rita," she said, and pointed at the woman in the back with us. "That's Lulu—"

"*Colonel* Rita and *Captain* Lulu," Tristan said, and the colonel sighed.

"I'm all for cats talking," she said, "but you're very pedantic, Tristan."

"They're all a bit like that," Callum said, and I growled.

"*Corporal* Dudley Greenwood—" Tristan continued, ignoring the humans.

"Duds," the man on the floor put in, and saluted us. Callum gave a half-hearted wave.

"Yes. Thank you, Tristan," the colonel said. "And Noel in the front. You'll excuse him if he doesn't salute. He's concentrating."

Noel gave a lazy salute with one dark-skinned hand anyway, and the van veered wildly.

"*Hand on the wheel, sergeant!*" the colonel bawled, and Noel grabbed the wheel again.

"Soz," he said. "I forget sometimes."

"That you only have *one arm?*" I asked, putting my paws up on the seat in front of me so that I could see better. He shrugged, and I looked at the colonel. "Why's he the one driving?"

"He's a very good driver," she said, as we tore around another corner and I pitched off the back seat, winding up with Callum and Duds in a pile against the door. Tristan clawed wildly to stay in his seat, but Lulu didn't move. She had one foot up against the armrest and was peeling the potatoes. "Seatbelts, though," the colonel added.

Callum scrambled into the back seat, pulling a belt

around himself hurriedly, and I jumped up next to him, digging my claws more firmly into the fabric. Green Snake peered anxiously out of Callum's pocket at me, so evidently Callum had grabbed him on the way through.

"What're you all doing here?" Callum asked, as Duds settled himself next to Tristan.

"We've been staking out the house," Duds said.

"Yes. We'd have intervened yesterday, before you went in, but you went straight to the gate," the colonel said. "We weren't about to confront the magician, so we waited. Figured you'd make a run for it at some point." She paused. "Well, either that or we'd have to assume you were working with him, so." She didn't trail off, just finished the sentence there. *So.* I wasn't sure I liked the sound of it, and I eyed Lulu and her knife warily.

"But *why* were you staking it out?" Callum asked.

"Oh, we've been keeping an eye on things since the whole possession to-do. How're you feeling, by the way?" She leaned over the front seat again, and switched a small torch on. Callum raised a hand to shield his eyes as she shone it on him.

"I'm fine. What do you mean, keeping an eye on things?"

"Logs," Duds said triumphantly, and waved a tablet at us. "Always one of us about. We keep track of who goes in when, how long they stay, all that. Can't have ancient gods running around the streets of Leeds unchecked, you know."

"*Ancient gods.*" Lulu sniffed. "More like tyrannical luminescent power-hungry ghosties, if you ask me."

"The tyranny bit seems to be a common thread with any power-hungry sorts," I said. "Gods, politicians, CEOs, that sort of thing."

Lulu leaned around Duds' seat and offered me a fist. I nosed it, smelling frying bacon and cigarettes.

"Fist bump," Tristan said to me. "Use your paw."

"Cat," I said. "Use your brain."

"Logs?" Callum said, addressing Rita. "You've tracked *everyone?*"

Rita still had the torch on him, but now she switched it off, seemingly satisfied. "Yes. It wasn't like we could just pretend nothing had happened, was it? That woman and the magician – the old magician – tried to call up *something*, and then they just vanished." She gave Callum a severe look. "We may be old, but we're not senile. We did notice that they disappeared when the entity did, but no one knew where to."

"But what were you going to do if you did see them?" Callum asked.

"Is that what the garlic water was for?" I asked Duds. "They're not vampires."

Duds patted his water cannon. "I got a thingy off the internet and blessed it, too. Can't hurt, right?"

"A Bless-O-Matic," Lulu said, going back to her potatoes. "Told him it was a waste of twenty quid."

"A *what?*" I demanded, and Callum gave me a sideways look and a little shake of his head. I subsided, but really. *Humans.*

"Can't hurt," Duds repeated.

"Maybe, but you've still not replaced my garlic," Lulu said, waving her knife at him.

Duds ignored her and hooked an arm over the back of the seat to look at Callum. "We've been doing research. And Tristan's been teaching us charms."

Tristan looked pleased with himself, and I examined the van more closely. Now that the chaos had eased, and away from the reek of wolves and magician, there was a whiff of magic about the place. Clumsy, easy stuff, but enough that the van could probably park outside the walls of even the poshest houses without being noticed, and definitely enough that a bunch of oldies would pass even further below the attention of the average human than they usually did. Doubly invisible.

"Is that a good idea?" I asked Tristan. "You know the Watch are even jumpier than usual at the moment. If they decided to clean up it could end badly." Part of how the Watch keep the human and Folk world separate is by suggestion, which is most definitely a euphemism. Humans don't believe in magic, so even when they see Folk or unusual things, they tend to explain it away to themselves. Fauns don't exist, so that barista just had a weird horn headdress and some seriously strange shoes. Fashion these days, right? Faeries don't exist, so that man running for the bus just has a really bad humpback covered in a weird leather jacket, and some sort of scary false teeth. Takes all sorts. No one beats a human for self-deception. It's almost an art, and one Folk take full advantage of.

But every now and then there's a hiccough, and a human will actually see what's right in front of them and won't be *able* to explain it away. And cats have a talent for fixing those sorts of situations, a kind of nudge to the mind that couches the world in terms humans are more ready to accept. The problem is that once people *know* what they've seen, that nudge becomes more like a scouring. It's risky on young, elastic minds, let alone on the demographic of the OAP army.

Tristan narrowed orange eyes at me. "The Watch never even came looking to see what happened at the magician's house. And you can't tell me they missed it, not with that amount of power being flung around."

"True," I admitted. "But that doesn't mean they'll be happy about humans playing with charms."

"I don't think they want to know about any of it. Or they don't care. The Watch are pretty paws-off these days, if you haven't noticed."

"Not with me, they're not," I grumbled. I was still sore from the injuries they'd inflicted on me in Whitby. Sore in both the literal and the *I wish they'd stop doing this* sense. Plus my tail hadn't had time to heal from the beast of the Inbetween they'd tried to feed me to. *Again.*

Tristan examined me, then said, "Well, they haven't been making their presence felt around here. Whatever they're up to, they've got their own agenda."

"That's hardly news," I said. "They *always* have their own agenda."

"Do you have any idea what it is?" Callum asked Tristan, while the ginger tom tipped his whiskers at me in grudging agreement. Green Snake was hanging from Callum's pocket, examining the van, and Duds offered him a mint. The snake recoiled, but Callum took it.

"Not me," Tristan said. "I'm just some stray hanging out with humans. Think they've got bigger things on, to be honest."

"Like what?" I asked.

"All I know is that we can't rely on them to keep this world safe anymore. We need to have our own defences." He paused, then added, "Maybe even against them. Not that *that's* anything new, either."

"And so, Bless-O-Matics," Lulu said, and cackled. Rita snorted from the front seat. She was still watching Callum, and the van shook and shuddered as we lurched through the night-time streets, leaving the posh suburbs behind and heading for patchier, more well-worn places.

I was silent, and it wasn't entirely because Tristan was saying what I'd been trying not to think about for … well, a while. It felt like longer than it could be, the words setting up reverberations in my memory that echoed in past lives and past deaths that were nothing more than the shape of pain washing out across the years. At some point a sneaking sense that it wasn't just me that the Watch had a problem with had surfaced in the back of my mind, and I'd been trying to ignore it, but now it marched out into the light and demanded to be seen.

But I was also waiting to see if the Watch were going to pop out of the ether and snatch Tristan up for such traitorous statements. When that didn't happen, I asked him, "Do you remember your past lives?"

"Of course," he said. "Everyone does."

Which was the second time I'd been told that, and I was starting to think there was something really wrong with my memory. Maybe I'd hit my head at some stage. Repeatedly. I poked the blankness at the back of my mind, and it swelled toward me, writhing with tentacles and the promise of pain, and for one moment the sound of the engine was so distant I could barely breathe.

Then Green Snake flopped down next to me and tried to tap my nose with his, and I batted him away with a hiss. He hissed back, and Tristan said, "Oi! Settle down, soldiers!" so we both hissed at him instead. He snarled, and Lulu said, "Get that blessed water ready, Duds."

"Got it," Duds said, and grinned at us. I managed not to hiss at him, since he was pointing the water cannon at me. Pure favouritism, not pointing it at Tristan.

"Sorry," Callum said, and looked at Rita. "So you know *everyone* who's been in and out of Ifan's?"

"Sure. Saw you come and go a few times a month or so ago, which made us a bit suspicious, but a couple of cats vouched for you." Rita sighed and looked at the roof of the van. "I don't know when that became something I could count on."

"What cats?" I asked.

"Your hairless lass," Lulu said, putting her knife down and

taking a cigarette packet from her apron pocket. "And the big one."

Pru and Tam. "Have you seen them recently?" I asked. "Are they okay?"

"They're fine," Rita said. "Although I have apparently become designated cat lady, and there's hair *all over* my flat." She scowled at Tristan, who shrugged.

"It's not right for young ladies to meet in a man's apartment."

"They're *cats,*" Rita said. "You're *all cats.* I don't think etiquette applies quite the same."

"I said I'd chaperone," Duds said. "But he said I wasn't suitable."

Going by some of the tattoos, Tristan probably had a point, but I thought it was more likely to have something to do with the fact that Rita looked like she could afford a better grade of canned tuna.

Lulu offered her cigarettes to Callum, who took one.

"No smoking in the van," Noel called from the front, wrestling us around another corner without touching the brakes. "Had enough to explain after the whole orange ghosties incident, when I came back with mud and blood-stains all over the seats."

"And that's better than cigarette smoke?" I asked.

"No one likes a smoker."

I looked at Callum. "He makes a good point."

He tucked the cigarette into his pocket and said, "So where are we going, then? And is there someone still watching the house now?"

"There's always someone keeping an eye on things," Rita said. "Just not necessarily a human someone. We had an idea we might be needed when you turned up, so we were pretty ready to go. Then when those wolves surfaced a couple of hours later we got in position. It seemed prudent to have transport and backup available."

"The wolves weren't there before?" Callum asked.

"No." She gave him a look as sharp as the torchlight had been. "Somehow doubt that's a coincidence."

"No baby goats," I said, and Duds peered over the seat at me.

"What do you have against baby goats?"

"No *kidding*," I said.

"I wasn't kidding. I was asking about the baby goats."

I blinked at him, then addressed Rita. "Who's watching now we've left?"

"I know some cats," Tristan said.

"*Cats?* What if they're Watch?"

"They're not," he said, and fixed me with that orange stare. "I'm no fan either. You think you're the only one they've killed off for having an independent thought?"

I blinked at him, and that stray idea regarding the Watch's vendetta not being just about me felt like it was being smug in the back of my mind.

"Come on, soldier," Tristan said. "Use your brain! The Watch don't tolerate dissent. You know this! You toe the line, you're all good. You stick a whisker out ... well, you know how it goes."

"Right. Well, yes. Sort of." I *did* know. I just couldn't bloody well remember how, or why, or *anything* beyond the fog of my last death. And I *wanted* to, or thought I did. But there had been Whitby, and Black Dogs, and kraken, and bloody mermaids, and I hadn't even had time to think. There was never time to think. "Boiled sprouts with mould on," I said with a sigh, and Lulu gave me a startled look.

"What?" Tristan demanded.

"I can't remember," I said, looking at him. "I mean, I know

the Watch are a bunch of untrustworthy parasitic radishes, but I just can't remember *why*. I think they did something to me, cleaned my head or something. And if everyone would stop trying to kill us for five minutes I might be able to remember. But it's just one bloody thing after another at the moment."

Callum scritched the back of my neck. "True. But there's *always* one thing after another, so you should be used to it by now."

"I'd really rather not be."

"*I* remember," Tristan huffed. "Just bloody excuses, is all. So the Watch killed you off. Happens to all of us. Toughen up, soldier!"

I opened my mouth to ask if *he'd* had his skin removed by the beasts of the Inbetween at least once, and possibly multiple times, and also if he'd like me to demonstrate what it was like, because I was perfectly willing to do so, but before I could manage more than a hiss the van screeched around a corner and came to halt so suddenly I pitched off the seat and onto the floor.

"We're here," Noel said.

"Where's here?" I asked, jumping back up next to Callum and shooting Tristan a narrow-eyed look. He didn't notice.

"We figured we were best not basing operations at the retirement village," Rita said. "Didn't want to bring trouble to the doorstep and all that."

We'd stopped with the headlights washing over a set of high, long-barred gates, held shut with a heavy chain and an equally industrial-looking padlock. Lulu tucked her knife into her apron pocket and clambered out of the van, going to deal with the lock. I smelled damp river water and crumbling tarmac creeping in on the night, the whiff of old silent places overlooked by the city. Lulu pushed the gates wide and Noel crept through, stopping to wait for her to re-lock them and climb back in.

Before she could even pull the sliding door closed he took off again, tearing past straggling rows of shipping containers and a collection of black-windowed cabins of the sort that always seem to be scattered about on construction sites. Some of them were a bit wonky, as if their foundations weren't quite stable, or they'd been removed from said construction sites somewhat unceremoniously. Long grass and leggy weeds grew up at the edges of the drive, and tracks branched off among the containers and cabins at irregular intervals and angles. A big building clad in corrugated iron loomed up to our left, but we continued past it, jouncing violently through potholes and over crumbling speed bumps, into a spreading net of alleys formed by caravans resting wearily on concrete blocks. Most of them had moss growing on the walls, and one had a small tree getting a start on its roof.

"Nice place," I observed.

"Unpopulated place," Rita said. "Storage centre, essentially, but one of their selling points is no cameras or security guards, no monitoring of any kind. Cash payment dropped into a mailing box in Leeds once a month, and no contact with anyone else at all. It's a real lock-and-leave-at-own-risk type thing, all word of mouth to find it. Plus it's priced high enough that anyone who *wants* monitoring would never choose to come here over somewhere more secure."

"Ninety percent certain there's a fake antiques manufacturing operation going on in the containers on the north side," Lulu said. "And there's definitely stolen cars being done up in the boat shed just down from us. Cabin 423 does a nice fry-up of a morning, though."

"Just don't mention caravan 1292C," Duds said, and they all shuddered.

"Why, what's in that?" Callum asked.

"I just said don't mention it," Duds said. "Come on, soldier! Get with the program!"

Callum looked at him blankly, but didn't protest.

The caravans gave way to sheds built in the same corrugated cladding as the main building, and I caught a glimpse of the moon shining off a canal or river through the gaps between them. Noel finally slowed and pulled up in front of one, and he and Rita clambered stiffly out. She slid open the back door of the van and stood there looking at us, leaning on a stick. "Come on, then," she said.

"Want your scooter, Duds?" Noel asked.

"No, just give me one of those sticks," he said, and we followed Lulu and Tristan out into the damp-smelling night as Noel helped Duds down. A faint wind whispered in the trees on the other side of the water, and the sheds hunkered over their secrets, backs bland and windowless.

Rita limped to the shed door and unlocked another padlock, shooting a heavy bolt open and pushing the door wide, then vanished into the darkness beyond. I could smell charms and stale smoke and cats. A moment later the cold glow of florescent lighting washed over the threshold.

"Welcome to the resistance, brothers," Tristan said, walking past us.

"I'm not sure about this," Callum said to me.

"Me either," I said. "But I also don't fancy being hit upside the head by someone's walking stick, so let's just go with it. At least we can find out who they've been watching. And maybe why we almost ended up as midnight snacks for a couple of weres."

"That's a good question," he said.

"So's why Ifan didn't seem too surprised to see wolves chasing us."

"You couldn't tell that from the van."

"Well, he wasn't running and screaming, so there's that."

Callum bent down to show me his phone screen, which showed nine missed calls and twenty-seven messages, all from the magician. "I think he might want to talk to us."

"But do we believe anything he says?"

He *hmm*-ed, then clicked his messages open. "There's this, too." He angled the phone toward me.

Cal. We have to talk. Call me. Ez.

I looked up at him. "*Ez?* How does she have this number? No one's got this number." Then I growled, my tail twitching. "Bloody Ifan. He got it off you, didn't he?"

"I gave it to him," Callum said. "But why would he contact her?"

"To get her off *his* back. Gets him in as her favourite magic-worker, too. I don't believe any of that steaming mulch about how sad he is to be the most powerful magician in the north, with his fancy car and fancy house and ... and fancy *biscuits.*"

Callum made a doubtful sound. "I don't know, Gobs. It's never been his style."

"He likes power just fine."

"Maybe, but he's never been a fan of responsibility." He pocketed the phone. "And there's another way Ez could've got the number."

"*How?*" I demanded, then stopped, my spine stiffening. "We called Gerry."

"We did," Callum said, and we were both silent for a long moment, while some night bird cried over the river, and the stars burned pale distant scars in the sky.

"But she couldn't ..." I started, then trailed off. She could. Ez was nothing if not inventive, and one way or another, she could. We both knew it. "Hairy mung bean sprouts."

"Pretty much."

We both stood there, with the cold night sharpening its claws on us, feeling exposed and lost and bereft, until Lulu leaned out of the shed door and glared at us. "Are you coming in or not?" she demanded. "You're not *both* cats. You can't just stand in the doorway forever."

"Sorry," Callum said, and we hurried over the threshold into the headquarters of the OAP army.

6

IF THE LITTER BOX FITS

I HADN'T REALLY THOUGHT ABOUT WHAT WE MIGHT FIND INSIDE the shed. A kettle and some camping chairs, maybe, just some place for the veterans to meet in private, away from the retirement village. I could understand their desire to keep this separate. Combining work and home hadn't ended super-well for us, after all.

But I hadn't expected what lay inside the shed.

They'd apparently either raided an army surplus store, or they'd smuggled much more gear home with them upon retirement than was probably strictly permissible. A large camouflage-green tent that looked bigger than our entire old flat took up the majority of the space inside the shed. Hooks had been drilled into the concrete floor for the guy lines to attach to, and all the window flaps were rolled tightly down so we couldn't see inside. A little speedboat on a trailer was positioned near the doors, where it could be easily hitched up to the van, and I was certain there'd be a slip to launch it from not far away. Shelves made from planks resting on old bricks ran around the walls of the shed, and they were stacked with army-green packs, coils of rope, large jerry cans, cases of water, boxes of canned food, and crates stuffed with dried goods in plastic and foil packaging. One corner held enough camping gas cans to fuel a summer music festival, and there was a bench set up next to it with stacks of pots and plates resting next to an industrial-looking gas cooktop. More crates were labelled *First Aid,* and *Spare Parts,* and still others said *Winter Gear* or *Waterproofs.* There were also a number of soft bags with various tools poking out of them that looked suspiciously like they might not be used for home improvements.

Duds hobbled past us with a fresh bottle of whisky tucked under one arm and ducked into the tent, the heavy canvas of the flap getting tangled around his stick and setting him muttering and cursing.

"This … this is a lot of stuff," Callum said to Noel, who was checking the little boat's trailer tyres. "You collected all this?"

Noel gave a small *hmm.* "Yes?" he offered.

"I don't think we have to worry about these two running to the authorities," Lulu said, and grinned at us. "And yes. We've been *collecting* for a while." She chuckled, and lifted the tent flap. She'd left her potatoes in the van, but she still had the knife in one hand. "Come on in."

In contrast to the fluorescent glare of the shed, the inside of the tent was lit with soft yellow light from hanging bulbs suspended under the canvas roof. A brighter spotlight was directed onto a board standing at one end, and the floors were covered with heavy carpets in deep reds and intricate patterns. A heater purred, already pumping out warm air, and there were four hefty chairs positioned around a low, finely-carved coffee table at the opposite end of the tent to the board. Beneath the board was a more utilitarian but still not at all camping-standard table, with six matching chairs surrounding it. A tall fridge and a workbench topped with a microwave and an electric cooktop stood away from the canvas walls between the table and the seating area, and Noel made straight to it, topping a kettle up from a container of water that stood on the floor. He plugged the kettle in and switched it on, then looked at us.

"There's water," he said. "And a toilet. Out in the shed, I mean. But you try carrying four cups of tea in from out there."

I looked at his missing arm, and at Duds and Rita with their sticks. Only Lulu looked like she could manage four cups of tea, and I was willing to bet no one had ever asked her to be the tea lady.

Callum had, rather uncharacteristically, lost interest in the tea, and walked to the board at the end of the tent instead. Rita and Duds were already sitting at the table in front of it, and I padded over to join them. The carpets were heavy and soft under my paws, and the warm scent of them drowned the concrete tang of the shed floor beneath.

I tugged at Callum's jeans, and he crouched down to let me jump to his shoulder so that we could examine the board together. A map of Leeds was centred on it, with coloured drawing pins stabbed into it in various places. Matching pins held scraps of paper to the board just beyond the map, and I read a couple of them.

Reports of numerous lost pets linked to a pin stuck in the river Aire where it snaked past Stourton.

Reports of zombies were tied to pins in Harehills cemetery and Leeds Market.

Scary dogs pointed to Chapeltown.

Warehouse fire in Belle Isle.

And a large red loop was drawn around the area where

Dimly lurked, with a question mark in the centre. Pins ringed it, with printouts attached to them. River monsters. Hallucinations. Strange noises. Unusual smells. Weird fish. Headaches. Reports of floods that were suddenly retracted.

Rita leaned back in her chair and regarded us with bright, thoughtful eyes. "So," she said. "As you can see, we've done our research. So I'd really recommend you don't fob us off like a bunch of oldies with too much time on their hands. Something's happening in Leeds. And you two are right at the centre of it."

There was silence for a moment, then Callum said, "I'm not sure how much we know—"

"Rubbish," Lulu said, so close to us that Callum jumped and almost tipped me off his shoulder. "Sit down, lad," she said, and pointed at the nearest seat with her knife. He sat, and she stood over us, scowling. "We've got grandkids, see. And we're not letting the world be taken over by some orange lot that seem very into the whole enslaving thing."

"Been there, done that," Noel agreed, putting a couple of mugs on the table then going back for more.

"But I don't—" Callum started, and Lulu cut him off with a wave of the knife.

"How about we ask the questions, you just go on and answer them?"

"Lulu," Rita said, and the other woman gave her a questioning look. "Try not to take the boy's eye out, will you?"

Lulu looked at the knife in her hand as if startled to find it there, and put it back in her apron pocket. "Right. Sorry."

"I suggest you tell us everything from the beginning," Rita said to us. "Then we'll tell you everything relevant that *we* know, and we can take it from there."

"Sharing intelligence," Duds said, tipping condensed milk straight from a can into his mouth. "It's the only option," he continued, somewhat indistinctly. "No secrets."

I jumped to the table and looked up at Callum. "May as well," I said. "They're all bonkers, but I'm pretty sure they're not necromancer, Watch, or Ez bonkers. And they're definitely not weres, so there's that."

"How delightful," Rita said. "Now get off the table. It's mahogany."

"Sorry," I said, and jumped to one of the chairs. "Pretty cheap that, is it? On an ex-services pension and all."

"I said we'd tell you everything *relevant*," she said, and swirled the teapot Noel had put on the table. "Do we still have some of those biscuits we got the other night? Harrods, weren't they?"

"Not sure," Noel said, going back to poke in the crates stacked under the workbench. "Lulu was scoffing them."

"*Heresy*," she said, and sat down next to me, spinning the knife on the table absently.

And somehow it still felt a whole lot safer than the magician's house had, which just goes to show that my reference points were really off.

It took a while to tell the whole story. We skipped the Whitby part of things, as our issues all seemed to be centred on Dimly, and pretty much boiled down to *everyone's out to get us*. The Watch. Ez. Necromancers. A certain portion of the were population of Leeds, although hopefully not all of them, since we still needed to get the sorcerer's dentist off them. And then there was Ifan, whose motivations were maddeningly unclear. Callum insisted the magician wouldn't have called Ez, and might not have known about the weres, or that if he had they might've been there to protect the house and we'd misunderstood the whole situation. I argued that it was more likely they were there to keep us prisoners until he handed us over to Ez, or simply to gnaw off vital bits until we agreed to be magician pets, and everything got a bit heated until Lulu slammed her hands on the table and yelled, *"Enough!"*, shocking us both to silence. Green Snake stared up at her from where he'd taken cover in the empty teapot.

"Anyhow, I still don't trust him," I said, once my ears had recovered.

"Everyone's *very* clear on that, Gobs," Callum said. "I'm reserving judgement, okay? I don't think we know everything that's going on."

"Clearly," Tristan said. "You two have no discipline whatsoever." Noel had found a folding canvas chair among the supplies, which was a little lower than the others, and all I could see of the ginger tom across the table were the tips of his ears.

"What's *that* got to do with anything?" I demanded.

"You haven't investigated things in any sort of methodical manner. Aren't you meant to be professionals?"

"We are," I said, at the same time as Callum said, "Eh," and seesawed his hand. I glared at him. "We *are*. Best magical PIs in Yorkshire."

"I really think you need to stop saying that, considering there's not exactly any competition, is there?" he said.

"Can't see any other way you'd be the best," Tristan said, and Rita flicked his ear. *"Hey!"*

"We're the best OAP army in Yorkshire," she said. "Zero competition also, but that changes nothing."

"Yeah, chins up, lads," Duds said. "Can't let a little setback like losing an ancient god weigh on you too much."

Callum and I looked at each other, then Callum said, "Sorry, *losing* one? We banished it."

"We don't think you did," Rita said.

"But Ifan and I—"

"Ifan the magician you don't entirely trust?" she asked,

raising her eyebrows. "Whose house you just ran away from and where you almost got eaten by wolves?"

Callum frowned, and there was an edge in his voice when he answered. "True, but he wouldn't be involved in Old Ones. Ifan's ... Ifan, but he hasn't got a death wish. And *everyone* knows there's nothing good that could come out of Old Ones coming back. All they ever wanted was to enslave humans and the majority of Folk, and raise themselves above all other kinds. No one would want to bring them back except another Old One."

"And yet the magician's father and that necromancer woman were doing just that," Noel said. "Remember?"

"Sure, but Lewis thought he was getting Ifan back. He didn't know it was about the Old Ones," Callum pointed out.

"Not a very good magician, then, was he?" Lulu asked. "To not realise that?"

Callum didn't answer, and Duds chuckled into the silence, then hauled himself off the chair and tottered over to a cabinet in the corner. He came back with five stacked tumblers with thick, cut-glass sides, and set them next to the bottle of whisky.

"But we still stopped the Old One," Callum said, waving off the offer of whisky and taking another biscuit instead. Green Snake abandoned the teapot and went looking for crumbs. "We pushed it back through the door, or portal, or whatever it was."

"How do you know?" Lulu asked. "You done it before?"

"What makes *you* think it didn't work?" I asked.

"Stuff's been happening," Duds said.

"Specifically, *magical* stuff," Rita said. "Even allowing that we didn't know about it before, the incidents of unexplained phenomena and sightings of strange creatures has skyrocketed."

"We had to join clubs," Noel said heavily, and swigged

whisky. "*Clubs*. For *research purposes*. I've been on UFO tours. Out hunting the bloody Yorkshire Beast. Even looking for damn *Nessie*."

"And every weekend warrior with a monster guide thinks they're bloody special forces," Lulu said. "Running about in surplus camouflage and painting their faces." She shook her head. "You just want to …" she trailed off, pounding a fist lightly on the table.

"It hasn't been that bad," Rita said mildly.

"It's fine for you! You've just been in the chatrooms and so on. Noel and me have been out there in the field!"

"And yet you somehow survived."

"Surprised anyone else did," Duds said, and grinned at Lulu when she scowled at him.

"Wait," Callum said. "You think the Old One hasn't gone because you've been seeing more magical happenings?"

"Do you have another theory?" Rita asked, raising an eyebrow.

"I don't know." He took his cigarettes out, turning the packet over in his hands. "But if an Old One was actually here, they'd be bringing others. They'd open a path through to wherever they come from, and after that I don't think there'd be any sort of control. There wouldn't just be a few extra creature sightings. The world would be coming apart at the seams."

"Unless they haven't had the power to open a way through," I said. "We interrupted their nine cats with nine lives sacrifice thing, and you definitely did *something* when you tried to push it back. Maybe the Old One did manage to cling on over here but they've been too weak to open another door. Maybe they need a little extra firepower."

Callum looked at me. "Scythes," he said.

"Scythes," I agreed. Scythes, like the ones that had been

stolen from the reapers in Whitby by the Sea Witch and given to the drowned dead. Scythes that could cleave a soul from the world and cut a hole in reality.

"Scythes?" Rita asked. "We're not talking farming implements here, are we?"

"Reapers," Callum said.

"As in the Grim Reaper?" Lulu asked.

"Well, Reaper Scarborough and the East Yorkshire Marine Division," I said. "Grim Yorkshire's still got his, and so does Reaper Leeds, but she's in a bit of trouble over the whole mini-break thing."

Rita looked at me blankly and took a sip of whisky, while Lulu *hmm*-ed thoughtfully.

"I missed this bit," Duds said. "We don't have to deal with reapers, do we? Seems a bit dicey, given ... well." He waved at himself, his tattoos jumping alarmingly.

"Speak for yourself," Lulu said. "Some of us are still in *excellent* shape."

Rita put her glass down. "Reapers are *actual people?*"

Noel chuckled. "Not that we should be surprised by that these days."

Rita acknowledged that with a tip of her head, then looked at Callum and me. "And reapers are what? Also out to get you? Allies? Please tell me we've got *some* allies."

"Neutral," Callum said. "They're mostly just concerned about souls."

"Except that reapers did stand with the Watch way back when," Tristan said. "They were worried enough about the Old Ones and the necromancers and what they'd do to the souls that they fought with the Watch against them."

"With their scythes," I said. "About the only thing that'll work against an Old One."

"And now these scythes are missing?" Noel asked.

"Missing, and as well as being used for souls, reapers' scythes can cut through anything," Callum said. "Even the fabric of the world. So if the necromancers have them, they'll be able to open the way to the Old Ones pretty easily."

No one spoke for a moment, and despite the heater huffing away in the corner it suddenly felt cold in the tent, as if the night had curled tighter around us. I shivered.

"Well, they can't have done it yet," Lulu said finally. "Otherwise there'd be nasty orange ghosties all over the place. Like you say, it wouldn't just be some extra sightings. Maybe those are just a side effect of having one of the things here, like we thought."

"When did these scythes go missing?" Rita asked.

Callum and I looked at each other. "Not quite sure," he said. "Not more than a week or so, I think, because Grim Yorkshire had just been notified about souls being missed by DHL when we saw him in Whitby."

"The delivery people?" Duds asked.

"Departed Human Logistics," I said, and he choked on his whisky. Lulu thumped him briskly on the back until he calmed down, although he was still chortling happily when Rita spoke over him.

"The necromancers could've tried them already, then. What're they waiting for?"

The silence this time was longer, and I could feel uneasy currents moving around outside, fumbling charms tripping and sparking against each other, threatening to reveal us at any moment. Green Snake lifted his head and looked at me, and I tipped my head in acknowledgement.

"You," I said to Callum.

"What?"

"You stopped the Old One last time. They don't want to risk it happening again."

"Well, it was Ifan—"

"And didn't you say Norths are basically conduits? Bet that power would come in handy. Or they definitely don't want it available to work against them."

He shook his head. "Not even a proper North could do anything to stop Old Ones coming through. It can't be that."

"Maybe not exactly. But think about it. We got rid of the book of power that got dimensions all wobbly to start with. Put down the first lot of undead. At least slowed Ez getting a grip on Dimly, and you can't tell me she isn't in the middle of all this. Stopped the Old One coming through. Kept the sorcerer's dentist out of the teeth of some bad weres, which means *she's* still safe somewhere, and so still a threat to the necromancers. Stopped the dead in Whitby taking any more scythes."

"Well, maybe," Callum started, and I talked over him.

"Dude, we're the worst sort of flies in the pudding. Or the best. We're awesome, anyway."

"Ointment," he said automatically.

"They're totally after us." I thought about it, then sighed. "Hairy jam toasties. They're *totally* after us. We keep messing things up for them, and they won't risk it happening again."

The OAP army had been watching us with interest as we talked, and now Noel laughed softly and gestured to Duds to top up his glass. "I think you've nailed it, lads."

"Wish I hadn't now," I muttered.

"I'd just point out that stopping the Old One was a joint effort," Tristan said. "Don't get your tail too big."

"I'm very happy for an Old One to chew on your bones instead of mine," I said, and he put his front paws on the table so he could bare his teeth at me. I returned the favour.

Rita leaned forward, steepling her fingers over her glass. "Alright. So tell me about allies. Tell me you have some. Tell me *we* have some."

"Well, there's a sorcerer we can't find who's probably on

her own side rather than anyone else's, a missing troll, his troll kids we have no way of contacting, the reaper who's off being re-educated, and ..." I trailed off, looking at Callum. "I mean, I know some rats who are good sorts."

Duds started laughing again, and poured himself some more whisky. Green Snake hissed at him.

Rita nodded. "And us." She considered it, then looked at Tristan. "The Watch? Any help there?"

"No," I said. "Well, not since Claudia went missing, anyway."

"Does anyone *not* go missing around you?" Lulu asked, and Noel tutted. "What?"

"Harsh, Lu."

"Not really."

Tristan glared at me. "The colonel was talking to me. I have contacts."

I bared my teeth at him. "In the *Watch?* I thought you said they'd had your tail, too?"

"It doesn't mean I lost all my contacts," he snapped. "You use what you've got, man."

"You're talking to them?" My heart was going too fast, and my muscles were bunching almost against my will. "What is this? You some Watch informant, you soggy bloody week-old rhubarb crumble?"

"*What?*" he demanded. "What did you call me?"

"I called you a soggy—"

"You called me an *informant!*"

"If the litter box fits—"

Lulu slammed her hands down again, hard enough that the contents of Duds' whisky glass made a break for freedom and Green Snake dived for cover in the biscuit packet. "You want to take it outside?" she asked. "Because I'll take you both by the scruff like a couple of damn kittens, see if I don't."

"Sorry ma'am," Tristan said, and I stared at her for a moment, then muttered, "Yeah. Sorry."

"The Watch can't be trusted," Callum said. "Some cats are fine, but our experience – well, Gobs' experience – is that overall the Watch isn't doing what they should be."

"Which is?" Rita asked.

"Keeping the Folk and human worlds apart. Preventing anything that might upset the balance, but also making sure all kinds live as equally as they can." He looked at me. "That's meant to be their deal, right?"

"Right," I said.

"Been a long time since it worked like that, though," Tristan said, and gave me a grudging look. "But I do still keep contacts I can trust."

"Know your enemy," Noel said absently, reclaiming the whisky bottle from Duds.

"So what's happening, then?" I asked Tristan. "Since you've got this inside info, tell us. What are they playing at? Where are they now we've got actual sodding necromancers about the place? Where were they in Dimly when things got bad? When a godsdamned Old One popped into a bloody *basement?* They all off on their hols?"

"I'm not sure," Tristan said. "I've not been able to get any info from anyone for weeks, and when I did it wasn't good. Watch cats were vanishing. They've got their own problems."

"Yeah, well. That doesn't help much," I said, trying not think of hungry voids and the cats that had attacked me in Whitby. There was something sickeningly familiar about this whole thing, as if everything had been leading to this point, the unicorn horn weapons in Dimly and the magical spills in Headingly and bloody magic-workers gathering power like two-for-one coupon books and just *everything.* "With all the stuff they've been ignoring, it's like they've just stopped caring if humans get a whiff of Folk."

"They can't have," Tristan said. "Even if they're playing with necromancers, they wouldn't want humans getting wind of it. It'd be war, if humans discovered Folk. Humans can't help themselves."

"Fair," Rita said, and Duds grunted agreement.

"It makes sense if they think there's no going back," Callum said quietly. He'd swapped his cigarettes for the piece of jet. "That's what you mean, isn't it, Gobs?"

I stretched where I sat, arching my spine up, less to get the kinks out of it than out of my mind. Out of my *memory*. "Maybe? Doesn't it feel like they've been waiting for this? Letting things go little bit by little bit, letting resentments grow between kinds. Making them worse, even. And anyone who questions how things are, or tries to make things better – to make things easier between kinds, or more equal, or …" I trailed off, unable to find the words. I could feel the Inbetween pressing around me, closer than the walls of the tent, full of teeth and tentacles and things that rend and tear, and my mouth was suddenly dry. I licked my chops and looked at Lulu. "Hey, have you lot *collected* any sushi-grade tuna? Maybe some free-range pheasant? Or is it all just whisky and posh glasses?"

Callum tapped the chair by my paws. "Finish what you were saying."

I looked up at him, and said, "The Watch aren't targeting the ones that are making things worse. Ez and her unicorn horn. The necromancers and all those cats they took. No one's done *anything*—" I was cut off by a touch on my spine. Not a touch, a *burn*, a talon laying flesh open to the bone, and I was there again, there in the non-dark emptiness of the void, held in place by the shifting claws and teeth of one cat then another, swapping grips but never letting go, never giving me a chance to escape, pinning me there while the beasts ripped and snatched and tore, shredding skin and devouring flesh, and my screams were lost in the nothingness even as it swallowed me.

Everything was lost.

7

ALLERGIC TO MEMORIES

"GOBS. *GOBS.*"

Cigarette smoke and old books and quiet, aching loss, and that remote undercurrent of power, closer now. Callum had hold of me, and my teeth and claws were buried in his hands, the carpets heavy and silent under my back. I stared up at him, my breath rattling in my throat.

"Alright?" he asked.

I unlatched myself from his arm, tremors running across my limbs. "Sure. Stop *touching* me. Grabby bloody human."

Callum rocked back on his heels, his face unreadable and his hands laced with the heavy red lines of scratches, already starting to spill over.

"What was *that?*" Tristan asked, appearing over me.

"Allergic reaction," I said, rolling onto my belly but not trusting myself to get up yet. "I never did like ginger."

Tristan growled, and Lulu laughed softly. I glared at her, and she smiled. "First time I've seen an allergic reaction look like a flashback."

Callum made a *hmm* noise and took a blue-trimmed

hanky Noel offered him, dabbing the blood off his hands. "I think we know why you were killed in your last life, at least."

"Because I asked for pheasant?" I suggested.

"Because you figured it out," he said.

"Did I?" I asked, then added, "I mean, of course I did, but I was a bit distracted there, so enlighten me."

"The Watch has been playing a long game, sounds to me," Rita said. "And maybe there've been enough good sorts to keep it all in check, but now there's not."

Lulu nodded. "And so now you've got one of your Old Ones about, and some reaper's scythes to help them bring more through, and it's all going to go a bit Armageddon."

I thought about it. "So, what – I keep figuring this out and they keep killing me?"

"Seems about right," Duds said. "Maybe you've been a fly in their pudding before. Certainly something happened to you that's connected with figuring it out, else you wouldn't have had your little turn there."

"I didn't have a *little turn*," I snapped. "Something tried to drag me into the void!"

"It didn't," Callum said. "This wasn't like the flat. You just ..." He hesitated.

"Had a little turn," Tristan said, with a purr at the end of the words.

I glared at him, then at the humans gathered above me. "*Well?* Pheasant? Something? I'm not going to recover without it, you know."

"Cats," Lulu muttered, and everyone returned to the table except Callum. He stayed crouched next to me, and scratched the back of my neck gently. The dark edges lurking at the edge of the room retreated bit by bit, and I sat there with my limbs trembling, panting quietly. Green Snake slipped off the edge of the table and dropped down next to me, and when he curled himself around my legs I didn't even kick him off.

I might not have gone anywhere, but I could feel the echoes of the times that I had, ringing on the edges of my consciousness, calling the beasts in. There was nothing little about that.

LULU FOUND some vacuum-sealed fish of some description in one of the crates outside, as well as a tub of caviar, which is weird salty stuff and not at all a substitute for pheasant. Green Snake seemed very impressed by it though, and pretty much immersed his entire head in the jar. The fish was delicately filleted and doused with oil that Lulu insisted on rinsing off, as she said she didn't think it was any good for cats. I doubted a little oil was the worst of my problems right now, but I wasn't about to argue with her. She had a knife peeking out of her sleeve.

While I waited on the fish, Callum promised me I hadn't gone anywhere when I'd felt like I was back in the Inbetween. No accidental shifting, not that that had been an issue since I was a kitten, and nothing had reached out to snatch me. So it wasn't the Watch, and it hadn't been a repeat of the flat, either. That had been something else, some nasty little trapdoor to unknown places that seemed likely to be set by necromancers, when I looked at it in the context of everything else that was going on.

So if it hadn't been either of those, maybe it *was* just memories. It had felt bloody real, though. Toothily real, more to the point, and my paws prickled and twitched with it. I jerked away when Duds laid a twisted old hand on my back, baring my teeth at him, but he ignored it and just patted me, his touch heavy but oddly reassuring, deeply human and grounded in a world that had no knowledge of voids and void-beasts and the horrors of the Watch.

Plenty of his own horrors, though. Cats are hardly the only kind that are careless with their own. Duds' voice was low when he started to speak, his words meant for my ears only, and I stared up at the stubbled, ill-fitting skin of his face as he told me that sometimes he still felt the bullets hitting him, enemy fire taken in the backstreets and alleys of a hard-fought and unfair urban war. That sometimes he hid in corners with his arms over his head to ward off the beatings that had come after the capture. Beatings that still came calling in the empty hours of long nights, or pounced on him in supermarket aisles, invited back by the hard lights and cold floors. The memories were quicksand that swallowed him, ambushing him under the cover of everyday life. Under *normality*, whatever that was.

His voice was steady enough, but he passed his tremors to me as he petted my back, and when he stopped talking I rubbed my face against his hand until he laughed and said, "Bloody cats. Look at the weird face he's making!" He pointed at me delightedly, and the rest of the OAP army, who had been studiously looking at anything but us, laughed too. Duds drained his glass, and Rita topped it up, and Tristan lifted his chin at me. I returned the gesture and sat down as Lulu set a bowl in front of me, my whole being suddenly heavy with weariness.

While I ate fancy marinated fish fillets Callum went outside to smoke, Lulu padding alongside him with her head only coming up to about his chest. Tristan gulped his food down next to me, and Rita, who'd settled herself into a light-weight wheelchair, trundled around the tent collecting note-books on her lap. Noel and Duds remained at the table, drinking whisky and chuckling quietly about something.

When the bowl was clean I sat back and cleaned my face with my paws, using the moment to examine the tent more closely and to feel the weight of the charms surrounding us. I couldn't help but feel I'd made myself obvious with the flash-back, noticeable somehow, but maybe that was in my head, too, sharing space with the tentacles and the teeth.

"Alright, that cat?" Tristan asked, still hunkered over his bowl.

"Don't know," I said. "I get all the memory stuff, but it felt real."

"So do Duds' turns," he said. "Callum's lucky you only bit him. I've seen Duds take out orderlies twice his size in the rest home. He does better now, though."

"Better as in takes out more of them?" Although it was already pretty impressive, to be honest.

"No, better as in it doesn't happen so much. The more he talks about it, the easier it gets. He only told me about it at first, but now he tells everyone, and it seems like it makes it better for him."

I cocked my head. "How long've you been with him?"

"Third life," Tristan said. "Others were decent long ones, too. More so than this one looks like being, anyway."

"Dude," I said, and wondered if I could put up with Callum for that long. He'd have to stop being such a bleeding heart and get us some actual money first. And stop smoking. Tristan went back to munching contentedly on his fish, and after a moment I asked, "So what info have your super-reli-able, not-at-all-dodgy Watch contacts come up with, then? Anything useful?"

"Not as much as I'd like," he said. "Cats have been less and less welcome in a lot of places."

I licked oil off my chops. Lulu might've had a point about rinsing it off. "Less welcome as in *all* cats are being kept out of places? Doesn't seem like the Watch would stand for that."

"They'll have their own ways around such things. They *always* have their own ways around things." He sounded suddenly tired, then shook himself. "Anyway, I should have a couple of contacts arriving soon. Maybe they'll know something."

"Are these your Watch contacts?" The hair was rising on my back just at the idea, even though, now I was thinking a little more clearly, Tristan was hardly Watch material with his OAP buddies and makeshift charm school. But just because he likely wasn't Watch didn't mean the Watch couldn't use him to get what they wanted, and all a cat would need to do was call him sir and he'd cough up his last hairball on command.

He narrowed his eyes at me. "No, of course not my Watch contacts. I told you, they've all vanished on me. Did you hit your head when you fell off the table?"

"I have no idea. I was busy reliving being torn limb from limb at the time."

He snorted, and we stared at each other, then he said, "I kept in touch with some of the cats from the whole Old One incident. We've formed a bit of an alliance, us and a few others."

"Pru? Is she coming?" I said immediately. "Tam?"

"Meant to be," he said. "They were really keen to see you, for reasons that escape me." He turned to address the room as Lulu and Callum came back inside, trailing the reek of cigarette smoke. "Alright, chaps," Tristan said, and if he could've clapped his paws he would've. I could see it. "The COR will be here any moment. Let's look sharp, shall we?"

"Core?" Callum asked.

"Like 'Cor, guv, look what we have here'?" I suggested.

"No, you muppets. COR as in Cats of the Resistance."

"Wouldn't that be COT-R?" I asked. "Or Cotter? Coater?"

"*No.* One doesn't include the … the things. The little words."

"Articles," Callum said, but no one paid him any attention.

"What about 'of'?" I asked. "That's a littler word than 'the'."

"But then it'd be CR, which isn't a word," Tristan said.

"*Krrr*," I said.

"*No.*"

"Good to see things are progressing as usual," a new voice said, and I spun around to see a slim, hairless cat padding across the soft carpeting, a bright pink puffer jacket turning her softly rotund. A brindled tabby at least twice her size (even given the jacket) strolled next to her, ragged ears setting off a perpetually enraged expression.

"Pru! Tam!" I managed not to bound forward, and settled for a casual trot to touch noses with each of them. Pru smelled of some sort of floral oil and good tuna, while Tam had the whiff of damp nights and old wood and dark alleys, and both scents were glorious.

Callum crouched down to offer his hand for them to head-bump, and the OAP army nodded at them. Noel put the kettle on again, and I looked at Tristan. "Wait – this is it? This is COR? Not to be rude or anything, but ..."

"It's not all of us," Pru said. "We've had to be careful. There's the cats we were in the cages with – Astrid won't have anything to do with it, she says she's got the one life left and she'd rather make it comfortable. Mitzi comes and goes. She's adopted some other old cat and is more concerned with keeping her in one piece than dealing with the Watch. But there's us, and the brothers, not that we've heard from them for a while, and a few others we trust. Plus Gordie's very enthusiastic when he understands what's going on."

"Gordie? Is he still with Rav?" Callum asked. Gordie was a very old and somewhat senile tom who'd been adopted by a necromancer heavy after the showdown with the Old One. The heavy had quit necromancing, but he'd then been nipped by his werewolf boyfriend, which wasn't exactly an improvement. "We should talk to Rav."

"Should we?" I asked. "Doggy scent and big teeth and all that."

"He might know where Malcolm is," Callum pointed out. "And what weres tried to jump us at Ifan's."

Pru arched her non-existent whiskers, turning her forehead into a canvas of wrinkles. "Good to see you two haven't wasted any time getting back into the swing of things. How long have you been in town?"

"Two days," I said.

"Not even 24 hours," Callum admitted.

"Spread over two days," I protested.

Tam huffed soft cat laughter and leaped to the table with an easy, muscular grace, making Rita jump when she appeared at her elbow.

"Bloody hell, it's like being stalked by a pint-sized tiger. Sorry, Tam."

Tam just sat down and started cleaning her paws. No one told *her* to get off the table.

I'D REALLY LIKE to say that we had a level, productive discussion regarding the almost-certainty that the Watch were somehow in league with orange almost-gods and filthy bloody necromancers, but that would fail to take into account the fact that four humans, one sort-of human, and four cats of varying affiliation had a *lot* of opinions. Plus a certain portion of the gathering had partaken pretty heavily of the whisky.

Within ten minutes Rita was slamming her fist on the table, holding forth at a commanding volume about the need for careful reconnaissance and planning. Duds had taken his jacket off to reveal his collection of very adult tattoos and was limping in circles with the whisky bottle in one hand, shouting that we should take the battle to the necromancers, and Lulu was sharpening an alarming collection of knives with grim determination and occasionally snarling a "Seconded!" to Duds' suggestions. Noel was jabbing his finger wildly at a map laid out on the table, talking about routes of attack and retreat and the need for better transport, and Callum had retreated to sit cross-legged on the floor under the whiteboard, out of the worst of the crossfire as he scrolled through a tablet.

Tristan, meanwhile, was bellowing that COR was meant to be in charge of these things, and as the humans couldn't really be expected to be up to speed on Folk issues, they needed to step back. He hated to be thrust into the limelight, of course, but as leader of COR he would if he had to. The OAP army were ignoring him, and Pru was hissing that she'd thrust him into *something* if he didn't sit down and shut up. Tam had eaten all the remaining fish and finished off Green Snake's caviar, and was now asleep in the centre of the table, Noel's map lying over her like an over-starched sheet, and I was just sitting in a chair watching it all with a slow, twisting dread in my belly.

Eventually I jumped down and padded over to Callum. He looked up from the tablet and said, "Alright?"

I could barely hear him over the shouting from the table. "Well, yes, but also no. This is who's going to help us stop scheming bloody necromancers and Old Ones? We're stuffed like Sunday dinner."

He took a mouthful of tea from the mug sitting by his leg and set it back down before he answered. "Is that what we're doing?"

I hesitated, then said, "I don't think we've got much choice. I don't think I've *ever* had any choice." My mind almost sneaked back to find a memory, but I clamped down on it. I'd bitten my tongue in my panic earlier, and once was enough in one evening for that sort of thing.

"There's always a choice," he said. "We don't have to stay in Leeds, you know. We can leave again. Go back to Whitby, or somewhere else. We'll figure it out."

I considered it, but not for long. The Watch have paws everywhere, and if the Old Ones really were coming back, nowhere would be safe. Not for anyone. Besides, there was still Gerry to worry about, and Gertrude off being disciplined or whatever, and leaving the OAP army unsupervised seemed likely to end up with them declaring war on the city's magic-workers and invading Dimly. "No," I said aloud. "Too many bloody gulls in Whitby."

He smiled slightly at that. "Well, then. We're going to have to be a bit more proactive."

"As in?"

He tapped the tablet, and Green Snake, who'd been flopped over Callum's leg like an exhausted ribbon, craned his head up to take a look. "This is the log from Ifan's house. Their reconnaissance has been really thorough, but it's also pretty cat-based. Tristan must've organised a lot of it."

"So? That's good, right?"

"Yeah. Not really. We have photos of delivery drivers – Ifan eats a lot of takeaways by the looks of things, and has an unhealthy home shopping habit—"

"I had no idea you could order tongue of gnat and toe of dog online."

"—and other than that there's just been the occasional person going in. I don't recognise them." He turned the tablet to show me a series of photos, one lot of a tall, broad man in a well-made suit, and another set of a slight woman in a sleek wool coat. I sniffed the screen but there was no way to tell anything from it.

"They could be necromancers," I suggested. "Or weres. Other magicians."

"Sure. Or they could be his accountant, or lawyer, or pretty much anyone."

"Could be human sacrifices," I suggested. "Or dates."

"They come back out, so the human sacrifice is unlikely," Callum said. "No Ez, though," he added pointedly.

"Probably wouldn't be silly enough to meet him there."

"Maybe."

I narrowed my eyes at him. "You haven't messaged her, have you?" He hesitated just long enough that I hissed, startling Green Snake. "You sodden radish. What d'you think she's going to tell you?"

"Maybe something useful," he said, and took his phone out. "She sent me this: *Can't talk on here. Meet me 10 a.m. at the old spot. Don't come to Dimly.*"

"The old spot?"

He smiled slightly, dimples appearing then vanishing. "When we were kids we used to sneak off and go to this games arcade in Leeds. Play video games and eat chips and just be ... I don't know. Normal. *Human.*"

"When she wasn't exploding pigs' heads, you mean?"

The look he gave me was sharp. "I haven't forgotten, Gobs."

"Good. Because she'll probably have half a dozen necromancers ready to jump you."

"I know. But we need more information. We need to know what's happening in Dimly."

I acknowledged that with a huff. "Walking straight into a trap seems like a dubious method of gathering intelligence, even for us. Wasn't Ifan and the hungry house enough?"

"Ifan's done nothing wrong." He looked back at the tablet as I turned my huff into a snort. "Certainly nothing that's in these logs anyway. That was pretty much it for the human notes, then we've got the cat ones, as told to Noel." He swiped the photos away and read, "'Female human-ish green shoes'."

"Ah," I said, suddenly remembering my own problems with describing humans.

"'Human sort in car'."

"Right."

"'Pigeon hair'."

"Okay, okay. So not useful. And they'd have been too far away to get a scent off them."

"I've not found any mention of scents yet, so it'd seem that way." He paused, then said, "But couldn't you recognise necromancers from a distance? I mean, that's a strong *feel*, right?"

"Eh. Yes and no. Depends how strong they are." I'd been literally on top of Sonia, the boss necromancer, before I'd known who she was. But she'd been in the magician's house when Ifan's dad had still had it, so the sense of her would've been masked, overwhelmed by the old magic of the place. "Any mention of weres? You can usually whiff those out two streets over."

"A few, but sounds like they were just prowling. They didn't try and go in. So they might've been just keeping an eye on the place too."

"Or they sniffed out the surveillance and thought better of things."

Callum nodded and picked up his tea again. "So we've still no reason to suspect Ifan."

"We've no reason to trust him, either."

He nodded. "Fair. But what do we do now, then?" He looked at his phone, lying on the rug next to him.

"Ez isn't going to help," I said. "You heard what Ifan said."

Callum met my gaze steadily. "So you trust him on that bit, then?"

"I just prefer to assume worst case scenario. It's rarely wrong."

He snorted. "Fair point. But we need some help if we're going to find Gerry. *And* Malcolm. And what about the scythes? We can't just ignore that."

I looked back at the table. Duds and Rita had stopped shouting at each other, and were instead arguing with Noel, and Tristan had given up on Pru and was snarling at Lulu. She was tapping the point of a knife into a notebook, and Tristan looked like he was about to launch himself across the table at her. Pru was watching with her ears pricked forward and her front paws pressed neatly together, and Tam was still just a mound under the map.

"What about this lot?" I asked. "How do we keep them out of it all? We can't let them get involved, or go up against the necromancers. Look at them."

Callum nodded. "Agreed. I'm not sure how easy it's going to be to stop them, though."

I thought about it. "They're not the sort of help we need, anyway. We need someone with more than Bless-O-Matic garlic water and potatoes."

"So we're back to Ms Jones, and that means Malcolm, and that means finding Yasmin."

"Or," I said, and hesitated. It was true that we didn't have the best track record with those who helped us, but we also didn't have a lot of choices, and it felt like they were narrowing down every moment. There was one kind out there who could actually take on an Old One, and we had a direct line to one of them. Or to her partner, anyway. "We need to go and see Emma," I said.

"We can't," Callum said. "Gertrude's not even there. And the last time we saw Emma we ended up losing her to the Sea Witch."

"We got her back," I pointed out. "And that was the time before last, anyway."

"She specifically told us not to come around."

"Cat," I said, with as much conviction as I could. My uncertainty was due to not wanting to drag Emma into anything, though, not because I was bothered about disobeying instructions. Cat was an accurate description, after all.

"Human," Callum said.

"Not entirely," I pointed out, and he sighed. "Also, I'd feel much better about hitting up some weres with a reaper on side."

"There is that," he said, and looked at Green Snake. The little reptile lifted his head from the tablet, looked at each of us, then pointed his snout at me.

"See?" I said.

"I shouldn't be outvoted by a cat and a snake," Callum said, but without much conviction.

8

A GLIMMER OF A PLAN

So we had a plan, as far as that went. The only thing now was to shake our suddenly acquired team of OAPs and squabbling cats. I suggested we tried simply walking out while they were still fighting among themselves, but Callum pointed out that unless we wanted to steal the van from at least one person with an excess of knives, we'd just end up as necromancer bait on the road. So we went back to join the table before anyone lost an eye. Or a tail.

"I didn't notice you arrive," Tristan was saying to Pru. "I *should* have felt you arrive. Did you break the charms?"

Pru just gave him a look through half-closed eyes that indicated she was both unbothered by the accusation and inclined to inflict violence on his person if he continued, and a moment later, when Tristan wondered aloud if *someone* had been large enough to bust the charms accidentally, Tam erupted from under Noel's maps with her head low and a growl already rumbling in her chest.

"Enough, enough," Rita said. "We're not getting anywhere. Look, we've got our primary targets—" She stopped, and

Callum and I stared at her. "Targets in the best possible way," she added.

"I'm not sure there is a best possible way," I said.

"Would you prefer we left you for the wolves?"

"No," I admitted.

"I didn't think so."

Callum took a seat at the table. "And thank you for that. Really. You know as much as we do now, but we need to get on. We've got a plan and we're going with it." He looked around the table. "Alone."

There was a moment's silence, and Duds was the first to break it by laughing. Lulu joined in, and a moment later the entire OAP army were wheezing and chuckling and waving at Callum like he'd been brought in as afternoon entertainment in the retirement home.

"That went well," Pru said.

"Even I wouldn't have bothered trying that on this lot," Tam said, her tones oddly precise for a cat who looked like she mostly slept in hedges. She yawned when I blinked at her.

"Oh, hello," I said. "Thought you'd gone back to your vow of silence there."

"Didn't have anything to say to you before." She stretched luxuriously and closed her eyes again.

Rita leaned her forearms on the table and grinned at us. "We've hardly spent the last six months poking around with monster groupies and camping outside magicians' houses just to potter off home now. Bless, though. It was a good effort."

"But this is too dangerous," Callum said. "We can't ask you for help."

"We weren't waiting for you to ask," Noel said.

"Or give permission," Rita added.

"Do you know how boring retirement is?" Lulu asked.

"That whole necromancer summoning thing was the most excitement we'd had in years. We've been on the trail ever since."

"Oh, *fantastic*," I said. "You couldn't take up bloody crochet like everyone else?"

Lulu pointed a knife at me warningly and I put my ears back. Green Snake ducked back into Callum's sleeve, which shows how much help a snake is.

"I like crocheting," Duds said. "Very meditative."

"So what's this plan?" Noel asked. "Who do we tackle first?"

"I've got some ideas for the magician," Lulu said, thumbing the edge of a blade.

"*No*," Callum said, apparently hoping for a better result this time. "For a start, we don't know if he's actually the one we need to worry about, and also *none* of us are equipped to go up against a magician." He shook his head. "We're going to start with the reaper. If we can get in contact with her, maybe she can convince Grim Yorkshire that this is something they need to be involved in. And failing that, we can at least warn them about the scythes. See if they can, I don't know ... deactivate them or something."

The OAP army looked at each other, then Rita said, "That actually sounds like a reasonable course of action."

"Thanks?" Callum said.

"Any news on Claudia?" I asked Pru.

"Nothing," she said. "But I've not been near the Watch since you were here last. Being aligned with Claudia has been making some cats twitchy."

"Claudia is kitty non-grated," Tristan said. "As are all those who held to her."

"Non-grated?" Lulu asked. "They didn't grate her? What did they do to her?"

Tristan blinked at her. "I don't know what they did to her.

But why would they grate her? How would they even do that?"

"*Persona non grata,*" Rita said.

"*Claudia,* not Persona," Tristan said. "I did tell you about hearing aids."

"It means she's out of favour," Callum said, rubbing his forehead.

"I *know,*" Tristan said.

"She was last heard of with Ms Jones," Pru put in, before things could deteriorate further. "So maybe she's still with her." She glanced at Tam. "Hopefully, anyway. Although it's possible the Watch got their paws on her."

"Last thing my contacts told me was that the situation in the Watch was pretty sticky for anyone who held to Claudia's ways," Tristan said. "Or even the old ways – you know, some rough semblance of equality and maintaining balance."

"*His contacts* meaning Charlie and Harvey," Pru said.

"The brothers?" I asked. "They're missing?" They had been annoying, impossible to tell apart, and part of some Watch schism that Claudia headed – the Watch's watchers. Not the sort of cats that would have walked away from trouble.

"I have other contacts," Tristan protested. "Just no one who'll talk to me."

"There's cats vanishing like kibble in a nip frenzy," Tam observed.

Pru looked at me. "You were in touch with Ms Jones. Has she said anything about Claudia or the Watch?"

I licked my chops, my mouth sticky, and said, "She hasn't. We never have long to talk."

"What about the Watch leader?" Callum asked. "I thought she was sort of aligned with Claudia's ideas."

"Missing," Tristan said, his voice quiet. "Charlie and Harvey told me that much, before they vanished too."

"The Old Guard has fallen," Tam said softly. "Now come the end times."

No one spoke for a moment, then Duds said, "Well, I'm having another drink in that case."

"Damn straight," Lulu said. "No point going out sober."

SITTING on the table with my back as straight as I could make it, my tail curled over my toes, I met Pru's gaze. She regarded me curiously, eyebrow ridges raised. Callum was rolling his piece of jet in his fingers, but he seemed oddly calm, his movements relaxed as he leaned back in his chair with one ankle resting on his opposite knee, watching the OAP army sharing out more whisky. I hoped Noel wasn't planning to drive any of them home, because the bottle was all but empty.

"How was the seaside?" Pru asked me.

"Wet," I said. "And there's such a thing as too much fish."

She snorted, and nodded at the bald patch on my tail. "Restful, was it?"

I examined the newest addition to my collection of scars. "That was the Watch. They tried to chuck me in the Inbetween again."

Tam growled slightly, and Noel leaned toward us. "What happens if there's no leader? Is there a second in command or something?"

"Technically," I said. "But cats aren't really into the whole rank and file thing. Usually there's just a bloody great scrap and everything's chaos until it gets sorted out."

"That seems ideal when there's all sorts of trouble going down," Lulu said.

Rita pointed at me. "This Claudia – has she got some authority?"

I looked at Tam and Tristan. Tam shrugged. "She has respect," she said. "For those who still think equality between kinds matters, anyway."

"Then we need her," Rita said. "We need your reaper, and it sounds like if we get Claudia, we might get some pull in the Watch, *and* get a sorcerer too. That seems like a good start."

It did sound like a good start. But it also sounded like more out-of-body experiences. I sighed. "I don't really know how to contact Ms Jones, but I can try. The only thing is that she still insists she needs bloody Walker. Every time I see her – Walker, Walker, Walker. He's a *dentist*. I don't get it."

"That little man at the house?" Lulu asked. "He was a right weedy specimen. I'm sure we can find her something better." She gave Callum a speculative look, and he shifted uneasily.

"If she wants that human, she wants that human," Pru said. "There's no accounting for it."

I purred agreement, although privately I thought that there *was* some accounting for Pru's human, who seemed to invest heavily in wild sea trout and organic partridges and such things. She also looked like a Norse god, but that's of less interest to cats.

"There's our plan, then," Callum said. "Start with Gertrude. Then find Malcolm. Take him to Ms Jones, or at least tell her we've got him. Then hopefully she'll help us with both Claudia and … everything." He waved vaguely.

"Just like that," I said.

"Just like that." He grinned at me. "I even know where we can find a couple of weres."

"You could just phone this Walker," Rita pointed out.

"No one seems keen to answer us."

"Give me the number and leave it with me." She tapped the table. "I'll track the dentist down. You two deal with the reaper and the sorcerer. The rest of us—"

"Gerry," I said. "We need to check on him."

"Really?" Pru said. "He's a *troll*."

"Something's up," Callum said. "We had a message that we think was from Poppy. But we don't have a way to contact her, and Gerry's not answering his phone."

"Who's this Gerry?" Rita asked. "I'm assuming we're not talking an internet troll."

"No, a proper one," I said. "Mayor of Dimly."

"Of course he is. And he's missing?"

"Possibly," Callum said.

"We evidently need some old age and cunning on the case," Noel said.

"Yeah, you young lot – 'oh, they won't answer my texts, so we may as well give up'." Duds snorted.

"I mean, we tried," Callum started, and Lulu waved at him, almost jabbing him with her cigarette.

"Just give us all the details then go and find your reaper. Let us get on with the good stuff." She cleared her throat and said in a suddenly cut-crystal voice, "Oh, yes, darling. I should like to speak to the Lord Mayor. It's concerning a *very* important dinner. Do be a sweetie and put me through, *hmm?*" She shoved the cigarette back into her mouth and coughed around it. "Should do it."

"It's dangerous," Callum started.

"And we are very old and have very little to lose," Rita said. "Now go and grab a few hours kip. There's camp beds in the shed you can bring in here. No one's going anywhere tonight. No one human," she amended, as Tam arched her whiskers.

"Yes, ma'am, as you say, ma'am," Tristan barked, and promptly jumped off his chair, going to curl up in a pile of floor cushions.

"Won't they miss you at the retirement home?" Callum asked Rita.

"Do you know how much the staff in those places make?

Not enough to worry about a few of us going on a night out. Especially if we drop a few pounds in the right places."

"I need to get the van back first thing, though," Noel said, getting up. "Bowls tournament."

Rita clicked her fingers. "Damn. Forgot. Never mind – I'll just have to miss this one." She grinned at us. "Bigger things at stake."

Callum and I looked at each other, and he said, "I'll drive you back. The camp beds don't sound very comfortable."

There was a pause, then Lulu said, "S'true. Last time we slept here I had to go to the chiropractor every other day for three weeks."

"Don't think anyone should be driving," Duds said, waving the whisky bottle at us. "Police are so bloody picky these days."

Callum raised his mug. "I don't drink."

All four humans stared at him, and Lulu muttered, "Young folk these days."

He shrugged. "It comes in handy. You get some sleep, and the van's back when it should be. I need to get my car anyway—"

He was drowned out by a chorus of protest.

"Absolutely not," Rita said, raising her voice over the others. "You're not going back to that house."

"Weres," I said to Callum. "Did you forget the weres?"

"And the magician," Duds pointed out. "You'll have to go in and face him and all his ..." He waved his hands in what was presumably meant to be a mystical manner.

"Get the lad out of trouble, and he's straight back to it like a bloody dog," Lulu said, scowling at Callum.

"I can't just *walk* everywhere," Callum protested. "How're we meant to cover any sort of ground like that? Bus?"

Everyone started arguing again, and Rita shouted over them, "Noel, let him take your car."

"Absolutely not," Noel said. "Have you seen him? If he treats his clothes like that, how's he going to treat my car?"

"It's a *car*," Rita said, and both Lulu and Noel made the sort of teeth-sucking noises that always indicate both disagreement and that things are about to get expensive. "You never even drive it," she pointed out. "If it really is the end times, it may as well get a run out."

"If it is the end times, I'm going out driving her myself," Noel said, and scowled when Rita tipped her head to one side. "I can manage the gears! It's just a bit awkward."

"He can take my car," Duds said.

"We're trying to help him, not kill him, Duds."

"My car runs just fine," Duds said. "And if she winds up with a few more scratches, it really makes no difference."

"Well, that's a fair point," Rita said, and they all looked at Callum.

He tapped his fingers on the table. "I'd really prefer my own car."

"You're not going back to the magician's," Rita said. "Take Duds' car."

WHICH IS how we ended up, an hour or so later, puttering down the lanes of the retirement village in an ancient VW Beetle that was made up of a variety of mismatched panels in different colours, all tied together with liberal applications of rust and gaffer tape. One headlight pointed at the road just in front of us, and the other was apparently trying to call aircraft in to land, and we backfired so loudly on the way out of the shoddy garage attached to Duds' little unit that Callum stalled it.

Duds leaned in the driver's window and said, "It's fine.

Everyone around here's deaf or half dead. They won't notice."

So we rattled and backfired our way out of the village, scraping the underside of the car on the speed bumps, then turned onto the early morning roads of Leeds on threadbare tyres.

"Is this thing safe?" Pru asked. She, Tam and I were wedged together on the front seat, where we seemed marginally less likely to get asphyxiated by exhaust fumes than in the back. Tristan had stayed with Duds, declaring he'd supervise that end of things, which in theory was going to consist of trying to track down Walker, the weres, Gerry, and Poppy. We'd handed over every phone number we had in the hope that it'd keep them busy until we had a better handle on things. And hopefully Tristan might be able to stop them rolling straight into Dimly on their mobility scooters first thing in the morning. Or at least give us advance warning if they did.

"Probably not," Callum said, wrestling with the gears. He seemed to be having trouble getting it out of second and the car was belching noxious black smoke everywhere.

"Awesome," I said. "So we can add risk of exploding cars to the list of things to worry about. You know, if weres, necromancers, magicians, Ez, and the Watch weren't enough."

"Don't forget the Old Ones," Pru said.

"I'd like to," I said to her. "I really would like to."

"We've got to get our own car back," Callum said, finally finding another gear. It seemed to be a little too high now, and the VW struggled a bit before finally picking up speed and chugging down the quiet streets.

"Two of the things we're worrying about are hanging out where our car is," I said to him. "Plus I'm not sure our car really runs any better than this one."

"If you hadn't sneaked out we'd *have* our car," he said.

"I felt it was too risky for you to leave. It was a judgement call."

"Leaving me with the dodgy magician in the hungry house with the scary cellar and the weres at the gate?"

"To be fair, I didn't know about the weres."

"Can you two save the domestics?" Pru said. "We have a car. And since only some of us are any good without them"— she didn't look at me when she said that, but rather at Callum, which I appreciated. The not being able to shift hadn't become any less of a sore point—"let's start with tracking down some people who can actually help before you go running back into the claws of the enemy, shall we?"

"She speaks sense," I said.

"Ifan's not *the enemy*," Callum muttered, as he pulled up at a red light. The engine was settling into a throaty rumble as it warmed up, sounding as if it'd be more at home on some secret racetrack in the depths of an abandoned industrial park somewhere than in the empty streets of the city.

"Let's just hope Emma hasn't decided *we're* the enemy," I said.

"Why?" Pru asked. "What did you do?"

"Harsh," I protested.

"We did almost get her eaten by a kraken," Callum said, and Tam gave a huff of surprise.

"That was an accident," I pointed out. "And we were the ones being eaten by the kraken. She was just fending off the advances of the Sea Witch."

"*Just*," Callum said.

"*Kraken*," Tam said. "I always miss the good bits."

We were quiet for a moment, the windscreen wipers creaking slowly and painting the world outside in the curling, melted outline of dreams and fevers.

"There's something wrong with all of you," Pru said

finally, and settled herself more securely into the seat, her puffer jacket riding high around her ears.

"You love it, really," I said.

"There's probably something wrong with me, too."

THE STREETS around the Dead Good Cafe were empty and silent, the parking spaces taken up by compact little city cars that were either electric or looked like they should be. Streetlights cast the clean pavements in a warm glow, and the collection of cafes and specialty shops and organic locally made micro-whatever bars turned dark windows to the road. Here and there light leaked through from back kitchens, and I caught a whiff of baking bread over the stink of the exhaust.

Callum pulled into the alley that ran behind the cafe, parking with our nose to the white half-size van Gertrude and Emma drove. There was a light on behind the high window that led to the kitchen, and something in me settled a little. Gertrude must be alright, if she was baking as usual. Callum knocked on the back door, but no one answered. He gave it a moment, then knocked again, a little louder.

Still nothing, and he looked at me.

"I'll try the window," I said, and jumped to a big commercial bin leaning below it, then up to the narrow sill. The paint was slippery, and it took me a moment to get myself settled, but then I was pressed against the glass, looking down into a stainless-steel expanse of worktops and cabinets and fridges below. All of that was the same, and nothing suggested there had been trouble, exactly. There were no smashed plates or overturned mixers or anything like that.

But it wasn't *right*, either. Instead of immaculately polished surfaces and neatly kept cupboards, with maybe just one cake-in-progress left out to prove that someone did actually cook in there, bags of flour and sugar were scattered across the kitchen island. Cabinet doors stood open, half the contents stacked on the worktops in front of them. The sinks were filled with unwashed bowls, a cake sagged at a terminal angle on a cooling rack by the ovens, and a bag of walnuts had fallen on the floor, spilling its contents everywhere.

Above all, though, there was no reaper with a frilly, cat-themed apron pulled on over her robes, applying icing with the same precision she used to take souls. There was just Emma, standing in the middle of the floor and clutching a tea towel to her chest, flour dusting her hair. She flinched as Callum knocked again, her hands twisting in the cloth until her knuckles went white.

I scratched the window cautiously and she yelped, the noise audible through the double glazing, her gaze snapping up. Her eyes widened when she spotted me, and she shook her head. I scratched again, and she waved. *Go away.* I sighed, and scratched harder.

Emma flung down her tea towel and ran to the window, standing on her tiptoes to push it open. I almost fell off the sill as she did, but managed to cling on. I peered in at her, smelling butter and burnt chocolate and a shining thread of anxiety.

"You alright?" I asked her. "Looks like you fell in the mixing bowl."

"What're you doing here?" she hissed. "I told you not to come."

"We wanted to make sure you were okay," I said, not adding, *and we hoped Gertrude might lend us her scythe.*

"Do I look alright?" She glared at me, and I examined her. Under the dusting of flour she had dark circles below her eyes, and a small sore blooming just under her nose. That thin, ugly thread of fear and worry was clearer, too. More a skein than a thread.

"Well," I started, and she spoke over me.

"*It was a rhetorical question.*"

"I'm a cat."

"That really—" She jumped as Callum banged on the door again. "Can you tell him to stop that? Just go away, can't you?"

"What's happened?" I nodded at the kitchen. "You don't normally do this, do you?"

"What gave you that idea?" she said, and gave me half smile that was more like the old Emma. It faded quickly, though. "Whatever you want, I can't help you, Gobbelino."

"Full name. That sounds serious," I said, as the banging started up again. Callum was really going for it.

"I *am* serious. Gertrude got in a lot of trouble for being out of Leeds, and even if she kept her scythe, she still went in the water, and ..." Emma shook her head. "She's not been home, and all Ethel – Secretary Reaper – will tell me is that Gertrude is being re-educated, and I just have to be patient." She eyed me. "And stay out of anything that might make Grim Yorkshire think Gertrude's impartiality is compromised."

"Re-educated? That sounds ..." I didn't want to say *brain-washy*, but I was definitely thinking it, and going by the way Emma rubbed a hand over her face, adding some cake batter to the flour, she was thinking the same thing.

"I know. And all I can think of to do is to keep the cafe going and hope she comes home. Plus look after the ghoulets. Ethel's taken on Gertrude's reaping duties, and she keeps bringing me more of the bloody things. I mean, I love them, I do, but we're up to thirty-six now."

"Gods."

"I know. And Gertrude was the one who always bought

the chickens for them, and I can't access her accounts." The sound of someone hammering on the door rang through the kitchen again, and Emma screamed, "*Will you just **stop it?***"

I leaned around the windowsill, intending to yell to Callum to give it a rest, and found him standing just below the window, looking up at me. "Is she alright?" he asked.

I looked back at Emma. "That's not Callum."

She stared at me. "I told you not to come. I *told* you."

And I couldn't even say it had nothing to do with us. We were never that lucky.

9

OUT OF THE GHOULETS, INTO THE FIRE

"Can you see who it is?" Emma asked. "Is it a reaper?"

I glanced back at Callum. "I can't tell. It's not the back door."

Emma said something that didn't really go with the pastel green cardigan and kittenish apron combo she was currently sporting over her pyjamas. She snatched up the nearest wooden spoon, still dripping batter, then discarded it in favour of a large knife she'd been chopping nuts with.

"Don't," I said. "I'll go and have a look around the corner, see who it is. Let Callum in, alright?"

"I don't need someone protecting me," she snapped.

"No, but you can use him as a human shield," I said. "He's a bit skinny, but he's tall enough."

Emma snorted, and I didn't wait to see if she let him in or not. I slipped off the ledge straight to the ground, looking up at Callum. "Someone's at the front door."

Tam turned wordlessly and headed for the end of the alley, Pru trotting next to her, and Callum started to follow.

"Wait," I said to him. "Let us take a look first."

"What's going on in there?" he asked, nodding at the kitchen window.

"Gertrude's been taken off for some sort of reaper indoctrination, and Emma's trying to hold down the fort. She also has a really big knife, so I wouldn't be too quick to stick your nose in there."

"Noted."

I ran after Tam and Pru, the yellow light of the streetlamp turning her puffer jacket a deep rose colour and rendering her bare ears translucent.

We stopped at the corner of the alley, peering down the dim-lit street to the cafe door. There was nothing to obscure our view, and nothing to hide us if the unexpected visitors turned our way, either. The little table and chairs and blackboard that usually stood outside had been taken in for the night. I guess even in the fancy parts of Leeds things have a tendency to walk off if left unattended. Two people stood at the front door, not much more than silhouettes in the night. They weren't reapers, not even of the Gertrude variety. They were far too *real,* too anchored to the world to be the escorts of souls. The still night had no breeze to carry their scents to us, and in the shadows I couldn't tell much about them other than the fact they were human-shaped, which covered a whole range of possible problems.

And then one turned just enough for the light to catch on their face, spilling across shadowed eyes and catching on the lines of a familiar jaw, and I blinked, bewildered.

"Why's *she* here?" I muttered.

Pru and Tam both looked at me. "Who?" Pru asked.

"Kara." Kara, besties with Ez and dedicated fan of unicorn horn, who had tried to get all stabby at me with it the last time I'd seen her. Well, shooty, actually. She was standing on the reaper's doorstep with her hands in her pockets, while a taller figure next to her in a long purple coat raised their hand to pound on the frame one more time. I wondered if it was Ez, but she was as rangy as Callum, and Purple looked more solid than that.

Kara shook her head. "No one's here."

"They are," the other said, the voice warm and rounded on the edges. "I can smell baking."

"Then let's try around the back."

The other nodded and turned toward us, and Tam, Pru and I shot back into the alley before they could spot us. The cafe door was open and Callum was standing well back, so presumably Emma hadn't given up her knife.

"It's *Kara*," I hissed as we bolted toward them. "We need to make ourselves scarce."

"Kara?" Emma asked.

"She works with my sister," Callum said, already turning to the car. "Don't answer the door."

"Pretty sure she's trying to kill him," I said to Emma. "His sister, I mean. Bit of a fraught relationship."

"Oh, awesome," she said. "*Awesome.* This is just what I need." She waved at us. "There's no time. Get in here." Callum started to protest, and she hissed, "*Now!*"

I don't know if it was the knife or the grim look on her face that did it, but Callum gave up on the car and ran for the door. We cats shot into the well-swept hallway with him hurrying after us, mumbling apologies, and Emma shut the door softly, careful not to let it slam. She turned the lock and slid an extra couple of bolts across it. The inside of the door was lined with stainless steel, as were the other doors that led off the hall, one marked *Private*, another *Toilet*, a third lying open onto the kitchen and a fourth unmarked.

We'd been here before, and I knew that fourth door led into the cafe itself, all deep purple curtains and red candles and soft sofas, with the gnawed bones left by the ghoulets scattered about the place like bloodthirsty confetti. Somewhere there was a special ghoulet room too, knee-deep in graveyard dirt so that they could sleep peacefully and grow to be big strong horrifying ghouls. I guessed it was probably in the cellar, and likely reinforced with even more stainless steel than the rest of the place, to stop them gnawing their way out.

We stayed where we were, waiting, and a moment later someone knocked on the back door. It wasn't overly hard, but there was something of a snarl to it, like the knock of a bailiff. We all jumped, with the exception of Tam, who was cleaning her paws. She did look up, though, so she must've been startled. Emma swapped her knife to her other hand, wiped her palm on her apron, and switched back again. There was a pause, then another knock, deliberate and slow.

Knock. Knock. Knock.

The pause between each knock was long enough to set the hair shivering on my spine, and I looked at Callum. He was frowning at the door as if he disapproved of its methods, but didn't move toward it.

Knock. Knock. Knock.

No one spoke outside or in, and my tail was doing its bottle brush thing, even though I couldn't smell anything more than some baking mishaps and the tang of heavy cleaning.

Knock. Knock. Knock.

I forced myself forward, paws soft and silent on the hard floor, and stepped onto the mat at the door. My muscles felt like they'd been strung with wire, whether from the fraught day or sleeplessness or the weight of the city around me.

Knock. Knock. Knock.

I put my nose right down by the gap under the door and snuffled softly. For a moment all I could smell was chilly tarmac and rain waiting beyond the horizon, the greasy stink of the old VW and the whiff of the bin.

Knock. Knock. Knock.

Maybe it was her movement as she knocked. Maybe her irritation at not being answered meant she stopped guarding herself for a moment. It didn't matter how I smelled her, just that I did. Deep forest mulch and blood and bone fertiliser, power old and rich and brutal and cruelly *spoilt*. The last time I'd smelled that scent, she'd been attempting to shove an Old One into Callum's body, and power the transition with the lives of us cats. *Necromancer.* And not just any necromancer, either. Sonia. The big boss.

I started to step away from the door to warn the others, to suggest we run out the front door and leg it at a house-on-fire pace, or barricade ourselves into the ghoulets' secure room, or just generally do the best vanishing act we possibly could, when her voice came from right beside my ear. I bounced away, spine arching, picturing her crouching outside with her purple coat pooling around her feet and her soft dark hair curling over her cheeks, framing the neat features and bright eyes of the sort of people who go on telly and tell you how to organise your shelves and therefore your life.

"Well, hello, Gobbelino," she said, her voice low and warm. "I can feel you in there. And Callum." She paused. "I think I recognise a couple of other cats too. How wonderful! We weren't expecting all of you to be here."

"No one here of that name," I said, unable to think of anything else. "Wrong number. Sorry."

Sonia chuckled, a delightful little sound, and Emma strode to the door, knocking the blade of the knife against the stainless. "We're closed. You'll have to come back tomorrow."

"Ah, that's who we've come to see. I can smell the reaper taint on you."

Emma gave the door a disgusted look. "You can't come

back at all, actually. Sod off and sniff someone else's door, you weirdo."

"She's some sort of necromancer high priest type thing," I said.

"Definitely a weirdo, then," Emma said, and knocked the knife on the door again. "I've got quite enough to deal with right now."

"Callum?" That was Kara. "I've a message from your sister."

"How did you know we'd be here?" Callum asked.

There was a pause, then she said, "We heard you'd been hanging out with the reaper in Whitby."

Emma muttered something about not letting anyone in ever again, and shifted her grip on the knife. I opened my mouth to say something about blind luck not being the same as knowing we'd be here, and movement in the kitchen caught my eye. Tam spun toward it at the same time, spitting, and Pru yelled, "*She's inside!*"

Callum grabbed Emma's arm and hauled her toward the door that led to the cafe. I ran to join Tam and Pru in the kitchen doorway as Kara shouted from outside, "*Hey!* Let me in!"

Sonia swept out of the kitchen into the hallway, her purple coat swirling over neatly tailored white trousers and pointy-toed pink boots. Behind her, the kitchen window yawned open, the gap far too narrow to admit a human without a lot of huffing and struggling, but I guess maybe necromancers have different relationships with the world.

"Kara, go to the front door," she called as she tried to step around us and follow Callum and Emma, who'd left the cafe door open in their wake.

"I'm not a *doorman*," Kara snarled from outside, and I launched myself at the necromancer, swarming up the folds of her coat. She batted at me irritably, and Tam lunged for her arm, a matted, barrel-shaped ball of growling fury. She latched on with all four limbs, biting down on the necromancer's hand so hard I heard the crunch of skin and cartilage.

Sonia clicked her tongue irritably, stopping as she tried to pry Tam off. I took the opportunity to scramble up to her shoulder and bury my teeth in her ear. She gave a snarl that was as feral as anything Tam could come out with, and grabbed for me. Pru chose that moment to launch herself at the necromancer's legs, landing mid-thigh with all claws out and snagging her way upwards enthusiastically, her naked tail lashing as she hissed her fury.

"Oh, *cats!*" Sonia said, in the tone of someone addressing a puppy who's been chewing the rug. I bit down harder, and she simply shook us all off. Which sounds quite gentle, and also as though we weren't trying to remove as much of her skin as possible, which is entirely inaccurate on both counts. My teeth tore out of her ear, taking a gold earring with them, and I flew across the hall to hit the wall so hard it knocked the wind out of me. I lay there, trying to catch my breath, and watched Pru vanish into the cafe with a yowl, leaving Sonia's white trousers dotted with bloody marks from her claw-work. Tam tumbled into the darkness silently, still with a large chunk of necromancer in her teeth.

"There now," Sonia said, and I tried to yell, *she's coming*, but I couldn't find the air. All I could hope was that Callum and Emma were already out the door and away. They could handle Kara. Well, assuming she didn't have her unicorn horn crossbow.

And then Callum stepped into the faint light coming through the curtained windows of the cafe, his hands in the pockets of his tatty coat, and said, "Emma's got nothing to do with anything."

Old Ones take bleeding heart partners. If the necromancer didn't get him first, of course.

I rolled to my belly and crawled forward, my legs working about as well as can be expected for a small cat that's just been smashed into the wall by a freaky necromancer with well-shaped nails. I couldn't quite get to my feet yet, but it was coming, and nothing seemed to be broken. Not that I was sure what I could do, but a few well-placed bites before she turned me into a pastry twist would go a long way to making me feel better, whether it bought Callum and Emma any time or not.

I pulled myself over the threshold into the cafe as Sonia smiled at Callum and said, "That's my business. Now you just keep a handle on your little monsters." She touched her torn ear, which was dripping blood onto her coat, and I gave a small growl of satisfaction.

"What do you want?" Callum asked.

"Well, I *did* want a little chat with Emma," she said, adjusting her hair. "But how wonderful to find you here! I've been waiting for you to come back. Kara assures me that you could be quite useful, given the right motivation."

"I'm not looking for a job."

"Are you sure?" Sonia asked, tipping her head as she examined his tatty coat and old jeans. "Let's be quite honest here, Callum. You've made things terribly awkward for me. It took a lot of work and power to open that doorway at the magician's house, to invite our glorious ones through, and it hardly made me look good when you turned it into such a shambles. You owe me."

Callum shook his head. "Did you not *see* that thing? It would've devoured you as soon as it was finished with us. They don't care about you. You're just another human for them to enslave."

"I'm a *necromancer*," Sonia said severely.

"So not worth boasting about," I managed, and Callum's glance flicked to me. Sonia didn't look around.

"A necromancer is still human enough," Callum said. "And it doesn't matter anyway. You're not an Old One. Anything that isn't the same as them is beneath them. You must know this."

Sonia waved imperiously, splattering blood off her damaged hand. "Old Ones were necromancers once themselves. They respect power. And I shall show it to them. I admit I was a little unprepared last time, but that's what comes from working with idiot magicians." She snorted. "He honestly thought we were bringing his son back."

"You kind of did," Pru said, from the arm of a sofa. "So that's score one for the magician, zero for you, if we're keeping track."

"We totally are," I said. I could breathe without wheezing now, and some strength was coming back into my legs. Pru looked unruffled, which I supposed came from having no fur to ruffle. The collar of her coat was a bit skew-whiff, though. I couldn't see Tam, but I reckoned she could hit a tanker truck at twenty metres and bounce, so I was fairly sure she was okay. I also couldn't see Emma, which seemed good. Hopefully she was either hiding or already out the door. I didn't like to think what business Sonia had with her, but it likely involved reapers and scythes.

"You can't imagine you can control an Old One," Callum said. "That's …" He looked around, as if trying to find a better way to put things, then gave up. "Ridiculous."

"What's ridiculous is you, running about in your tatty clothes, with your tatty car, and tatty cat—"

"Hey," I said.

"—thinking you're something special because you've turned your back on your family. Your *destiny*."

Callum, Pru, and I all snorted, and another snort came

from somewhere behind the cafe counter, so that was Tam accounted for.

"Calling it destiny is how the rich and powerful justify doing really crappy things," Callum said, taking his cigarettes out. "The rest of us just have to make choices and live with them."

"Well, you *would* be rich and powerful if you stopped listening to cats and Folk," Sonia snapped. "You could take your rightful place as the head of the Norths. Actually *do* something."

"Such as?" I asked. "He joins your little death cult, raises some ancient gods, and rules the north happily ever after?"

"The north? You're thinking too small." She kept her eyes on Callum. "I underestimated you before. Thought you were just a nuisance to be dealt with. But that's not right, is it?"

"It probably is," he said, taking a cigarette from the packet.

Sonia looked puzzled for a moment, as if things had gone off-script, then shook her head. "I have an offer for you. We work together. You can run things as you see fit. All ethical and equal and so on." She waved a little distastefully. "Homes for delinquent elves and hospital beds for kitties, or whatever."

"Don't you already have a North?" Callum asked.

"Esme is proving difficult," Sonia said.

"That's a family trait," I said, and Sonia gave me an irritated look before turning back to Callum.

"If you were to join me, she would fall in line," the necromancer said. "Should you wish, of course. Otherwise I can simply ensure Dimly is yours. Dimly. The north. More. As much as you want."

"Right. Sure." Callum looked at me. "What d'you reckon, Gobs? Shall we run the world?"

"You're the wrong gender," Pru said. "It's girls who run the world."

"Don't be making assumptions," I said. "He might be flexible."

"Right. Sorry," Pru said. "The new cat-sitter's like that."

"A new one? What did you do to the last one?"

"He couldn't hack it."

"It's not as easy as it sounds, cat-sitting."

We both made thoughtful noises, and Sonia tapped one pink-booted foot, sending a ripple across the floor that shook the glasses behind the counter. "Be *quiet*."

"Unlikely," I said.

Callum lit his cigarette, despite the fact that I was sure Emma would take to him with the wooden spoon, if not the knife, if she saw. "I'm not so keen on world-ruling," he said. "Sounds stressful."

"Come with me and we'll discuss it," Sonia said. "Away from *cats*." She gave me a sharp look, and I bared my teeth at her.

"Will you leave Emma alone?" Callum asked. "This is nothing to do with her, you know."

"Oh, she'll be fine. If I have you, I don't need her." Sonia smiled, a wide and insincere smile, and I could see Callum knew it as well as I did. She'd still want Gertrude's scythe, and Emma was leverage – or bait. Even if Sonia left Emma alone, just for now, it wouldn't last. No one's peace was going to last anymore. It might not be end times, but it was certainly looking like distinctly uncomfortable ones.

"Alright," Callum said. "Here's the deal. You and Kara leave, and once I know Emma's safe, I'll come and meet you."

"No. You come with me now. You have my word she won't be hurt."

"Oh, that's reassuring," I said. "Do you cross your heart and hope to die?"

"I need to make sure Emma's alright," Callum said.

"She won't be alright if you don't come with me," Sonia said, and smiled. "Cross my heart and *someone* dies."

Callum stood there, smoking his cigarette, and I could see him considering it. I wanted to yell to him to not listen, to not go, but that was as good as saying, *here necromancer lady, have our friend Emma instead.* Pru was looking at me, as if waiting for me to do something, but I couldn't think of any way to get Callum and Emma both safely away. Three cats can do an awful lot, but taking down a necromancer was another level entirely.

"Why?" Callum asked finally. "Why do you even need Ez *or* me? Why not just get rid of us if you're so all-powerful already?"

"Not an invitation," I said. "Just in case you thought it was."

Sonia ignored me. "Because I need the north. And to have the north, I need *a* North. And Esme, as I say, is proving difficult."

"Probably help if you didn't call her Esme," I said.

Callum took a hefty lungful of smoke then said, "Alright."

"What?" I asked. "What d'you mean, *alright?*"

He smiled slightly. "I don't have a choice, Gobs. I can't let her hurt Emma."

"And I really will," Sonia said, smiling that sweet, warm smile.

"I know," Callum said.

"*How many times?*" Emma demanded, emerging from the shadows at the back of the room. "How many times do I have to say it? I don't need *anyone* to protect me! Just because I'm *human* doesn't mean I'm helpless!"

"Emma," Callum started, and she cut him off.

"And put that cigarette out! Honestly!"

"Necromancer, Emma," I said. "I mean, I totally believe

you could take out a couple of muggers or home invaders, but *necromancer.*"

"Don't you go condescending at me," Emma snapped, and glared at Sonia. "Get out of my cafe, you ..." She looked her up and down. "Overdressed bloody Avon lady."

"I like the Avon," Tam said from behind the counter. "Nice river."

"*Out!*" Emma shouted at Sonia, pointing at the front door.

Sonia stared at her. "You're wearing penguin pyjamas."

"And?"

"And an apron with kittens on it."

"*And?*"

"And you're really going to criticise my clothes?"

"*Get. Out.*"

"Emma," Callum tried again, and it was the necromancer who cut him off this time.

"For the Old Ones' sakes! Enough of this." She pointed at Callum, and he yelped as his arms locked to his sides, and he was spun on his heel toward the door. "Off we go."

"Callum!" I yelled, and tried to run after him, but an invisible hand clamped me to the floor, so hard the yell turned into a squawk.

"You too," Sonia said, looking at Emma.

Emma's whole body jolted as she was gripped in the same manner and twisted roughly toward the door, but she didn't fight back. She just grinned at the necromancer and said, "Sic her."

"What?"

"*Sic her.*"

The ghoulets washed out of the shadows in a delighted frenzy of weirdly jointed limbs and fleshy, pale-haired bodies, grunting and slobbering and flashing jagged teeth, bearing down on the necromancer without so much as a glance at the rest of us, and Sonia's grip on us vanished as she held out a hand to repel the onslaught.

"*Everyone out!*" Emma shouted, and Pru and Tam bolted for the door to the hallway. I waited just long enough to make sure Callum was following, then shot after them. We skidded into the hall, bright-lit after the dimness of the cafe, and Callum half shut the door, keeping it open just enough that we could see Sonia pressing her hands out toward the ghoulets, creating an unseen barrier. The creatures kept piling up against it, a frenzy of determined, flabby limbs and oversized teeth, and there were too many for even her to hold back. They were gaining ground bit by bit, pressing in on her. She gestured, sending pale bodies flying everywhere, and one hit the wall next to us. It slid down with a grunt and gave us a baleful look, then gathered itself up and rushed back to join the fight.

The cafe was suddenly lit with orange light as Emma opened the door to the street, revealing Kara with her hands still raised as if they'd been cupped on the glass.

"Get out," Emma said again, her voice flat, and this time Sonia broke for the door, the ghoulets surging after her. She stopped on the threshold, starting to say something, and Emma shoved her, sending her stumbling into Kara, then snatched up a ghoulet that was in hot pursuit and slammed the door again. She shot the bolts with the ghoulet still tucked under her arm, while the rest of them grumbled and pawed hungrily at the door and windows. She turned and looked at us where we still huddled behind the door.

"I *told* you I didn't need anyone to protect me," she said.

"Well, other than ghoulets," I pointed out, then immediately regretted it when she scowled at me over the surging backs of her creepy little horde.

But then she laughed, and said, "Okay, fine. But they did a damn sight better than you lot."

"Fair," I said.

"Is something burning?" Pru asked, and Emma dropped her ghoulet and bolted toward us.

I turned around to see smoke seeping across the hall ceiling from the kitchen door.

"Out of the ghoulets, into the fire," Tam observed, and Callum dived into the kitchen, one arm over his face.

"The adventure never stops," Pru said, as we watched the two humans vanish.

"No wonder you missed us."

10

HOLD THAT THOUGHT

THE OVEN WAS LEAKING GREY SMOKE, WHICH TURNED INTO A belch as Callum opened the door.

"Don't do that!" Emma yelped, waving wildly at the smoke detector with a tea towel. "You'll set it off!"

Callum hurriedly slammed the oven door again, turned the dial to the off position and grabbed another tea towel, then the two of them flailed around the kitchen, trying to encourage the worst of the smoke to head out the still-open window. Pru, Tam and I sat in the doorway, safely under the smoke, and watched. I mean, it wasn't as if there was a lot we could do, was there?

A few minutes later things seemed marginally more under control. Callum went to bolt the back door closed again, and Emma vanished into the cafe with two buckets of unidentifiable chicken parts. I could hear the ghoulets slobbering and whining in the moment before she pushed the door closed behind her, and it set my hair shivering away from my spine.

Callum wandered back into the kitchen, looked around, then flicked the kettle on and started picking up the scattered debris of Emma's cooking from the worktops and floor. I padded in to join him, and said, "What now?"

"Tea," he said.

"Well. Obviously," I started, then realised he was addressing Emma, who'd come back in swinging the two empty buckets.

"Please," she said, dropping them in the big commercial sink and using a stainless hose to rinse them out.

"Are you alright?" Callum asked, finding the mugs and setting two on the worktop. They both had some combination of kittens and flowers on them.

"Not really," Emma said, leaning against the sink. "Gertrude's being *re-educated*, a necromancer just tried to grab me, which presumably has something to do with the scythes, and I sicced ghoulets on her, which doesn't seem like a good thing to do to anyone, even if they are seriously unpleasant." She paused, and added, "Plus, I now have *thirty-nine* ghoulets, and I don't know where the extra three came from. They're too young to breed, right?"

Callum looked at me, and I shrugged. "Ghoul breeding habits are outside my area of expertise."

"What can we do?" Callum asked. He'd found the teabags and topped the mugs up with water, and was now picking up bags of nuts and dried fruit and stacking them together neatly. Which didn't go far to actually tidying things away, but at least got all the mess together in the same spot. Green Snake stuck his head out of Callum's pocket a little warily to watch. He had the pink seashell in his mouth, and he looked around for a moment, then vanished again.

Emma took the milk from the fridge and said, "I think you should leave."

"But if she comes back," Callum started, and Emma shook her head.

"If she does, I have the ghoulets. And I'm going to call

Ethel. I don't know how worried they'll be about me, but the reapers need to know someone's after them. It is the scythes they're after, isn't it?"

"I think so," Callum said. "And I know the ghoulets worked this time, but she'll be prepared if she comes back. *When* she comes back. It's not safe here."

Emma slopped milk into the mugs, spilling some on the worktop, and sighed. "Damn. Look, I see what you mean, but where am I meant to go? We *live* here."

"We know somewhere kind of safe," I said.

"Kind of?"

"That's about as good as it gets these days."

Emma pushed a mug toward Callum. "How reassuring."

"Situation normal," Pru said, almost to herself.

Callum looked at me and said, "Are you thinking of the OAP headquarters?"

"*Excuse* me?" Emma had been poking around in the fridge, and now she looked at Callum. "You've got a bunch of oldies mixed up in this?"

"Don't let them hear you call them that," I said.

Emma pulled out a Tupperware and set it on the worktop, taking the lid off to reveal half a chocolate cake. It looked slightly gooey in the middle, and the icing had mysterious lumps in it. "That doesn't seem any safer than a cafe full of ghoulets. *At all.* And not for them, either. What if that necromancer finds me, and they get hurt?"

Callum put Green Snake on the worktop, took the seashell off him after a moment's struggle, then said, "They're pretty well hidden."

"And defended," Pru said. "I'm sure I saw a cannon the other day."

Emma stared at her, then shook her head. "If I can get Ethel to come and help out, it'll be fine. No one's going to mess with a reaper."

"Eh," I said. "Wouldn't be too sure about that. Remember the lovely Sonia *wants* to get her hands on your reaper."

She sliced off two large chunks of cake and tipped them onto plates, handing one to Callum. "But what if Gertrude comes back and I'm not here?" For the first time her voice wavered, and the corner of her mouth twitched down. In that moment I saw what she'd looked like before she'd known who she was. Lost, and scared, and adrift in an unknown world.

Green Snake had been investigating the cake, and now he pointed his nose at Emma curiously.

"Hi," she said, and her voice caught on the word. She swallowed and looked around the kitchen vaguely. "I think we have some tuna—"

"Please," I said, at the same time as Callum said, "No."

"You've *just* eaten," he said, when I glared at him.

"You're about to have cake!"

"I didn't have fancy fish," he said, and took a gulp of tea. "Emma, I know it doesn't sound ideal, but at least no one will look for you at the OAP headquarters. The only other option is Ifan's—"

"No," I said. "Talk about out of the necrophiles into the taxidermy army."

"Ignore him, but also he's not entirely wrong," Callum said, as Emma stared at me. "How about if you call Ethel, tell her what happened so they know someone's targeting them, and then pack up and go?"

"What about the ghoulets? I can't just leave them."

"Survival of the fittest," Tam said, gazing thoughtfully at the nearest wall.

"What? *No*," Emma said.

"Tell Ethel to feed them," Callum said. "You can't stay here. You really *can't*."

She started to say something, stopped, then took a bite of

chocolate cake instead. "What're you going to do?" she asked around it, a little indistinctly, and gave a crumb to Green Snake. No one pointed out *he'd* been munching on fish eggs.

Callum rubbed a hand through his hair, and I said, "Dentist. If you can get reapers, and we can get dentists – I mean, sorcerers – a sorcerer—"

"Dentists might be more scary," Tam observed, still intent on her wall, and I wondered if she'd been at the nip.

"They have drills," Pru added. "And weres."

"The weres have *him*," I said. "And he only had chopsticks, last time I saw him."

Emma took another bite of cake and said, "I'm not sure that clarifies anything."

"It never does," Callum said. "But Gobs is right. That's our next step. If you can get the reapers on board, then stay safe—"

"I don't need—"

"I just mean that if you're safe, they can't use you to get to Gertrude."

They looked at each other for a moment, then she nodded and fed another morsel of cake to Green Snake. "Alright. That's fair."

Callum took his phone out, frowned at it, then put it away again. "It's almost five. I'll help you clean up, then we can go."

She shook her head. "No. Get on and find your dentist. I'm going to call Ethel now, so she can get here before the sun gets up. Just give me a pin drop for where to go after."

"You can't just turn up—"

"We'll go with her," Pru said. "You two can survive looking for weres on your own for the moment, can't you?"

"We're very capable," I said.

"Appearances are so deceptive," Tam said, still addressing the wall. I considered baring my teeth at her, but I had a feeling she'd know I was doing it somehow. I really had preferred her not talking.

⸺

CALLUM FINISHED his tea and piece of cake, then reclaimed Green Snake, who was cleaning Emma's plate while she leaned against the worktop under the window with her phone, talking to Secretary Reaper.

Finally she set the phone down and looked at us. "Alright. She'll be here soon."

"And you know where to go?" Callum asked.

"Yes." She looked around at the half-tidied worktops. "I'll see you later."

And just like that we were dismissed. We left Emma, Pru and Tam in the wreckage of the kitchen and headed out into the persistent chill of the winter pre-dawn. Callum pulled the back door shut behind him, the latch locking into place. He gave it a little shake to make sure it was secure, then checked the alley warily. The moon had vanished, and while the sky was just a dully indeterminate ceiling beyond the city lights, a fine drizzle had come in from somewhere. It turned to haze in the warm glow of the streetlights, and the old VW was sitting at a strange angle in the dimness.

"Oh, *come on,*" Callum muttered, crouching down and poking the flat tyre as if that would help anything.

"We can't even *borrow* a decent car," I said. "Should we try stealing? Stealing might give us better options."

"How about instead of worrying about the car you figure out how we're going to find some weres," he said.

I wrinkled my snout. "Muscles, I suppose."

"And how do we find him?" he asked, opening the boot and frowning at it. He closed it again and went around to the front of the car, where a grunt indicated that he'd found the jack.

"Poppy."

"And how do we find her, since we've got no phone number?"

"Yellow Pages," I suggested, then went to keep watch down the street while Callum muttered and clanged about with the spare tyre. The nuts on the wheel were as old and rusted as the rest of the car, but Duds was apparently better at keeping things in working order than he was at keeping them in pretty condition. Callum got the tyre swapped over without too much trouble and only the minimum of swearing, and before long we were puttering back out into the streets of Leeds on three threadbare tyres and one almost completely bald one.

"We need our car," Callum muttered.

"We're not going back for the car," I said.

"We can't drive around in this."

"It runs," I pointed out. And it did. The more we drove the smoother the engine seemed to become, and we pulled away from the lights with a nippiness the old Rover would have envied.

"I just don't feel being done for driving an illegal car is going to help much," Callum said.

"Do we know it's illegal?"

"You saw the tyres."

I sniffed and stared at the roof. "There's a leak. It's dripping on me."

"Of course there is," Callum said, and sighed.

We were silent for while, except for the growl of the engine, then I said, "Where're we going, anyway?"

He didn't answer, and I shot him a suspicious look.

"Callum? Tell me we're not going to some bloody amusement arcade to meet your dodgy sister."

"It's too early," he said.

"She messaged you again, though, didn't she?"

"Yes," he admitted.

"Did you message *her?*"

He took his cigarettes out. "I asked her what Kara and Sonia were up to, hunting for reapers. She said she didn't know, that she was trying to keep a handle on things in Dimly. That she and Kara fell out after the whole unicorn incident and she hasn't really seen her since, and that she's been trying to keep Sonia out of town."

"Likely story."

"Sonia did say Ez was being difficult."

"I doubt that means she's going to be helpful to us."

Callum sighed. "Probably not. But like I say, it's too early to meet her yet anyway. I was going to try out where the weres' club was. There might be some signs for where they meet now, like the ones we found last time."

"And we're not going to meet Ez *at all*, right?"

"Let's just start with the club. Maybe we'll get lucky and then we won't have to even discuss it."

I thought that was about as likely as Sonia deciding to give up necromancing and take up needlepoint, but at least it was a start that didn't involve his sister. So I didn't answer, just watched the traffic lights and stop signs pass almost without noticing them, the streets empty in the strange gap between early morning deliveries and the last of the night traffic fading. Callum turned off the main road, working his way through the side streets and quiet lanes that were hopefully less likely to be patrolled by keen police with an eye for scruffy cars.

There was something almost hypnotic in watching the lights, the constant whisper of tyres on the steadily dampening tarmac, the grumble of the engine and the shake of the car's frame. Callum lit his cigarette, declaring that with the amount of fumes washing around us he was hardly going to make things worse. The smoke melded with the exhaust, comforting in a throat-squeezing kind of way, and the last of the night stretched on toward the dawn. I yawned and stretched, my nerves still strung tight with the events of the night, yet lulled by the noisy rhythm of the car. And at some odd, still point, I stopped hearing each individual noise. They all melded into one, then drew distant, leaving me in a strange limbo, my ears full of a roaring that could have been the car, or the distant sea, or the blood in my veins. The lights blurred and spread, then blinked past me, and I sank into a half-dreaming daze, wondering where the sorcerer was, and how we were supposed to get her dentist back for her.

Callum's phone dinged, and he checked it as he drove. "It's *Poppy*," he said, a note of astonishment in his voice.

"Win," I said, or tried to, because instead of climbing out of my slow lethargy I seemed to be falling further into it. I couldn't feel my legs, and my ears had gone numb, and I seemed to have become one with the seat. Then I was sinking *through* it, and I thought, without much urgency, *Bloody Ms Jones again, isn't it?*

And there she was, standing at a sink below a set of white-framed windows with her hands in the soapy water, thick dark curls hanging past her shoulders and lines of strain at the corner of her mouth. She was wearing fluffy boots and soft loose trousers, and was unaccountably unfamiliar because of it. The kitchen was warmly lit, the world beyond the windows dark, reflecting only her own face, and she looked up sharply. Her gaze locked with mine in the reflection, and she spun around, reaching out. In the next moment the world snapped into focus, and she was holding me by the scruff of the neck, suspended over a stone-flagged floor in a kitchen that smelled of coffee and wood smoke.

"Ow," I managed.

She changed her grip, using both hands to hold me straight out in front of her, examining me as if she'd never seen a cat before. "Where the hell did you come from?" she asked.

"I was puttering along perfectly happily in a car," I said. "Well, other than the exhaust fumes and some mild bruising from a run-in with head lady necromancer. And a narrow miss with some weres earlier."

"But how did you get here?" she asked.

I looked around. We were in some sort of low-ceilinged farmhouse-style place, all heavy wooden beams and white walls and thick-silled windows. The kitchen sported a big cream AGA stove, and a curving wood-topped bar separated it from a lounge area stuffed with beige, soft-looking sofas framing a chunky wood burner that was belching out heat. The lounge was glass-walled, and the ceiling looked to have blinds on it, so it was probably some sort of conservatory.

"Where's here?" I demanded. "Is this your subconscious? It's fancy."

"No," she said, still examining me. Her eyes were even darker today, full of shark-like shadows. "Does it look like my subconscious?"

"Well, it's not *mine*." I wrinkled my snout at her. "I don't think even my subconscious wants sorcerers grabbing me by the scruff."

She poked me in the stomach with one long finger.

"*Ow!*"

"You're here," she said.

"*Obviously.* You dragged me here again, right?"

"No," she said. "I've never dragged you anywhere."

"You have."

"Have not." She shook her head and set me on the

smooth, polished expanse of the kitchen bar. "I just summoned your consciousness, remember?"

"Oh, is that all? Just a little out-of-body ..." I trailed off and looked at my paws. I extended the claws, scratching at the wooden worktop tentatively.

"Stop that. I'm not losing my security deposit for you."

I looked at a bowl of fruit resting on the end of the bar, then padded over to it and bit the end of a lemon. My teeth scraped through the bitter pith, and oil from the skin squirted into my nose. *"Ugh."* I sat back down and stared at her. "I actually am here. How did you do this?"

"I didn't do anything. What did *you* do?"

"Nothing! I was just in the car, and I was wondering how we were going to find the dentist, and ..." I shook my head and looked around as the sorcerer leaned against the sink and picked a mug up. It had uneven, pale blue stripes on it, and I could smell coffee as she sipped from it. If this was my subconscious, it was very detailed. "Where *are* we? This is posh. I thought you must be being held somewhere, like a dungeon or something. Attic, maybe."

She frowned at the mention of an attic, and shook her head. "Doesn't matter. What's happening? Are you back in Leeds?"

"Well, I was," I said, trying to get the lemon taste off my teeth. "D'you have any biscuits or something?"

She sighed and opened a cupboard next to the sink, taking out a packet of cat treats. Stacked cans and boxes splashed with cat pictures looked back at me in the instant before she shut it again. She shook a small serving into a bowl and set it in front of me.

"Why d'you have so much cat food?" I asked her.

"Because I've learned it's the only way to get anywhere with you lot," she said, picking her mug up again. "Are you in trouble?"

I ate a couple of biscuits while I considered it. "More so than usual, you mean, or ...?"

"Did you shift here because you're in immediate danger? Is that what caused it?"

"I didn't *shift*," I said sharply. "I can't. You must've pulled me here."

"I was doing the dishes," she said. "I was thinking about you, but I didn't bring you here."

"I was thinking of you, too," I said. "So you must've done it by accident or something."

"I don't do anything by accident. Well, anything much," she amended.

I supposed she didn't, at that. Under the low, comforting scent of warm house and old fires and, somewhere, a hint of wide wild spaces, I could smell her. A heavy, muscular scent, feral and ancient and considered. "But I can't shift," I said. "And I remember shifting, from when I could. It doesn't work like this." It was long, and tortured, and filled with the terror of the Inbetween, or of what lurked there. It wasn't a nicely sleepy bop from one place to another.

She shrugged. "I suppose it doesn't matter. Tell me what's going on in Leeds. You haven't found Malcolm yet, then?"

"No. We've only been back a day, and so far we've run away from the magician, been chased by weres, got rescued by the OAP army, and the necromancer high priest whatsit threatened both Callum and Emma, but Emma sicced ghoulets on her, so that's sorted."

Ms Jones' gaze sharpened, those shark-like forms suddenly closer, and she said, "You saw her. The same necromancer the old magician was working with."

"She does not get any more pleasant."

"What did she want with Emma and Callum?"

"Scythes," I said immediately, finally shaking off the strange lethargy of the car. "You need to get back to Leeds.

High Whatsit Sonia's after all the reaper scythes. That's why she wanted Emma, to get to Gertrude. And she wants Callum because ... well, we're not so sure on that bit, but she seems to think he's useful. More useful than his sister, anyway."

Ms Jones sipped coffee and said, "You saw weres but you haven't found Malcolm."

"Did you not hear the rest? Bigger problems."

She crossed the gap between the sink and the bar, leaning on it with her arms wide so that she could stare down at me. This close, the scent of her made my paws twitch, the way they do when the wind comes in from savage places. "You need to find Malcolm. I *need* Malcolm."

"*Why?*" I demanded. "Look, we went to Yasmin's bar and she's not there anymore. There were weres at the magician's house, but we've no way of knowing if they're Yasmin's lot or not. We can't just march up to any old were and say, *Hey, have you seen the sorcerer's human?*"

"Callum has a phone, doesn't he? Call Malcolm. Or Yasmin."

"We've *tried.* And why don't you just do it, anyway?"

She shook her head. "Because he'll fuss, and I don't need the hassle right now. I just need to know where he is."

I took a deep breath. "Well, we're just trying to stay alive for now. We've got Gerry and Emma to worry about, *and* Poppy and William, and, oh yeah, the Watch is falling apart and no one knows where Claudia is. So I'm sorry, but finding your pet dentist isn't high on my list right now. *We need help.* Why can't you come back?"

She looked at me for a long moment, then said, "I will, but not yet. There's a reason behind it, Gobbelino, but right now I just can't. And when I do, I need Malcolm there, in Leeds. With you, preferably, so I don't have to hunt for him. That's why I wanted you to keep him safe."

"I guess he thought the weres were more promising than us."

"Can't imagine why," she said.

"Rude. Although, Yasmin does smell nicer than Callum."

"Yes. I just hope Malcolm hasn't worn out his welcome with them." She straightened up. "Go and find him."

"What about the necros? And Emma? And Gerry? And—"

She pinched the bridge of her nose, and said, "Gods. Do you have *any* leads?"

"Poppy," I said.

"Hold that thought."

I opened my mouth to ask why, and she grabbed me up in one richly scented hand and hurled me unceremoniously across the room. I squawked, tumbling nose over tail as I searched for a landing, bracing myself to hit a wall or a sofa and promising any small god that would listen that if I landed in one piece I'd make sure she never got her security deposit back.

Then the world parted around me, folded in on itself, and opened up again. I bounced off a seat, hit a gear stick, and slid helplessly past a set of legs to end up on the floor.

I had one blissful moment when I thought they were Callum's legs, then realised that the trousers were ironed to a painfully neat crease and the boots were highly polished, and someone said, in tones of astonishment, "Cat!"

The owner of the shiny boots slammed the brakes on, almost trapping my tail, and I cursed Ms Jones with hairballs for all eternity.

11

DOES A COW EAT CABBAGES

"Gobbelino?" the voice said. "Is you?"

I blinked up from the shelter of the driver's legs, still too confused by my sudden arrival to recognise the voice, then yelped as a large and horrifyingly toothy head lunged toward me. The teeth were stacked up in shark-like rows, and the creature was drooling around them with the sort of enthusiasm that suggested their owner thought dinner had just been delivered. It also had five eyes, which were alternately rolling in excitement and fixed in a bulging stare as the beast strained to reach me, whining and scrabbling at the seats. They weren't going to last long with that sort of treatment, given that the thing's claws were as excessively sharp as their teeth, but before I could even manage a hiss, the car's passenger put out a heavy arm and pushed Toothy McTooth-face effortlessly back. The beast whined plaintively.

"Sit, Strawberry," the passenger said, and peered down at me. She had one extra eye than is usually expected, but was thankfully much less toothy than the creature, even though she was showing off a jagged collection in a grin of delight. "Is Gobbelino! Look, William! Gobbelino!"

"I sees," the driver said. "You moves, please, Gobbelino? I no can—" He stopped, took a breath, and said, "I can no drive with there you." He growled, the heavy, armoured plates of his forehead clashing as he scowled. "You there."

His three-eyed passenger patted him heavily on the shoulder. "You speaks good, William. Gerry be proud."

William growled again, and six months ago being stuck in the footwell of a car with two young trolls – one of whom was having some trouble expressing himself – would have been right up there with Situations Not To Be In, especially as trolls' usual methods of expressing themselves tend to be loud, explicit, and painful for bystanders. But that was before meeting Gerry and his two young charges. Right now I couldn't think of many people I would've been happier to crash-land on.

I clambered out of the footwell, trying not to shed on William's immaculate trousers, and looked for somewhere to sit that wasn't troll lap. But even small trolls take up a lot of space, and Poppy patted her knee, grinning at me broadly. "You sit."

"Alright." I gave SharkDog a suspicious look, and Poppy clicked her tongue.

"Strawberry good dog. He no bite you."

I was less worried about being bitten than eaten whole, but I jumped onto her lap. Strawberry watched me with three eyes, panting, while the other two checked Poppy in case of treats.

"Seatbelt?" William said.

"Seatbelt," Poppy said, tugging at hers in demonstration. "Strawberry has harness."

Strawberry whined. He was the size of a Rottweiler, with a spine of spikes running from his shoulders to his tail, and his harness had a strawberry pattern that clashed somewhat with the threat of his teeth.

"Gobbelino?" William asked, looking at me with his forehead plates all crunched up in concern.

"Um, yeah. Good to go."

"Mirrors," he declared. "Indicator. Mirrors. Check road. I drive." He headed off again, surprisingly smoothly, then I realised that it was an automatic. Probably wise. Trolls aren't known for their fine motor control, so I just hoped that their motorised vehicle control was better.

"Where are we?" I asked.

"Going to meet yous," Poppy said. "I calls Callum and we makes plan, then you appears. Does Callum appears too?" She looked down in the footwell as if expecting a gangly PI to materialise at William's feet.

"I don't think so," I said. "Can you call him? He might be wondering where I am."

"You no tell him you leaves?" she asked, and William clicked his tongue.

"It was unexpected," I said.

"Is rude," William said. "Always leave note."

"Yes," Poppy said. "Or people worries." She frowned down at me, and although William was keeping his gaze firmly on the road, I could feel the disapproval radiating off him.

"Got it," I said. "Won't happen again."

"Good," Poppy said, and petted me with surprisingly gentle hands.

WILLIAM DROVE CAREFULLY around the centre of Leeds, keeping to quieter streets and away from the slow build of morning traffic on the main roads. His heavy hands were carefully spaced on the wheel, and he drove with such care that there was no chance of being done by any speed cameras. He also indicated so far ahead of any manoeuvre that we passed at least two possible turnings before actually taking one, which resulted in us being honked at by at least one impatient white van. William's only response to that was to wave as they overtook us and say, "Have a better day."

We slid slowly into quieter, dirtier streets that offered glimpses of river or rubbly, weed-choked wasteland, leaving behind the bits of city that had done the whole regenerating thing and heading into the parts the developers hadn't reached yet. No whiff of roasting coffee or grind of raw juice bars here. Just betting shops rubbing shoulders with pubs that leaked the sort of smells that raised the hair on the spine, and discount stores that sold everything from international phone cards to TV sets, as long as you didn't ask too many questions about where they came from. It was very like the area around our flat, and it made me momentarily homesick. Not for the flat itself, which had been tiny, draughty, cold, and afflicted by weird smells and strange noises even before the sorcerer's book of power had got its pages on it. But homesick for a time that seemed horribly distant now, when our worst concern had been being beaten up by an unhappy client.

Finally William pulled into a scruffy-edged side street sporting a mix of run-down shops and tatty terraced houses. The only light came from the front windows of a greasy spoon, the species of cafe that sprouted in every neighbourhood like this. They'd serve strong tea in thick-walled, chipped mugs for a pound, instant coffee (or some filter stuff with weird oil slicks on its surface if they were feeling fancy), and huge plates of eggs, sausages, bacon, and beans, all served up with a side of fried bread or sliced white toast. Cooking options would be fried or fried (I suspected even the beans met the same fate), and everything would have a faint film of grease to it, including the air. They'd be frequented by the terminally exhausted, working strange shifts, and the terminally different, walking the world in strange ways. They're the sort of places Folk are very familiar with, as they turn a blind eye to just about everything. They're safe havens for those who have lost their place in the world, or never had it to begin with. Certainly no one was going to notice a cat or a five-eyed SharkDog. Or they wouldn't say anything if they did.

The old VW Beetle was already parked across the road from the greasy spoon, looking very much at home among a line of parked cars of similar condition, if not vintage. Callum leaned against it with a cigarette in one hand and the other twisted into his tangled hair, looking around as if he thought I'd somehow fallen through the floor of the car and he just had to figure out where. William indicated, and inched slowly into the space behind the VW, performing a surprisingly tidy parallel park. When he turned the engine off the rain on the roof was a gentle chatter, rendering the inside of the car a peaceful cocoon against the world.

Callum had stubbed out his cigarette as he watched us pull in, and now waited warily with the VW driver's door already partly open and his hand resting on the top of it. Although I wasn't sure what he thought that would do – even given how it had seemed to perk up a bit while we were driving, making a quick getaway in that car hadn't been possible since about 1972. William opened his own door and gave Callum a huge, craggy troll grin.

"William," Callum said, his shoulders sagging. "There you are."

"Hello, Callum," William said. "How is you? No, how you are? No—"

"I'm alright," Callum said, before William could try every possible word combination. "How are you?"

"Bad," William said solemnly, and Poppy snorted.

"Is philoscoffical question, William."

"What?" William looked at her.

"Philoscoffical. Not possible to be answered."

"But I cans answer it," he pointed out, climbing out of the car. "I is bad."

Poppy looked doubtful. "But maybe we do not look at the question properly."

"You might mean rhetorical," Callum said. "But I did mean it."

"You've been talking to that addled bloody donkey, haven't you?" I asked Poppy, and she patted me again.

"Kent is very smart dinkey. He thinks lots."

Callum bent to look in William's door at me. "Bloody hell, Gobs. How—"

"Long story," I said, because *no idea*, while more accurate, was a bit embarrassing.

"Right," Callum said. He took his cigarettes from his pocket, and Poppy made a *tsk*-ing noise.

"Is bad for you," she told him.

"It is," he agreed, cupping his hands as he flicked his lighter. The flame gave his face hard, exhausted angles. "It's good to see you two."

"We got your message," I added to Poppy as she opened the door and I jumped to the ground. "In Whitby. See you got Strawberry back, though."

She bent down toward me, cupping one hand over her mouth so she could troll-whisper loudly enough to be heard down the block, "Is pretend. Is not Strawberry is missing."

"*No*," I said, and Callum scowled at me. "Sorry. I mean, yes, it was code. We got that."

Poppy gave me a puzzled look that made me feel vaguely guilty, but before she could answer William spoke up, beeping the car locked as he did. It was quite a nice-looking Audi SUV.

"We no speak here," he said, waving at the sleeping

terraced houses lining the sides of the road. A couple had lights on in bedroom windows, and somewhere a dog barked as it was let out into a pocket-sized garden. Leeds was starting to wake up.

"Is Gerry," Poppy said. "Gerry is missing." There was an unevenness to her voice.

Callum rubbed the back of his head. "Things are bad, aren't they?"

"Yes," Poppy said simply.

"We not talk here," William said again. "We go in." He pointed at the cafe.

"Is that safe?" I asked. "Won't we be more likely to be heard in there?"

"No," William said.

"I do need a cuppa," Callum mumbled, more to himself than to us.

"Surprise," I said.

Callum gave me a half smile, then looked at William. "Is it the sort of place where they mind cats?"

"They not mind anything," William said, and checked the car door was locked before leading the way toward the steamed glass of the cafe door.

Callum crouched next to me for a moment, smoke drifting over his lower lip. "What happened?" he asked in a low voice. "Did Ms Jones grab you again?"

"Pretty much," I said. Which wasn't a lie. It had involved Ms Jones, after all. I just hadn't worked out the rest of it.

"What did she say?"

"That she still wants her bloody dentist." I sighed. "I guess we should've hung about and seen if any of those weres at the magician's were smart enough to talk to after all."

"Why can't she just go and find him herself?"

"Oddly, I didn't question the scary sorcerer too much. She just said she couldn't yet, and that she needed him to be with us so that when she comes back she doesn't have to go looking for him."

He gave me a sideways glance. "You never vanished like that before."

"How do you know? You've only seen it happen once. Maybe it's variable."

"You keep calling it an out-of-body experience, so that seems unlikely."

"I might've been wrong. It's not entirely conducive to clear thinking, you know, being hauled about the place by sorcerers. Be nice if she picked on you for a change."

"I imagine you're easier to deal with. More compact."

"You do have an excessive amount of limbs."

"Not really. Four is pretty usual."

"Excessive expanses of them, then."

He snorted, then stood up as William paused at the cafe door, waiting for us. Poppy was holding Strawberry's leash in one big hand while the dog checked a lamp post for messages.

Callum glanced at me as we crossed the road. "So did Ms Jones seem alright? Did you get any idea of where she's being held?"

"I'm not sure she is."

"What?"

"Well, everything was kind of beige and stone, and there were those dead sticks in vases people seem to like so much, and she kept going on about her security deposit."

Callum frowned at me. "Security deposit?"

"Yeah. Maybe she's recharging or something. Doing research. Who bloody knows with sorcerers." I didn't want to think about the sort of recharging Ms Jones might be doing, or why she might need a remote cottage to do it at. That way lay sleepless nights, even for a cat.

Callum took a final puff on his cigarette, then paused to

stub it out and drop it into an overflowing bin. "That's very weird, Gobs."

"*Everything* is very weird. That seems to be our situation normal right now."

"You say *right now* as if it's ever been any different."

"Fair point." I sniffed the early morning air as William pulled the door open. "I need bacon *and* sausage after a sorcerer visit, though."

"Of course you do," Callum said, and we followed the troll into the cafe, its white-silled windows glowing behind a sheen of grease and condensation like a promise.

IF A REGULAR GREASY spoon can look past the odd cat, William's greasy spoon could've looked past ten cats, five pigs, and a travelling circus full of monkeys. Callum was the closest to human in there, other than an exhausted-looking man sitting in one corner, a striped black and white jacket zipped up to his chin and his head resting against the wall. He was snoring softly, a large bacon sandwich with one bite out of it congealing on a plate in front of him, and someone had carefully moved his mug far enough away that he wouldn't knock it over if he face-planted on the table. A second table was taken up by two goblins with a plate piled high with sausages set between them, which they were eating without any recourse to utensils. The final table, set near the window, had a faery huddled over it, clutching a large fried egg sandwich. She glowered at us as we walked in, yolk and red sauce decorating her chin, and Callum gave her a polite nod.

"Wills!" a dwarf behind the counter shouted, and came out to give the young troll an enthusiastic hug at about waist-height. The dwarf's beard was plaited and tidied away over their shoulders with a neat green ribbon to hold it in place, and they reached up to pat William's back so enthusiastically I could almost hear his body ringing like a barrel. "Go on through," they said, barely glancing at us. "There's tables out the back."

"Thanks, G," William said, and led us through a low, broad door, more suited to dwarf dimensions than human or troll ones. William and Callum both ducked, but Poppy wasn't looking and gave a little *oof* of surprise as her head hit the frame, accompanied by the sound of wood splintering. Strawberry promptly tried to attack the door, and there was one hairy moment when I thought G the dwarf was going to chuck us all out, but Poppy picked the SharkDog up in a bear hug and held him until he calmed down, and William apologised so effusively I was certain he'd been listening to Gerry mayor-ing about the place. To be fair, G didn't seem particularly alarmed, and there looked to be other cracks in the frame anyway. They waved us through, mumbling something about the hazards of a varied clientele.

The back room was twice the size of the little kitchen and front room combo, done out in the same old grey lino floor and discoloured, white-painted walls of every greasy spoon everywhere. A couple of framed prints had been added as a nod to atmosphere, looking very much like photos torn from an old calendar, and a skeletal plant sat on one windowsill.

There was some messing about while Callum and William ordered, and Poppy restrained Strawberry from stealing fried bread from the table next to us, which was occupied by three fauns scoffing eggs and beans and swigging unsubtly from some bottles they kept beneath the table. Another table was taken up by a couple of dwarfs eating full breakfasts while going over some sort of plans they'd spread on a chair between them, their beards tucked inside their shirts out of harm's way. No one paid any attention to us at all.

"Right," Callum said, once he was seated with a large mug of tea. William had the same, and Poppy had a large glass of suspiciously luminous orange juice, which Strawberry seemed determined to sample. Green Snake had emerged from Callum's pocket, still clutching the seashell, taken one look at Strawberry's snake-like tail, and dived for cover. He peered out again now as Callum talked. "What's happening? We didn't expect to see you – someone said you'd been sent away from Dimly, so I thought you'd be *away* away, you know."

"Such clarity," I said, around a piece of bacon. I had both bacon and sausage, as requested, although I was vaguely jealous of William, who'd just grinned broadly and said, "Everything," when asked what he wanted. He was working his way methodically through a full English breakfast that had evidently been upgraded to troll-sized. There were six sausages and eight slices of bacon, an inordinate amount of black pudding, and a tub of beans, and his plate was more like a serving platter.

"We is sent away," William said. "Gerry says no is safe, we must go to country."

"But if no safe for us, is no safe for Gerry," Poppy said, picking up her fried egg sandwich. It was a quadruple decker, and I stopped eating to watch what happened when she bit into it.

"So we stay," William agreed. "But secret. No tells Gerry we stays. We knows people, so if we can't goes in Dimly, we asks them to tell us what happens."

Which was some astonishingly clear thinking for trolls. Also astonishingly sneaky and *strategic* thinking. I hoped that if any other trolls started thinking as well as Gerry and these two, that they also shared their dispositions, otherwise things were going to get mighty unpleasant for a lot of kinds.

"So what happens – happened?" Callum asked, taking the seashell off Green Snake as he tried to sneak it onto the table. I had a suspicion the reptile was missing his buddy the kraken.

"At first, all is same," William said. "Gerry tries to keep things okay for all peoples, but some peoples no like. They wants changes."

"Bad changes," Poppy said. "Before we leaves, nasty peoples come and say is no place for animal rescues. No place for modern trolls. Trolls is trolls, and no can have cafes or animal rescues. And animals must survive by selves or die."

She frowned at me, and I said, "Hard disagree, there, Poppy."

She nodded. "I knows. You is ..." She hesitated. "Good cat. Not always nice, but good."

"Fair," I said.

"Generous," Callum said, and grinned at me over his mug.

"So I closes cafe," William said. "Poppy closes animal rescue."

Poppy waved urgently, and we waited while she carefully chewed, swallowed, and wiped her mouth with a napkin.

"Excuse me," she said. "I no closes animal rescue. I pretends. I hides animals, especially unicorns, but if peoples calls me I still answers." She grinned. "Is how we have your phone digits and finds you. A nice lady calls me and says, oh, I has skinny human and cat needs rescue and I knows is you."

"Accurate description," I said, wondering how Rita had found the number of a Folk animal rescue. I was starting to wonder a lot of things about the OAP army.

William nodded. "Yes, Poppy is clever."

"Thank you," Poppy said, and tipped more red sauce onto her sandwich.

"I'm glad you called," Callum said. "And I'm glad you got the message to us in Whitby." He looked back at William. "And so Dimly …?"

"Ah, yes. After Gerry tells us go, Poppy and me … I … we be careful. Quiet. Gerry is still mayor, but people no like. And more people say, oh, troll cannot be mayor. Is wrong. Troll can no wear dresses. Is wrong. And if other peoples say, no, is okay, we like Gerry, suddenly their business is robbed, or they windows break, or sometimes—" He stopped, struggling to string the words together properly. "Ugh, I speak bad now!"

"You speak great," Callum said quietly. "Some people made it bad for anyone who supported Gerry?"

"That," William said. "There are lots who no like us." There was no self-pity in his voice, but Poppy gave his arm a troll-sized squeeze.

"Anyone who say all kinds are same have trouble," she said to us. "We knows all kinds is same. Different, but same. Some good, some bad. Gerry always say, and we always see. Is easy to see when you look." She shrugged. "But some peoples no say same."

"What peoples?" I asked.

"There is lots. Human sorts, and Folk sorts, and peoples with magic." She hesitated, looking at Callum. "Always more and more, and then all sudden Gerry is not mayor and your sister is."

"Ez is mayor?" Callum asked.

"She call it something else. Like she no really mayor, is just helping until new mayor is choosed."

Callum rubbed his mouth and looked at me. I twitched my ears at him meaningfully. She hadn't exactly mentioned *that* in her texts. Green Snake looked from one of us to the other, then tried to steal a piece of my bacon. I batted him, and he hissed at me, then took the bacon anyway.

"Where's Gerry now?" I asked the trolls. "Do you know?"

"We no know," William said. "Now our friends is scared to talk to us. They blocks us on phones. And we can no see them because maybe is bad for them."

Poppy looked at us, then at Callum, her three eyes huge and grey in the harsh light of the room. "You helps us? Please?"

And I answered before Callum could. "Does a cow eat cabbages?"

They all looked at me. "Not really," Poppy said. "Why?"

"Oh. Well, never mind. Yes, we'll help. Of course we will." Because the one thing the world couldn't stand to lose was a troll who not only saw the best in everyone, but believed in it even when they couldn't see it. There was little enough of that to go around as it was.

12

RISK TO LIFE

So we had a missing Gerry, a missing dentist, a missing Watch lieutenant, and a deliberately absent sorcerer to find, all while dealing with a reaper-hunting necromancer and her various, as yet unseen but likely to be unpleasant (certainly if Kara was anything to go by) sidekicks. Not to mention a Schrodinger's magician who was at once working with necromancers and not, plus Ez and her sudden bout of sibling loyalty.

All of which was troubling enough, but on top of that we were still going to have to go through weres to get any help. And finding the right weres, as much as there could be any such thing, was going to be an issue. According to the trolls, there were packs of them in Dimly, but they weren't the sort of weres we were after.

"Before things go bad, Gerry tell Yasmin Dimly is safe place for her now, but she say no," William said. "She say change is not sticky."

"She's pretty bright for a dog," I said.

Callum ignored me and said, "Do you know who the weres are who did come to Dimly, then?"

"We not know them," Poppy said. "They is strange. No talk to other Folk. Only to Ez and the naked mans magic people."

"What?" I said. "Naked magic-workers? I thought all that nude dancing around fires was just the fevered imagination of some repressed sorts."

"Necromancers," Callum suggested.

"I says," Poppy said.

"Oh. That makes more sense." I considered it. "So the weres only deal with them?"

"Only human sorts," William said, his voice level.

"Cool," I said. "Species-ist weres."

"And they're working with Ez?" Callum asked.

Poppy and William looked at each other. "Maybe?" William said. "Is hard to have truth."

Callum thought about it. "It'd make sense," he said, his voice tight. "The Norths have used weres before. Anyone convenient, really, but weres are pretty easy to employ. They don't tend to have many allegiances."

"So how we starts?" William asked. "How we find Gerry? We go in Dimly?"

"*No*," Callum and I said together, then looked at each other. "No," he said, more gently. "Gerry was right. It's not safe for you. We'll do some digging around and see what we can find out."

"How?" Poppy asked. "Ez and her bad friend and naked man lady don't like yous. *You* no can go Dimly either."

"Well," Callum started, and I spoke over him.

"She's right. Walker has to be our first stop. We get him, we get the sorcerer."

"You make it sound so easy," Callum said, poking his phone.

I glanced around the cafe warily. Strawberry panted away under the table, whining every time someone came and went to the toilets in the corner of the room. But he wasn't attempting to eat anyone, even me, which made a nice change. Green Snake had crept around the table to sample some of William's beans, still carting the damn shell with him, and you'd think we'd have been noticeable as keeping unusual company even in a Folk cafe, but no one had so much as glanced at us. One of the first rules of being Folk is that you don't notice other Folk. They spend enough time hiding themselves from humans. They don't need others paying them too much attention as well.

Callum put his phone down with a sigh. "Malcolm's phone still goes straight to messages," he said. "I don't know if it's off, or …"

"Or Yasmin finally got sick of him and bit his face off?" I suggested helpfully.

"You have a fixation with that."

"I'm of the opinion that many people could do to have Yasmin give them a good nip."

"Some of them would probably enjoy it, though," he pointed out, and I wrinkled my snout.

"*Humans,*" I said, and he snorted, going back to scrolling through his phone as if he might find the helpline for missing dentists.

Poppy sipped a giant mug of hot chocolate William had fetched her to wash down her sandwich, the heavy slabs of her hands engulfing the sides. She was wearing blue gingham dungarees with daisies embroidered on them, and a red puffer jacket was slung over the back of the chair. Somewhere she'd found a daisy-print headband that was almost troll-sized, and it was stretched to breaking point across the top of her broad, bare head. She looked at me and gave a small, jagged grin.

"Alright, Poppy?" I asked.

"No," she said honestly. "But better now yous is here."

I hoped her faith was only slightly misplaced and not completely. "What's happened with the animal rescue, then? How did you hide everyone?"

She sighed, sending the discarded napkins on the table fluttering to the floor. Callum picked them up absently, still staring at his phone. "The unicorns is problem. Ez's bad friend want their horns agains."

"Her bad friend?" I asked. "Do you mean Kara?"

"Yes," Poppy said, scowling. It was an impressive sight, and the daisy headband set it off nicely. "We had to move quick-quick, because we hears she come to takes them. Is *very bad*, Gobbelino."

"It is," I said, with feeling, although I had an idea that she was mostly worried about her precious unicorns being maltreated. I was more worried about that fact that unicorn horn can kill *anything*, and take every one of a cat's lives in a single blow. Also its powdered dust gives people the sort of high that transcends space, time, and the laws of the universe, but I was less interested in that than in keeping my skin on. "So you hid them?"

"We finds place," William said. "Is no perfect—"

"The unicorns is very angry," Poppy said.

"Unicorns is always angry," William pointed out. "But for now they are safe."

"That seems like a good start," I said, and looked at Callum. "Who're you trying now?"

"I don't know," he said, and I narrowed my eyes at him. "I was hoping I'd think of something."

Green Snake set the seashell next to Callum's plate and craned his head up at him, tilting it curiously.

"Thanks," Callum said, pocketing the shell again, and Green Snake flopped down to the table, then tipped his head at me. I don't know what passes as love in reptile circles, but he was definitely pining for the kraken.

Poppy scratched her chin and said, "Why you no call Rav?"

"I don't have his number," Callum said, putting the phone down with a sigh. "Besides, he's only just become a were. He'll still be figuring things out, *and* he didn't actually know Yasmin or Malcolm. I don't want to put him in the middle of anything."

"His boyfriend might know something, though," I said. "He was in with the pack at the club. He could know where they're hiding out."

"Sure. And then he'll have betrayed a were pack as well as put himself at odds with the necromancers. Seems a lot to ask."

"We can *ask*," I pointed out. "Doesn't hurt to do that. You know, considering the whole end of the world thing."

"He'll feel he has to help." Callum ran his hands back over his hair, staring at his phone. "I really don't want to drag anyone else into this, Gobs."

Poppy looked from one of us to the other, then pulled her own phone out of the chest pocket of her dungarees. It was a huge slab of a thing, one of those industrial style models designed to be dropped from a crane on a construction site, driven over by a forklift, and to still work when dug out of the concrete three days later. Troll-proof, in other words. "We asks," she said. "Rav helps with unicorns, because I helps with were bite, but he can say no, because is friend. Friend can always say no."

I thought that Poppy's recourse to hydrogen peroxide as the cure to all ills, even an infection that causes you to become a wolf at inopportune moments, had maybe not been as much help as Rav – also known, far more accurately, in my opinion, as Muscles – had been hoping for. But if he was hanging out with Poppy herding unicorns then he presumably wasn't one of the weres trying to tear our heads off outside the magician's house. Hopefully.

Poppy hit dial and held the phone out to Callum, who took it in both hands. I jumped up on the table next to him so that I could listen in, and a moment later we heard the click of connection, and Rav said in a voice still smudged with sleep, "Yeah?"

"Rav? It's Callum," Callum started, and Rav yelped. There was a dull thud, then a clatter, as if he'd dropped the phone then knocked it off the bed, and someone else asked something. There was a lot of whispered muttering in the background, but no one came back to the phone.

"Rav?" Callum tried. "Hello?"

"*Oi!*" I bellowed into the phone, making Callum jerk away from me and one of the fauns at the other table yelp. "Pick up, Hairy Maclary!"

"Shut up, Gobs," Callum said. There was some rustling on the phone, then a pause. "Rav?"

"Sorry," he said. "Wasn't expecting you."

"Evidently," I said. "How's Gordie?" The old cat Muscles had adopted might be halfway senile, but he was a decent sort for all that.

"Um, yeah. He's fine," Rav said. "Keeps telling me off for shedding, but I can't help that. He's just as bad anyway."

"Bitten anyone lately?"

"*Gobs.*" Callum pushed me away and said, "Sorry. Look, Rav, don't want to put you on the spot, and you don't have to help, but Poppy said you might know where Yasmin is. Well, Walker, really, but we're assuming he's still with her."

There was a long pause, and some scuffling that suggested he'd put his hand over the phone. We could just hear some whispered discussion, then Rav came back on and said, "Yeah, look, I can't help you."

"At *all?*" I said. "*Really?* We saved Gordie for you, remember?" We'd also got his flat burned down, but that hadn't been on purpose.

"*Gobs,*" Callum snapped. "Sorry, Rav. I get it."

"I don't," I said.

"No surprises there." Callum and I glared at each other, and Rav sighed over the phone.

"Look, we haven't had a lot to do with anyone else. Things got really weird after the fire and that, and Gabe reckoned we were better off keeping out of it."

"Is Gabe your mum?" I demanded.

"No, he just doesn't want me getting hurt."

"Dude, you're the size of a bloody charging bull. *And* you're a were now. Tell Gabe you can make up your own mind."

"Do cats have relationships?" Rav asked. "Because I'm thinking not."

"Not adult ones," Callum said, and I bared my teeth at him.

"Callum, the dude could break a necromancer over his knee."

"He has someone who worries about him. Leave it alone, Gobs."

"You're all too *human*," I grumbled. "Not picking up your lost cat again, dude."

Rav sighed again, then the sound changed, as if he'd walked out of whatever room he'd been in into something larger and more echoey. "Look," he said, his voice quiet. "Yasmin's got property on the edge of Ilkley Moor, on the Keighley side—" A voice rose behind him, and he added, "No, Gabe, I'm telling them. They *did* help me."

Gabe said something in the background, the words unclear but the tone suggesting pretty clearly that he was throwing his hands up in exasperation.

"I'm sorry," Callum started, and Rav cut him off.

"I don't know if that's where Yasmin's staying, but that's where a lot of the pack go to run. So be careful. Wait outside. Don't just go in."

"They run?" Callum asked.

"As wolves," I said. "That's what you mean, right?"

"Yeah. Yasmin's always been big on embracing wolf nature, apparently." His voice faded, as if he'd taken the phone away. "*You* told me that, Gabe. It's hardly a secret, anyway. And they're friends. They're not going to hurt anyone." His voice came clear again. "Are you?"

"No," Callum said, and I wondered what Rav thought we could do against a were pack. It was kind of complimentary, in a weird way.

"Good. I don't have an exact address, but I'll send you a pin drop to the area." He paused, then added, "I better go."

"Why, is Gabe coming to check you've washed behind your ears?" I asked.

"No, we already did that this morning," Rav said, and disconnected while Callum snorted.

"Humans. Almost humans. *Whatever*," I muttered, and looked at Callum as he slid the phone across the table to Poppy.

"So we're going to Ilkley Moor?" I asked. "That seems very wolfy."

"Looks like," Callum said. "Best lead we've got."

"We come," William said.

"After feed dragons," Poppy said, and I stared at her.

"You have *dragons?*"

"You know dragons. From Dimly. They is difficult if hungry."

"Oh, *those* dragons." Not the clever, fire-breathing sort that you could have an actual conversation with, if you didn't mind being pontificated at about how when *they* were young, back in the Jurassic period or whatever. Which, to be fair, was still more appealing than Poppy's dragons, who were actually Komodo dragons rescued from guard-lizard duty in the weapons stores of Dimly. They were very toothy, not very clever, and I definitely didn't want to see them hungry. "You'd best sort them, then. You'll be down a unicorn before you know it."

"I knows." She looked expectantly at William, and he sighed.

"Okay. We feeds dragons and checks all is safe. Then we go see weres."

"No, we'll call you," Callum said, getting up and holding a hand out for Green Snake to slither onto. "We're only going to talk to Yasmin, and the quicker we are, the better."

"Are you sure?" I asked him. "I quite fancy some troll backup when dealing with weres."

"Let's just get going," he said, and looked at William and Poppy. "You two go and sort the animals out, then lay low. We're going to find Gerry, I promise. This is just the first step. In the meantime you stay out of Dimly, alright?"

"Alright," Poppy said. William nodded, looking slightly unimpressed. Callum evidently needed to work on his technique when it came to giving orders.

DUDS' car rattled and sang as we hit the dual carriageways, but the rush of air through all the gaps around the doors and in the floor was refreshing, and the engine seemed to be surprisingly happy with being out on faster roads. Rush hour had started, but heading out of Leeds we were going against it, bumbling past queuing cars and creeping lines of traffic all bound in the opposite direction. Callum kept checking the fuel, and finally he said to me, "Either this car has a truck engine or we've got a leak."

"Maybe it's broken."

"I don't think so."

"Can't we risk it?" I asked. "It's not like we can afford to fill it up if it keeps running out all over the road."

"You're going to be complaining plenty if it runs out when we're in the hills somewhere," he said, pulling around a roundabout and accelerating away with a belch of exhaust.

"Good point," I said. "Be just our luck that it runs out with a were on our tails."

"Exactly," Callum said, and indicated to turn into a garage.

"Get me snacks," I said, as he climbed out.

"How you're not round, I don't know."

"It's my active lifestyle."

He snorted and went to wrestle the cap off the fuel tank.

The pin drop led us to a road in one of those edge places, where the city had crept up to nibble on the edges of farm-land, housing developments and industrial parks making incursions into the swathes of green land, and stolid-looking farmhouses looked resignedly over the dual carriageways and B-roads that had sprouted in the fields. It wasn't wild land, but it still remembered when it had been, and as we turned off the main road and wound our way up through clusters of flat-faced stone houses, we started to glimpse drystone walls and bored-looking sheep taking over from tarmac car parks and looming warehouses.

Another couple of turns, and we found ourselves on a one-lane road, lined on both sides with an unpleasant mix of sharp-edged walls and brambles. Here and there were little gravelled bays to allow cars to pass each other, and we pulled into one, Callum waving politely, as a tractor appeared around a corner. The driver gave us a suspicious look as he passed, then the road was empty again.

"Are you sure it's down here?" I asked.

"No," he said, the engine grumbling throatily as he pulled out. "The pin's in there somewhere." He waved toward the wall on our left. The fields had given way to crowded trees, pressing close to the wall and reaching winter-skeletal branches hungrily toward us.

"So what're we doing? Driving around till we see something?"

"Pretty much," he said. "You want to go out and have a sniff around?"

I looked at the overhanging limbs of the trees and shivered. "Not really."

The road didn't change, and we didn't see anyone else. Earlier I'd thought the land only remembered being wild, down there where the city gave to farmland, but up here it was all but untouched, too steep and rough for farming, and in the cold air that swept through the car the scent of forgotten places was more immediate than memory. There were footpath signs pointing over some of the walls to our right, and gates leading to farm tracks that offered glimpses of more familiar fields, good enough for sheep if nothing else. But to our left was nothing except those trees, crowded and twisted and moss-encrusted, pushing against the drystone wall as if determined to burst through and reclaim their land from the intruding tarmac. Some of them were so heavy-limbed and gnarled that they might have been there before cities had sprouted, been there as long as Dimly, holding firm against the onslaught of progress and hunching jealously over their secrets. Nothing invited the outside to enter. No gates, no stiles, no footpaths.

The road kept steadily climbing until we breached some unseen crest, where passing bays opened to both sides of the lane. To the right, past a gate with a national parks plaque and a footpath sign above it, we could see farmland tumbling down toward the towns that sprawled around Leeds and

Bradford, offshoots that the cities slowly crept out to embrace. There was a bin in the bay, and a sign saying, *Parking this side only.*

Callum pulled in next to the sign, and we stared across the road at the bay on the left. There was a gate there too, big enough for a vehicle to go through. It was padlocked shut, and had a rather wider selection of signs.

STRICTLY NO PARKING. Vehicles will be towed.

NO ENTRY. Private property.

DO NOT ENTER. Hunting in progress year-round.

DANGER. Risk to life. No trespassing.

"That seems promising," Callum said.

"I'm not sure I share your definition of *promising.*"

He pushed his door open and got out, tugging his coat tight around him as wind rushed up the hill to grab us. I followed, my ears flat to my head, and we walked across the empty road to stand in front of the supposedly promising gate.

"Anything?" Callum asked.

"Yes," I said. The heavy forest aroma of softly rotting leaf mulch, warmly organic. Old wood and new growth and the sweet sharp tang of fresh water. A whiff of the city still reaching us on the wind, plus crumbling tarmac and the distant scent of sheep.

And something feral, fierce, and deeply layered, full of wild, delighted abandon, all teeth and claws and hairy glory.

"Definitely wolfy."

"Thought so," Callum said, and climbed over the gate. Green Snake stuck his head out of his sleeve, looked around, then vanished again. How a thing with a head that size was smarter than either of us, I don't know.

"*Callum!*" I hissed. "What're you *doing?*"

"Going to find Yasmin," he said, jumping down on the far side.

"Did you not see the very big signs telling us how very, *very* bad it is to go in there? It's going to be teeming with bloodthirsty bloody wolves, and we're not going to help anyone if we're torn to bloody pieces!"

He looked at me, then said, "You think it's going to be bloody, then?"

"I hope you do get eaten."

He snorted and turned down the track, his coat swirling in damp, stained folds, and after a moment I slipped through the bars and trotted after him, my ears pricked for signs of stalking wolves and my nose full of the faint, layered traces of their scents.

The rutted trail curled through the trees and headed still further uphill, the gravel ground deep into the earth from the passage of cars and vans. The trees hung low, the gaps between their trunks shadowed and crowded with under-growth, and everywhere was the soft, dank green smell of mulch and plant life. There could've been anything in there watching us, and we wouldn't see them until they were on top of us. But birds sang, and the wind played through the bare branches, and old leaves flitted across the track, and nothing else moved. Maybe it was a down day for the weres of Leeds.

We'd been walking ages – well, I said it was ages, although Callum reckoned it was only ten minutes, but his legs are longer, so that makes things shorter – when the trees finally thinned, opening up onto grassy slopes that rose to rocky outcroppings on top of a sharp ridge to our right, and tumbled down into a steep valley on our left, trees and scrub and rocks all fighting for supremacy. A spring jumped and chattered from the rocky heights down to the valley below, and an old stone cottage with an equally ancient-looking barn stood between us and it. The barn was stone as well, with new windows lining the walls and big glass doors that looked over the valley. A stone patio extended from the front of it, with a built-in fireplace and outdoor bar-type area, and overall it looked as if it had had the full remodelling treatment, the sort that costs twice as much as building a new house. The cottage looked mostly untouched, although that could've just been very expensive renovations, too.

An old green Land Rover and a snazzy pale blue car that looked electric were tucked around the side of the barn, so as not to spoil the views, and there were lights on against the dull day in both buildings.

"Fancy weres," I said.

"Did you think they'd be living in caves?" Callum asked.

"Well, all that stuff about embracing the wolf within. Should be sleeping in the woods and rolling in the mud, really."

"Well, you can tell Yasmin you're disappointed in her commitment to authenticity, then."

"Eh." We'd stopped where the trees did, reluctant to emerge into the open just yet. There were no weres milling about outside the buildings, poised to gobble up small cats, but they could be waiting just inside, or hidden behind a rock or a tree or something. There was no telling with weres.

"Ready?" Callum asked me.

"Always ready to be torn limb from limb by ravening beasts."

"That's an advantage in our line of work," he said, and we set off down the track again, heading for the barn simply because it was the closest. I thought about retreating to Callum's shoulder, but decided dignity was more important than safety right now. Besides, I could run faster than him, so it might give me a head start. Hopefully, anyway.

We made it about halfway to the barn before one of the huge bifold doors swept open, and a hulking, heavily muscled man emerged, his bare forearms and smoothly shaved head dark against his tight pink shirt.

"Oi," he shouted, and the pink shirt seemed to be clinging on for dear life as he strode across the patio, at least as tall as Callum but twice as broad. "Who the hell are you?"

"Hi," Callum called, giving a little wave like he'd just dropped by with a sponge cake to welcome the scary weres to the neighbourhood. "Xavier, right?"

Xavier didn't answer at once, his head raised and tilted slightly. I could almost feel him sniffing for our scent, and suddenly he nodded. "Callum. And the kitty."

"Gobbelino London, PI," I said. "Not *the kitty*."

"Sorry," he said, and looked around warily. "What're you doing here?"

"Looking for Yasmin," Callum said. "Well, Malcolm, actually, but we thought he might still be with her."

Xavier ran his tongue across his teeth at the mention of Malcolm, and I wasn't sure if that was a flashback to a traumatic teeth cleaning, or in memory of the taste of dentist. "You'd better come in," he said.

"Is Yasmin there?" Callum asked, and Xavier tipped his head suddenly, looking toward the track to the gate.

"Come in *now*," he said, waving at us urgently, and my ears twitched as I caught the sound of an oncoming engine.

"Someone's coming," I said.

"*Hurry up*," Xavier hissed. "You want just any were to find you here?"

Callum didn't ask any questions, just ran for the patio, and I sprinted past him, sliding around Xavier's bare feet and into the airy, warm interior of the old barn, all done out in heavy wood and black metal and white walls. It smelled of coffee and hewn wood and weres, which was an unsettling combo.

Xavier slid the door shut behind us and pointed across an

open-plan kitchen and dining area to a sliding door near the fridge. "In there."

"Where does it go?" I asked, as we hurried across the room. "Back door?"

"Pantry," Xavier said, ushering us in.

I stopped so hard I stumbled. *"What?"*

The were slammed the door behind us.

13

RISK TO LIMB

THE LOCK TO THE WERE'S PANTRY ROLLED SHUT WITH A FINAL clunk, leaving us trapped in a long, narrow room that seemed to run the length of the kitchen, behind the cabinets on the other side of the wall. It was stocked with boxes of water filters and multipacks of crisps and peanuts, with sacks of flour and rice and onions and potatoes, and stacked crates of soft drinks and beer of the posh sort that you get from little breweries where everyone has a beard and/or tattoos. There were also cans of baked beans, tuna, pineapple slices, and half a dozen varieties of soup.

I pawed Callum's jeans and said, "He put us in the pantry, Callum. The *pantry*. That can't be good."

"*Shh.*"

I looked around and said, "Where's the chew stick supplies? Maybe we can distract them."

"Shut *up*," Callum whispered. He had his fingertips against the door, listening, and I cocked my head as I caught the squirt and hiss of something being sprayed in the room outside. A strong reek of some sort of essential oil came rolling under the door, making me snuffle. Callum shushed me again, and I just about strangled on a sneeze as we heard the smooth whisper of the bifold doors sliding open, followed by the squeak and scrape of feet as people came in, two by the sound of things.

"Alright, Lani," Xavier said, and I wrinkled my snout. Lani was by far the one were who seemed most inclined to want to eat small cats, going by previous encounters.

"Where's Anton?" Lani asked, not bothering with the niceties.

"Sleeping, I imagine," Xavier said. "Not seen him this morning."

"Any change?"

"No."

So that likely meant Anton, the big boss wolf with his tattoos-and-shirtsleeves voice (when human) was still stuck in wolf mode, thanks to Ifan. Not just wolf form, wolf *mode* – he couldn't even communicate with his pack using whatever mind meld stuff weres usually did. Which was unlikely to be making anyone too happy, and also very unlikely to make us flavour of the month. Or it might mean we were at risk of *becoming* flavour of the month, as Ifan had been very quick to blame the whole thing on us. Well, on him doing it to protect Callum, which was really the same thing.

"Had any visitors?" Lani asked.

"No," Xavier said. "We expecting someone?"

Lani growled, a low, angry sound. "There's a car parked at the end of the lane, and someone's been over the gate. Bit faint, but I got a whiff of cat, too."

"Really? I haven't seen anyone," Xavier said, far too brightly.

There was a pause, and I could just imagine Lani glaring at him. "Sure? You and your little cat fetish?"

"It's not a *fetish*. They're just all … small. And soft. And their feet are so cute."

Callum and I looked at each other, and it was a good thing we were worried about being overheard, as I was pretty sure he was going to say something about Xavier having misguided notions about cats.

"And just bite-sized," a new voice said. I didn't recognise it, but it was deeper than Lani's. "With you there, Xav."

"*No*," Xavier said.

"What is *wrong* with you?" Lani asked. "They're sneaky little monsters. Have you seriously let one in here?"

"No," Xavier said again. "No cats, and no one else, either. You sure they weren't just walkers? Took a look over our gate then headed off on the path across the road?"

A silence, and I wrinkled my snout, forcing back another sneeze. That oil was *strong*.

"With a cat?" the unfamiliar voice said.

"Takes all sorts," Xavier replied.

"Seems unlikely," Lani said. "That bloody North and his cat are back in town. Odds are it's them."

"Well, I haven't seen anyone," Xavier said.

Lani grunted. "Suppose he'd be sneaking around the woods rather than walking straight up to the house. No one's that stupid."

Callum and I looked at each other again, and I arched my eyebrow whiskers.

"Come on," the other were said. "If he's on our land, we'll find him. Be a bit of fun taking him down."

"In one piece," Lani said. "Kara wants to get her hands on him before Ez or Sonia do."

"If you really think someone's here, I'd better get Yasmin," Xavier said. "She'll want to know."

"*No*," Lani said sharply. "She's all touchy-touchy politics. She'll want to discuss it or vote on it or some bollocks. I say we get out there and get him. You coming?"

"I've not had breakfast yet."

"Gods," the second were said. "*Really?*"

"Look, let me get sorted, and I'll get a few others up, then we'll join you. Cover more ground."

"No," Lani said. "You'll send Yasmin after us."

"I won't."

"You're like her bloody lap dog," the second were said, and I could hear the sneer in his voice. "Do you lick her toes at night, too?"

"So what if I am, Johan?" Xavier demanded. "*She's* not doing party tricks for bloody Norths and necromancers."

There was a snarl in the kitchen, something that was human yet not, and the hair on my spine shivered to attention.

"We're not doing *tricks*," Lani said, her voice low and dangerous. "We're aligning ourselves with those most likely to come out of this mess in one piece."

"Really? That Sonia doesn't care about the pack's needs. We're disposable to her type. How do you see this working out? "

"I've got my plans," Lani said. "Now we're going to see if we can catch ourselves a North. You coming or not?"

"No."

"Then we'll get Angela. She'll want in."

"*No*," Xavier said again, and I heard the scuff of his bare feet on the wooden floors as he moved. I could imagine him putting himself between the were and the way deeper into the house, broad and solid and cat-fixated. "Angela stays out of all this. She's too young to be dragged into your mess. But you two suit yourselves."

There was a pause, then Lani said, "Being a soft little bleeding heart never gets you anywhere, Xav. One day you'll have to be a proper wolf."

"I am," he said. "I'm just not a wolf like you."

There was the soft thud of boots on the floor, then the

sound of the big doors sliding shut. We stayed where we were, and a few minutes later Xavier opened the pantry door and looked down at us.

"You can come out now," he said. "You want a coffee?"

"Tea, if you have it," Callum said.

"You want some milk, Kitty?"

"*Gobbelino.* Even Gobs, if you must. Not Kitty."

"Sorry." He scratched the back of my neck, and despite the raw, savage scent of him I arched my back, purring slightly. "Milk?"

"No," Callum said. "He can't digest it. And you don't want to smell the end result."

"I *like* milk," I muttered, and Xavier said, "What about goat's milk? I'm lactose intolerant, but I can drink that."

"Sure," I said. "Got any camel milk while we're at it?"

Xavier gave me a curious look and went to get our drinks. "Why didn't you just call?" he asked. "Sneaking into a were property is kind of ... well, not very smart," he amended, putting a ramekin of milk in front of me and going to fiddle with a fancy-looking coffee machine.

"We didn't have a phone number," Callum said, while I gave him a pointed look.

"You're friends with that magician, aren't you? He could've passed a message. Yasmin calls him about every other day to ask when he's going to sort Anton out."

Callum gave me a pointed look back.

"We don't trust him," I said.

"Obviously," the big were said, topping a mug up for Callum's tea and going back to the coffee machine. It seemed needlessly complicated. "He's a *magician.* But aren't you buddies?"

"No," I said, and Callum sighed.

"Is Yasmin here?" he asked.

Xavier put a mug in front of him. "I'll call her. She's over in the old house with the cubs and Anton. This place is too nice for cubs when they get all chewy and stuff."

"Thanks," Callum said, and I sampled the milk. It wasn't awful, but it wasn't custard, either.

WHILE WE WAITED FOR YASMIN, Angela appeared on the stairs, looking even younger than she really was with her fine braids loose down her back and her muscular shoulders swamped by a pyjama top that read *You've got to be kitten me.* There was a grumpy-looking cat on it.

She looked from us to Xavier, then back at us, and said, "Oh." Callum got a nod, I got a scratch, then she sat down at the big wooden table with a mug of tea and a piece of toast, yawning. I could see her canines, just slightly longer and sharper than a human's. Green Snake slithered over to her and they stared at each other, then she gave him a scrap of toast.

We didn't have long to wait before Yasmin appeared, striding up the steps to the patio with a long, multicoloured skirt swirling around her in the wind. Her feet were bare and brown on the hard stone, and a gold anklet shone on one ankle. A ruby stud in her nose caught the faint brightness of the day, and did nothing to lighten her expression, which was leaning toward *caution, will bite.* A wolf stalked next to her, heavy-shouldered and broad, his colours running with shades of deep grey. I suppose the only thing we could be happy about was that Anton the wolf was sticking more with Yasmin the political were rather than Lani the *off with their heads* were.

She came in the door with the scent of wild heather and shadowed places on sunlit days, and the damp of the day swirled in after her and the big wolf. Xavier handed her a mug of coffee, and she sat down at the table directly across from us. Anton prowled the room restlessly, ears twitching.

"Callum," she said. "Gobbelino."

"Alright," I said.

"Sorry to barge in," Callum started, and she snorted.

"Do you ever do anything else?"

"Not really," he admitted.

"Are Lani and Johan going to find the magician lurking around the place?"

"No."

"Any cats? Anyone else?"

"No."

She nodded, not looking particularly convinced. We didn't have the best track record with her. "What d'you want?"

"Is Malcolm still with you?" Callum asked.

"He may still be enjoying our protection," she said, and Angela made an irritated noise. Yasmin looked at her, eyebrows raised.

"'Enjoying our protection'? He's like the worst house guest *ever.* One that never goes home and never tidies up after himself."

"Sounds like him," I said.

Yasmin sighed. "Yeah. It's not ideal. And yes, he's still here. We're not entirely sure what to do with him, but he pays well. And as someone blew up Anton's bar and forced me out of mine," she added, looking at Callum, "*and* we've still got a pack to feed, money's a bit tight."

"Yeah, we met the new owner of your place," I said. "How come you didn't bite his face off?"

"Same reason I've not made you into a cat sandwich," she said, showing me her fangs and setting the hair bristling along my spine. "Some of us are civilised creatures."

"That guy's not," I managed, and Anton snorted, so close to me that I almost fell off the table.

"Still not a reason for biting anyone's face off, as satisfying as it might be," Yasmin said. "Why do you want Malcolm?"

"The sorcerer wants him," Callum said.

"And where's she?"

Callum looked at me, and I shrugged. "Somewhere beige."

"Sorry?"

"Like, all beige walls and stuff. Dead flowers and stone floors and things."

"Like a show home?" Angela asked, as the rest just stared at me. "Not somewhere anyone really lives, so it's just all stuff that no one can ever really love or hate? Just boring?"

"That," I said. "Only she said something about a security deposit, so I think it's a rental rather than a show home."

"Holiday cottage," Angela said. "They love that whole beige thing." We all looked at her, and she said, "What? I like design magazines. Sue me."

"She's on holiday?" Xavier asked. "Really?"

"I think more hiding out," I said. "She said she couldn't come back yet, but when she does she wants the dentist with us so she can find him easily."

"Why does she want him so much?" Yasmin asked.

"No idea," I said. "Maybe she's lost a filling."

"It's more than that," Callum said. "I just don't know what, exactly."

"Proof?" Yasmin said.

"What?"

"We're meant to be protecting Malcolm. That's what he's been paying us for. To keep him safe from whoever attacked the sorcerer's house. Attackers who smelled of Dimly and the Norths." Yasmin narrowed dark eyes at Callum. "So prove to us that the sorcerer's really the one who wants this, and you're not just going to take him back to the magician, or the necromancers, or your sister, or anyone else."

"Well ... we can't," Callum admitted. "But Anton smelled me." He turned to look at the wolf. "You know I'm not a North anymore."

The wolf looked back at him with unreadable golden eyes, unmoving.

"Anton may have made that judgement, but that was before he was stuck as a wolf. Before he was no longer able to communicate, and before I had to take on leadership of this pack." Yasmin set her mug down, and I spotted a curl of fresh scar tissue inside her forearm. I had an idea she'd less *taken on* the leadership than fought for it. "I want to hear from the sorcerer herself before we let Malcolm go anywhere with you."

"Shouldn't that be his choice?" I asked.

Yasmin looked at me. "Have you met him?"

I snorted, and Callum said, "He's right, though."

"No. If you tell him Ms Jones sent you, he might waltz off with you happily, then two days later I've got an enraged sorcerer tearing this place apart. Tearing *us* apart." She shook her head. "Proof first. Get her to call me."

"*How?* We don't even have a phone number for her that works!"

"You're in contact with her somehow." She got up and found a piece of paper on a shelf in the kitchen. She scrawled a number on it, then came back to hand it to Callum. "Get her to call me on that. And don't bother trying Malcolm. We had to take his phone away. That man likes his online shopping *far* too much."

"He sounds more like a prisoner than a guest," Callum said quietly.

"And you smell like a North *and* that damn magician. You're lucky Lani didn't sniff you straight out."

"She did," someone said, and we spun to see the woman in question standing in the shadows of a hallway beyond the kitchen, near an open door that looked like it led to a utility room. A utility room and a back door, most likely. She had a towel wrapped around her, but even as she spoke she dropped it, collapsing to the floor in a stomach-churning crunch and snap of shattering bones and tearing muscles. I'd seen it before, but it still sent every hair standing to attention, and I gagged as Lani became nothing more than a splodgy, gruesome mess of flesh and bone. Then the mess surged upward, knitting and reforming into a wolf. The whole thing took less time than a breath, and as wolf-Lani emerged she was already lunging for Callum. A second wolf sprinted in the door behind her, and a third, then a fourth, and from all around the table came the clamour of bodies tearing their way out of human form and into wolf.

The fancy new house wasn't going to stay fancy for long.

WERE fights are not like dog fights. Dog fights are all snarl and muscle, fury and fright, pure instinctual chaos. And while there was a certain amount of fury and muscle going on in the kitchen currently, there was also a lot of strategic thinking, which when combined with the teeth made for something much more terrifying than your average dog fight. I mean, we're not talking advanced strategy here, because they were still more beast than thinking creature when they got to this stage, but breaking things up wasn't going to be as easy as throwing a glass of water over them.

Which is pretty much what Callum did when Lani lunged for him.

To be fair, it was his still-warm tea, and he lobbed the whole mug with it, so she caught it straight between the eyes with a yelp that quickly became a snarl. It did slow her enough that he could swing himself up onto the table before she resumed her rush, and he met her jaw with his boot and his own yelp of "Sorry!"

"Stop apologising to things that want to eat us!" I shouted at him. I'd shot to the top of the open shelving that lined one wall of the dining area, and as wolf-Johan lunged at me, scrabbling at the shelves with his paws, I knocked a plant pot straight onto his nose. He yelped, and Anton hit him from the side, shoulder-barging him back and away from the wall, snapping without making contact.

"I don't like kicking people," Callum yelled back, then added, "Sorry," as he booted another wolf in the face, then stooped to snatch up Green Snake, who was doing his cobra impression without much effect. Yasmin had already taken Lani to the floor, and Xavier lunged to meet the wolf Callum had just kicked, surging over the table and past him in a rush of sleek dark fur. Angela was backed against the door as the fourth attacker circled and snarled at her. It was a male, bigger and bulkier than she was in her half-grown wolf form, but she had her hackles up and her ears back and was growling back like she wanted to remove his head. She probably did, but that didn't mean it was going to happen.

"Hairballs," I muttered, and launched myself straight from the shelves to the table. I hit once, hearing a snarl as one of the wolves twisted to snap at me, then was airborne again. I came down straight onto the back of the wolf confronting Angela and clawed my way grimly toward his head. He spun with a startled yelp, then kept spinning, trying to get his teeth into me. It wasn't easy to keep a grip, but I didn't have any of Callum's reservations about not hurting anyone. They were all about ten times my size, for a start.

Angela rushed the wolf as he was distracted trying to throw me off, and closed her teeth on his ear. It wasn't exactly a deadly move, but it did set him howling and twisting as he tried to get away from both me *and* the young were. He staggered, feet muddled for an instant – I doubt you can switch between biped and quadruped and expect to keep everything straight. Angela braced her back legs and *lunged,* and the bigger wolf went sprawling to the floor, the young were letting go of his ear and snapping for his throat instead. I threw myself clear just as Anton surged over the table and knocked Angela off the other wolf before things got terminal.

Callum had snatched up one of the heavy chairs and was wielding it like a lion tamer, and I ran to join him. He was puffing and lunging and letting the chairs legs rest on the table every chance he got, so it was more like a lion tamer who hadn't been putting in the upper body work, but that was currently enough. Yasmin and Lani were all teeth and chaos and flying fur, skidding across the kitchen in a vicious dance that was as strangely graceful as it was terrifying. Xavier was battling both Johan and another wolf, fast and graceful despite his bulk, and Anton was dealing to Angela's wolf while she dashed and nipped and whined in delight. Currently no one was paying any attention to us, and I looked at Callum.

"Run for it?" I suggested.

"We can't just leave—"

"Do you actually think we're doing any good here?"

"No, but I mean Malcolm." He swiped at Johan, who'd given up on Xavier to make another run at us, but the big wolf was directly behind him, and before the chair even looked like making contact they were both rolling away again.

"I don't think we're going to get away with sneaking upstairs for a look around," I said.

"No," he agreed. "Lift?"

"Sure. That way I've still got a chance to make it while they're chewing on your legs."

"My thoughts exactly." He crouched, keeping a wary eye on the scrapping wolves, and I leaped to his shoulder, digging my claws into the familiar, smoke-scented material of his coat.

I thought he was going to go for the bifold doors, those being the nearest, but instead he jumped off the table on the opposite side, breaking into a sprint as soon as he landed, the hard soles of his borrowed boots squeaking on the floor. He bolted for the door the wolves had come in through, head down and arms pumping, and a sudden, roaring silence fell behind us as the weres turned their attention from fighting each other to watching us. It was barely a moment, not even a breath, and then came an explosion of movement. Claws scraped on hard floors, bodies collided, teeth clashed and snarls and growls flooded the room. Lani came up and over the heavy kitchen table, teeth bared and snout wrinkled in fury, Yasmin surging after her. Anton thundered out of the kitchen, muscles moving smoothly under his heavy pelt, and Xavier and Angela were lost in a tumble of wolfish bodies as the others bolted after us.

Yasmin wasn't going to reach Lani in time to stop her. Neither was Anton. And Callum wasn't going to reach the door. Lani hit the floor and exploded up again, a smoothly muscular leap that would take her jaws to the back of Callum's neck even as he grabbed the door frame to swing himself around and into the utility room.

He wasn't going to make it. *We* weren't going to make it.

So I leaped from his shoulder to meet the damn wolf, screeching as I went. *"Mangy lettuce-brained snaggle-toothed bloody **mutts!**"*

Which wasn't super imaginative, but I was under duress.

I saw Lani's eyes widen in the moment before I hit her,

but she was already committed to the leap. I slammed into her snout, grimly making every part of me that could be sharp and pointy as sharp and pointy as they were possibly able to be, and clawed wildly. She still crashed into Callum, but rather than teeth-first it was front paws-first, as she twisted to try and fling me off. He stumbled into the utility room and hit the wall with a yelp while Lani and I tumbled to the hallway floor, sliding past the door in a tangle of limbs. I scratched and bit frantically, far too aware of the size and proximity of the were's teeth, and she snarled and surged back to her feet, shaking her head to try and fling me off. I clung on tighter. Letting go was likely to have dire consequences.

Anton caught up with us in an explosion of pure wolfy muscle, and in the next instant I had two sets of were teeth uncomfortably close to my vital bits. But Anton wasn't interested in me. He had Lani's throat in his jaws, and she froze. I stayed where I was, still attached to her snout, my heart hammering so hard I could almost see my pulse at the edges of my vision. Callum dived out of the utility room and grabbed me in one hand, tearing me free, then turned to see Yasmin watching us. An expensive-sounding crash came from the kitchen behind her, and she twitched one ear, then looked at us and jerked her head toward the utility room.

"Gotcha," I said, but Callum didn't move, and I looked up at him. "Run?"

"Malcolm," he started, and Yasmin snarled. "Right. Run."

We ran.

Or, rather, Callum did, diving into the utility room and slamming the door behind us. There was no lock, but it hardly mattered – even fancy house internal doors aren't made to withstand weres. The utility was a similar shape to the pantry, just a long thin hallway, this one lined on one side by white cabinets and a sink and a worktop, and a washing machine and drier with fancy displays. There was a hanging rail on the opposite side, with various shirts and jumpers dangling from clothes hangers, and the whole thing smelled of soap and sunshine. More importantly, though, there was an exterior door at the other end of the room, and Callum ran to it. A moment later we were out in the wet, damp-smelling day, full of low cloud and mud and an absolutely beautiful dearth of weres.

Not for long, though.

14

JUST A LITTLE LIGHT PROPERTY DAMAGE

WE HAD A CLEAR PATH AROUND THE BARN TO THE TRACK OUT, but Callum hesitated, looking at the stone cottage next door.

I growled and said, "Do you want to be turned into doggy dinner?"

"But we don't—"

"We know he's still with them, and that they're not handing him over until we have the sorcerer. And we *can't fight weres.* Haven't we tried it enough already?"

Callum started to say something else, and was interrupted by the sound of a heavy body hitting the door we'd just come through. The fight was following us. "Fine," he said, and broke into a run, skirting the building. I wriggled out of his grip and jumped to the ground, the sound of the scrap setting my ears twitching as I tried to check every way at once for attack and still keep running.

We made it around the barn without anyone rushing us, but as we reached the drive there was the unmistakable sound of a door being smashed open and hitting a wall. A howl went up, rich and deep and tasting of bleak moonlit fells, and I shuddered, turning my lope into a sprint. Callum angled abruptly away from the track, heading for the corner of the barn as if he were going to circle it.

"What're you *doing?*" I screeched at him as more howls went up, the ones behind us being answered from the stone cottage and, even more alarmingly, from the hills beyond.

"We can't outrun them," he shouted back, not slowing. I sprinted after him, risking a glance over my shoulder to see Lani coming around the barn with her head low and blood on her shoulder, her stride long and sure.

"Hairballs," I muttered, then added in a shout, "You better have a plan!"

Callum reached the old Land Rover and grabbed the door, giving a yelp of triumph when it opened easily. He swung himself in and I shot over his lap, going so fast that I hit the opposite door before I could stop. Callum slammed the door and scrabbled beneath the front seats, coming up empty-handed. Lani reached us, lunging up with both paws on Callum's window, snarling and slobbering.

"Not so clever now, are you?" I shouted at her, and looked at Callum expectantly. He'd tried behind the sun visors, and was now digging in the glovebox. "Well?"

"Well, I need keys, Gobs."

"Can't you just grab some wires and squidge them together?"

"Keys would be better – I'm not sure this thing's old enough to hotwire. It might have an ignition lock."

Lani threw herself against the Land Rover, making it rock gently, and Johan appeared next to her. They looked at each other, then lunged at the car in unison. It bounced rather less gently.

"Don't like that," I said, and peered into the back seat. It was folded down, and there were what looked like fence posts lying across the open boot, plus a couple of tubs of hefty-looking u-shaped nails. We bounced again, even more enthusiastically this time, and I looked back at the weres. The third wolf had joined them, and the fourth was on its way. Yasmin, Anton, Xavier and Angela were standing back, watching. Apparently they'd decided they'd done enough, which I couldn't exactly fault them for. Anton had blood around his mouth and Xavier was limping, and we were, after all, trespassers.

The fourth were crashed into the Land Rover, and this time there was definitely a *lean* along with the bouncing. Callum said something I filed away for future reference, and I leaped into the back. There was an empty tub of sheep wormer, so that was nice. They kept their prey parasite-free. There was also— I lunged forward as the vehicle rocked again, then scrambled into the front seat carrying my prize. Callum was sprawled across the seats with his head under the wheel, presumably trying to find some wires to squidge, and I said, "Oi! Look!"

He looked up hopefully, then sighed. "Well, it's not keys, is it?"

"I've seen it work," I said as he straightened up and snatched the screwdriver off the seat, shoving it into the ignition.

"On TV?"

"Maybe," I admitted. The SUV shook again, and this time I was sure the wheels on that side left the ground.

"Can't get much worse," he said, which I thought was one of those things we'd always agreed not to say.

But the engine revved into smooth, grumbling life as he turned the screwdriver, and we had one moment of shared triumph before the weres renewed their attack on the car and we lurched so badly I thought we were going over. Callum shoved the car hurriedly into reverse and backed away from the barn, then swung around to head for the track.

"Go faster," I said. "We've got to get a head start or they'll have us at the gate."

"They're in the way," he said, trying to skirt Lani as she stepped in front of us. The other three were crowding around too, forming a furry barrier between us and escape.

"They'll move."

"I'm not hitting them, Gobs," he said.

"They'll move."

He tried to speed up a little, swerving to avoid Johan, but as quick as he turned the big car, the weres were quicker. There was no way forward that wasn't blocked by broad backs and narrowed eyes, and he eased off again. So I did the only thing a smart cat can do in such circumstances.

I dived into the footwell and shoved myself against the accelerator as hard as I could, wedging myself between it and Callum's boot. He yelped, jerking his foot away, and tried to get to the brake, but I had my hindquarters firmly in the way, so all he did was squish me a bit instead. I howled in outrage that was mostly faked, and heard answering howls from outside.

"Gobs, get off!" Callum yelled.

"Just steer!" I bellowed back, as the Land Rover swerved and shook and juddered, and the engine screamed, and as far as I could tell we hit nothing at all.

I stayed where I was until the erratic course smoothed out, and the light dimmed in the cover of the trees. Then I scrambled free, letting Callum take over. He shifted up through the gears without speaking, quieting the shrieking engine, and I put my paws up on the back of the passenger seat to check out the rear window. The weres were sprinting after us, but they were losing ground as Callum sped up.

"That went alright, then," I said.

"I could have hit one of them."

"They were very keen to roll the car and pick our carcasses," I pointed out. "And I did say they'd move."

"Hitting one of them would not have been helpful. Yasmin doesn't currently intend to let them eat us, but I'm not sure she'd feel the same if we ran someone over."

"True," I admitted. Yasmin was on the pack's side, and no one else's. She didn't want Lani starting things, but she wouldn't tolerate us doing it, either. "Got us out, though, didn't I?"

"I suppose." He kept his eyes on the track. The Land Rover handled the rough ground easily, but we weren't going to have a huge window for escape when we reached the gate. We couldn't go *that* fast.

Even so, it was a lot quicker getting to the road by car than it had been on foot. A couple more curves and the gate was ahead of us, the road dull beyond it and Duds' patchy car painted almost glossy by rain just across the empty stretch of tarmac.

"Ready?" Callum asked, checking the rear-view. The weres weren't around the last corner yet, but they wouldn't be far off.

"Can't you just drive straight through the gate? That'd be better. Through the gate and just keep going."

"I'd rather not add property damage to the reason the weres don't like us."

"Well, you've already stolen some property," I pointed out. "It's not a big jump."

"The car's still on their land," he replied, checking his pockets. Green Snake stuck his head up, holding Duds' key, and Callum said, "Thanks." He folded it into his hand, then brought us to a screeching halt with the Land Rover's nose almost touching the gate. He wrenched the hand brake on and swung out of the car in almost the same movement, leaving the engine running. I piled out after him and we sprinted for the gate as a howl went up behind us.

I shot though the bars, feeling the shiver of charms passing across my skin, and Callum swung up and over the top with unnatural grace, given the weird length of his limbs. We were side by side as we bolted across the road, and I shot into the car as soon as he'd got the door open wide enough. Callum dropped in after me, and I put my paws on the dashboard so I could peer out the windscreen.

The wolves washed around the Land Rover as Callum cranked the key and the old VW burst into life, growlier and louder than the 4WD had been. The wolves stopped at the gate, watching as we backed onto the road and peeled away, belching black exhaust like a smokescreen as the worn tyres fought for traction on the damp tarmac. Then we were off, and I clambered into the back to check for pursuit. But the weres didn't human up and grab the Land Rover, or even follow on paw. Only Lani walked out into the road to watch us go, her ears pricked and her head high. One turn in the winding road and they were gone.

It should have been a relief. But all I had was the niggling sense that Lani wasn't following because she knew she'd be catching up to us soon enough, and that was no relief at all.

"Smooth getaway, nicely executed," I said, and Callum glanced at me. He'd pulled over in a passing bay once we were sure no one had followed us, and was leaning against the car smoking a cigarette. He didn't answer, just rolled his piece of Whitby jet in his free hand. It made me uneasy, it and the pink seashell Green Snake was so fond of. I kept wanting to say that either or both of them might be a charm or a tracker of some sort, that our luck never lent itself to *keepsakes,* but there had been few enough good things in life recently. And maybe it didn't even matter. The jet had been given to us as a going away gift by a small hairy creature of dubious parentage whom we only knew as Housekeeping from a boarding house that had dubious standards of the same. Even if the jet summoned them, what was the worst that could happen? They'd dust something?

The seashell was more questionable, but even if it had something to do with mermaids, the same question applied. It wasn't like a mermaid could do much here. We were pretty much slap bang in the middle of the country, and I'd never heard they took much to rivers.

"No Malcolm without Ms Jones, no Ms Jones without Malcolm," he said, and sighed, tucking the stone away. He ran a hand through his messy hair, scattering a soft dusting of drizzle from the ends. "No Gerry, no Gertrude, no anything."

I considered it, then said, "We've got a car that runs."

"Our car runs."

"Sometimes. This one seems marginally more reliable, even if it is still leaking." I lifted one paw to show him the passenger seat was moving steadily from *damp* to *soggy.*

He gave me half a smile and ground his cigarette butt out on the ground, then tucked it back into the packet. "This holiday home you reckon Ms Jones was in – did you get any idea of where it might be?"

I considered it. "No. It was dark, and I couldn't see anything outside. It was just some place. Although there were beachy things – not proper beachy things, but all that tatt people *think* is beachy. Starfish and little wooden boats and so on. So maybe near the sea? Or the house people just like the sea. Not sure."

"Well, it's not like the UK has a massive coastline," he said, and I looked at him for a moment, then huffed.

"Look, even if we knew where she was, we probably couldn't find her. She'll have so many charms on that place it'll be like a mirage."

"True." He checked his cigarette packet, apparently considering another, then put it away again. "Can you try reaching her again?"

I made a reluctant noise and watched him strip his coat off and throw it in the back of the car, pushing the sleeves of his jumper up before getting in. The jumper was some knitted black thing he'd rescued from the lost property on our Whitby pirate ship, and it was unravelling at the neck-line. It also smelled faintly of fish.

"Are you pining for Whitby?" I asked him.

"Pining for a time where all we had to worry about was getting one person back off mermaids, rather than negotiate with half the Folk of Leeds."

Which was fair enough. Even if we had had Black Dogs, vicious cats, angry pirates, and flirtatious mermaids to deal with. Plus a parrot of seriously questionable character. I thought of standing in Ms Jones' kitchen while she said, *I didn't bring you here,* and licked my chops quietly.

"Stop changing the subject," he added, as he pulled back onto the empty road. "Can you reach Ms Jones?"

I shivered, my back suddenly cold with the void. "I'd really rather not."

"We don't have a lot of options."

"Gah. Why do we *always* end up with no options?"

"Poor life choices," he suggested.

"Fair," I agreed, then sighed. "We need somewhere."

"What sort of somewhere?"

"Somewhere to hole up while I try a couple of things."

He gave me a curious look. "You mean to try and reach Ms Jones?"

"Yes. Sort of." I took a breath. "I think ... I think I might've shifted."

He frowned. "That last time, you mean? From the car?"

"Yeah. She said she didn't drag me there. I just turned up."

"But you can't go through the Inbetween. You've always known that."

"Have I, though?" I asked. "I can't remember *anything*. When I try all I get are images of being held there by the Watch, of the beasts tearing me to pieces – I can't see past it, and every time I think of shifting that's what I remember, too. But maybe it's ... in the way or something."

Callum nodded thoughtfully. "It would make sense. It was a huge trauma."

"You're a huge trauma," I said immediately, then wrinkled my snout. "Sorry."

"It's fine." He was quiet for a moment, then said, "And that's kind of fair. I'm not being much help, anyway. The only thing I can do is hang around and ask you to go and relive something no one should ever have to go through once, let alone repeatedly." He glanced at me. "All that time in Dimly when I was a kid, and I could've been learning things that were actually useful, *North* things, and instead all I did was get high and drunk and do all I could to run away from everything."

"Isn't that just being a human teenager?" I asked. "Plenty of Folk, too, really."

"Yeah, I think I took it rather to the extreme, though."

"No point being half-hearted about stuff."

He snorted and scritched my head. "Do you think that particular life philosophy could have something to do with why you keep getting killed?"

"Maybe. But really I think it's just that no one appreciates quite how delightful I am."

"Yeah, that's definitely it," he said, and grinned at me when I narrowed my eyes at him.

THE PHONE RANG while we were making our way a little aimlessly down the hill and back toward Leeds, for the simple reason that there didn't seem to be anywhere else to go. Callum took it from his pocket and stared at it for a moment.

"What?" I asked. "Who is it?"

"Ez," he said.

"Don't answer it. *Don't.*"

"It might be about Gerry," he said.

"It won't be anything good about him, if it is."

He shot a quick look at me, then hit answer, putting the phone to his ear. I growled, and scrambled to his shoulder so I could hear.

"Cal?" Ez said, her voice cautious.

"Here," he said.

"Which is not at the old place." A touch of amusement lifted the tightness in her tones. "I'd be able to hear if it was."

"Is it even still there?" he asked.

"No idea."

"Why mention it, then, you grease-spotted draining board?" I demanded.

"See you've still got the cat," Ez said.

"He hasn't *got* me. I'm not bloody foot fungus. I—" I squawked as Callum hefted me off his shoulder and onto the seat, pulling the car over into a lay-by as he did so. "It was a fair question!"

Callum put the phone on speaker as Ez said, "You remembered."

"Hard to forget."

"Explain," I said.

"It's what we'd tell each other when things were really bad at home," Callum said. "A kind of promise of what we'd do when it was all over."

"Meet at the old place," Ez agreed. "No one's going to tell you to break a faery's wings there."

"You what?" I said, but I couldn't get any fury into my voice. Not when the edges of hers had the same shadows Callum's did.

"How bad is it?" Callum asked.

"Bad. And going to get worse."

"What d'you want from me, Ez?" His voice was quiet, and he took his cigarettes out, putting the phone down on his knee so he could find his lighter at the same time.

She sighed, the noise a whisper on the line. "You need to come home."

"Dimly's not my home."

"You don't get that choice. The town needs the Norths."

"It's got you."

There was a pause, then she said, "Some people feel that's not enough. That it's risky for them, you being out there. And them thinking that makes it risky for *you*. Come home. Work with me. It'll keep you safe – keep us both safe – and we can stop things getting too out of hand."

"Like necromancers breaking into cafes out of hand?" I demanded.

"I didn't know she was going to do that. Look, there's going to be … some changes. Cal, if you're here, we can protect what needs protecting. We can control it. And we have to, because otherwise we're going to lose the north. We're going to lose *everything*."

Callum snorted, sending twin jets of smoke out of his nose. "You're working with necromancers, Ez. There's *nothing* can be controlled in that. You're way out of your depth."

"I wouldn't be if you were here." Her voice was abruptly sharp. "I wouldn't have even had to have anything to do with them if you'd been here to help. And you want to know how fun it is, what I'm doing to try and keep this place together? I'm in the bloody loo because it's the only place I can get a *second* of privacy, and she's probably got frogs listening in the drains or something. I have to fix this."

"If it's that bad, walk away from it. Let go of all the old stuff and walk away, and *then* we can talk about working together."

There was a long pause, then she said, "I can't."

"No," he said. "I didn't think so." And he hung up even as she said his name again, her voice sharp. He started the car and pulled back onto the road, the cigarette clamped between his lips and his mouth pulled tight at the corners.

"What—" I started, and he shook his head.

"She's just trying to get us to go in because they didn't get Emma at the cafe. Like you said, we're the flies in the pudding. Ointment." He looked at me. "You're catching."

"Delightfully so," I said, then added, "So no change?"

"No change," he agreed. There was a burnt orange scent of hurt on him, and I wondered if Ez smelled the same, if she carried that the same way she carried the matching shadows in her voice. Wondered how the arcade had become a haven, and when – and in what terrible way – it had been taken from them. I examined Callum for a moment, then started grooming the mud from between my toes.

There are times for asking questions, and times for cleaning your toes. And this was evidently the latter, since he was already pulling another cigarette out to light from the butt of the other. I was going to asphyxiate before the necromancers got me at this rate.

A QUICK PHONE call confirmed that Poppy and William had dealt with the hungry dragons, and that the unicorns hadn't stabbed anyone recently. They wanted to know what to do next, but Callum just told them to stay with the animals and look after them for now. When he hung up, I looked at him with my eyebrow whiskers arched and said, "D'you think they'll listen?"

"I don't know," he said, his voice quiet. "But we can't let them get in the middle of this. It's the least we can do, after all Gerry did."

I thought about that for a moment, then said, "Did. You think something terminal's happened."

Callum's mouth twisted, and he shook his head. "I don't know. But Ez got our number from somewhere, and I *had* been calling his phone. And I know that it'd break his heart if Poppy or William got hurt. So we keep them out of it if we can. They're ..." He trailed off, frowning.

"Good sorts," I said, and sighed. "Yeah. Let's keep hold of that sort of thing as long as we can."

Callum went back to his phone, and a moment later Emma answered, her voice bright over the speakerphone. I could hear Tristan shouting behind her, and Duds cackling, and some weird whistling noises that I couldn't quite place.

"Are you alright?" Callum asked her.

"I'm learning how to use a crossbow," she said, sounding both impressed and horrified.

"Right," Callum said. "That's ... good?"

She dropped her voice to a whisper. "I mean, they're all wonderful, but why do they have *so many weapons?*"

"What's so many?" Callum asked, frowning.

"A lot. And that's just what I've seen. I think they've got stashes all over the place."

"That doesn't surprise me," I said. "Just make sure they haven't planted any mines on the road in, will you?"

"I don't even know if you're joking," Emma said.

"Has Ethel said anything more?" Callum asked.

"Just that she'll look after the ghoulets, and that they're taking the necromancer situation *under advisement*," Emma said, and I could hear the scowl in her voice. "I mean, what good's that? I wish Gertrude was here. She'd sort them out. Her and Ms Jones. I mean, they sorted out the zombies, didn't they?"

"With help," I protested.

Callum didn't say anything, just ran his tongue over his teeth. He hadn't been much help then, either, since he'd had a bit of a case of undeadness of his own.

"Have you got Ms Jones yet?" Emma asked. "I mean, maybe she could talk to Grim Yorkshire."

"We're working on it," Callum said, not looking at me. "We'll see you soon."

"Don't forget to check on the mines," I said, before he hung up. With Emma gone the silence hung heavy in the car, and finally I said, "*Fine.* But let's get to the OAP headquarters, so if it all goes mushroom-shaped someone'll have a flamethrower or something."

Callum looked at me, and I knew he was thinking of that first, distant meeting, when I'd been just a kitten, of the things that had been reaching out of the Inbetween to drag me back in. Things with tentacles and teeth and things that hurt the eyes – although not as much as they hurt small cats.

"Sounds like a plan," he said.

15

A LOT, ALL AT ONCE

THE ROAD TO THE OAP ARMY'S STORAGE FACILITY BASE WAS deserted and darkened with rain, and Pru and Tam were waiting outside the gate for us when we arrived, Pru with her ears back against the damp. She must have been home, as she'd traded her pink puffer jacket in for a khaki utility coat with a surprising amount of pockets for a cat, and the water beaded on it like captured gems. Tam just dripped stolidly next to her. Callum opened his door and looked at them.

"Hi," he said, and Tam looked at him thoughtfully, then opened her mouth and disgorged a shiny, drool-covered padlock key onto the muddy drive. "Ah, thanks?"

"Dude. That has *got* to hurt," I said.

"Not a dude," Pru said. "But I'm with you otherwise."

Tam just looked at us with an expression of self-satisfaction, and Callum went to unlock the gates.

The drive was free of mines, which was nice, and before long we pulled up in front of the OAP army's headquarters. As Callum opened the door to the shed I could hear raised voices from inside the tent.

"I'm telling you, we need a water-based unit. One border

of that town's on a canal," Noel was saying, his voice as strident as I'd heard it.

"How many of us do you think there are?" Lulu snapped back. "Even given our new recruits, we can't surround the whole damn town!"

"You're discounting us cats, as usual," Tristan put in. "I can pull in some more reinforcements still, you know. Not everyone's happy with the Watch."

"And what d'you think you're going to do then?" Lulu asked. "Bite some necromancer toes?"

There was a sharp intake of breath from what sounded like both Duds and Tristan, and I looked at Callum. "You go on in. I'll be right with you."

"Sure you will," he said, but headed for the tent anyway, probably lured by the siren song of tea. He hadn't finished his one at the were house, after all.

I looked at Pru. "Want to hang about out here for a bit?"

She shrugged. "Why not. I can't listen to Tristan anymore. He's giving me a headache."

"Do cats get headaches?"

"Well, he's making my head hurt, so I guess we do."

"Seems reasonable." I padded around the outside of the shed, heading toward the river so that we'd be out of sight from anyone who came down the drive. Tam followed as well, and a moment later all three of us were standing in the tenuous shelter of the shed's overhanging roof, staring at the dimpled green surface of the river. The drizzle was strengthening steadily to something a bit more committed, and the world was drooping at the edges under the weight of the day. Although I supposed it was only about lunchtime, if that. Our day had started excessively early.

"Now what?" Pru asked. "Are we just taking in the sights?"

"Not as nice as the Avon," Tam said.

I blinked at her, and Pru shook a couple of rogue rain-drops off her bare ears.

"There's a duck, though," Tam added.

"That's nice," Pru said.

"You decide to talk, and these are your contributions?" I asked, and they both looked at me until I said, "Sorry."

"Should think so," Pru said.

"Two ducks," Tam said.

I resisted the urge to ask her if she'd been hitting the nip, licked my chops, and said, "When you shift, how long do you spend in the Inbetween?"

Pru and Tam looked at each other, then at me. "You don't," Pru said. "No one hangs about in there."

"No, but I mean as you pass through. How long does it take? Do you see the beasts?"

"No," Pru said, and her voice was soft. "You can't see anything in there, for a start. But the beasts don't have time to see *us*, Gobbelino. We could bounce off their snouts and they'd still be too slow to catch us. The Inbetween is a door-way, not a hall. You step through it to where you're going, not *into* it."

"But ..." I wanted to say I *remembered* the Inbetween, that vast and crushing emptiness, wanted to say I'd always known it, but maybe I hadn't. Maybe all I could recall was my death in there. "Right. That's not how I remember it, is all."

"We don't always remember things the way they were," Tam said. She'd gone back to watching the ducks. "Just the way they felt."

I licked my chops, then said, "I think I shifted. By acci-dent. I was thinking about Ms Jones, and then I was *there*. Properly there, not the whole out-of-body thing."

"You might have," Pru said. "If you weren't thinking about it, it might've just been instinctive. And you've got a really strong connection to her, so you wouldn't have needed her trail."

"I suppose," I said. "But I wasn't thinking of *shifting* to her. Shifting gets me killed."

No one spoke for a moment, then Pru said, "Seems like lots of things can get us killed at the moment. Maybe it was a desperate situation type thing."

"The situation's not *desperate*," I said, although, to be fair, I was probably arguing in degrees of desperation these days. "And I didn't have her scent or anything to follow. I was just *there*."

"No, but were you thinking that you really needed a sorcerer?"

"I seem to be in situations where I think that quite a lot, but I don't usually wind up on her kitchen bar."

Tam snorted and said, "Maybe she doesn't think of you quite as much as you think of her."

"That's it," Pru said. "You both thought of each other at the same time, and it overcame your resistance to shifting, because you weren't thinking of the shift, just of having a sorcerer handy."

"Her thinking of you would've got you through her lock charms, too," Tam added. "Opened a door in them."

I wrinkled my snout. "I'm not sure I'm a huge fan of randomly turning up in front of people. What if I end up on Sonia's kitchen bar?"

"She'd be delighted. Probably fancies some cat fur mittens," Tam said, and Pru gave her a disapproving look.

"Not helpful."

Tam shrugged.

I stood and shook myself off. However it had happened, it was no help if I couldn't recreate it. "Will you help me?" I asked them.

"You want to try properly?" Pru asked.

"I need to talk to Ms Jones, and if I can shift, if I can actually do it without getting stuck in the Inbetween, maybe I can remember why the Watch are out for me. Maybe if I can get past that, I can get past everything else."

"Lot to ask from a shift," Tam said, but she got up and pressed one shoulder to mine. She smelled of silent streets and darkened corners and secrets.

"You lead," Pru said, stepping up to my other side. "If you get stuck, we can pull you through."

It was how you shifted old cats who couldn't remember quite how things worked, how you shifted kittens who might get distracted mid-shift. How you shifted anyone who might falter in the Inbetween and linger, drawing the attention of the beasts. It was safe, it worked, cats did it all the time, but I still hesitated.

"What if the beasts really are waiting for me? I feel them sometimes, you know. Like they're just beyond the edges of the world, waiting for me to slip. Or looking for some little tear they can reach out and grab me through. They tried to follow me once before. In this life. When I was a kitten. There were tentacles and things. Callum saved me, even though we didn't know each other then. I was trying to get away from some other humans, and I had them on one side and the beasts on the other, so, you know, he had really good timing. Oh, and then there was the time I dropped Ms Jones' book in there. The book of power? I mean, I *meant* to stop in there, because I wanted a beast to take it, but then I couldn't get started again, and Claudia had to help, and if they *are* still waiting, and you go in with me—"

"Now *my* head hurts," Tam said, sitting down again.

"You shouldn't have been on your own as a kitten," Pru said. "And a book of power? It would've been like a beacon in there. The beasts would've swarmed it. Plus you said you meant to stop, so there we go."

"But what if they're right there? As soon as we go through?"

Tam looked at me and said, "You really think they're waiting just for you? They're vast. Eternal. One cat is nothing."

"Oh." I wasn't sure if I was reassured or not. "I mean, that's good, but tentacles, you know? Are you sure about this?"

Pru looked like she was sharing my long-time wish that cats could roll their eyes, and Tam just inspected one paw.

"Oh, hairballs," I muttered, and thought of the long polished kitchen bar, and Ms Jones with her dark carelessness of hair and eyes that changed like solar storms and her well-worn Docs, because even if she'd been in fluffy boots when I last saw her, that wasn't the sorcerer who lived in my head. I could almost smell the fragrantly raw, muscular scent of her, see the worn texture of her skinny jeans and feel the coolness of her fingers when she touched my back and whispered *remember*.

"For the Old Ones' *sakes!*"

I opened my eyes, which I hadn't even realised I'd closed, and found myself standing nose to nose with the sorcerer, who was sitting at the kitchen bar. We glared at each other from very close quarters, and she said, "You're standing in my lunch."

I looked down and found my front paws pressed firmly into what looked like a rather nice kipper. "I shifted," I said.

"Congratu-bloody-lations. How did you get through my locking charms?"

"Same way as last time?"

"I wasn't thinking of you," she started, then shook her head. "No, I was. Dammit. I'm going to have to be more careful about that." She cocked her head. "Who's with you?"

"Pru and Tam."

She made a puzzled noise.

"Bald cat from the zombie apocalypse. And Tam's ... Tam."

She swung off her stool with a sigh and went to the kitchen door, opening it to reveal a back garden that was neat and trellised but winter-dull, colours subdued in the grey morning. Pru and Tam were standing just beyond a small wooden gate that punctuated a low stone wall. "Come in," the sorcerer said, and there was shiver in the air that I felt rather than saw. Tam jumped the gate and led the way up the path, shoulders rolling under her heavy pelt, and Ms Jones nodded at her. Tam nodded back, and came to join me on the bar.

Pru stopped just short of the sorcerer and examined her with pale, narrowed eyes, her skinny tail twitching and curling under the khaki cloth of the utility jacket.

"Where's Claudia?" she asked.

Ms Jones inclined her head at the kitchen, and Pru watched her for a moment longer, then padded in and jumped up next to Tam and me. The sorcerer checked the garden, then closed the door again and locked it, turning to face us.

"We need help," I said.

"I need more time," Ms Jones said.

"What for?" I asked. "You seem fine." Whatever that grimace had been when she'd given me my last out-of-body experience, there was no sign of it now. She moved easily as she came back to the bar, with a smooth gait that wasn't unlike Tam's in its hint of threat.

"Not for me," she said.

"Where's Claudia?" Pru asked again. "You know, don't you?"

"She's here," Tam said. She was sniffing the air carefully,

and I lifted my own nose. Under the heavy, all-pervading scent of the sorcerer, there was the whiff of cat. *Cats.*

"She's the one that needs time," Ms Jones said.

"Well, not me, exactly," a new voice said, and we turned to see a slim calico cat standing in the doorway to the hall. Her tail was kinked, her flanks marred with twists of fresh scars and still-raw wounds, and one eye was sealed shut. "They're the problem." She tipped her head to the hall behind her, where a trail of kittens of various ages padded after her, all of them trying to look tough. A small black one sat down next to Claudia and looked at us severely, then was distracted by her own tail and fell over trying to catch it.

"*Claudia?*" I said, as Pru jumped off the bar and went to touch noses to the other cat. The kitten recovered in time to touch her nose to Pru's as well, then went back to her tail. "Are you alright? What happened?"

"A lot," Claudia said, looking at Ms Jones.

"And all at once," the sorcerer said.

"And you have kittens?" I asked.

"In a manner of speaking," Claudia said, watching the kitten tumble away. "Meet Anna, ousted Watch leader."

"Oh, sodden parsnips with seashells on," I said. "They killed the Watch leader?"

"Not just her," Claudia said, looking at the other kittens exploring the room with wobbly authority.

"Hairballs," I said.

Ms Jones nodded, taking a sip of coffee. "Yes," she said. "A couple more months would've been nice."

"How did ... I mean, they're *all* kittens," I said, watching them spreading across the room. There were at least fifteen of them, tabbies and gingers and everything else besides, and only about half of them were at the age where they'd be starting to remember their previous lives. That doesn't come back right away, even for those who do eventually remember properly. There's something about our mother's milk, perhaps, or simply the structure of kitten brain, that means the memories don't start returning until we're weaned, and we're full-grown before we remember everything. If we do.

I looked around for more grown cats, then at Claudia. "Are they ... they're not all yours?"

She gave me an amused look from her single eye – it was the green one, her blue one shut in a persistent wink, although I couldn't see any injuries around it – and shook Anna off, jumping up to join me and Tam on the bar. "No. I'm good, but I'm not good enough to birth the entire Old Guard."

"What happened?" Pru asked, following Claudia and inspecting the wounds on her flanks. Some of the older ones were distinctly sucker-shaped, and I had matching ones on my own shoulder. That had been a beast of the Inbetween.

Claudia yawned and hooked a piece of Ms Jones' kipper off her plate.

"Sure," the sorcerer said. "Go right ahead. Stand in my lunch. Steal it. I wasn't hungry anyway." She stepped over two brawling black and white kittens and took a bottle of whisky from a cupboard above the fridge, bringing it back to the bar with her. "And everyone thinks witches have cats as familiars. I've yet to meet *one* actual witch who puts up with cats."

"The Watch has been in flux for a while," Claudia said, ignoring her, and looked at me. "You remember anything yet?"

"I shifted," I offered.

She waited, then looked at Tam and Pru.

"Yeah, that's it," Pru said. "He's going to have to sit in on history lessons with the kittens."

"Not these ones. The older ones are all trying to remember already. Never mind a couple of months – a few more weeks and we'd have been fine." Claudia clawed up another piece of fish. "Right, so. The Watch has always had factions. Those who think the world is best as it is – Folk and humans completely separate, with the Watch enforcing the divide. The Old Guard, basically. Then there's those who think that yes, it's essentially fine, because humans aren't good with things they don't understand, but there has to be nuance. No hard-lining, and above all we still keep to the original spirit of the Watch, which is that all kinds are equal and deserve safety." She thought about it. "That's less a faction than just the average cat's view, I think, though. Anna, myself, a few others – we were pushing to get the Old Guard to fully accept that with more humans, there's going to be more overlap with Folk. We have to adapt, to allow more mixing and blurring of the boundaries of the worlds."

"And this lot?" I asked, looking at a small ginger and white cat who was giving me a hard stare from eyes that were still a murky, undecided blue.

"A mix. Some felt we were right, others felt that if the old ways had worked for centuries, why change."

Ms Jones leaned on the bar, looking at us all. There were a couple of stools pulled up to it, but she hadn't bothered to sit down again. "And then there's the new hardline."

"Yes." Claudia licked her chops. "They feel that humans are a problem. Breeding too wildly, careless about every-thing, just charging on like they're the only ones who matter. Tearing the world apart and remaking it in their own image, with never a thought for those they think are lesser, or even the survival of their own species, really."

"Some have always thought that," I said. "It's not entirely

wrong, either."

"Sure. But it just used to be a thing cats or Folk would talk about, about how in the good old times it wouldn't have been allowed, that humans would have been reined in. Reminiscing about a world that never really existed. About how wonderful it was when humans weren't so prevalent and Folk were more so, when cats were gods and magic was law, etc., etc."

"And no one ever had enough food, a torn claw could kill you, and most cats whipped through their nine lives in the time it takes us to live one these days," Tam observed. "Wasn't blood sacrifice a big thing, too?"

"No one ever remembers those bits," Ms Jones said, taking a sip of whisky and picking up a small tabby kitten. She cradled him in one hand, tickling his paws with one long finger while he tried to grab her. "Only the *we were gods!* bits." She looked up at us. "I mean *we* in the general term, not just cats. Sorcerers were gods too, and there's enough magic-workers think a return to old times is just what's needed."

"And everyone kind of knows that you can't go back," Claudia said. "But there's a certain faction who think things can be the same as then, but also the same as now. Pick and choose the old bits they want, get rid of the new bits they don't."

"Wait," I said. "'*Get rid of the new bits*'? As in, humans? I mean, I know we can deal with the odd troublesome human, I've—" I stopped. "I've done that?"

Claudia huffed soft cat laughter. "You have, Gobs."

"Really? I mean ... it was an accident, right?"

"Twelve cats to shift them, and drop them in the Inbetween. It takes a bit of organising."

I stared at her. "I did that to someone?"

"They deserved it," Claudia said.

"Did they?" I had a nasty taste at the back of my mouth,

like a hairball was trying to come up.

"Yes. And as to your question – no, of course cats can't wipe out humans."

"But necromancers can," Ms Jones said. "Especially if they raise the Old Ones. The original necromancers, who have never forgotten that they would have ruled all, if the cats and Folk hadn't stood together to resist them."

"We don't do being ruled," Tam said.

"But the Watch are ignoring that bit and working with these new necromancers?" Pru asked.

"They were doing it on the quiet," Claudia said. "Then while I was distracted tracking down Polly—"

"Who?" Tam said, and Claudia nodded at Ms Jones. "Really?"

I shared her opinion that Polly was a really unsuitable name for an ancient magical being who had basically been a god once, but Ms Jones just shrugged and picked up the story.

"After I hefted that bloody young magician back your way—"

"Yeah, thanks for that," I said. "He's a *gem.*"

"Did he sort out your necromancer problem?"

"Well." I looked at Pru and Tam. "Sort of. Temporarily, like."

"Good enough," Ms Jones said, raising her eyebrows at me and taking another sip of whisky.

"Maybe him, maybe Callum," Tam said.

"Callum?" Ms Jones examined me, and I shrugged.

"Maybe. Joint effort sort of thing."

"Interesting." She tapped her fingers on the worktop, then continued. "So I booted him back toward you – his dad was summoning him anyway, so all I had to do was break his hold on where he was – and then Claudia and I went to poke around and see how deep this necromancer thing went. How serious it was, because people are always running around swearing they're going to bring back some god or other and rule the world and blah blah blah. Turned out it was pretty serious, because we got nabbed."

"*You* got nabbed?" I demanded.

She shrugged. "It happens. I was still weak from confronting the older magician. He drained off a fair bit of my power." Her lip curled at the memory. "I needed to recharge before I could get us out, and I didn't have time to properly recover even then."

"They were sacrificing Anna and eight others," Claudia said. "Me included. Ms Jones was meant to be the vessel for the Old One."

"So we were, what, a trial run?" Pru asked.

"I think so," Ms Jones said. "So they're zero from two, which you'd think would cause at least a small rethink in the approach, but these are necromancers."

"Oh, they're rethinking," I said. "They've got a shiny new plan. With scythes."

"Scythes?" Claudia asked. "As in *reaper* scythes?"

"We think they've got three already," I said. "And we're trying to warn the reapers, but they don't seem to have much sense of urgency."

"That's what spending eternity playing with souls does," Ms Jones said. "Not much rush there." Claudia looked at her, and she waved her glass. "*Yes. I know.* Scythes are a bad development."

"Exceptionally so," Claudia said, then looked at me. "Anyway, we got out, but things got messy. The new hardline in the Watch were helping. When things started to go south – when Ms Jones threw the Old One back – they shifted the cages into the Inbetween and dropped them, I suppose so they'd be rid of us for now. A lot of the Old Guard had already been outright killed."

"The only one I managed to snag was Claudia," Ms Jones said. "I didn't know the rest well enough to be able to find them. I can't go into the Inbetween, but I can push things in and pull them out, if I can feel them."

"And the kittens?" I asked.

"We tracked down most of the Old Guard before the Watch could. They won't tolerate them living. It's too much of a threat to what they're doing. They can't take all their lives at once unless they've got someone handy with some unicorn horn about, so they'll just keep killing them over and over again, preferably as kittens, so they never have a chance to become a threat."

I shivered, and curled my tail over my toes. "I know someone who's back messing with unicorn horn."

"Hardly surprising at this point," Ms Jones said. "I think we left the usual state of play about three turns back." She topped her glass up.

"And you …?" I nodded at Claudia, at her scars and fresh wounds.

"Should've seen the beast," she said, her voice light, and glanced at Ms Jones. "Even my eye's healing."

Ms Jones made a dubious noise. "I'm not a healer. I just gave the cells a little tickle. It might work again, or it might just stay sealed over, or you might end up with some extra teeth in there or something."

"*Ew*," Pru and I said, and Claudia huffed laughter. Tam just sat up straighter, suddenly interested.

"Alright," I said, as Ms Jones drained her glass and gave the whisky bottle a suspicious look, as if she suspected it of short-changing her. Sorcerer metabolisms are distinctly different to human ones. "So the Watch really has fallen."

"So dramatic," Claudia said.

Which, fair, but I wasn't sure there was any way to be *un*dramatic about it.

16

RED RIDING HOOD & THE WOLVES

"The Watch has fallen off a cliff?" Ms Jones suggested, giving up on the whisky and getting some chocolate in a fancy box out of the fridge instead. "Fallen over? Stubbed their toes?"

Pru and Tam snickered, and I growled. "You know what I mean. It's blown straight past compromised and into *let's get a bit genocidal and bring on the end times.*"

"That's a pretty good summary of things," Claudia said.

"They're also working with the necromancers."

"Correct."

"And the only senior Watch cats who might've been able to influence anyone are currently more interested in pompoms and long naps."

"Also correct."

I thought about it, then said, "They're going to do it now."

"Do what?" Claudia asked.

"The whole thing. The *full* thing. Bring the Old Ones back and wipe out all the humans and Folk they don't want to use as free labour and pets. Bloody Ez has given them Dimly, which is basically a magical power pack, they've got the scythes, Ms Jones is out of the picture, and the Watch is either kitten-sized or working with them. It's the perfect time. We *have* to stop them, and you have to help."

"This is why I need Malcolm," Ms Jones said.

"*Why?* He's a bloody *dentist!*"

"Because I do, Gobbelino."

"The weres have him. They won't so much as let us see him until they hear from you. So you have to go to them. Or call them, if not."

She made a *hmm* sound, then said, "Do you have a number?"

I looked down at myself. "It must be in my other pockets. You're a *sorcerer.*"

"I can't magic someone's phone number."

"Some sorcerer," I muttered. "Callum has a phone number, okay? Just come back. Gerry's missing. Ifan's up to gods know what. Gertrude's being re-educated. There's a bunch of oldies about to launch a military assault on Dimly, and we can't seem to stop them. *We need help.*"

Ms Jones tipped her head to one side and said, "You're very invested for a cat who was so determined to stay out of trouble when we first met."

"I did try. Didn't work."

"Never has," Claudia said. "Not in any of your lives."

I looked at her properly. "Why did the Watch kill me? And why didn't anyone help? Was it because of the … the human thing?" I still couldn't quite imagine myself doing it, subjecting someone to the pure horror of the beasts. But the knowledge of it was there, even if the memory wasn't. It ached like a broken fang.

"No, Gobbelino. The Watch has never had a problem with that. They killed you because you stood in their way. Because the Watch wanted Dimly, and to take it they needed to wipe out a whole family."

I stared at her. "The Norths."

"The Norths. And they weren't good people, but you didn't think dropping them in the Inbetween was right."

"I did it to someone before, though."

Claudia regarded me with her one pale eye for a moment, then said, "You did. But what that human did to cats, and what they did to other humans .... No one could prove anything. They were insulated by power and privilege, and even the humans that suspected something couldn't touch them. You could, though, and you were right to. As bad as the Norths were, they were never that bad."

I considered that, not sure if it made me feel better or not. I couldn't decide, so finally I said, "Why were the Watch out for the Norths, then? Was it for the unicorn horn? It was, wasn't it? They wanted to ... what, control it?"

"The Watch are meant to be neutral, but something changed," Claudia said. "The new hardline, the necromancers, whatever came first – they wanted Dimly and the horn trade, and they didn't want any of the older, more established Norths around to cause any trouble."

"Which is unfortunate," Ms Jones said. "They've not really been guardians for generations, in the sense of having power, but the Norths had loyalty in plenty of places. The Watch broke all that. "

"And Ez and Callum?" I asked.

"Callum was long gone. And having Ez as a figurehead meant they could keep up the pretence that Dimly and the north were still independent, while really the Watch had their paws all over them. Which everyone knows, but no one's going to challenge it. Not after what happened to the family."

I thought of Ez back in Dimly, saying to me, *I felt it.* Felt the Inbetween, when the Watch threatened to fling her after the rest of her family. I couldn't really blame her for cooperating. I might have too, given the choice. "Is that why I went and found Callum when I was a kitten?" I asked.

"Maybe," Claudia said. "Who knows what kittens are thinking." As if hearing her, the two black and white kittens went charging across the floor, shoulder to shoulder. They were mirror images of each other, and as they ran their movements matched perfectly, furry, fluid reflections. They shot under a sofa and vanished.

"And no one helped me," I said, trying not to sound accusing. I don't think it worked that well. I *felt* accusing.

"We didn't know. You followed your own path, and you never came back."

"And my other lives? I feel like the Watch was always killing me, but is that a real memory?"

"Eh. Portions of the Watch were," Claudia said. "I told you, there's always been factions. And you have always, *always* been good at getting in the way of things."

"Nothing changes there," Ms Jones said, and popped a chocolate in her mouth. "This Callum thing interests me, though."

"Me too," I said.

She shook her head. "No, not your bestie thing. The bit where he helped throw the Old One back."

"It's something to do with being a North," I said. "He's not a magic-worker."

"Of course it's to do with being a North. But those two things aren't mutually exclusive. And you didn't even think he had magic at all at a point."

"He hides it really well."

"He does," she agreed. "I could tell there was power around you, but I thought maybe you were playing with necromancers yourself initially. Then I thought it was the magician association. Now it seems it might be your scruffy friend."

"You can ask him when you come back to help us."

"I will," she said, and looked at Claudia.

"They're too young," Claudia said.

"So we leave them."

"We can't *leave* them. Kittens are so bloody slippery, even the shift locks won't hold them. They need watching so no one falls into the Inbetween, or pushes someone else in, or inadvertently summons the whole bloody Watch and gives us away. Otherwise why d'you think I've been stuck in this bloody place for weeks?"

Ms Jones waved at her own face, indicating her eye, and Claudia growled.

"If you think losing an eye can stop me—"

"Right," I said. "Well, while you two are arguing about babysitting, I'm going back to tell Callum we've got the bloody apocalypse coming to town. Just as a heads up, you know."

"We'll come," Pru said. "Before anyone mentions cat-sitting."

Tam got up with a yawn and jumped to the floor, scattering a couple of kittens who were playing with a pen. I looked from Ms Jones to Claudia. "I'm glad you're alright and all that," I said. "But can we just get this sorted now? I've had enough of feeling like someone's about to skin me at every corner."

"You always had that effect on people," Claudia said, and Ms Jones snorted.

"Get me the phone number for the were," she said. "We'll sort the kitten situation out and follow, but you know how to find me now."

"Follow the scent of kippers and whisky," I said.

"Close enough. Go." She waved her hand at the door. It popped open on the increasingly heavy rain, and Tam batted casually at a kitten who tried to run out. The kitten rolled twice and came up hissing. "Stay in one piece until I get there."

I jumped from the bar, giving her a final, suspicious look. Not that there was much I could do. Either she was coming or she wasn't, and if she wasn't we were just going to have to handle things on our own. Again.

One of the kittens we passed on the way to the door was playing with a hair tie, and I snatched it off her as unobtrusively as I could. She hissed, and glared at me in a manner that made me suspect I'd be answering to her when she grew up a bit, but for now I was bigger and older, so I just twitched my ears at her in a half apology and kept going.

We left the warmth of the kitchen and ran for the gate, the charms parting for us with a hiss like water sparkling on a hotplate. Over the gate we found ourselves on a skinny country lane, empty in both directions and heavy with the smell of the sea and damp sand. The cottage was the only building in sight, the windows full of mellow light, and even crowded with rain the sky felt high and broad and empty. I dropped the hair tie, breathed in deeply and looked at the other two.

"Was that progress?"

"Some," Pru said. "You know you've always been annoying, at least."

"Harsh."

"Boring would be worse," Tam said, and I nodded at her.

"Yes! Thank you."

"Less likely to get you killed, though," Pru pointed out, and yawned. "Are we going? I should probably put in an appearance at home again, but we best not drop you in the Inbetween, seeing as you're like the last of the Old Guard or something."

"I don't do all that regimented stuff," I said. "You can call me sir if you want, though."

Tam huffed laughter so hard that she choked a little, then nudged me.

"What?"

"Thief," she said, and I looked at the hair tie.

"I mean, yes, but that kitten had already stolen it."

"Bully," the big she-cat said, and I was almost sure she was joking. Almost.

"Desperate times and all that. It smells like Ms Jones. Maybe that'll be enough for the weres, because I'd rather get hold of the dentist ourselves. Seems a good plan to have something the sorcerer wants that much."

"Definitely not a *bad* plan," Pru admitted. "Shall we go?"

"Onward," I said, and reached out for Callum, feeling the sense of him like an echo across the void of the Inbetween. I never even saw it as we passed through, though. Never felt the beasts. Pru had been right.

But I had no time to triumph in my newly rediscovered abilities, because we emerged into a war zone.

THE SHED that housed the OAP headquarters was burning. Actually, several sheds were burning, with the distinctive whiff of the sort of magic that meant the rain had no chance of damping things down, raising a clamour of cracking glass and falling wood above the hungry roar of the flames. Wolves and humans were running in various directions, seemingly at random, the humans shouting and the wolves silent but for the odd snarl. The entire front of the OAP army's shed had been curled back like the top of a sardine tin, and the tent inside was burning as well. The OAPs themselves were nowhere to be seen, but the bark of a gun followed by the glaring arc of a flare suggested at least one of them was taking shelter behind the van. The van already had some scorch marks on the side, which someone was going to have fun explaining to the retirement home.

"I always miss the good stuff," Tam said, and Pru and I dived for cover behind a wheel-less, rusting car skeleton that smelled like someone had been keeping chickens in it. The big she-cat ambled after us, apparently unconcerned about being spotted.

A hooded figure in a heavy coat emerged from the cover of a row of sheds and walked toward the burning OAP head-quarters. Another shot went off, and the figure flung an arm out dramatically, giving the impression that they felt they should be wearing robes rather than a coat. The flare swerved off-course, slammed into a caravan and showered embers everywhere.

"Give it up," the figure shouted. I strained to see through the shifting light, examining the scattered humans – or human-shaped forms, anyway. Most of them had hats or hoods pulled over their heads, and one was wearing a full-on balaclava. They didn't seem bothered by the wolves, so they were either weres themselves or working with them.

"Recognise anyone?" I whispered to Pru and Tam around the hair tie still gripped in my teeth.

They shrugged in almost perfect unison, eyes on the milling forms. Both wolves and humans seemed to be hunting for someone, but every time anyone approached the burning OAP army shed they were subjected to a barrage of cans, well-aimed potatoes, and even some arrows that weren't quite as well aimed. The flares were being let off at rather more circumspect intervals, so presumably there wasn't an endless supply of those. There seemed to be plenty of potatoes, though.

I set down the hair tie and put a paw in the middle of it, then gripped it in my teeth and pulled it up my leg. A little fiddle, and I got a twist into it, then my paw back through it again. I shook my leg experimentally. It wasn't too tight, but it felt like it *should* stay put.

I slipped out of the shelter of the ancient car, keeping my belly low to the ground and sticking to the long grass, and eased over to an undamaged caravan with weeds growing through its wheel arches. A quick scramble over the gas bottle locker at the rear (my tail twitching with the potential for a badly placed flare or fireball to create a *boom* situation) took me to the roof, where I could hunker down and keep on eye on things without worrying about a wolf sneaking up behind us. Tam and Pru joined me as the dramatic figure called, "Lay down your weapons. We're not interested in you humans."

The voice was familiar, but for a moment I couldn't place it, amid the snarls of wolves and the yelp of a magic-worker whose spell had backfired and scorched their hand.

"We might be interested in you," Rita shouted back. "Crimes against humanity and all that."

"And cats!" Duds shouted.

"Crimes against humanity and cats," Rita amended. "We might just have to do a citizen's arrest."

"Don't be ridiculous," the figure said, and pushed their hood back.

"Oh, you rotting, hairy cucumber," I said. *Kara.* Of course it was bloody Kara, and I put good odds on Lani being out there on four paws. I wasn't sure why Ez's bestie – or ex-bestie, if we believed Ez, which I wasn't inclined to do – was talking about *you humans*, though, as she was as human as anyone Folk-adjacent can be. Although she'd definitely sent that flare off-course, which was an interesting development. Interesting in a bad way.

"Have you seen how outnumbered you are?" she asked, her voice light. She wiped her nose, a quick nervy movement. "I have wolves and magic-workers. You have a couple of cats and a wheelchair. *And* you're all going to need a nanny nap before long."

"So why d'you need all that backup?" Lulu called. "Seems like overkill to me. Why don't you send your pets away, since we're so harmless?"

"Because I don't want you hurting yourselves thinking you can fight me. Understand you're outnumbered. Sit down, drink your tea, and let us take what we've come for." She did the nose wipe again.

"What've you come for?" Rita called back. The wolves and magic-workers were circling back to Kara, grouping behind her. I wasn't entirely sure her confidence in her magic-workers was that well-placed. The one with the balaclava had their hands on their knees, puffing hard, and another held their burned hand out in front of them, blowing on it like it was a too-hot toastie. Two others were lying on the ground in camouflage gear that they'd stuck some twigs to, pretending to be bushes. They'd have done better if they hadn't apparently used the remains of an old Christmas tree. A fake one, with tinsel branches. Green tinsel, admittedly, but still.

But the wolves were enough to worry about, even if the magic-workers were substandard. I couldn't pick one were scent from another, but there were half a dozen of them, including a lean sleek beast that could easily have been Lani.

"Send out the North," Kara said, her voice tight and sharp.

"What, you need a compass?" Rita asked, and Lulu cackled.

"Callum, then. Whatever he's calling himself. The tall one."

"Me?" Noel asked, peering around the back of the van. "I'm the tallest."

"*No.* Don't be foolish. We know he's here. Him and his cat."

"There's a few cats." Noel looked down as Tristan marched out from behind him, ginger chest puffed out and tail high.

He stood with his four paws planted firmly and bellowed, "Sergeant Tristan Mallow! OAP army! I do *not* surrender!"

Kara made an irritable noise and waved her hand. Tristan went flying, rolling twice in mid-air before crashing into the burning frame of the shed. He threw himself out again with a yowl, and Duds shouted, "Tristan!"

"Send them out," Kara said. "I'm losing patience."

"Get the OAPs moving," I said to Tam and Pru. "*Hurry.*" Then I walked to the edge of the caravan roof and shouted, "Oi, cabbage face! Looking for me?"

Tam and Pru slipped silently away as Kara turned to face me. Her eyes were too bright, and she wiped her nose again. My belly tightened in sudden, painful recognition. Callum had kept to the human range of illicit substances in the days before he'd become heavily invested in tea and biscuits, but I knew those eyes. I even knew that sniff, and it wasn't allergies. Given Kara's suddenly acquired magical skills, though, I doubted she'd been sniffing anything human-centric. But unicorn dust, as previously noted, has a whole range of weird side effects before it turns you inside out.

"Not looking for you so much as Callum," she said. "But you'll do." She started to raise a hand and I shot off the roof, landing hard on the half-frozen ground and sprinting into the thicket of sheds and caravans. I wasn't going to test how effective her unicorn dust magic was. "Oh, for the gods' sakes," she shouted, as I swerved around a man in a camouflage headband. "*Get him!*"

"The cat?" I heard someone ask over the scuffle of paws as the wolves launched themselves after me.

"*Yes, the cat!*"

The pound of boots joined the paws, and I wound my

way wildly between old, flattened wheels and narrow, nettle-filled ditches that served as both drains and separation of the plots. Something hit a shed wall above me hard enough to dent the metal, leaving a scorch mark and the whiff of basic magic behind it. Some of them did have a bit of skill, then. Enough to squish a slow-moving feline, anyway. But I had no intentions of being slow, and I was more worried about the wolves and their noses. I shot to the roof of another caravan, sprinted across it and leaped to the next, narrowly avoiding falling into the interior as the rotten metal crumbled beneath my paws.

A wolf howled below me, and the fur on my tail went to full attention as the little, primal voice in the back of my mind screamed wordlessly. I kept running, eyes on the roof ahead of me, and soared across the gap between the caravans as teeth propelled by a huge, hairy form exploded out of it. I somehow bounced straight off its snout, snagged the roof of the next caravan with my claws, and hauled myself on before the were could grab me. I skidded to the centre of the rickety expanse, heart pounding so hard it seemed my whole body was reverberating with it, and braced myself as the caravan shook under the assault of wolfish bodies.

"Hairballs," I whispered, wishing this hadn't worked quite so well, then the caravan door slammed open.

"What the *hell* is going on?" someone bellowed, only it was put a little more strongly than that.

A wolf growled, and there was the sound of a solid impact, and a yelp. I sidled to the edge of the roof and peered down to see a squat, bald-headed man in a filthy singlet rolling a cast iron frying pan by the handle in one hand. "Anyone else want one?" he asked, and the wolves looked at each other as the first of the magic-workers came jogging around the corner of the nearest shed. Singlet turned to face them, then shouted, "Is that *fire?*"

"Um, no?" Balaclava said, glancing behind them at a merrily burning shed.

"Well, it's not the bloody aurora borealis, is it?" Singlet demanded. He charged forward, slamming the nearest wolf aside with his frying pan almost casually. "Fire!" he roared as he ran. "*Fire!*"

I was already sprinting back the way I'd come, keeping to the roofs of the caravans and the tops of the odd container, and I was too busy watching for gaps, holes in roofs, and sneaky wolves to see who he was shouting his warning to. A wolf howled behind me, and the pack bolted in pursuit, but I had a head start. And, as it turned out, Singlet wasn't the only one who'd been disturbed by the fight in the yard.

I leaped to a final container, slid across its grime-slicked topside with my claws out, and came to a teetering stop at the far edge. I found myself looking back at the OAPs' shed, which was still burning merrily. The van had been flung into it and had its nose stuck in the remnants of the tent, and Noel and Lulu were standing beside Rita in her wheelchair. Duds leaned on his stick next to them clutching his water cannon in one hand, and Emma had a cricket bat on her shoulder, looking like she couldn't wait to hit *someone*. Kara stood facing them, her arms loose at her sides and her face painted in raw colours by the fire, while Rita kept the flare gun levelled at her. Noel was hanging onto a crossbow (that explained the wild aim. I didn't imagine it was easy to steady it with only one arm), and Lulu was bouncing a potato in her right hand, an oversized slingshot gripped in the other. But Callum stood in front of all of them with his hands extended, palms forward in a *stop* gesture. Or possibly an *I'm unarmed please don't eat me* gesture. Neither seemed likely to work.

"Let them go," he said.

"I *probably* will," Kara said. "They're not much use to me. But they really are a pain, so then again ..." She shrugged.

"Kara," Callum started, and was interrupted by a shout from deeper in the park.

"*Oi!* Who's having bloody Guy Fawkes down here? People got businesses to run, you know?" An alarmingly thin woman strode into the light, all hard angles, with a gas mask swinging from one hand and her hair tied severely back. Two skinny teenage-looking lads trailed after her. Skinny but well-armed, and not with flare guns or potatoes.

"None of your business," Kara said.

"Damn well is," Singlet roared, appearing with the magic-workers trailing after him. Two of them were using their sleeves to wipe blood from their faces, and another was limping, being helped along by their buddy. Apparently Singlet's frying pan wasn't limited to wolf-related usage, and going by the scorch marks on it, it was also good at fending off spells. I had a sneaking suspicion it wasn't a *usual* sort of frying pan. My paws were still tingly from his roof. "This is *our* park! Get that bloody fire out before it spreads!"

"They set it," Rita shouted, waving at Kara and the magic-workers. "Picking on us old folk!"

"That is so not cool," one of the teenagers said.

"I'm not interested in them," Kara started, and more shouting interrupted her, accompanied by some heartfelt yelps.

"Who's got wild bloody dogs loose in here?" A tall man in a boiler suit marched through the containers, a heavy pipe clenched in one hand. "We do *not* do dog fighting. Or *any* animal fighting. That's in the contract!"

"They're *wolves!*" Kara shouted, as the beasts in question loped to join her, their eyes on Callum.

"Even bloody worse. Who d'you think you are, Red Riding Hood?"

"That doesn't even make sense!"

"There's gas in there!" Rita shouted, pointing at the shed.

"It could go up at any moment! Someone help! Make her go away! She's scaring us!" She put a surprisingly convincing wobble in her voice, that was only slightly undermined by the fact that her flare gun never wavered at all.

"*Save the elders!*" Singlet roared, and charged. The other residents of the storage park gave a roar of approval, and launched themselves forward, and the OAP army cheered and broke into something that was almost a charge of their own.

Kara raised her arms and shouted, "What the hell is *wrong* with you all?"

I mean, unicorn dust aside, it was a fair question, really.

17

EVERYONE NEEDS A LOGARITHM

THE WOLVES SURGED TOWARD CALLUM AS THE NEW ARRIVALS ran to protect the OAP army. The magic-workers, apparently hoping they'd be easier prey than Singlet had been, rushed to meet them. Callum spun toward Emma, hands still out, and she threw the bat to him then grabbed a slingshot from the top of a big pack that was lying at her feet. She loaded it with a potato and let fly at the nearest wolf, scoring a direct hit on its snout that made it huff and stumble.

Callum whirled back and met the next wolf with a swing of the bat, and I came flying off the shed to sprint across the path of another. It just about turned a somersault as it tried to stop and turn to catch me all in one movement, and I was half aware that Tam, Pru, and Tristan were flashing about the place like little furry missiles, emerging from nothing to bury teeth and claws in the wolves, then diving back into the Inbetween before the beasts could retaliate. I'd have liked to do the same, but I didn't trust my control enough for that yet.

The storage park's residents weren't bothering to ask any questions. As far as they were concerned, their entire compound was under attack, and they were *not* having it.

They went straight for the magic-workers, swinging tyre irons and two-by-fours and the sort of fists that have seen a lot of practice. Kara's gang of magic-workers had apparently not prepared for that variety of resistance, and they rapidly resorted to flinging rocks and reclaimed potatoes to fend them off, punctuated by the occasional belch of a badly formed spell.

I pelted out of the surging mass in time to see Noel set a boot into a wolf's face, then hand Callum a set of keys.

"Go," he said.

"But—"

"We're going to be absolutely fine," he said, and grinned at Rita. She swung the flare gun toward the shed and gave Callum a matching grin.

"There's going to be a *boom*. Take advantage of it."

"*Save the elders!*" Singlet roared again, and appeared out of the melee with one of the teenagers in tow. He tried to grab Lulu and she jabbed his hand with a knife. "*Hey.*"

"Lulu," Rita said. "Don't stab the nice man."

"Sorry," she said. "Grabby men make me stabby."

"*Go,*" Noel said again, gesturing at Emma.

Callum nodded, grabbed Emma's arm and said, "Come on."

"No," she started, and Lulu slapped her shoulder and shouted, "*Move out*, girl!" She'd given her slingshot to Duds and had a knife in each hand, and rather than waiting for Emma to answer she spun back to the fight and threw one then the other, raising yelps of pain from a wolf and a magic-worker. Two more knives appeared in her hands, and I didn't want to know where she was hiding them.

"Got it," Emma said, grabbing the bag, and followed Callum as he sprinted toward the shed.

"We can't hide in there," I shouted, racing after them. "It's on *fire.*"

"No—" He raised his bat as a camouflaged magic-worker popped up in front of us, his hands raised like he thought he was going to shoot sparks from them, but a stocky young woman in baggy jeans and safety goggles flung a syringe at him like a dart, and he pitched to the ground with a very small squeak. She gave Callum a suspicious look then turned away, and Callum skidded to a stop next to the little boat, already positioned on the ramp next to the shed. Evidently the OAP army had anticipated a getaway was going to be needed.

"Oh, not bloody boats again," I said, as he fumbled with the trailer then managed to find the brake.

"Seconded," Emma said, but she grabbed the front of the trailer with Callum, and they both heaved, inching it back toward the slipway.

"Get in," Callum said to me.

"This life sucks," I announced, but I jumped in as Pru and Tam appeared at a sprint, followed by two wolves and Kara. "Heads up!"

Callum and Emma heaved again, and the trailer shot abruptly backward into the water. Emma yelped and ran with it, splashing into the shallows, and Callum almost face-planted onto the slip.

"*Callum!*" Kara shouted as she ran to intercept us. "You're only making things worse!"

Pru leaped from the bank as the boat bobbed free, bounced off Callum's shoulder, and landed on the bow next to me. Tam followed, making Callum stagger, and he yelled, "*You're welcome,*" at both of them as he scrambled to haul himself aboard. Emma had already rolled in over the low sides, and now she grabbed her slingshot and let a potato fly at Kara's head. It missed, but the thought was there.

Water caught the boat, and we slid free of the trailer, the light current tugging us.

"Last chance," Kara called, pressing her hands together as if she were begging us. "You and dead-lover there come with me, and everything gets *much* easier."

Callum ignored her, fiddling with the keys and trying to figure out the gears.

"Who let you off your leash?" I yelled at her. "Bloody dust-sotted attack cabbage."

Kara scowled at me, wiping her nose in a quick, instinctive reaction, and I saw Callum's face twist into something that was half recognition, half pity. "It just lets me tap into my own power. I'm not an *addict*."

"And I've just got an affection for black fur. I'm not a *cat*," I snapped back.

She pressed her hands together a little harder, and I could almost feel the warmth of them from here. "I don't care what some cat thinks. And he's going to be so pleased with me when I drag your sorry tails back—" I lost the rest of what she was saying as the engine roared into life. The prop was still lifted out of the water though, and we just bobbed in place while Callum poked desperately around, looking for the engine tilt button. Kara stopped talking and closed her eyes, apparently doing a little more power tapping, and the air gave a crackle that was almost physical, filling my ears with ringing pressure.

"Oh, spammy biscuits," I said. "That's actually working."

Callum found the button, and as the prop sank into the water, the engine's scream turned into a hungry burble. He jammed the gear lever into reverse and we lurched back, then came to a screeching halt with the stern fishtailing. We were still attached at the bow. He put the boat back into neutral, swearing, and scrambled forward to free us. Emma tried for another potato, but she couldn't seem to get it into the slingshot. I could hear her ragged breath, edged with panic, as the magic built around us, pulling my hair to attention.

Kara grinned as she opened her eyes and her hands, power pooling in her palms like softly luminescent syrup. She raised them toward us. "I gave you the option to just come quietly," she said. "No one can say I didn't."

And at that moment the shed exploded.

The noise shattered against my ears, stealing the pressure of the magic and replacing it with something brutal and physical, and debris shot across the river, tearing watery gouges in the surface. Metal screeched and tore, wood splintered and windows exploded, and Kara went face-first into the ramp as if someone very large had shoved her from behind. A wolf howled, and someone screamed, and a babble of shouting rose above the hungry crumple of the fire.

Noel appeared at a shambling run, still toting his crossbow, and stepped over Kara into the water. He leaned forward, did something at the bow, then pushed us off.

"Get moving," he said.

"But," Callum started, and Noel interrupted him with a quick gesture.

"That's an order and you'll bloody well take it. *Now.*" He turned his attention to Kara, who was starting to sit up, and pushed her back to the ramp. "*Stay.*"

She said something about his parentage, but the crossbow was pointed straight at her head, and even with one arm I doubted he'd miss from that range.

"Do it, dude," I said to Callum. "I see zero chance they need our help."

"But there's wolves. And Kara—" He stopped with a yelp as Tam jumped up next to him, throwing the weight of her body against the controls. The engine slammed into reverse again, and this time we went spinning wildly into the river,

Pru and Emma and I all tumbling to the floor and Callum barely saving himself from going overboard.

"Alright, alright! Bloody hell. Cats need to stop driving." He managed to get control of the boat while Tam looked around with a satisfied air, and a moment later we were purring off downstream through the darkness, the glow of the fire fading behind us.

Emma sat up in the bottom of the boat, looked around, and said, "I've spilled my potatoes."

"What happened to the crossbow?" I asked her.

"Apparently my aim was questionable."

"Bold claim from what I saw of the shooting earlier," I said, inspecting the boat. "Now what?"

"We can't get lost, at least," Pru said, putting her paws on one of the narrow seats. There was one on each side of the boat, and forward of the helm was a tiny cabin with another seat set into the very bow. It looked too low-ceilinged and small for anyone other than a cat. "Canals are quite useful for that."

"Locks, though," I said. "There'll be locks."

We both looked at Callum, but he'd taken his phone from his pocket and was frowning at it.

"What now?" I asked, and he looked at me. "Wait, no, I don't want to know. Not unless it's the offer of a nice house in the country. Or at least a comfy, dry bed for the night, where no one's trying to eat us or blow us up."

Without speaking, Callum turned the phone so we could see the screen.

"Oh, sugar-plum parsnips," I said, and Emma gasped.

It was a photo of Gerry, the big troll stripped of his floral skirts and pearls, clad only in a pair of what looked like over-sized jogging bottoms. Welts and gashes criss-crossed his shoulders and chest, and he was kneeling on a stone floor, but his back was still straight and his head up. His horns had been filed down, and heavy manacles and chains attached him to a ring on the floor.

There was a single word below the photo. *Dimly.*

SO THERE WENT any hope of making a quiet getaway and hunkering down somewhere until the cavalry in the form of Ms Jones rocked into town. Instead we puttered on, not speaking, Tam, Pru and I squeezed together on the little bow seat under the shelter of the boat's dinky deck while Callum guided us along the flat green waters of the canal. Rain slicked his hair to his head and cheeks, and dripped from his nose and the sleeves and bottom of his jacket, but he didn't seem to notice except to grumble when he couldn't get his cigarettes lit. Green Snake offered him the seashell instead, then vanished back to drier territory in his pockets. Emma discovered an army-green waterproof jacket in the pack and pulled it on. It came down to her knees, and had a hood so deep she looked like she was cos-playing a reaper, but she looked distinctly more comfortable than Callum did.

We went through one lock, Callum slinging a bit of rope – sorry, a *line* – around a bollard to hold us in place while he got out and cranked laboriously on the big old winches, the water gates slowly opening in front of us. Emma untied us and moved us carefully into the lock, then tied us up again while Callum closed it, opened the sluices on the other side to let the water level drop to match that of the next stretch of canal, then cranked the gates open and climbed back on board again. He peered in at us as Emma got us puttering off down the canal.

"Comfortable?"

"Relatively," I said.

"Good, good. Don't want anyone straining themselves."

"It's not our fault all this stuff is human-centric. That's on you lot."

Not long after, we pulled into the shelter of some overhanging willows, and Callum looped the line over one of the old bollards that pocked the canal wall, switching the engine off. Silence rushed in to fill the space it left behind, all shaded in greens and greys and dull afternoon hues. The towpath that ran alongside the canal was empty in both directions, and we hadn't seen so much as a dogwalker since we'd left the OAP headquarters. It wasn't the day for it. Callum sat down on the opposite side of the boat to Emma, rubbed his hands together to warm them, and plucked his cigarettes out. He regarded the sodden packet with a disgusted look, and put them away again.

I padded out of shelter, wrinkling my nose. The trees were letting a lot of rain in.

"So what do we do?" Emma asked. "That was your friend, wasn't it? The troll in Dimly?"

"It was," Callum said, looking at me. "I suppose at least it means he's still alive."

"Or he was when they took the photo." I shook rain off my ears. "They took his horns. They don't grow back."

"I know. That's a terrible bloody thing to do to a troll."

"It's a way of showing power," Tam said, strolling out to join us. "They used to do it to troll prisoners all the time. It doesn't hurt physically. Just in all the other ways."

"What's the next move?" Pru called. She had, rather wisely, decided to stay in the bow. She didn't even have any hair to keep her warm, although judging by the way I could feel rain weighing down my fur, she might've done better than me with her utility coat.

"You should go home," Callum said. "Katja'll be worried."

"Some things are more important than worried humans,"

Pru said, poking her nose out and wrinkling it even more deeply at the rain.

"You barely even know Gerry," I said.

"I know you two. And you can't be trusted to be left alone. Look what happened when we left Callum. It wasn't even an hour!"

"It was at least an hour," he protested.

"That's not as good an argument as you seem to think," she said, and he laughed softly, scrubbing a hand through his hair. It sent water droplets everywhere, and left him with a rumpled crow's nest, almost black between the shadows and the wet.

"I can try Ethel again," Emma said. "They *have* to start taking this seriously. That woman back there was blowing things up!"

"I'm not sure that'll make much difference," I said. "Reapers are worried about souls, and that's it. And Kara certainly doesn't have any scythes, or she'd have been using them. Although the fact she's got her hands on unicorn horn is bad enough."

"I still want to see a unicorn," Emma said.

"You really don't."

Callum leaned forward with his forearms on his knees and said, "I think you should go back to the cafe, though, Emma. Or wherever Ethel is. It's pretty obvious that Kara's going to keep coming for both us and you, and at least the reapers will do *something* if it happens on their doorstep."

"Oh, good," she said. "I'll just be bait, shall I?"

"It's still safer than this," he said, and looked at Pru. "You go home too. Make sure Katja's okay. You're not foul of anyone yet, not really. Keep it that way."

She narrowed her eyes at him, and before she could speak I said, "He's right. And you as well, Tam. I'm in it up to my dewclaws with the Watch, and apparently always have been, and Northy here's got family issues coming out his eyeballs, but the rest of you can keep out of the whole thing."

Tam and Pru looked at each other, and Pru said, "Shall we head off then, Tam? Nibble a little smoked salmon in the dining room and watch a nature documentary?"

Tam rumbled thoughtfully. "Caviar for me. The documentary sounds good, though. One on wildebeest. I could take a wildebeest, I think."

"We can lie back among the cushions with the heating on and think about those less fortunate than us."

"Poor, poor souls," Tam said. "But nothing to be done."

"No, no. None of our business."

"We could send flowers, perhaps."

"Yes, quite. Maybe a nice card."

They both looked at us, and after a moment Callum said, "Is that some sort of cat sarcasm?"

"*Yes,* you soggy vol-au-vent case," Pru snapped. "A) don't try to tell cats what to do, which you should know by now, and b) don't try to tell your *friends* what to do, which *anyone* should know. *Honestly.*"

"I'm with them on all counts," Emma said. "Especially the bit where Pru said you can't be trusted to stay out of trouble on your own."

"The wildebeest bit wasn't sarcasm," Tam said, before I could even think of how to respond.

Pru blinked at her. "What?

"I think I could take a wildebeest. Maybe not a big one, but a medium one, say."

"Aren't they all kind of big?" I asked, mostly for something to say.

"Maybe. Am I thinking of antelope?"

"There's all sizes of them," Emma said.

Tam made a thoughtful noise, and Callum said, "I think it is an antelope."

"What is?" I asked.

"A wildebeest."

"It's a *wildebeest.* You just said."

"Yeah, but a wildebeest's a kind of antelope," he said.

"That seems unnecessarily confusing."

"Not really. You're a kind of cat."

"I'm a *cat,*" I said. "Nothing kind of about it."

"What's a gnu, then?" Tam asked.

"Isn't that a wildebeest too?" Emma said. "I seem to remember that from somewhere."

"You said it was an antelope," I said to Callum accusingly, and Pru sighed. I looked at her, then padded over and bumped her shoulder with my own.

"You're all impossible," she said.

"Fish, kettle, etc."

"What?"

"He means pot," Callum said, and Pru just stared at him.

"I think I have a headache," Emma said.

"You get used to it," Callum replied.

"You don't," Tam said, and I looked at Pru.

"I'm so glad you got Tam talking. It's delightful."

Tam growled. "I'm a retiring flower is all."

I looked at the hulking great she-cat, who might not be able to handle a wildebeest, but I was quite certain would try to, and thought that seemed unlikely. But then many things in life did, and often it was the most unlikely that was the most beautiful, and sometimes even magical. Like friendship, both in the general sense and in particular.

"Right," I said, once Tam, Pru and I had retreated into the bow again, and Emma and Callum were hunkered down so we could all see each other, Callum playing with his Whitby jet. It was glossy as deep ocean in the wet, and Green Snake was hanging out of his pocket watching it with flat green eyes that swallowed the dim reflections of the trees and canal. "So you lot have even less sense than us, since we at least have no choice in things. But fine. Callum, you and I have to go to Dimly. We can't ignore that photo."

"No," he agreed.

"But walking in there utterly unprepared is probably not wise."

"Although it's also our usual mode of operation." He rubbed his thumb over the stone absently, then put it back in his pocket. Green Snake dived after it. "I suppose the boat might be handy, anyway. They won't expect us to come that way."

"That's a start," I said. "But we don't know where Gerry's being held. We don't know anything about Dimly as it is now – unless you do?" I addressed the last to Tam and Pru. Tam shrugged, and Pru shook her head.

"Last time we went for a nose around we couldn't even get in," she said. "Weres on all the borders."

"Aw, dudes," I said with a sigh.

"Not dudes," Pru said automatically.

"What?" Callum asked, looking at me. "What is it?"

"There's a way in. Just not by the streets."

He wrinkled his nose. "The sewers? I could still smell you for a week."

"Try being in my fur."

"What does it get us, though?" Pru asked. "If we go in through the sewers? Callum can't, so we can't sneak him in, and as much as Tam could maybe or maybe not take down a wildebeest, I'm not sure the three of us are enough to disable any necromancer or were guards and bust Gerry out."

Tam made a thoughtful sound that suggested she had higher expectations of us than Pru did.

"But Callum can't go in at all," I said. "It's a trap, right? He goes in, and then ... well, whatever Scary Sonia wants out of you. It's got to be her who sent the message. Ez had a go at trying to get you to go willingly, and now Sonia's having her turn."

"I suppose," Callum said. "But how else do we get Gerry back if I *don't* go in?"

"So are Sonia and Kara working against each other now?" Emma asked. "Because surely Kara wouldn't have bothered with the camp raid if she'd known Sonia was going to use Gerry to get to you." We all looked at her, and she spread her hands. "Don't you think?"

"Kara said *he'll* be so pleased," I said, and looked at Callum. "You still so sure about Magic Boy?"

"Yes," he said, then frowned. "Sort of. But isn't it more likely that she means the Old One? If we never really got rid of it, maybe she thinks it'll reward her with more power if she brings us in."

"Or more unicorn dust," Pru said. "She was just about vibrating with the stuff. Give her six months and her brain'll be paté."

Callum didn't say anything, but I saw the corner of his mouth twitch down, an unconscious little grimace. I could smell the hurt on him like dark corners in abandoned halls, damp and gritty.

"We don't have six months," I said. "And whatever – Gerry's a trap."

"We can't leave him," Callum said. "I can't ignore that photo."

"And you can't just walk straight into it," Emma said. "Why don't we all go to Ethel? Maybe she'll listen if it's all of us."

"Not a bad idea." I pawed at the hair tie on my leg, then growled and held my paw up to Callum. "Little help, please."

"What?" He plucked at the hair tie. "What is that?"

"Sorcerer's hair tie."

"You accessorising now?" He tugged it off and examined it.

"Put it down before it smells of tea and cigarettes," I said, and looked at the others. "We can't leave Gerry, but going in alone's out. We need backup *now*. I'll take that to Yasmin and get the dentist."

"Not on your own," Pru said.

"Yes. You have to go to Ms Jones and tell her the weres are bringing her dentist to meet her in Dimly, and she can't wait anymore. Not for the kittens, nothing."

"Kittens?" Callum started, then shook his head. "Never mind. Look, I've got Yasmin's number still. Take it to Ms Jones, she can call Yasmin, and you don't have to go shifting around weres."

I looked at the hair tie blankly, then said, "I'm not used to having a simple option."

Tam snorted, startling Green Snake, who had slithered out of Callum's pocket and onto the side of the boat with the seashell in his jaws. He stared at her for a moment, then dropped the shell over the side and went back to Callum's coat. Evidently he'd fallen out of love with his souvenir.

"It should be here …" Callum dug into his coat, extricating wet cigarettes, a silver lighter, Green Snake, and the piece of jet, all of which he put on the seat, then checked his jeans. He finally came up with a sodden piece of paper, stained blue with run ink, that looked as if someone had been chewing on it. "Oh. Think she can get something off this?"

Emma peered at it. "You didn't put it in your phone? Take a photo of it?"

"No," he admitted.

"Ah," she said, which seemed polite.

"Right," I said. "Back to my plan. I take the hair tie to Yasmin as proof Ms Jones is on board. Tam and Pru tell Ms Jones to get her bike out."

"We don't know where she is," Pru said. "What if she's in Cornwall or something? It could take her a day to get here. More, even."

"She's a sorcerer. She'll get here fast as she needs to."

"Why don't we go and get the car?" Callum said. "We can drive up to the weres."

"And risk getting nabbed by Ifan? We don't want to be anywhere near that poisonous bloody cauliflower."

"We don't know—" Callum started.

"We don't *not* know," I said flatly. We glared at each other, and finally Pru spoke up.

"If we're shifting, there's time to do both. Tam and I'll go to Yasmin with you, then to Ms Jones, then come back here. Then we'll all go and see if we can convince the reapers things are getting a bit end times. That works, right?"

I huffed air, and squinted at her. "Who died and made you logarithmics?"

"Well, you're making things twice as hard as they need to be," she said, which was fair.

"Logistics," Callum said, with the air of someone solving a tricky crossword clue.

"You do need a translator sometimes, don't you?" Emma said, and Pru, Tam and I glared at her. I opened my mouth to point out that she could give Cat a go, when there was a clear, unmistakable *bloop*. We all looked at the side of the boat, where Callum had piled the contents of his pockets.

The jet was missing.

So was Green Snake.

18

OUT OF OPTIONS. AGAIN

"Green Snake?" Callum asked, leaning over the side and peering up and down the hull. I jumped up to the seat to join him, my nose twitching.

"He can't have gone over," I said. "Why would he go over?" Unless he'd suddenly regretted giving up his damn shell, but surely he wasn't that besotted with it.

"Maybe he's gone into the hull," Emma said. She was checking in the little seating area forward. "There's so many gaps a snake could get through."

"But there was a splash," Callum pointed out.

"It might've been the jet," I said. "Maybe it fell."

Callum frowned at me and pocketed the rest of his debris. "We need to find him."

"I know." My mouth felt tacky and hairball-ish as I said, "But we also have to think about the end of the world and all that fun stuff. About Gerry."

Callum groaned and rubbed his hands through his sodden hair. "Bloody *hell*. Why's he gone *now*?"

"That damn jet," I said. "I *knew* there was something weird about it."

"What, you think it ate him?" Callum asked, and I bared a tooth at him.

"*No.* But maybe it got his tiny head all muddled and he thinks he's a sea serpent now."

"We don't even know he went over," Emma said. "Do we search the boat?"

Callum and I looked at each other, then he shook his head. "No. You lot get off. I'll look while you're gone."

"What're you going to do?" I asked him. "Crawl through the bilges? I don't think you're small enough for that."

"I'll go through all the lockers while you go to Yasmin and Ms Jones," he said, inspecting his cigarettes.

"Just that," I said.

"Just that." He shoved the packet in his coat pocket. "Go on. We need to get moving."

"How do I get back to the cafe?" Emma asked, while I stared at Callum suspiciously.

"There'll be a road nearby," he said.

"I'm not *hitchhiking*." She looked as horrified as if she hadn't just taken on a pack of weres and a job lot of magic-workers with a slingshot.

"Get an Uber."

She gave him a blank look, then said, "I don't know why that feels like the weird bit in all this."

Callum snorted and looked at me. "Alright then, off you go. On with the plan."

"I'm a bit unclear on the plan, really," Emma said. "Other than the reapers."

"Get the weres," Tam said. "Weres have the dentist. Dentist means sorcerer, who can do sorcery things at the Old One. Rest of us bite as many of the other weres and baby necromancers we can. Plus rescue the troll in distress."

"It's not much of a plan," Pru said.

"To be fair, it's more of a plan than we usually have," I pointed out.

"That's unfortunately true," Callum said, and Pru sighed.

"How have you two stayed alive this long?"

"I haven't, really," I said.

"I'm starting to see why."

"Let's go," Tam said. "It's wet."

Callum nodded. "I'll see you soon."

I took the hair tie off him again and got it back on my leg, in the hope that weres might be less likely to gobble me up if I smelled of sorcerer, then looked at him with narrowed eyes. "Stay here. My aim's not great."

"I've got a snake to find," he said, and lifted one of the seats to poke into the locker beneath.

Which wasn't exactly convincing.

IT WAS easy enough to get to the weres' compound. Some things are ingrained, a muscle memory carried over from shift after shift in previous lives. Just because I'd never shifted in this one didn't mean I didn't know how. I'd never eaten custard, either, until I first sniffed it out, and I knew perfectly well what to do with it once I did. The trick was not thinking about it, otherwise no one would eat something that was basically eggs and milk made weirdly wobbly. Or, in the current situation, think about it too much and I'd end up getting stuck halfway and turned into someone else's custard.

But the shift itself was easy, leaving the boat huddled beneath its trees and stepping into nothing. Of course, the charms at the were house meant we couldn't just pop into the living room at a handy vantage point and give Yasmin a wave. Instead we stepped out of the Inbetween onto the hard gravel just outside the gate, smelling wolf and magic and damp dark woods, which was all a bit fae and creepy for comfort. Rain glommed together into heavy droplets that spilled through the branches overhead, splatting on our coats, and the day was dull and heavy under their shelter.

Tam padded forward and sniffed the gate, her pupils so wide they all but ate the green of her eyes.

"Anyone nearby?" I asked, my voice low as I joined her. She didn't answer, just slipped through the bars and set off at a steady lope along the track. Pru and I glanced at each other, then followed. My spine prickled with rain and the heavy scent of weres, and as soft as my paw-falls were, the minute shift of gravel still seemed thunderous in my ears.

We ran.

The drive snaked muddy and pale between the trees, the bank high to our right and the hill falling away to the left. The shadows under the trees were deep and opaque, and wind and rain plucked at the branches, setting up a chorus of moaning voices and chattering teeth. But nothing emerged from the shadows. Nothing stepped in front of us, barring our path. Nothing exploded onto the track behind us, all teeth and fury. And their simple absence felt like a trap, but still we kept going.

I smelled it before we reached the end of the drive, before the trees gave way to open land. Tam and Pru did too, slowing to a trot as they looked at me. Not that I could do or say anything to change it. We had to know. I ran harder, my lope turning into a sprint, and I didn't stop until I was standing in front of the smouldering ruins of the barn, smelling scorched wood and singed fur and fear, and the ugly taint of unpleasant magic. For a moment I thought the cottage had survived, but then I saw the broken windows, and smoke still drifting from the upstairs ones.

"Oh, godsdammit," I said softly, standing there with the

rain parting my fur. Cubs. There had been *cubs*. I couldn't see any bodies, and after a moment I padded slowly up to the wreckage, picking my way past fallen stone and discarded clothes and broken glass. There was blood here and there, but not a lot of it, and what I saw confirmed what my nose was telling me. This hadn't been any accident, no gas explosion or electrical fire. And it hadn't been villagers with torches, ether. Spent magic scratched at the back of my throat as I watched the rain slowly drowning the embers.

"They got out," Pru said. Her ears were back, and her teeth were showing.

"I think so," I said.

"Or they took their dead," Tam said. "They wouldn't leave them. Not a pack."

I stared at her, wanting to tell her to take the words back, but it was too late for that. Too late for anything. I turned back to the track, pushing myself up to a sprint that made my limbs shake, and when I shot through the gate I was already reaching out for the Inbetween, not caring if the others were with me or not.

This was *enough*.

BUT IT WASN'T. Of course it wasn't. Instead of appearing with my paws in her lunch I hit the shift locks at Ms Jones' cottage so hard I was thrown back, colliding with Pru and Tam as they emerged from the Inbetween just behind me. We went down in a tangle of limbs and tails, Pru hissing furiously, and I yelped, "Sorry!"

"A little control, Gobs," she said, rolling away from me.

"Right." I scrambled to my feet, bellowing, "*Oi, sorcerer!*"

There was no answer. No answer because the charms were down. Not the shift locks that had thrown me so effortlessly back, but there was nothing to stop us simply walking in. None of the heavy, living magic that had been woven so deftly around the cottage when we'd left. We slipped through the gate without encountering any resistance, looking at each other and the garden nervously and waiting for some sort of freaky magical defence to kick in. Likely one with claws and stabby bits.

But nothing did, and my stomach was turning slowly over by the time we reached the cottage. We'd arrived at the back door, the same way we'd left, and after peering in the windows to see the whisky glass in the sink and nothing else amiss, we kept going around the building. The wind was stronger on this side, ruffling my damp fur and pressing the brine of an unseen sea into the corners of my ears, but I barely noticed it. I just stared at the front door, which had been torn off its hinges and was lying at the opposite end of the hallway. Rain had blown in over the mat, and mud scuffed the floors, cat prints and wolf prints and human prints all mixed up together.

"This … she has to be alright. They all have to be alright," I said, and looked at Tam and Pru. "She's a *sorcerer!* And Claudia … I mean, the two of them, together. Nothing gets past that, right?"

Neither of them replied, and after a moment I turned away. There was nothing here. The house was empty of cats, kittens, and sorcerers alike. So much for my plan.

Pru touched her nose to mine as we stopped outside the gate. "They'll turn up," she said.

"In one piece?" I asked.

"If they don't, then it was something even a sorcerer can't fight," Tam said. "And there's not much any of us can do about something like that."

I nodded. "Well, yeah. Cheers for that."

"Sure," she said, shrugging.

I reached out to Callum, but I was distracted and the shifts still weren't as automatic as they should be. My focus seemed to slide right off him, so I thought of the boat instead, dripping softly under the willows, and felt it drift toward me. I stepped to meet it, and turned to give Callum the news that things were already going radish-shaped, and we hadn't even started.

He wasn't there.

I leaped to the bank, *wanting* to see him sheltering under the trees, but already knowing he wouldn't be. It was in the hard, sickening turn of my belly and the thin whine in my ears.

The bank was empty, and I staggered as the world went dark at the edges.

Tam had to bite my tail to stop me tumbling back into the Inbetween, which was an undignified way to prevent the demise of the entire firm of G&C London, Private Investigators.

But it was effective.

WE JUST STOOD THERE, in the rain, looking at each other.

"Maybe he went with Emma," Pru said.

"I told him not to go anywhere," I said. "I *told* him." Neither of them replied to that, and after a moment I said, "Can you track him?" I knew I couldn't, not in the state I was in. Maybe not at all, not yet. It's a delicate art, and I may have overestimated my rediscovered shifting ability a teensy bit.

There was a pause, then Tam said, "No. He's hidden."

I took a deep, shaky breath, and said, "You didn't even try."

"Don't need to," she said.

"He's always hidden," Pru said, her voice soft. "We track

you. You're always easier to find. He's sort of a bit ... unclear."

"Sounds right," I muttered, and sat down, scratching my ear with a back paw. It was more to have something to do than anything else. I didn't like the way the other two were looking at me. A *what now* look was one thing. A sympathetic look was something else entirely. "How about Emma?"

"We'll look," Pru said, glancing at Tam.

"Good," I said. "Yes. See if he's with her."

"Are you coming?" Pru asked.

"No." He wasn't going to be with Emma. He'd be on the way to Dimly, willingly or not. Dragged there, maybe, but just as likely under his own momentum, trusting to his North-ness, his *Callum*-ness to keep him hidden, because he could. Because he hadn't been able to use who he was for anything else. Because he was relying on others to fight what he thought was somehow his battle. Because he felt he'd let us down in some obscure, human way, and now he was going to make up for it. Likely by having an ancient god shoved down his throat. And all of that meant I was going to Dimly too, and I didn't need anyone else getting hurt on the way. "You go on. I need to calm down before I try shifting again."

"Sure?" Pru asked.

"Yeah. I'll be here. I just need a minute." I took a breath. "Get some cheese too, while you're at it."

"Cheese?" Pru asked.

"Good stuff. For the rats."

She acknowledged that with a tip of her head, and Tam was the one who touched noses with me this time. I took a moment as they stepped away, leaving nothing but slightly less damp patches on the boat behind them, to think that everyone got a lot more affectionate when the apocalypse was underway. Then I got up and focused. Not on Callum, because he was as undefined as he had been when I'd tried from Ms Jones'. And no matter if he was hidden from Tam and Pru, he never was from me. I could always feel him, a smoke-stained constant in a shifting world. So if he was hidden from me now, he was either deep into Dimly already, or someone who cast a heavy shadow across the worlds had him.

Either way, I wasn't going to find him, and that meant I had one option.

I was going straight to the heart of the beast.

I shook my fur out as I readied myself to shift, the thought of Dimly's tattered borders lingering like a sour taste in the back of my mouth, and a small green head poked over the stern of the boat. It stared at me with an expression that should have been guilty, but it's really hard to tell with snakes.

"*You,*" I hissed at him. "What're you playing at, you skinny green snot string?"

He slithered into the boat and tilted his head at me.

"Where's Callum? It's your fault we left him here, you know."

Another head tilt, and he glanced at the river.

"What? He went that way? You saw where he went?"

Green Snake tipped his head from side to side, a little seesaw motion.

"Stick to kraken," I told him. "You're no help with anything else."

He reared up, doing his cobra impression, then opened his mouth. For one moment I thought he was going to strike me, and I scuttled back, wondering what sort of ideas the seashell had given him, then he disgorged something onto the floor of the boat, his jaws stretching alarmingly wide.

"Ew. Hairball?" I asked him. "Scale ball?"

He looked at me, and tilted his head.

"Yeah, yeah," I said, imitating him, then went to investigate. If it was the shell I was going to shove it back down his throat.

It wasn't the shell.

It was a key. An old, slightly ornate, marginally rusty and now snake-flavoured key. I looked from it to him, then said, "The magician's got him?"

He stared at me blankly.

"He's at the magician's house?"

Still nothing.

I sighed. "You want me to go to the magician's house?"

Head tilt.

"Roasted parsnip balls," I said, and pawed the key a few times, trying to get the worst of the snake bile off it. "He's as trustworthy as a vet with a thermometer."

Green Snake gave a sudden wriggle, coiling over and around himself a few times, fluid and luminous, and I stared at him.

"You were in his pocket for a bit."

Wriggle wriggle.

"You trust him."

Blank stare.

I sighed. "Yeah, me either. But you think he'll help. For Callum."

A stare, then a head tilt. Which pretty much summed up how I felt about the magician, too. But I was out of options. No sorcerer. No weres. No reaper. No troll. And, as has been previously noted, sometimes the only option is a bad one. I picked the key up delicately in my teeth and stepped toward Green Snake, intending to let him curl up over my shoulders and hitch a ride, but he uncoiled and spooled himself back off the stern of the boat, vanishing silently.

"Well, cheers to you too," I said to the empty boat, and wondered if he had a pet kraken down there somewhere. That might be handy.

But there was no time to find out. I had a dodgy magician to deal with.

🐈

I STUMBLED AS I SHIFTED, the void rising up to engulf me, and for one panicked moment I thought it had been Pru and Tam's momentum that had carried me through before, that I really *couldn't* do this, that I'd been lying to myself to think I ever could. Then there was a flicker of *something*, a mass in the un-dark, a thickening of nothingness, and I slammed straight back out of the Inbetween. I landed hard, somersaulting twice, and came up with my ears back and my teeth bared in a snarl.

Nothing rushed me. Nothing attacked. The street was broad and sodden and nastily familiar, and I turned to look at the gates. They still hung at a strange angle, the gap between them clear, but I had a feeling the magician would've beefed up the protection there, and I didn't fancy testing the key on something that might fry my eyeballs. So I took an old route, because no one ever looks up.

I scaled the tree closest to the wall, checking for rabid squirrels as I went, but it was still raining, and they were obviously much smarter than I was, tucked up somewhere dry with their big tails wrapped around their necks like ruffs. Which sounded very cosy and lovely when I was out here dripping and cold and wet enough to feel it in my bones. I padded along the branch that ran toward the magician's property, jumped from it to the wall itself, then slid my paws down the damp old bricks and jumped to the weedy flowerbeds beneath. Charms spat and whispered, things with weight and indignant fury, but the key cleaved them, dragging me behind it like a stone falling through the turbulent waters of a river to the stillness beneath. Nothing stopped me or flung me back, and no weaponised badgers or armoured hippos came galumphing around the corner of the house to greet me.

I stalked across the garden toward the front door unimpeded, head low. Our car was still sitting next to the corpse of the Bentley, and there wasn't a lot between them, to be honest. It was even possible that the Bentley looked better than the Rover did.

There were lights on inside, and I wasn't surprised when the door opened before I even reached the steps. I stopped and set the key down, glaring up at Ifan. He was wearing a red T-shirt that read *Magic AF*, and he *did* look surprised.

"Gobs?"

"Who were you expecting?"

"Not you." He looked past me. "Where's Callum?"

"I was hoping you could tell me."

His gaze shifted from the gates to me, a frown tugging weary lines into his face. He didn't look like he'd slept much more than we had recently. "What?"

I stared at him, at his bare feet and close-cropped dark hair, at his long-fingered hands and the shadows under his eyes. I could smell the power on him, but I could smell weariness and worry and a bright worm of fear as well. "Who are you?" I asked.

"Ifan," he said simply. "Magician. Quite accidentally the most powerful one about. Would rather not be. Much preferred hanging on a beach in Mustique drinking fruity rum drinks."

"With umbrellas?" I asked.

"With umbrellas."

I sighed. Someone was going to have to explain the umbrella thing to me properly at some point, but it wasn't the time. "The necromancers. What happened when you faked your death?"

His mouth twisted. "You want to come in?"

"No."

"Alright." He hugged an arm around himself against the cold. "I joined a little local group. It was fun. I lent them a little magic without them realising, so they thought it was them doing it, and it was cute, you know? They were just playing with stuff, wearing lots of black clothes and silver rings and getting all excited about moving a cup across a table. Then I got a text saying we had a meeting, but I was the only one from the group who turned up to it. It was in this house where something big had happened. Something nasty. Something got out that shouldn't have, or almost did – not sure. I never got the full story, but there was power there, and people with actual power, too."

"Sonia?" I asked, and he shook his head.

"Not then. But there were real necromancers, and they wanted me to know it. Know that the group was just a way to find those that they could use, and either take their power or train them up if they seemed useful. They wanted me to know that they were the real deal, and they had real plans. And it was pretty clear they already knew who I was. They weren't going to leave me alone until I joined up. I refused, and they said they'd go after Dad unless I jumped on the necromancer train. I said good luck on that, but I also knew they weren't going to stop." He shrugged. "So I got out."

"By faking your own death?" I demanded. "Seems a bit of an overreaction. Couldn't you have, I don't know, just told your dad?"

He gave me a smile that had no humour in it. "You didn't know him. And I kind of liked the idea of disappearing, anyway. I've been known to partake in recreational substances, so an overdose wasn't out of the realms of possibility, and it's easy enough to magic things up a bit. I kind of was dead, really. Enough to fool even Dad. I had it in my will that there wasn't to be any embalming, because the chemicals were bad for the earth, and therefore I had to be buried immediately. And then I just popped on back."

"And now?"

"Now I can scratch *buried alive* off my bucket list." His smile was fleeting. "I've had nothing to do with the necromancers since. I can't get close to them since Cal and I shoved the Old One back, anyway. They won't trust me. So I've stayed clear, but I've been working on making contacts. Weres, magic-workers, whoever I can."

"So you know they want Callum."

"Yes. Also why I told you two to stay here, but, what – the chicken not up to standard or something?"

"What about the weres outside the house?"

He shook his head. "Nothing to do with me. I know they watch me sometimes, though."

"What did you do to Anton?"

"That was a genuine backfire. I think bloody Walker was fiddling about with his chopsticks and something went sideways."

"Why didn't you fix it?"

"I've tried. I can't seem to undo it, and now I'm a bit scared to try. If it goes wrong again and all his hair falls out or something I think he might rip my throat out. And Yasmin *definitely* will."

I sighed. "Firebombs at Rav's house?"

"Again, not me."

"We saw your car."

He grimaced. "I may have been following you, in case you got into trouble." I growled, and he spread his fingers. "Seriously. I can be really handy."

"When you're not freezing people as dogs."

"Ouch. But fair. Although I probably wouldn't refer to the great big wolf as a dog if he's in earshot."

I walked up the steps and stood on the broad, cracked expanse of the top one, looking up at him. "What do you want with Callum?"

He looked back at me, his gaze level, and said, "To be friends again. He was my *best* friend. He's the only one who just doesn't care about the stuff other people do. Doesn't care if I'm rich, or a magician, or anything. He never has. He makes me feel *normal*. And I want that back. But even if I can't have it, I won't let him be hurt if I can help it, because he'd do the same for me."

We regarded each other for a long moment. I still didn't trust him. I couldn't. There was too much that was tangled and complicated, all the human stuff said and unsaid, the twisted threads of family and friendship and history that Callum would've been able to put his hand on and say, *this I understand.* I didn't. Even if he'd explained it to me, I wouldn't have understood it. But I understood that we both wanted Callum in one piece, and for at least some of the same reasons, and more than that, I understood that Ifan had power, and I needed it.

"Get your keys," I said. "Let's go."

19

BRINGER OF MAD TIDINGS

ANNOYINGLY, IFAN JUST STOOD THERE LOOKING AT ME. "Where to?"

"To find Callum. Come on."

"Find him where?"

"If I knew that I wouldn't have to find him, would I? He's gone."

"You've lost him?"

I glared at him. "Look, the sorcerer's missing. *Again*, I mean, because we found her. Sort of, anyway. Yasmin's weres are gone. Scary Sonia's on the hunt for us. Ez is trying to play the family card to get to Callum. And Gerry's being held prisoner, so now Callum's either gone after him alone or someone's nabbed him."

"Wow. How long have you been back?"

I growled. "Also had a slight run-in with Kara, who might or might not be working with Sonia, but has definitely figured out how to use unicorn dust to go all magic warrior on us. Plus she's got her own weres and magic-workers, so definitely a problem."

"Alright." He still looked at me a little blankly.

"Well? Get some shoes on! Hurry up!"

Ifan shook his head, but he vanished inside, leaving the door standing open on the hall. The taxidermied animals peered out at me with dull glass eyes, and a lizard-type thing at least as big as I was scuttled jerkily toward the door. I stayed where I was, my fur drenched and my ears full of water, wondering if Pru and Tam were back by now. I hoped they stayed out of Dimly. I hoped they didn't try taking my planned route in. Dimly's sewers had been bad enough last summer, infested with things that were there for the precise purpose of hunting cats and intruders. I hated to think what they were like now. Plus the rats weren't *entirely* friendly.

Ifan came back, boots squeaking on the marble and a dark wool coat hanging heavily from his shoulders, a towel bundled under one arm. He nudged the lizard back inside as he pulled a soft grey wool hat down over his ears and closed the door behind him. "I tried Callum's phone. He's not answering."

"Shock, surprise, etcetera," I said, and he scowled at me. "What? I *told* you he was gone."

"Excuse me for checking. How much magic's it going to take to get your car going?"

"Our car? What about yours?"

"You don't think it might be a touch recognisable?"

I wrinkled my snout. "Doesn't yours have cool magician weapons or something?"

"Nope." He opened the driver's door of the old Rover and let me jump inside, then swung in after me, less gangly and more solid than Callum.

"This is disappointing," I said. "I was hoping to make an entrance."

He dropped the towel next to me on the passenger seat and said, "You might want to dry yourself first."

"Thanks." I curled into the towel as he adjusted bits and

poked around the dashboard, making little disbelieving sounds, then finally turned the key.

Nothing.

He ran a hand over the dashboard, and I could feel the warmth rising from his fingers. He gave the car a final pat and tried the key again. The engine turned over, first choppily, then settling into a reasonably steady grumble. He wrestled with the gears for a moment and finally got us moving, only to stall halfway to the gate.

"Bloody hell," he muttered, but a moment later we were off again, more smoothly this time. The gates swung open in front of us, one side dragging a little on its broken hinge. "Do you ever service this thing?"

"Do you ever fix your gates?" I shot back.

"It's been a *day*." He glanced at me and reached across. I flinched away from him, but he just pulled the towel over my back and gave me a brisk rub. I growled, but his hands really were very warm, and I was abruptly a lot drier.

"Don't you magic at me."

"Oh, bite me." He pulled through the gates and stopped with the nose of the Rover touching the road. The gates clanged shut behind us, a metallic shiver that I felt in my ears. "Which way?"

I sighed. "Dimly."

He gave me a sharp look. "Callum's in Dimly?"

"I don't know," I admitted. "But Gerry's in trouble, and the odds are he's still in Dimly, and I can't find Callum. I can always feel him, but ..." The words dried up, and I licked my chops.

"Oh," Ifan said. "*Oh.*" Then he said something else, as well, but it was mostly drowned out by the clash of gears and the rev of the engine as he pulled onto the road, pushing our poor old car faster than she'd had to go in possibly ... well, since our last displeased client. A pity, too, because whatever the magician had said was very inventive and would've been a good addition to my vocabulary.

☙

WE MADE it two blocks before Ifan pulled into a driveway. Most of the houses around here were hunkered down behind big walls, maintaining their distance and difference. This one seemed to have been made into flats, though – sorry, probably *executive living options* or something – and there were half a dozen cars parked on the gravel drive that curled around the front of what must have once been some sort of mini-stately home. Not mini as in pixie-sized or anything, just mini as in it had probably only had one ballroom instead of a matching set.

"What're we doing?" I demanded as Ifan drove up and parked in front of an old stone garage with a *Groundskeeper Keep Clear* sign on it.

"I can't drive anywhere in this."

"It was your idea to take it."

"I didn't realise how bad it was. I can't even tell how much fuel you have." He pointed at the gauges. "The needle's gone. How do you lose a fuel gauge needle?"

"The car isn't my area," I said. "Callum always managed though."

"Yeah, well, it's not the day for worrying if we're going to run out of fuel, or, from the sounds of things, the gearbox is going to fall out on the road. I can't hold the whole thing together with magic. And does it always run with the temperature like that?" He pointed again, and I squinted. The needle had gone off the scale on the red side.

"We did have a couple of problems on the way down from Whitby," I admitted.

"Jesus. Come on." He climbed out, leaving the car with the

keys in it. I glanced at the sign again, but neither of us was a groundskeeper, so I supposed it was fine.

Ifan surveyed the cars, settled on a sleek, low-slung MG, and put his hand on the bonnet. There was a muted click as the locks popped, and he opened the door, looking at me.

"Dude," I said. "This is how magicians get so rich, huh?"

"Eh. Not the cars. But similar techniques."

"Nice for some." I jumped in, catching a whiff of yappy little dogs and heavy cologne before the magician followed me, and then all I could smell was the snap and spark of persuasive magic as he started the engine. A moment later we were purring out of the gates and down the road, and I put my paws on the door handle to peer out at the muted, dark day, reaching out for Callum.

I still couldn't feel him.

DIMLY LURKED on the edge of Leeds, coiling itself around a tributary of river that invited no boaters, no walkers on the overgrown canal paths. It held tight to roots that had been old long before Leeds had been anything more than a scruffy hamlet ringed with fires to keep the wolves out. The human cities had continued to expand voraciously long after Dimly's growth had stalled, but pockets have their own ways of protecting themselves. Town planners in sweater vests and urban developers in shiny shoes skirted it the same way the occasional misdirected human did, eyes and feet and wheels turning away before they even touched the borders. Pocket towns are old, and steeped in power, and their ancient boundary charms are less cast by modern magic-workers than cautiously maintained, dusted off and given a quick polish, but largely left to their own devices. Some things are so old they have their own sort of consciousness, and it's best not to mess with them too much. Just in case.

The streets of Leeds were snarled with traffic, with shoppers and workers and delivery vans, but somehow every light was in our favour, and traffic melted away before us as Ifan took the fastest route he could around the centre, curving toward Dimly. I was starting to see that there were *lots* of advantages to being a magician.

"How come you didn't want to be a magician?" I asked him.

He turned the music down. It was some sort of club stuff that I didn't recognise, and didn't really want to. "It wasn't that I didn't want to be one at all. Being a magician is fine. I just didn't want to be *the* magician, you know? Either Dad's little sidekick, or after he went taking over and having all these people coming to the house, wanting this or that, offering deals or politicking at me, or guilting me into helping." He shook his head. "It's too much."

"Sure," I said. "I can see stealing cars and lounging on Caribbean beaches being much more appealing than all that work."

He glanced at me. "I didn't *ask* to be a magician."

"And I didn't ask to be such a truly excellent PI, but there we go."

"It's why I always liked Callum. He gets it. He didn't want to be who he was, either."

"His family are a bunch of death-dealing, power-hungry murder merchants. It makes sense."

"And mine are a bunch of death-dealing, power-hungry magic-workers. See where we're going here?"

I huffed. I couldn't even begin to think of Ifan as being in the same situation as Callum. They were nothing alike. I peered out at the road instead. "We're almost there."

"Yeah." He turned down a side road, something that to the

casual observer would've looked like it was a dead-end, and more than likely the sort of place that brought about dead ends besides. Old buildings, the red brick stained black with the tainted city rain of decades gone, slouched on either side of the lane, radiating the energy of clumps of ousted drinkers outside pubs late on a Friday night. Windows gaped emptily or were boarded and blank, and the graffiti was monotone and indifferent, edges bleeding as if the painters hadn't been able to care enough to finish it. Weeds sprouted between broken walls and the patchy pavement, and a cat appeared in the middle of the road barely a car's length away, glaring straight at us.

I squawked, and Ifan slammed the brakes on so hard that I ended up in the footwell.

"Goddamn," he hissed, slipping the car into reverse. He'd barely touched the accelerator before he slammed the brakes on again. "Another one."

I leaped back onto the seat just as the two cats appeared on the bonnet, glaring in at us. Ifan swore, glanced behind him again, and floored it. The car went squealing backward, fishtailing for a moment before he got control of it, and I yelled, "*Stop!*"

"What? They're—"

"Not Watch," I said, as Pru stepped neatly out of the Inbetween and onto the seat next to me. There was a thud from the tiny back seat as Tam joined us slightly less elegantly, and Ifan brought us to a stop in the middle of the road, gripping the wheel in both hands. He leaned his forehead on it for a moment.

"Bloody hell," he muttered, the words slightly muffled. "My *heart*."

"Hey," I started, and Pru belted me on the snout with one paw. "*Hey!*"

She hissed, her tail whipping and her head low as she

glowered at me. With her hairless face all wrinkled up and her teeth showing, it was nothing short of terrifying. "You *sprouted mung bean,*" she snarled.

"Oh, come on—"

"You absolute *potato.* You ... you dregs from the bottom of a month-old litter box."

"Nice," Tam said.

"I was just—"

"You piece of mould on a beetroot sandwich. You insult of a vet visit. You ..." Pru drew herself up to her full height. "You cut-rate dog toy," she said, in tones of utter finality.

"Ouch," Ifan said.

"Does anyone really eat beetroot sandwiches?" I asked faintly, and Pru hissed at me again, close enough that I could feel her breath on my face. "Sorry. *Sorry!* But I knew you wouldn't agree with me going to Ifan, and I didn't even know if I should, or if we can trust him, and I wasn't sure if he might not try to turn me into a hamster, being a dodgy magician and all—"

"I am here," Ifan said.

"He *should* turn you into a hamster," Pru said. "*Cheese.* We've been carting stinking cheese over half of Leeds trying to find you."

"Sorry," I said again. "I hoped you'd sort of give it up when you realised I was gone."

"If you think that little of us, I'll throw you to the weres myself," she said.

"Or find you a human who likes crocheting little cat bonnets," Tam suggested. "With matching booties."

Ifan twisted in his seat to give her a curious look, but I just said, "Got it. I am the worst possible cat, and I deserve to never eat another roast chicken. *Ever.*"

"We should rub his nose in something," Tam said.

"Please don't."

Pru looked like she was considering it, then just said, "We were worried you might've gone into Dimly already, but we caught a bit of a trail from your shift. So we tracked you as far as Magic Boy's place, then lost you. He has a bit of a shadow – we couldn't really find you in it, and he's very hard to pinpoint, but we figured you'd come to Dimly. We've been following the borders while trying not to run into any weres or necromancers or anything else. *Very* safe."

"Sorry," I said again.

"Can you not call me Magic Boy?" Ifan asked.

"Trust me, it's the nicest thing I can call you," Pru said.

Ifan nodded, leaning back in the seat. "I've never done anything to you," he said, then shrugged when she glared at him. "I haven't."

"You don't need to," she said, her tail whipping. "I can *smell* you."

"What about Callum?" I asked Pru, before she could bite the magician. She looked tempted. "Any sign?"

"Nothing. But we were looking for you."

I hadn't really thought her answer would be any different, but my stomach still twisted sickly with it. I hadn't even pined for the cat biscuits left behind in our car, which shows I really was feeling unsettled. "Alright," I started, and Pru talked over me.

"If you do *anything* like that again I will personally feed you to a river monster. Got it?"

"The river monsters around here are pretty friendly," I started, then stopped again as she narrowed her eyes at me. "Right. No. Got it."

"You'd better. I'll find another river if I have to. Like the Styx."

"Understood."

"Dog sticks," Tam said, and huffed laughter. The three of us looked at her, and she looked back blandly.

"Right," I said. "Magic Boy says he's not in with the necros—"

"Will you *please* stop calling me Magic Boy?" Ifan said, and Pru spoke over him.

"And you trust him why, exactly?"

"Because we don't have any other options," I said. "We can't do this ourselves. And we can't wait for Ms Jones to find a bloody cat-sitter if Sonia and Ez have already got Callum. Or Kara does." I wasn't entirely sure which might be worst. "The OAP army might've fended her off, but you know they won't be able to keep hold of her."

"How do we know he won't just take us into Dimly and hand us over?" Pru asked, narrowing her eyes at Ifan.

"We don't," I said, and we all looked at the magician.

He shrugged. "I can't prove anything. You just have to trust me or not, but like Gobs says – you don't have many choices right now."

Tam looked at me. "Your call, Dog Sticks."

"Oh, come on. Gobs is bad enough."

"Try Magic Boy," Ifan muttered.

I looked though the windscreen, to where I could feel the edge of Dimly, its charms creeping across the earth, twining deep among the roots and worms and empty burrows, soaking the world around it with magic. Magic which was neither good nor bad. It just *was*, and it's what people do with it that counts. Like anything, really.

"You still got the cheese?" I asked.

"Left it by the bins," Pru said. "I was losing my sense of smell."

I turned to Ifan. "We can't just drive in."

"No," he agreed. "I was going to dump the car at the border and walk. I know some back ways that are usually less guarded."

"So do I," I said. "But you won't fit in them, so let's go your way."

"We could split up—"

"I definitely don't trust you that much," I said. "Let's get the cheese and go."

FIVE MINUTES later we stood at the border to Dimly, the crawling reach of the charms raising the hair on my back. At least my fur was dry – or had been. It was still raining, and while the MG had had some nice heated seats, it was the sort of dull rain that was already chilling my bones. Tam was drenched, but somehow rather than sticking to her and shrinking her down to normal cat size, she just shook herself occasionally and her fur stuck out in all directions, making her seem bigger than ever. She looked like an oversized, infuriated hedgehog. Pru just stood there with her ears back and rain dripping from her naked tail. Her utility coat looked to be warm as well as waterproof, and I wondered if she had a spare.

I shifted my grip on the cheese, the stink of it making my eyes water, then started forward. With no way to contact Yasmin or Ms Jones, we didn't have a plan other than *get in, find Callum, hopefully stop apocalypse while we're at it.* Which was a good plan overall, if rather lacking in specifics. But it wasn't like we had enough information to come up with anything better. All we knew was that there were necros about the place, Gerry was a prisoner, Ez (probably under the instruction of Sonia) was running things, and Kara was some sort of wild card. So not getting caught by anyone was high on the priority list, but everything else was in flux. However, a good PI is nothing if not adaptable. This was my cat house.

I walked forward, feeling the others following, and pressed through the barriers. I half expected to be thrown back, that Dimly had been locked against intruders, but there was just the familiar shiver of charms as I passed through them, a shift in pressure felt partly in my whiskers and partly at the back of my mind, and the feel of something dragging softly though my skin, prickly as midday sun. Then I was past them, into the strange light of Dimly, that was always just a touch brighter, or darker, or *something*-er than beyond its borders. Colours shifted a shade, edges were rendered a little sharper, shadows became a little deeper, and everything was made more real in a way I couldn't explain or define.

Which was all fine, but there was also the immediate reminder that one was in Dimly, which meant that I heard an explosion off to the left somewhere, a strange *pop* that suggested it hadn't quite occurred in this dimension, and a single yipping cheer went up that felt like it was probably accompanied by someone with too much hair and too few clothes dancing an angular, disjointed jig. Somewhere I could smell a cake baking, scented with a delightful under-current of burnt sulphur, and something with far too many legs went scuttling across a rooftop, only to be snatched into the sky by a drone with grabbing hooks that immediately vanished behind the roof again. The weeds leaned toward us hopefully from between the bars of a fence that seemed designed to keep things in rather than out, and Ifan pulled his woolly hat down over his ears, digging his hands into his coat pockets.

"Let's go," he said, and set off at a steady, sure pace, turning off the street into a tight little path that ran between the back walls of the houses, so close he almost had to turn sideways so he didn't scrape his shoulders. The pavement under-paw was cracked and slicked with mossy growth, and the houses were apparently trying to meet at the eaves.

Tam and Pru looked at me, and I took the deepest breath around the cheese I could manage without choking, then followed the magician.

Ifan led us in a winding, roundabout route that nevertheless tended inexorably toward the heart of Dimly. He stayed off the roads and kept to the winding footpaths and back ways that sneaked between houses and followed the beds of narrow little streams and drainage ditches, and cut through patches of unexpected wilderness that still flourished in secret, pockets in the heart of a pocket. Some were populated by trees so twisted and gnarled by age that they were more alien than familiar, pressing close to each other and cutting out the daylight even with their leaves thinned by winter, the earth under them dark and dank and cold. Things moved in the branches, chittered and whispered, and the scent of old earth magic was so deep and thick it made me lightheaded. Although that could've been the cheese, admittedly. At another point we waded through a field of grass and wildflowers that was midsummer high, insects buzzing and screaming, birds chattering, and despite the fact that I could look up and see the bleak winter sky, I could feel the weight of the sun on my back and the play of soft warm breezes about my ears. I didn't like it any more than the forest-y bits.

But finally we were into more familiar terrain, scuffed alleys that ran behind businesses and shops rather than houses, old pavement and dirt trails turning to cobbles, rambling yards and squat cottages giving way to taller buildings with featureless back walls and windows of wire-lined glass. The scents of bacon and beer and acrid potions, grease and engine oil and charms beaten into hot metal drifted from them, all muddled together and spilling across the cobbles. Ifan took one final turn then stopped, and we joined him, looking down a featureless stretch of alley with big commercial bins parked on one side of it. There was a T-junction at the very end, and the sheer wall of a big building rose up directly opposite it.

"That's the town hall," Ifan said. "I'd guess Gerry would be there, and they'll bring Callum too, if they've got him. Put them in the dungeons."

"The town hall has *dungeons?*" Pru asked.

"It's Dimly," Ifan said. "There used to be a torture chamber as well, but it got turned into a beer cellar a while back. Or they said it was," he amended. He adjusted his hat. "I don't know how we're going to find out if he's in there, though. Can't exactly walk up and say, hey, can we pop in and break out our mate?"

"You probably could," Pru said. "You did the whole necro thing."

"I did not," he said. "Not once I realised it was *actually* necromancers, anyway."

"Sure. Sounds convenient."

He scowled at her. "Do you have any idea how bloody tiring it is when *everyone* thinks you're a traitor? Everyone who's against the necromancers thinks you are one, and everyone who's with them thinks you're some sort of necro-hunter. There's not a single bloody person who thinks, oh, that's just Ifan, he's a magician who actually has no sodding idea what's happening, because *no one talks to him.*"

We all stared at him for a moment, then Tam said, "Aw. Poor wee Magic Boy," and Ifan gave her a look that suggested he might actually try turning her into a hamster, which I didn't fancy seeing. A giant, furious hamster was just what we didn't need.

So I hurriedly set the cheese down next to the grate in the centre of the alley and said as loudly as I dared, "Come on then, Pats."

"Pats?" Ifan demanded. "You want *pats* right now? What is *wrong* with you all?"

"No," I managed to swallow *you cabbage,* since he already looked like he quite fancied zapping a couple of spells at someone. "Patsy."

"Who?"

The answer came from the grate. "Ay up, Mogs. Bringer of mad tidings. What is it this time?"

"End of the world," I said.

"Can't get much madder than that."

20

ANARCHY! ANARCHY!

A SMALL, SNUFFLING NOSE EMERGED FROM THE GRATE, followed by a sleek rat body and a long, naked tail that was actually quite similar to Pru's. Patsy turned her good eye on us, the other lost to a scar that turned one side of her face into a permanent sneer. "So what're three cats and a magician doing loitering in the alleys of Dimly? Not very safe here for cats these days. Even less welcome than rats."

"Dimly's never been fond of cats," I said.

"No," Patsy agreed. "But there are cat catchers now. Traps and bags and wolves and men." She showed me her teeth, and I shivered.

"They're catching *all* the cats? Watch too?"

"You'd have to ask them. But you're the first I've seen in one piece for a while."

I looked at Pru, who just stood there with her tail twitching softly. It made no difference to us now, anyway. We had no choice but to be here. I turned back to Patsy. "We're looking for Callum. The tall gangly one."

"You lose him a lot. Bit careless, if you ask me." She

inspected the cheese, then passed it down into the grate, where small busy paws tidied it away. "Nice quality, that."

"I mean, *a lot*," I protested. "Not compared to how often I don't lose him."

"Compared to how often others lose their humans?"

"Well—"

"Do we have time for this?" Ifan asked.

"Yes," Tam and Pru said together, and he sighed, slumping against the wall.

"I guess cats work on a different timetable."

"The gathering of intelligence is the cornerstone of the PI business," I said, and he just raised his eyebrows and took his phone out, poking at it while I turned back to Patsy. "Have you seen Gerry?"

"Ah, the deposed mayor. The fallen emblem of a failed revolution."

"Sounds like him."

"He's in the dungeons."

"Is he alright?"

She made a non-committal sound, and a grey snout poked out of the grate next to her. "He's in *Dimly's* dungeons," the newcomer said. "What do you think?"

"Hey Ernie," I said, and the old rat dragged himself out, blinking at us myopically.

"Your boy's not in there, though."

"He isn't?" I tried to hide the disappointment in my voice. I'd been harbouring hopes we'd be able to march in with the magician, blast the town hall apart, rescue both of them at once and … Well, I hadn't thought beyond that, but *save the day* pretty much covered it.

"No, we've not seen him," Patsy said. "Plenty of his sister, though."

I growled, and she huffed rat laughter. "She's dancing to someone else's music, though. Most of them are. You need to find the piper, not the dancers."

"Sonia," I said.

"Unless she's just the pipe," Patsy said, and winked. "Thanks for the cheese, Mogs."

Ernie vanished back down into the grate, and Patsy turned to follow him. "Wait," I said. "What d'you mean, she's just the pipe?"

Patsy paused. "She plays the music, but she might not be the one who knows the tune, you know?"

"No," Ifan said. "Can you talk sense?"

She gave him the full benefit of her sneer. "Can you not piece it together, Magic Boy?"

"Oh, come *on*," he started, and I talked over him.

"How do we get into the hall, then? We need to get Gerry out."

Patsy looked down the alley at the building looming at the end, then at me. "Can't help you there, Mogs. But seeing as Gerry was pretty accommodating to rats, we'll meet you halfway. We can get him out of his cage. You get into the hall and take him the rest of the way."

"Done," I said. "I owe you an entire wheel of Stilton."

"For that we'll hang around a bit," she said, and winked her good eye at me. "It's always entertaining, anyway." Then she was gone.

I looked at the others. "It's a start."

Ifan nodded. "And then? We're going to need more than a start."

"Then we throw you at someone and see what happens," Tam said, and Ifan just looked at her for a long moment. Finally he laughed.

"You would as well," he said, and turned away, shoving his hands into his pockets. We followed him down the alley, heading for the town hall. So we still had no Callum. But at least if we could get Gerry out, the necromancers had one less card to play.

And having a troll handy was always going to be an advantage.

THERE WASN'T much point acting innocent about things. Unlike human towns, Dimly knew perfectly well that cats didn't just aimlessly wander about the place, accidentally turning up where they shouldn't because *oh, cats will be cats*. No, Dimly unfortunately knew that cats don't accidentally turn up anywhere, so we were going to have to go in fast, hope we weren't noticed, then bite anything that moved once we were. Of course, with my newly rediscovered shifting ability, that could've been a lot easier, but that option was somewhat curtailed by the fact that the entire town was shift-locked. No unfair advantages in pocket towns, although I'd argue shifting is pretty fair when you're a fraction the size of most of your opponents.

Ifan led the way around the pale stone of the town hall, the big, blocky building encircled by others more typical of Yorkshire – red brick and stone and a distinct dearth of fancy columns and double doors. The magician ignored the locked back door (it was *very* locked – someone had added three large hasps and padlocks to it, which was unsightly yet effective) and headed for the broad front steps that ran up to the huge double doors. No one stepped in front of us, or shouted to us to stop. The market square in front of the hall was surprisingly bereft of scheming necromancers or lurking wolves, which didn't make me feel as reassured as it might have. My whiskers were twitching with the sense of being observed, and the hair on my spine was at half-mast already.

Last time we'd been here there had been a market in the square, but now there was just a single cart selling jacket potatoes with various toppings. It was doing a desultory business, and the enticing scent of melted cheese and butter drifted to us in the damp air. The faun ladling beans onto a potato in a takeaway box didn't even look at us, and neither did the woman waiting, one scaly, clawed hand resting on the cart's counter. Dimly Folk were good at not noticing others.

Ifan didn't pause at the bottom of the steps, just walked straight up them with his hands in the pockets of his coat as if he were here on official magician business. I wondered briefly if he were simply delivering us into the paws of the enemy, but it was a bit late to worry about such things now. I trotted after him, and Pru and Tam came with me. I could feel their wariness in a twitchy echo of my own.

The building's columns and old stone walls were dull and damp with rain, and nothing seemed in any better repair than it had on our previous visit. Cardboard still blocked off a couple of broken panes in the big windows that overlooked the plaza, and some discarded beer cans and paper food bags were scattered along the stairs. Everything looked in need of a good clean, and I could see the faint shadow of writing that had been scrubbed off the doors. *Get Stoned Trolls*, it said, which was unlikely to be a friendly invitation to partake in some illicit substances.

Ifan pushed one of the double doors open, standing as well back as he could while he did it. It opened with a whine, letting onto a white-painted hall with a floor of old black and white marble tiles laid in a chequerboard pattern. A greeting booth sat off to the left, looking a bit lonely, and a broad set of stairs curled up to the floor above to the right.

"See if you can find the way to the dungeons," he said in a low voice, his eyes on the stairs, then walked in with his boots scuffing on the tiles and shouted, "Hello? Anyone home?"

We scattered without discussing it, Tam heading right, Pru though the open doorway to the left, and I shot straight ahead, to a door at the back of the hall. It was ajar, which was handy, as all the doorknobs in the place were those awful round ones that have no purchase for a cat's paws. Rude, but I understood Gerry's motivations in not changing them for something more cat-friendly. The Watch as it was now wouldn't have a lot of time for troll mayors. Even as it had been, really, other than certain more tolerant factions.

The door might've been ajar, but it was also jammed, and the gap was just a bit too narrow for me to wriggle through. I pressed my shoulder against the wood, squeezing my snout into the narrow space between door and frame and feeling my lips pull back from my teeth under the pressure. I scrabbled and clawed at the floor, and just as I heard someone shout, "*Hey!* What're you doing in there?", the door scraped reluctantly open enough to let me though.

I whipped through the gap, not waiting to check if it was me they were shouting out, or to see what was beyond the door, and found myself in a small white-painted room with dark blue, cracked tile floors and two big sinks. A drooping plant sat on a windowsill, leaves curling and brown, and three doors lined the wall on the left. One was open, revealing a surprisingly clean toilet, and I huffed in irritation. All that for a bloody toilet. I snuffled at the second door, but all I could smell was fake pine scent and bleach, so the odds were that was a second stall. I put my nose to the third door, prepared to be disappointed, and at first all I smelled was the same. But something snaked under the layered scents of cleaning products, something deep and dark and secret, and I hissed, "*Got you.*"

Then I looked at the door handle and realised that it not only had an annoying round knob, but a lock. Which made sense. I suppose there's not much point in having hidden dungeons if the door's left open. I jumped for the knob and tried grabbing it anyway, on the off-chance that some careless dungeon guard had left it unlocked, but I just slid straight off and back to the floor. I gave it another go, and this time managed to hang on for a bit, snarling under my breath, before my grip slipped and I dropped back down again. I glared at the knob, then turned and padded back to the bathroom door, poking my nose around to peer into the entrance hall. Ifan was standing just inside the front doors, his hands tucked into the pockets of his coat, while a skinny man and a woman with her hair pulled back in a thick plait stood with their backs to me, blocking his way further in.

"I want to talk to Ez," he said.

"She's not here," the man said.

"So I'll wait."

"You can't." The woman was poking at her phone.

"Pretty sure I can."

"Maybe you *can,* but we won't let you," the man said. He was wearing grey camouflage trousers and a utility vest with lots of loops and pockets that was nowhere near as fancy as Pru's. It also looked as though it'd slip off his skinny shoulders at any moment.

"I'm not sure you can really stop me," Ifan said, almost kindly.

The woman turned the phone toward the man. "It's him. The magician."

"I'd have told you that if you'd asked," Ifan said.

"Seize on sight?" the man asked.

"Please don't," Ifan said.

"Seize or incapacitate," the woman said, her eyes on the magician.

"Really, don't," Ifan said. "I don't want to hurt you."

The man barked laughter. "We're professionals, we are."

"Yeah, I know a couple of those," Ifan said, and his gaze

drifted to me. I jerked my head at the door, hoping he understood that I meant I'd found it, but was having some technical difficulties.

"Don't engage," the woman said, pointing at the phone.

"We should at least date first," Ifan agreed, and the woman gave him a glare I could feel from here. He grinned, then gave a sudden howl of pain, jerking forward as if someone had kicked the back of his legs. I smelled electricity and the singe of burned skin as he slammed to his knees, then pitched to the ground face-first, his whole body shaking.

"How's that for a date?" the man asked.

I blinked at Ifan. Neither of the two magic-workers had moved, but there were two wires protruding from the back of the magician's neck, and that had *not* sounded – or smelled – pleasant. There was a moment's silence, then a second woman slipped through the doors from outside. Bloody Kara. The OAP army definitely hadn't been able to keep hold of her, then. She'd swapped her long coat for an orange hoody that read *Old Ones Rise*, the shoulders damp with rain, and when Ifan moaned she keyed the device in her hand. He jerked again, giving a thin shriek.

"Incapacitated," she said, and the first woman fist-bumped her. I stared at them, unable to figure out what to do next. We'd had one advantage, and someone had shoved a cattle prod at him and taken him out without the need for any magic whatsoever. He'd not even let off one spell.

"Hairballs," I whispered, and on the floor Ifan shifted his head slightly, his gaze meeting mine. One hand twitched, and I heard the click of locks rolling in the stall door behind me, and something heavier clunked open beyond. I hesitated, wishing I could at least get Tam and Pru for some backup. But the two baby necromancers – or zap-happy henchpeople – were already trussing up the magician while Kara watched, her hand hovering over the controls of the zapper, and the odds were they'd be heading this way any moment to make sure their prisoner was still secure. If I wanted to try and get Gerry out, I was going to have to move.

I dived back into the bathroom, running to the third door. The knob had unlatched itself, and the door was resting on the jamb, allowing me to nose around it easily. A couple of buckets, a few mops, and a collection of industrial-sized jugs of cleaning stuff stacked on the floor greeted me, and shelves lined the back wall. They were stacked with paper towels and toilet rolls and cleaning sprays and air freshener type things, and the combined stink made me sneeze three times in quick succession. Once my eyes had cleared I scurried in, nosing around and searching for the thin trail of dungeon scent I'd caught before. For a moment I thought I'd been wrong, that I'd just broken into a cleaning cupboard and was going to come out of here empty-pawed. I could barely smell anything, the bleach-and-pine stench choking anything else, then I caught the whisper of a draught on my whiskers.

I followed it, pawing past stacks of unread *Dimly Monthly* magazines and *Folk Weekly* papers and dress catalogues, and found a crack that ran along the back corner of the room, across the floor and up the wall. I pushed my nose against it, and the crack became a gap. One more push and it was open enough for me to slip through, finding broad stone steps leading downward beyond. Excellent. Very dungeon-y.

I ran down the steps, taking them two at a time. The way was lit by old yellow bulbs in metal cages, set into the rough-hewn walls at regular intervals, and the floor was pretty well-swept for a dungeon. The stone was cold but dry, and the chill deepened as the passage dived deep under Dimly.

The stairs switch-backed twice, then opened onto a long, brightly lit corridor with metal doors to either side. They were more gates than doors, really, formed of old-fashioned iron bars with gaps more than big enough for a cat to pass through, should I have wanted to. The first one to my right was home to an astonishing array of kegs, barrels, and bottles of beer and spirits, and the smell was enough to set me sneezing again. To the left a whole other room had been built inside the cell, all glass walls and low lighting, and inside were shelves lined with books that looked as old as Dimly itself, as well as a large cabinet that seemed to hold cigar and tobacco boxes. Interesting, but unhelpful.

I moved on, finding a room full of filing boxes, the years labelled on them rather erratically, then another full of boxes that overflowed with tinsel, ribbon, fake tree branches, and baubles. Multicoloured glitter shone like ice on everything, including the floor of the corridor, and I could feel it coating my paws. Then there was a room that had a solid metal door rather than bars, and a whiff coming out of it that I tried not to smell. It felt like it could take root in my sinuses and haunt my nightmares, and I thought of Patsy saying, *there are cat catchers now*. I stuck to the opposite side of the corridor, which was given over to a cell where office equipment apparently came to die, stacked with computers that had to be even older than our long-lost laptop, plus a collection of dusty phones and dented filing cabinets and a couple of printers that looked a lot as if someone had been kicking them.

Finally I stepped out of the corridor and into a circle of cells that were definitely *cells,* short stone benches built roughly into the walls, and chains and manacles hanging above them. There were no windows, no cupboards, not even any toilets or basins, just drainage channels running around their perimeters.

"*Ew,*" I whispered, and heard some small movement to my right. I turned and saw Gerry.

His was the only cell occupied, and even with the halfway-decent lighting shed by the fat yellow bulbs above I'd almost missed him, his skin as grey as the stone. He knelt in the centre of the cell, head bowed, and the stumps of his horns looked dull and jagged in the unnatural light. I could see great scored wounds on his arms and shoulders, marring the intricate designs of his warrior tattoos, and I had an idea what had caused them. Troll skin's as tough as armour plating, but unicorn horn's as sharp as it is deadly. I couldn't even imagine how much it must have hurt.

I ran to the cell, slipping through the bars to stare up at him. "Gerry," I whispered, but he didn't look up. He didn't even move. Even close up he seemed smaller, despite his great slabs of muscle. Diminished without his pearls and twinsets.

"*Gerry*," I hissed. His hands and legs were manacled, just as we'd seen in the photo, and his eyes were closed. For one horrified moment I thought we were too late, then I saw the slow rise of his chest. He was breathing, slow and steady.

"Gerry?" I tried again, aware of Kara in the hall above, her hench-people probably already dragging the magician this way and finding the door open. "Gerry, dude, we have to go."

Although, having said that, I wasn't sure *how*. The magician's unlocking spell hadn't made it this far, and I could smell the charms and magic woven into the skin of the hall, locking it down tighter than the average cat lady's house (which is to say, Watch house, whether the cat lady knows it or not. Usually not). The cell was still locked, and, despite what Patsy had said, the manacles were still on, and so tight they'd worn gouges into his skin. A quick rescue wasn't looking like it was on the cards.

"Heads up, Mogs," a familiar voice said, and I turned to see Patsy had appeared in the drainage channel.

I made a little gagging noise before I could stop myself,

then said, "There you are. Have they knocked him out? What's going on?"

"Breathing practise," Ernie said, joining Patsy. "He's been teaching me. Pretty good really."

"Yeah. Breathing is," I said, wondering if Gerry wasn't as smart as I'd thought. Who had to practise *breathing?* Even trolls usually managed that. "What now? I thought you said you could help. I can't—"

I was cut off by a screech of metal and the crash of falling stone, near-deafening in the tight confines of the dungeon. I dived behind Gerry with a squawk as the entire front wall of the cell pitched forward, the metal bars ripping out of the ceiling and simply parting at floor level, as neatly as if they'd had a *tear here* label on them.

"Timmmberrr!" A chorus of rat shouts went up from the walls and ceiling, and when I looked up I spotted the channels they'd worked methodically through the mortar, until one hard shove was all it took. And enough motivated rats can make quite a shove. Most of them were still clinging to the stone above me, but a handful had ridden the bars to the floor and were chattering with glee.

"Anarchy! Anarchy!" one shrieked, and the rest cheered.

"I did say heads up," Patsy said, giving me that permanent sneer. She was definitely putting more effort into it right now though.

"How the hell," I started, and Gerry interrupted me.

"That was rather loud," he said, taking his wrist cuffs off. "Not terribly subtle, Patsy. I was going to cut through the others as soon as you got me a new blade. Shouldn't have been more than another couple of weeks."

I stared at him as he unlooped the manacles from his ankles.

"Sorry, Gaz," Patsy said. "Mogs here came charging in shrieking about the apocalypse—"

"I did not *shriek.*"

"—so your slow and steady escape had to have a rapid change of plans."

"Oh dear." Gerry stood up and stretched, wincing, then offered me a fist. I just stared at him.

"How—" I managed.

"Full story later," Gerry said briskly. "But one should always cultivate friendships with even the most overlooked of one's citizens."

"Right on," Ernie said.

I blinked at him. "The Anarchic Army sneaked tools in, okay. But the charms—"

Gerry grinned broadly. "Even charmed cuffs can be picked with the right tools, and even charmed metal can be sawed though with a decent supply of hacksaw blades and a very disgruntled disposition."

"Oh, hairballs," I said. "You didn't need rescuing at all."

"No," he said, and gave me his great craggy smile. "I had hoped you'd realise. But it was very nice of you anyway."

"Right," I shook my head, but there wasn't much else I could say, so I just went with "Right" again, more firmly. "Callum's missing, and I had hoped he'd be here. You haven't seen him, I take it?"

Gerry's smile vanished. "Oh dear. That's very bad news, Gobbelino."

"No baby goats."

The big troll nodded gravely and started to say something else, but Patsy interrupted him.

"*Heads!*" she bellowed, and I threw myself into the drainage channel, gross or not. Gerry dived for the back of the cell, and rats scattered everywhere as a fireball exploded right where we'd been standing.

"Bloody magicians!" I squawked, poking my head out of cover with my ears back.

But it wasn't the magician. He was still hanging mostly senseless – or appeared to be mostly senseless – between Skinny and Plait. Kara stood in front of them, her eyes fever-bright as she grinned at us. "Such a troublesome little kitty," she said. "In here breaking out prisoners. I think we'd better do something about that."

"For the gods' sakes, Kara," I complained. "Could you not have just stuck with unicorn rustling and a little recreational substance use?"

"You think too small," she said, and raised a hand. Fire dripped and coiled around it, and I flattened myself back into the drain. Thinking small seemed like a good move right then.

And then Tam came out of the corridor and hit Kara like she really thought she was a lion taking down a wildebeest, clawing her way straight up to the woman's neck. Pru was right behind her, and Kara's fireball gave a startled little jump, plopping off her hand and onto the ground, where it smouldered uncertainly.

"Your move, Mogs," Patsy said, by which I think she probably meant I was on my own now, but a certain portion of the rats had other ideas.

"*Anarchy! Anarchy!*" a very small one screeched, and half the pack took up the shout as they plunged forward, aiming for the hench-people, who promptly dropped Ifan and started stamping wildly at the tiny anarchists. Ifan's leg fell into Kara's fireball, and his jeans started to smoulder, and Gerry and I raced after the rats.

It was not going to plan, true. But it was going.

21

IN DIMLY, THE SIDE PICKS YOU

KARA MIGHT'VE BEEN DUST-SOTTED AND POWER-HUNGRY, BUT she wasn't silly. She caught the avalanche-like movement of Gerry as he barrelled toward her, gave up on trying to dislodge Tam and Pru, and sprinted for the exit. Skinny and Plait were still jumping around slapping at rats, and Gerry simply scooped Ifan up off the floor, tucked him under one arm, and thundered after Kara. Tam and Pru jumped clear of Kara as she fled, and the three of us loped after Gerry while the dungeons rang with shrieks of *"Anarchy!"* and *"Down with the establishment!"*

"Do you think they're enjoying that a bit much?" Pru asked me.

"It's always good for little anarchists to blow off some steam," I replied, as we reached the stairs and followed Gerry's charge up them. Above, there was a heavy slam as Kara tried to shut us in, followed by the sound of the dungeon door being removed unceremoniously from not just its hinges, but the entire wall. Something *whoomph*-ed, and hot light exploded across the ceiling. Gerry snarled.

Rather than stopping like sensible cats, we ran faster, in

time to see Gerry crash through the cupboard door and part of the wall that led into the bathroom. He had the heavy dungeon door from the back of the cleaning closet held out in front of him like a shield, clutching it by the handle, which looked like it was going to part ways with the rest of the door very shortly. Ifan was still tucked under his other arm, and another explosion of fire came from the hall outside.

"Stone-skinned *monster*," Kara shouted, her voice tight with fury, and fire licked at the corners of Gerry's door. The flames were catching, but he just kept marching grimly forward, shattering the edges of the doorway to the hall.

"Impressive," Tam observed.

"He did say he currently had a disgruntled disposition," I said.

"I'm going to be worried if he ups it to *mildly irritated*," Pru said.

There wasn't much we could do to help, so we just followed, keeping an eye out for Kara's hench-people to follow us, but apparently the anarchy was persisting in the dungeon. Screams of rat-induced panic were still drifting up the stairs. Gerry drove Kara ahead of us all the way out of the bathroom and onto the marble floor at the back of the entrance hall, and then I ran forward, yelling up at him.

"Gerry! Gerry, *stop!*"

"*What?*" He looked down at me, scowling. Never mind that Gerry without elegant drop earrings and a nice neckline just didn't seem like Gerry – scowling Gerry was enough to make my tail pouf and me take a step back.

"Do we have plan? We've still got some cover here. If we get right out into the foyer and she's got more backup, they might get around behind us."

Gerry started to say something, his brows drawn down heavy and furious, and the door handle chose that moment to give out. The door slipped and pitched to the floor, leaving us exposed to Kara, who gave a wordless yell of triumph. She hurled the fireball she'd had resting on her fingertips even as I bolted toward her, teeth bared. It skimmed my back, giving me a belt of heat and a whiff of scorched fur, and Pru yelled, "Gobs, *drop!*"

I didn't think about it, even though the missile had already passed. I just went down mid-run, throwing my side to the floor and rolling twice under my own momentum as I slid across the slick tiles. The fireball rebounded from something and roared back toward Kara, passing close enough that I squinted against the heat. I looked back and saw Ifan on his knees next to Gerry, one hand out, the other clutching his ribs as if someone had sneaked a kick in there at some point. It wouldn't have surprised me. They were that sort. And, to be fair, I would've been tempted too. *He* was that sort.

Kara had dived for the floor at the same time as me, the fire sweeping above her in a wave, stretched out by the impact with Ifan's blocking charm. It kept going until it hit the front wall, blowing the rest of the window glass out and setting the front doors alight.

"*Incoming!*" a small voice screamed from behind us, and Gerry bounded to his feet. He spun around, huge arms wide and the massive slab of his torso streaked with tattoos and dark smears of blood, seeming to fill the whole dim-lit foyer with pure, visceral troll rage. The effect was only slightly marred by the fact that he was sparkling with a light coating of glitter we'd picked up on the way through the dungeons.

He *roared* as the hench-people raced out of the toilets behind us, and my ears flattened and my back went up of its own accord. Someone screamed outside, and a piece of ceiling panel fell and smashed next to him, but, to give them points for bravery, Kara's buddies kept coming. I was definitely taking points off for having no sense of self-preservation though. Gerry took two strides forward, grabbed one of them around the waist in each hand, and strode back toward the toilets while they flailed like a couple of life-size dolls. He shoved them into the bathroom, picked the fallen door up and jammed it firmly into the gap, then turned back to face us.

Kara had retreated to the front doors, fire playing across her fingers, but it looked weak and uncertain, not congealing into a ball. Her face was drawn, and I was willing to bet she was in need of another hit of unicorn dust. She didn't have the power to keep going indefinitely, and she'd already been playing with magic at the OAP headquarters. Ifan climbed slowly to his feet, swaying, and Kara looked at him. "Come on, Ifan," she said, her voice wheedling. "What're you doing hanging out with cats and trolls? You're better than that."

Ifan looked at Gerry, then at us. "I don't have a problem with it."

"You should. They're not your sort. *Our* sort."

"I don't think I'm your sort either," he said.

"Of course you are. We were friends, remember?"

"You were just Art and Rory's little sister," he said. "And you were a pain then, as well."

She tried for a smile. "Come on, though. There's still time. Pick the right side. It's all you have to do."

"I don't *want* a side," he said, almost plaintively.

Tam snorted so loudly that it echoed in the hall, and she looked around as if impressed by the acoustics, then said, "Neutrality's not always an option. Sometimes sides choose you."

"Where's Callum?" I asked Kara, and she grinned.

"Has the poor little cat lost his human? I wondered why you were hanging about with the magician."

"*Where is he?*" I snarled, picking my way toward her with my ears back and my head low. "I swear to every cross-eyed, toothy god of small angry things that I'll take your eyes out through your toes unless you tell me."

"Nice," Tam murmured, falling into step with me.

"You can't threaten me. You're *cats*," Kara said, but her eyes shifted uneasily from me to Tam, then to Pru as she joined us, all of us full of teeth and claws and the promise of, if not mortal injury, then certainly a very painful and somewhat bloody interval.

"Tell them," Gerry rumbled, following us with his feet hard and bare on the slick floor, his arms hulking at his sides and his scarred body built of slabs of muscle on muscle on hard stone bone.

"Stop," Ifan said from behind us, but my eyes were on Kara.

"Where is he?"

She looked at me thoughtfully, then gave that grin again, curled so prettily at the corners but laced with cruelty. "No idea," she said. "But I know how we'll get him here." Her hand shot out, and I tried to go sideways, but Tam was there and it was like hitting a wall. Something closed around me so tightly it felt as if my insides were being crushed, and jerked me off my feet. I flew toward Kara, not even able to cry out, as spots swam in my vision and my breath locked in my throat. The force of the grip smooshed me into her chest, and I smelled soot and sweat and need and the sour, burnt energy of hard-won magic, sickly hot, and under it all a terrified, furious determination.

The vice eased enough that I could manage a breath, and she tucked me under one arm then grabbed for the door, heaving at it. It opened slightly, then slammed shut again, and she snarled, running to the nearest window. The edges were still crusted with glass, but she grabbed the sill with her free hand anyway. I don't know how she thought she was going to get over with me still in one hand, but I'd recovered enough to bite her, which put a crimp in matters, then Gerry lifted her away from the window with both hands under her armpits, like she was a toddler making a run for the road.

"Don't you touch me!" she shrieked, dropping me to concentrate on fighting Gerry, but she might as well have been fighting a stone gatehouse. Even the little splats of fire she managed to conjure just splashed across his arms, making him grumble but nothing worse. *"Get your dirty stone hands off me!"*

I took a couple of tentative breaths, checking for broken ribs, and looked at the troll. "Put her in the dungeons?" I suggested.

"Seems safe enough," he agreed, and turned to head that way.

"Wait," Ifan said, frowning.

"What? We're not *keeping* her," I said, watching the magician stagger to the doors. His feet didn't seem to be entirely under his own control just yet, and sweat beaded his forehead.

"No, I just … there's something," he said, reaching for the door, and I felt the pressure in the room change. Not drop, not rise, just *change,* as something arrived that shattered the fabric of the world, made it move in strange and unfamiliar ways.

"Don't!" I yelled, and the door exploded inward, taking Ifan with it as it flew across the room. Gerry dropped Kara and snagged Ifan before he could hit the unforgiving metal of the stair banisters, and Tam, Pru and I went skating across the floor as if it had suddenly become an ice rink, not stopping until we fetched up against the far wall. Kara tried to keep her feet, but after a moment's struggle she tumbled to the floor and was swept after us. Only Gerry stood solidly in the middle of the room with the magician in one hand,

looking a lot like he was considering skipping *irritated* and going straight to *ticked off*.

There was an instant of stillness as we all came to rest, and I could hear my breathing rattling. Nothing was on fire around us, at least. It had just been that sudden and ominous *change*, like a storm front coming in, which I could still feel in my trembling whiskers and the tightness of my chest. Then someone appeared in the doorway.

"Oh dear," Sonia said. "Kara, what *shall* we do with you?"

"They were breaking Gerry out," she said, scrambling up. "I was trying to stop them."

"Is that so? After your little scrap at the storage units this morning, I thought you might be …" Sonia trailed off, as if considering her words, but her eyes were bright and amused, and I was reminded of the way some cats will play with rats. Not for the fun of it. Just because cruelty was bred deep into their bones and they didn't care enough to overcome it. "Shall we say *playing your own game?*"

"I was showing *initiative*," Kara snapped, but I caught the flicker of fear in her face, and I was sure Sonia did too. "Not just sneaking around hoping no one noticed. We're *necromancers!* We shouldn't be *sneaking!*"

Sonia looked at her levelly. "Discretion, my dear, is not the same as *sneaking*. And *we?* You're a spoilt child playing in things you don't understand."

"This is *my* town," Kara said.

"Now we all know that's not true."

Kara started to say something, and Sonia flicked her hand lightly. There was the ringing sound of a slap, and Kara hissed, raising one hand to her cheek. It was reddening rapidly.

"Children need to learn their place," Sonia said. "Now, what on *earth* has happened here, Kara? Was it old people again, such as bested you at the storage unit? Very challenging, the senior citizens."

"Rats," I said, getting up and padding across the floor to stand next to Gerry. "Never underestimate a good anarchic rat."

"Rats?" Sonia asked.

"It was him," Kara said, pointing at Ifan. "He busted the troll out."

"To be fair, Ifan was unconscious for most of it," I said, and Kara glared at me. "The rats did most of the busting."

Sonia raised an eyebrow. "Really? *Rats?*"

Ifan chuckled. Gerry had set him on his feet and he was standing almost straight, but was clutching one of the troll's massive shoulders for support. "He's right. I was out cold for most of it."

"Well." Sonia gave that lovely, warm, *we're all friends here* smile. "You probably should have stayed out cold, to be honest."

"No," Ifan said, raising his free hand with the index finger up as if he were about to give her a good telling off. "No, I'm not—" His words became a shriek, his back arching as he was ripped away from Gerry and slammed to the floor. He made a small, aching noise and curled in on himself like a woodlouse exposed to the light.

"Yes, I don't think we want you conscious," Sonia said. "You'll be a very nice little vessel, but you're most troublesome."

Tam came off the stairs in one giant bound. I don't know how she'd got up there, but she was soundless as she plunged toward the necromancer. Sonia didn't even glance at her, just flicked her hand and Tam reversed direction mid-air. Gerry reached up and caught her as neatly as he had Ifan and set her on the ground next to the magician.

"Stop it," he said, his voice a grumble.

"I would not suggest you try making me, troll," Sonia said. "You have no chance." She looked at us. "None of you do."

"There's always a chance," I said, with as much conviction as I could manage.

She gave me that gentle smile again, and stepped away from the door. "Why don't you come outside and see if your opinion changes at all."

We looked at each other. Kara nudged Pru with a boot and Pru spun on her with her face contorted in such fury that Kara stepped back, bumping into the wall. I moved first, walking past Gerry and Ifan, who was motionless on the floor. I looked up at Sonia as I stopped on the threshold.

"Just for the record, I've met far better people in the bottom of Dimly's sewers than you. And I'm pretty sure most of the weird little shrimpy things living in the dark down there that I didn't *want* to meet would be better, too."

"Your definition of better and mine differs, I fear," she said, and waved me out like some besuited servant showing royalty into the room for tea.

"I'm glad," I told her. "I wouldn't want to share yours." I walked out the door with my head and tail high, even if my whiskers were twitching a little uncontrollably. I stopped at the top of the broad steps and waited while Tam and Pru joined me, then Gerry with Ifan over his shoulder.

"I'm so glad you brought the magician," Pru said, glancing at him. "He's been very useful."

"He was a good distraction," I said.

"I think we may need something more than that."

I looked out at the plaza, and I couldn't disagree with her.

The jacket potato van was still there, but the faun running it had vanished, and I could smell burning cheese. I didn't blame them for clearing out. The plaza was full, packed to capacity with people standing shoulder to shoulder. And those people weren't ... well. Maybe I'm using people in the wrong sense here. It was an army. Not lined up nice and neat like a human sort of army, or dressed in matchy-matchy gear, but an army nevertheless. I couldn't see down all the side streets, but the ones I could held even more figures, all still, all silently waiting. With such a huge, clustered mass of people, there should've been a whisper of shuffling, of clothes brushing against skin as weight shifted, or at least the sense of hundreds of hearts beating, hundreds of lungs filling and emptying, even the odd stomach gurgling its way through breakfast. There was nothing. The army was completely, utterly still, and the only noise was the very, very distant sound of glass breaking somewhere.

But to be fair, the only ones who were actually doing any breathing or heart-beating or digesting were a couple of dozen magic-workers standing on the steps, looking impatient. The rest, the entire army, were dead. Or undead. Not alive in the traditional sense, anyway.

"Have we got him?" one of the magic-workers asked. She was wearing an inadvisable amount of black leather under a broad-brimmed leather hat and a long leather coat, and I was certain she'd call herself something like *Hawk*, even if her mum had probably called her Ermentrude. For all that, I could smell power on her. Nothing like Sonia-level, or even Kara's fragile, dust-induced strength, but enough that she probably wasn't entirely delusional. The short, balding man next to her, on the other hand, wearing well-ironed beige trousers and a red waterproof jacket zipped up to his chin, looked like he was called Tony and smelled like he could probably break her in half with a thermos cup of tea in one hand and a cheese-and-pickle sandwich in the other. He coughed mildly into a handkerchief.

"No," Sonia said, and Hawk clenched both hands into fists.

"We're not still waiting, are we? We have the army, we have the town, we—"

"I hope you're not questioning me," Sonia said, her voice mild, and Hawk stopped speaking. I could almost hear her biting her cheek from here.

"She is right," someone else said, and I jumped, looking around for the speaker. "We shall start without him."

"I don't advise that, Lord," Sonia said.

"I will take that into account." A figure that looked an awful lot like Ifan's dad, and even sounded a little like him, unfolded himself from a golf cart that was parked at the bottom of the steps. He moved in the stilted, uneasy way of something not quite comfortable in its skin, and kept one hand on the cart for balance.

"Aw, dude," I said, and looked at Sonia. "That bloody Old One got through after all, didn't it?"

"Of course," Sonia said. "One small setback is not enough to stop what we've set in motion. You didn't think you were so special, did you, that you could stop such a grand movement?"

"Well, I am pretty special," I said. "How'd you get out of old Lewis' cellar, then? We were sure we'd closed the door through to your gloopy orange dimensions."

"A decent magic-worker always has an escape route and a backup plan," Sonia said, and smiled at me. "Lewis was a *very* good magic-worker. And I'm even better."

"And now you've got an undead army," I said, looking over the motionless, unbreathing mass. "Bit more well-behaved than the first lot."

"The technique needed a little refining," she said. "But now all we need to do is open the gate fully and allow the rest of the glorious Old Ones through to inhabit these vessels. The time of necromancers has come. The Watch is broken, all but wiped out. Humanity shall fall. Those who assist us will be rewarded. The rest shall be used as we see fit."

"You can't," Gerry said. "You can't pick and choose like that. No one kind is better than any other."

"But don't humans act as if they are? Don't they act like they're better than *you*, Mayor Troll?"

"Only because they don't know any better." He fixed her with a severe look. "*You*, however, should know better."

"I do," she said. "I know humans are remaking the world in their own image. They'll break it to pieces without a care for any of the rest of us. And there's enough Folk who agree with me, too."

"Are there?" I said. "I don't see any of them." The magic-workers were exclusively human, and the only other creatures in view were the dead.

"Well, they will agree with me," she said. "No one ever wants to get their hands dirty." She gave me pointed look. "Or paws."

"Gods," I said. "You've taken out the rest of the Watch, haven't you? You pretended you'd help them push through a military bloody coup in exchange for letting you kill off the Old Guard, and then you did them over. This isn't some grand Folk revolution against humanity. You're just some megalodon … megalithic … megalopolis …"

"Megalomaniac," Gerry said helpfully.

"That."

She laughed, a joyous little sound, and smiled at me. "Cats are ever blinded by their own sense of superiority, like so many others. Your grand Watch never expected they would be laid low by necromancers." She looked away. "And now we merely have your irritating North to deal with."

"We don't need him," Ez said, her voice flat, and I spun to look at her. She was standing to one side of the hall doors, her feet unaccountably bare and cold-looking, and her arms folded over her chest. I hissed, but she didn't look at me. "You've got me." She looked at Sonia. "I told you. Leave Callum out of it. I'll do what needs doing."

"You're nothing," Hawk spat from the steps. "Even I can see that. There's no magic in you."

Ez looked back at her steadily, and I could see dark shadows under her eyes. They made her look too much like Callum. "No. But I *am* the North."

"We will start," Not-Lewis said. He had tottered his way up the steps to stand in front of the wall of the town hall.

"We should find the other North," Sonia said. "He's been a problem all along."

Not-Lewis looked at her, then said, "I am tired of your *caution*. It is time."

Sonia looked like she was about to argue, then just tipped her head. "As you wish, Lord."

I felt that pressure shift again, and Not-Lewis reached a hand out, closing it around nothing. Then quite abruptly there was *something*, and a little groan nipped out of me.

"The *scythes*," I whispered.

"It's all we needed," Sonia said. "Just a little nudge."

Not-Lewis swung the scythe, and it slid straight into the wall of the town hall. He dragged it around, his arms shaking with the effort, forming an arch that looked drawn in some ink the shade of the void. The pale brick shuddered, suddenly less hard-edged and more pliable, as if the laws of physics had nipped out back for a smoke and left things unattended. I had the sense of the wall thinning – not the hall's wall, the *world's* wall – and a sickly orange hue started to crawl across everything, as if a nuclear sunset were rolling under the clouds, hours too early.

"Oh, not a-bloody-gain," Pru said, and rushed Not-Lewis with her ears back.

"*Pru!*" I shouted, and Not-Lewis lifted his hand casually,

flicking her straight into the soggy wall. There was a little *blip*, heard in the back of the mind, and she vanished.

"*You sodden great sandwich!*" I roared, and leaped at him, but Tam was ahead of me, and the Old One still didn't have great control of Lewis' body. He stumbled as Tam hit him, and fell sideways. I collided with them both and we tipped straight though the wall.

Everything went both intensely hot and painfully cold, roaring with deafening sound and so silent it almost broke me, and I was drowning in pressure and entirely weightless all at once. Everything was a confused whirl of sensation, and I didn't know if my mind would snap or my heart stop first, only that I couldn't stand it, *no one* could stand it.

And then it was thankfully, impossibly gone, and I was tumbling across the broad top step with the blissfully damp and grey Yorkshire air clammy as salt on my fur. Tam's legs were tangled up with mine, her ears flat and her eyes wide, and I looked around to see Gerry with everything above his hips immersed in the wall. One hand emerged with Pru cupped in it, her ears back and her teeth still bared as if she'd frozen that way, then he pushed himself out of the weird dimensional tear awkwardly, breathing hard.

I looked around at the unmoving army of the dead, who weren't looking at anything, and at the magic-workers, who were all watching us with their eyes wide. All except for Tony, who was buffing his fingernails with a metal file, looking bored. I decided I didn't like Tony.

"Right, then," Sonia said. "Shall we continue?"

I blinked at her. "We just shoved your Old One back. Gerry did. Game over and all that."

"Oh, no," she said, and smiled, nodding at the wall. "He returns. They *all* return."

I turned back to the wall in time to see Not-Lewis step through, no longer stumbling, walking tall and straightening his tie as he came, the scythe held casually in his other hand. And behind him, crawling and walking, oozing and scuttling, came the twisted golden forms of ancient, rotting almost-gods, the deathless memories of necromancers who had always, *always* known they were owed worship and sacrifice, and who would never, ever die.

"Oh, wormy lettuce in gravy," I whispered.

Tam said something I'd have tried to remember for later, if I'd thought there was going to be one.

22

HERE FOR THE SCRAP

THE MISSHAPEN, BLOBBY, GOD-MONSTERS SPREAD OUT, scuttling toward the waiting undead, and the magic-workers stepped aside hurriedly, making room for them. Even Tony put his nail file way, his mouth twisting in disgust. As the Old Ones reached an undead they'd sink into them, and the bodies started to jerk and flail as the creatures tried to figure out how to drive them. Not-Lewis walked among them, muttering encouragement. Or nasty spells, more likely.

I turned to Ez. "This is *your* fault," I hissed at her. "You let them in here!"

"Maybe if there had been more Norths we could've done something," she said. "Your lot didn't give me much choice in the matter."

"The Watch threw me to the beasts too. *I'm* not resurrecting dead monsters."

She looked around, her face drawn. "Where's Callum?"

"Doing stuff," I said, with as much conviction as I could. At least I could rule out him being trapped in some Ez-cage.

"Oh, great. You've lost him? Bloody hell." She rubbed one

hand over her face, then as Sonia turned to her she nudged me with one bare foot and said in a low voice, *"Find him."*

"Not for you," I hissed back, and ran to where Ifan was lying on the steps. I pawed his face. "Oi! Magic Boy! On your feet. We need some firepower."

Ifan mumbled, clawing at the ground. Gerry looked from the Old One to the wall, where creatures were still flopping and scraping through the suddenly porous stone, then lowered his head and charged. He didn't go straight for the gap, but hit the wall to the side, crashing into it with such force he rebounded, staggering a little. The impact sent splits sprinting across the wall, mortar crumbling and brick shifting. One of the splits ran right across the orange portal, and it hardened into a lightning strike of grey stone, forcing a couple of Old Ones to retreat, although more kept coming around it.

"Honestly," Sonia said, and reached out with one hand. I thought she was grabbing for Gerry, and I sprinted toward her, but she made a little twitching movement, and a scythe appeared in her hand to match the one Not-Lewis was wielding. She swirled it lightly through the air, and I heard the sound of dust motes parting under the blade as she turned to Gerry. "You're all such a bunch of annoying beasts."

I very much wanted to not rush the scary necromancer holding a stolen scythe, but I also had no intentions of standing by while she chopped Gerry into little bits. So I launched myself at her, teeth and claws bared, and just hoped she wasn't too accurate with the blade work. Tam and Pru rushed after me, and Gerry ignored us all. He charged the wall again, and from inside the hall I heard a rousing chant of *Anarchy!* growing in numbers and volume. I latched onto Sonia's arm as rats washed out of the double doors, poured down the steps, and surrounded the magic-workers like a rising tide. For all their big-magic looks, the necromancers were apparently not too keen on being swarmed by rodents. They squeaked and stamped and danced away from the steps, trying to shake off the united assault of far more rats than I've ever encountered in the sewers of Dimly. Told you they were good sorts, kraken cults aside.

Half a dozen of them swarmed Sonia with us, and she gave a growl of irritation, trying to pull us off with one hand while she clung to the scythe with the other.

"Disarm her!" I shouted, and Tam, who had apparently been trying to see if she could decapitate the necromancer by gnawing on her spine, scrabbled over her shoulder and onto her scythe arm.

Kara staggered toward us, her legs encased in a hairy mass of rats. Her eye kept twitching, probably because her jeans weren't giving her much protection against a load of sharp little teeth. "Give it to me!" she shouted at Sonia, pointing to the scythe. "Give it to me and I'll help you take them down!"

Sonia glared at her. "I'd no sooner give you a scythe than kiss that troll."

"Rude," Pru said, and Sonia gave a furious snarl. She threw her arms wide, and power came burning off her, a swell of charms that spread like an explosion, crisping fur and singeing noses. There was no way to hold on in the face of it. My claws tore out of the necromancer's sleeve and I was thrown down the steps by the pulse of power, Pru tumbling in the opposite direction. Even Tam lost her grip, and Sonia shook herself off, adjusting the neck of her fur-lined white jacket.

"Beasts," she repeated, and turned back to Gerry.

Gerry slammed into the wall again, and this time the window frame next to the wobbly portal collapsed, coming down in a tumble of stone that spread into the gap. It blocked it, a physical barrier to the tear in reality, and a squiggly golden creature was crushed beneath the debris with a startled squeal. I caught a glimpse of Not-Lewis turning back with a frown as I scrambled to my feet at the bottom of the stairs. He started to stroll through the crowd back toward the hall.

I looked around, my sides aching, and found myself eye to eye with Tony's sensible slip-on shoes. I felt his hand reaching for me rather than saw it, and jerked my head up to see a small smile curving his pale lips. I leaped at his face with my teeth and claws bared, making him stumble back with a snarl, then twisted away and raced up the steps, barely avoiding Gerry crashing down them. Kara was plucking at Ez's arm, but Ez was just standing there, arms crossed, not moving to help either side. Her face was pale and set, and her bare feet were planted wide on the stone. Sonia glared down at Gerry, and Not-Lewis drifted past her to place his hand back on the portal. The barrier Gerry had created crumbled to dust, and the way was open once more.

"Hairballs," I hissed, and turned to survey the crowd. The magic-workers were still trying to deal with the rats, but there were a lot less four-pawed anarchists now than there had been. My stomach clenched at the thought, and I hoped they'd taken their chance and run rather than … well, anything else. At least half of the undead were inhabited by Old Ones already, and more gold forms were passing down the chain of unmoving corpses and vanishing into the side streets. The ones that had started to figure out how to control their new bodies were moving unsteadily away, making wobbly grabs for the rats as they drifted out of the plaza in search of whatever nasty old god-things ate. Hopefully not rats, or anyone else, but I doubted they were after fish'n'chips.

And there were too many of them. We had no way to stop them, no way to fight them, and I couldn't even tell Callum that we'd missed our chance. That the end of the world was coming and we hadn't so much as faced it down together. Not that it would've helped, but it seemed like the sort of thing one should do. Tam joined me on one side, Pru on the other, and we stood shoulder to shoulder as we looked out over the orange-tinted crowd.

"Well, damn," Tam said.

"Seconded," Pru said.

Gerry pushed himself slowly up to sitting, and the magic-workers around him shuffled away, except for Tony, who had his nail file out again and was doing something fancy with it, teasing blood out of his fingertips.

"Gerry, move!" I shouted. "Anorak there's up to something."

Gerry looked at Tony and *roared,* and Tony bared his teeth in an ugly little grimace, but stepped behind one of the younger magic-workers, out of sight.

"*We rise!*" Sonia shouted, and the shout came back from the magic-workers, and the throats of those undead who were still around and had got a bit of a handle on things. Their speech was a little garbled, but the meaning was clear enough.

"*We rise!*"

"Steady on," a new voice said from behind us, and I jerked around to see Rita, Lulu helping her get the wheelchair across the rubble in the doorway. "I've got something to say about all this *rising.*"

"And why was the back door locked?" Duds demanded. "It's the only accessible entrance point to the town hall and it's *locked?* Standards, people. Standards."

"What," Sonia started, then shook her head. "What are the retirement home escapees doing here? How did you even get into Dimly?" No one answered her, and she glared at Ez, who shrugged.

"Charms are tighter than ever. I'm doing my bit."

"Your bit to bring on the apocalypse?" I asked her. "Nicely done, mange-worm."

"I told you I didn't have any help," she said, shifting her feet slightly. They were pale and pinched-looking.

"Isn't it a mite?" Pru asked.

"Possibly," I said.

"No, a mite. As in a little bitey thing."

"*Shut up,*" Sonia snarled at us.

"Or what?" I asked. "Can things really get much worse?"

"Stop," Not-Lewis said, and quite abruptly I was suspended in mid-air, without anyone's hand anywhere near me. I gave an undignified squawk.

"You had to say it," Tam said.

"*Put him down!*" Duds roared, and treated Not-Lewis to a generous squirt from his water cannon. The grip on me released, and I dropped back to the ground, panting. I'd caught a splatter from the water cannon, and I sniffed curiously. It didn't smell of garlic.

"The human things are annoying me," Not-Lewis said, and pointed at Sonia. "Deal with them."

"I am, Lord," she said.

"Quickly. The portal is not working properly, and I am ..." He thought about it. "*Irritated.*"

Sonia nodded and swung back to the OAP army. "How did you get here?" she demanded again.

Noel had walked out onto the steps and was standing rocking gently on his heels. He was wearing a black jumper with one arm pinned up, and black jeans, and had a hat pulled down over his ears. "Drove," he said.

"Oh, for the Old Ones' sakes— *Kara!*"

"I didn't bring them," she protested. "I had the situation in hand."

Lulu snorted so loudly that she broke into a wheezing cough and took her cigarettes out.

"I showed them," Tristan said, popping his head around the door of the hall.

"Oh, well done, then," Sonia snapped. "You've showed them to their deaths."

"Oh, no. We brought friends," Lulu said, and for a moment I thought she meant the knife she was twirling in her fingers, but Singlet appeared behind her, still wielding his frying pan. He looked at the crowd, sniffed, and spat on the steps.

"Excuse you," Gerry said. He had a magic-worker tucked under each arm, where they were struggling valiantly to free themselves, but with no sign of progress. Singlet looked at him blandly.

"Him?" Sonia said, and looked at Kara again. "This is what you had so much trouble with? A bunch of geriatrics and some base alchemist?"

"At least I was *doing* something," Kara snapped, and abruptly put two fingers in her mouth and whistled. It was a sharp, high sound, and off in the streets a howl went up. Others answered it, pocking the town, and she grinned as she looked at Not-Lewis. Her eyes were bright, the skin stretched taut on her cheeks, and I had an idea she'd helped herself to a unicorn dust top-up from somewhere. "And I've been making friends. Princess bloody Sonia there's just been hanging around in her flashy clothes, pretending to be some sort of queen of the undead. *I've* been working. *I've* been doing all the dirty jobs. *I'm* the one you should be counting on."

"Silly child," Sonia started.

"*I am not a child!*" Kara screamed, and threw one hand out, the strain visible in her neck and shoulders as she reached for something none of us could see. I saw Not-Lewis' eyes narrow just slightly, then he twitched one finger, a tiny, barely noticeable movement, and suddenly Kara had a scythe in her hand. She was so startled she almost dropped it, then clutched it to her chest fiercely. "Yes," she said, her voice suddenly soft. "See, I can claim one too."

"Rubbish," Sonia said, shooting a look at Not-Lewis, but his borrowed face was perfectly expressionless. Behind him, the gate continued to disgorge more Old Ones, and at the edges of the crowd wolves started to appear, heavy muscular beasts with sharp eyes and sharper teeth.

"Who holds to me?" Kara demanded, not looking away from Sonia. She raised her voice, a wild and furious note in it. *"Who holds to me?"*

"Not liking this development," I said to Pru.

"I haven't liked any developments today," she said, then considered it. "This last year, possibly."

"That's reasonable," I said.

Kara glanced at the crowd. "Well?" she demanded.

"I do," Hawk shouted suddenly. "I'm with you, K!"

"Me too!" Plait shouted, and then a smattering of other voices rose, uncertain but clear, putting their patchy magic behind the young woman with the enormous scythe, facing down a necromancer queen.

"How boring," Sonia said with a sigh. "Always someone getting ideas above their station, and always me having to deal with it."

"Come on then," Kara hissed. "Come on and give it a go."

Singlet scratched his chest, hoicked noisily, and spat onto the steps again. "I'm all for them offing each other, but I came here for a scrap, like."

"Oh, we're still going to have one," Rita said, grinning, and pulled her flare gun out from under the blanket on her lap.

THE STRANGE STILLNESS of the undead army had somehow turned the whole, Dimly-wide situation into nothing more than a localised tussle on the steps of the town hall, but as Rita turned the flare gun on Not-Lewis, everything exploded. The ranks of corpses lurched forward as one to protect their lord and master, and evidently the wolves that Kara had called did *not* approve of zombies. Either that, or they were invested enough in her that they took the surge forward as an attack on their baby necro. A howl went up from a lean, sleek wolf that I was almost certain was Lani, and on her signal the pack plunged forward, teeth bared. The dead didn't even try to fight them, just kept pressing toward the hall in their unfamiliar bodies, and as the wolves hit them, the walking corpses went down like old paper in a kitten fight, tumbling all over the place with their limbs flailing and taking out more of their buddies as they went.

It was *glorious,* and I'd have enjoyed it a lot more if we hadn't had a rather more pressing situation involving the magic-workers on the steps. Gerry still had one under each arm, and he was spinning in circles, using their flying legs to fend off other necromancers. Tony was standing well back, working away with his nail file, but others surged forward, rushing the steps and meeting a barrage of potatoes and something that smelled suspiciously flammable being squirted from Duds' water cannon. That suspicion was rapidly confirmed when one of the magic-workers conjured a fireball that turned into an unexpected case of spontaneous combustion. She shrieked and someone else threw her to the ground, flailing away at the flames with their jacket.

"That is *not on!*" Plait yelled.

"Neither's flinging fireballs at helpless old people," Lulu yelled back, and punctuated it with a thrown knife that Plait dodged, but which buried itself in a large, bearded man's upper thigh. He screamed and hurled a fireball back. It went wide of Lulu, and Singlet fielded it with his frying pan, sending it whistling back into the crowd, where it set a couple of the dead flaming. Duds promptly resumed his assault with the kerosene-laden water cannon, and there was a *whoomph* as spilled fuel caught. Above us, the upstairs windows of the hall crashed open, and someone shouted, "*Fire!*" Missiles curved out into the crowd, Molotov cocktails in old whisky bottles, and giant looted vases, plus bits of furniture and jars that burst to release clouds of thick, nasty-smelling gas that I'm sure would've been really effective if the undead had had any need to breathe.

"Impressive," Tam said, so close to my ear I barely managed not to jump.

"It's going to be more than that in a moment," I said, watching the fire leaping across the dead. "The whole town's going to go up."

"Is that a problem?" Pru asked from my other side.

"It is when we don't know who else is in here," I said. Which wasn't what I meant, exactly, but it sounded suitably concerning.

"Ah," Pru said, in a tone that said she knew I meant Callum.

A high, thin ring that could only come from the clash of metal that had been birthed from the very bones of the universe sent my ears back, and we all turned to look at Kara and Sonia. There was nothing fancy to their fighting, no magic involved, but I thought that was just because Kara knew she couldn't best the necromancer if it came to that. She was moving with a violent, frenzied speed, the scythe whispering though the air and shredding the day to dust, attacking hard, not giving Sonia a chance to do anything more than fend her off.

"Stop it," Sonia snarled. "What d'you think you're going to *do?*"

"Chop your head off," Kara panted, taking another swing. Sonia met it, and the blades slid off each other with a sound that made Tam growl at the back of her throat.

"That's rather specific," Rita said. She was watching the fight at the same time as she quickly reloaded the flare gun, then levelled it into the crowd, watching for the first of the magic-workers to make for the steps. Every time one tried she laid another flare at their feet, sending them scurrying back. Noel stood next to her, alternately catapulting potatoes at people and using a fire extinguisher to kill any flames that came sneaking up the trails of spilled kerosene toward them. Ez was crouched behind them, but I couldn't see what she was doing. Hiding, probably.

"My lord!" Sonia shouted, risking a glance at the Old One. "Put this child down!"

Not-Lewis just looked at the two women thoughtfully and said nothing.

"*My lord!*"

Not-Lewis turned back to the crowd and said, "Something is coming."

A shiver went through the undead, and the fallen clambered to their feet. Wolves still darted and snarled among them, avoiding the spreading patches of fire, but the corpses ignored them, turning to face the Old One, waiting for orders.

"Like a bloody hive mind," Lulu said, reaching into the sack of potatoes and coming up empty-handed. "Damn it, I'm out."

Hive mind. I looked from the crowd to Lewis, then at Tam and Pru. "He's controlling them."

"He's the boss type person," Pru said. "Of course he is."

"No, he's *controlling* them," I said. "Not ordering them. Whatever he thinks, they do."

Tam looked from me to Not-Lewis, and gave a thoughtful

little *hmph.*

"So we take him out, and then, what – they all just *stop?*" Pru asked.

"It's a working theory," I said.

Tam moved before I could even decide if it was a theory worth testing. She powered across the steps, pure muscle under her heavy pelt, and launched herself at Not-Lewis in one smooth leap.

"What's she *doing?*" Pru shouted, but I was already moving, sprinting after Tam. This was not what I'd meant. This was not *at all* what I'd meant, and Not-Lewis was already raising his hands lazily. He snatched Tam out of the air without even touching her, something unseen pinning her in the air like fruit in cheap jelly, and I saw her head tip as her body twisted out of true, her face contorted in a furious snarl.

I launched myself at the Old One, teeth and claws bared, and hit a wall before I could even get close enough to spit at him. It wasn't a slippery, slide-off wall either, but rather a grabby, wrap-you-up spiderweb-type wall, and no matter how I thrashed I couldn't get myself free of it. Pru came to a skidding stop just before she joined me, and now she yowled for Tam. I peered over at the big she-cat and met her bright green eyes, luminous with fury. But neither of us was moving, except as the Old One wanted us to. And the only moving he was interested in looked like it was about to remove Tam's head from her body.

"I say!" Tristan bellowed. "Stand down that, man! That is *not on!*"

"Save the cats!" Duds shouted, and shuffled toward us as fast as his cane would let him, only to hit the barrier that surrounded us. He staggered back, almost losing his balance, and Singlet grabbed him. Below, there was a sudden surge for the steps as Gerry's attention faltered, turning to us.

"Gobbelino!" he shouted, and threw two magic-workers back into their fellows before charging the steps.

Not-Lewis barely glanced at him. "This is very irritating," he said, almost to himself. "You are all so *irritating.*"

Tam let out a very small hiss of pain, barely audible over the clash of scythes and the snarl of wolves and the shouts of the magic-workers and the OAP army, and I watched helplessly as her neck went still further around. She couldn't breathe. No one could breathe with their head at that angle, and I yowled, *"Put her down, you power-sotted cabbage!"*

Not-Lewis ignored me, and he ignored Gerry too, as the troll collided with the barrier and bounced back, crashing into three magic-workers and sending them tumbling back down the steps. Gerry stayed standing, though, and came back for another try, bracing himself against the barrier this time and clawing at it, trying to push his huge arms through to grab us.

"Tam!" I yelled. Her eyes were still open, but they were losing focus, and her tongue lolled from her mouth, shockingly pink.

There was nothing I could do. Nothing anyone could do. All I could do was watch with my stomach sick and painful, and *I couldn't do anything.* I couldn't shift, couldn't—

"Someone break the charms!" I yelled. "Rats! *Rats!* Break the hall charms! Dimly's charms! Break *all* the charms!"

There was no immediate response, but somewhere on the edge of hearing I thought I caught urgent chitters, so maybe they'd heard. Maybe they could even do it, because if anyone knew the dark byways and under alleys of Dimly, knew the secret locks and fortifications of the town, and how to undo them, it was the rats. But it wasn't going to be quick enough. Not for Tam. I thrashed and twisted in the grip of the necromancer, not looking away from the big she-cat, even though I wanted to. If all I could do was watch, that was what I'd do.

And then Ifan, who had still been lying at the bottom of the portal, scrambled to all fours and launched himself at Not-Lewis, hitting him inelegantly but effectively at around knee-height with a distinctly painful-sounding crunch. The Old One gave a very human squawk of surprise and released both of us as Ifan took him down. Tam crashed to the ground, unmoving, and Pru bolted toward her. I wanted to as well, but I didn't. I raced for Ifan and Not-Lewis instead, Gerry thundering after me, and I shouted at the magician, "What now? What do we do?"

Ifan clawed at Not-Lewis, swearing and panting, trying to cling to the creature that was wearing his dad's body as it shoved and twisted and tried to hook the magician with the scythe without impaling itself. "Throw us through," he managed. "Gerry, *throw us through!*"

The troll hesitated, just for a moment, and that was long enough. I mean, I get it, hefting someone into another dimension isn't exactly the sort of modern troll behaviour Gerry was trying to embody, but given the fact that the world was ending, it seemed he could've done away with niceties, just this once.

With a hiss of triumph, Not-Lewis hooked Ifan through the shoulder with the scythe. The magician screamed, letting go of the Old One and grabbing his arm as if to hold it in place. Before Gerry or I could react, the creature had snatched Ifan up and hurled him bodily through the portal. The magician's scream cut off, leaving my ears ringing, and Gerry grabbed me, leaping back as Not-Lewis swung the scythe at us. It nipped Gerry's forearm, and the Old One dismissed us, looking around.

"*Enough!*" he roared. "*Take this world!*"

"Oh dear," Gerry said.

"You could say that," I replied.

23

NAUGHTY BOYS & END TIMES

THE UNDEAD MASSED TOWARD THE STEPS AND BROUGHT THE fire with them. They seemed indifferent to it, but the flames were spreading and catching, gobbling up their clothing and turning them into walking torches. The wolves retreated, their growls giving way to worried whines. The jacket potato cart was burning briskly, and the magic-workers broke out of the crowd, running up the steps to join Sonia and Kara, who had stopped their tussle to stare at Not-Lewis.

"Take this world?" Sonia said. "*Now?* Lord, I thought we agreed that in order to minimise resistance from the Folk and humans, we had to be methodical—"

"I do not need your advice," he said. He still had his own scythe grasped in one hand, but he clicked the fingers of the other. Sonia's scythe was ripped from her grip and spun across the suddenly silent steps to him. He grabbed it in his free hand, the two scythes meeting in an arch over his head. "And I do not need your foolishness. All this creeping around for what reason? Some cats and a human who yet evades you."

"A North—"

"A *human.*" He looked at Ez. "And if these Norths are such problems, put this one down."

Ez straightened up from her crouch, her face expressionless. Her hands were damp from being pressed to the ground, and she tucked them into her pockets. "I'm not a problem for you," she said.

"Evidently." Not-Lewis had got the hang of human sneers, if nothing else.

"I'm here because you need a North for the land to allow this," Ez said. "You don't need to worry about the other one."

"I do not worry about any of you. You are less than …" He considered it. "Very small things. *Minute* things. Tiny."

"Good grasp of imagery, there," Noel said, and Lulu cackled. "Very impressive."

"My lord," Sonia said, "Last time—"

"You were not here last time. I was. My brethren and I." He looked at Kara. "You will do."

"I will? I mean, *I will,*" she said, shifting her grip on her scythe and giving Sonia a triumphant look.

"I don't *think* so," Sonia said, and raised one hand toward Kara.

"This is good," Lulu said. "I always enjoy a good one-on-one scuffle."

Kara moved the scythe with more instinct than skill as Sonia unleashed a spell at her. The cold, thin metal shattered whatever had been flung her way, and I caught a whiff of something like burnt sugar as the spell crumbled. Kara gave a snarl of triumph, but Tony rose to his tiptoes and hurled a blast of power at her. She had her back to him, and it caught her between the shoulder blades. She cried out, falling to her knees, and Sonia swept in, wrenching the scythe away from her while the younger woman fumbled to grab it back.

"This is what happens when you get ideas above your station," Sonia hissed, and lifted the scythe, curving it into a smooth arc that would've taken Kara's head from her shoulders if three things hadn't happened in rapid succession.

Firstly, the wolves that had been trying to keep their distance from the burning undead finally broke for the hall, darting and sliding through the crowd. One hit Tony and took him to the ground, and two more made it halfway up the steps before Not-Lewis threw them back. It wasn't much, but it was enough to make Sonia hesitate, looking around. And that gave Kara enough time to simply throw herself down the stairs, tumbling away from the scythe.

Secondly, the distinctive, throaty grumble of something that sounded less machine than living thing rose from the streets outside the square, echoing off the walls at the sort of frequency that could shatter windows. I craned toward it with a wild hope rising in my chest.

"Is that the cavalry?" Duds asked. He was sitting on the steps, his stick gone and his hair dishevelled.

Thirdly, and before I could even put words to the hope, the noise of the engine was swallowed by the sound of ... a tidal wave? We all turned toward it, even Not-Lewis, his bland face puckering in some memory of concern, as the sound of rushing, crashing water grew. Glass shattered, and screams went up somewhere out of sight, and before I could even suggest that we might want to beat a hasty retreat to higher ground, green, foamy water surged into the plaza, bowling the undead off their feet, setting the magic-workers sprinting for the hall and capsizing the burning jacket potato van, which at least put the fire out. The weres and magic-workers charged up the steps to join us, and Gerry grabbed Rita's wheelchair with his free hand as water crashed toward us. The surge made it as far as the top step, swirling around the feet of those standing, then retreated, sucking most of the dead away with it. A startled silence descended on the square in its wake.

"What is happening?" Not-Lewis asked into the stillness, and glared at Sonia. "What is this?"

She gave him a cold look. "I'm not sure, Lord, but I imagine it's to do with that *foolishness* you were talking about."

Not-Lewis gave her a look that probably would've melted most people into a puddle of horrified goo, figuratively if not literally, but she just stared back at him, her scythe held at the ready, and all was quiet again.

In the silence I heard a splashing sound from one of the streets that led to the square, fast feet on wet ground, and more wolves appeared. They weren't running hard, because they were flanking a woman who was jogging in the manner of someone who's pretending they do a lot more running than they actually do, and the wolves weren't just keeping the undead away from her. They were keeping the pack of unruly, pale, floppy, and unnervingly teethy creatures that ran with her from escaping.

"Emma?" I said, from my vantage point in Gerry's arms, and I could hear the disbelief in my own voice. And if Emma was alright, then maybe ...

"Is this area clear?" she called, glaring around in a manner that suggested she couldn't *wait* to sic her ghoulets on someone. "Any dead?"

No one answered for a moment, then Ez said, "All clear, I guess?"

"Right," Emma said, and started jogging again, heading down one of the side streets. The ghoulets tumbled along with her, a wolf nipping at one to redirect it when it started toward the hall, and Gerry and I exchanged bewildered looks.

More footsteps, the sound of soggy boots taking long strides, and Callum followed the pack into the square with his coat hanging damply from his shoulders and his hands cupped as he tried to light a cigarette. He looked up, as if startled to find us there, and said, "Oh. Am I late?'

"Right on time," Rita said, and the motorcycle simply *arrived*, the quiet abruptly broken by the deep bass of the engine, the glass from the broken windows tumbling to the ground in fright. I understood how it felt. Motorbikes shouldn't be able to sneak up on you.

Ms Jones swung off the bike and pointed at Not-Lewis and the portal behind him. "Shut it," she said, her voice clear and ringing.

Claudia jumped lightly down off the bike, carting a small black kitten – who I was pretty sure was the Watch leader – by the scruff of the neck, and the bike just sat there, not on a stand. Waiting.

"No," Not-Lewis said, sounding bored. "Besides, it is too late. My brethren are here."

"You will shut it," Ms Jones said, walking forward with her rainbow-painted Docs squeaking softly on the damp stone. "And you'll do it now."

"No," he said again, and he didn't even raise a hand. Ms Jones flew backward, tumbling twice across the cobbles, and a collective gasp went up from the watchers.

"Grab him," Sonia said to the magic-workers, pointing at Callum, and Tony turned and ambled toward him, smiling.

I leaped from Gerry's arms and sprinted for Callum, glimpsing Ms Jones getting up as I did so. She looked more irritated than hurt. "Dude, do *not* trust Tony," I said as I reached Callum, and he grinned at me.

"Tony?"

"He's Tony," I said, nodding at the approaching magic-worker, who had his nail file out again. "He's all ... ugh."

"Got it," Callum said, looking at Tony warily. "You alright?" he added to me.

"*I'm* fine. What happened to you?"

"Tell you later."

By the hall, Ms Jones had taken the fight back to the Old One. Power surged back and forth between them, crackling and snapping and sending static electricity leaping across the square and exploding into sparks on anything metal. It was quite spectacular and was also threatening the structural integrity of not just the town hall, but possibly the universe. A few *oohs* were going up from the magic-workers – or those that weren't fighting among themselves. Kara was back on her feet and rallying her faction, and things among the junior necromancers were descending rapidly into a chaotic mix of the clumsy sort of scrapping that suggested no one had had much practice since nursery school, and misfired spells that splashed about the cobbles like living things. The distraction team was, quite wisely, abandoning stations and scarpering for safer ground in the plaza – or, in the case of Rita, being carried down the steps in her wheelchair by Gerry. Only Ez remained, crouching on the steps with her eyes fixed on Callum and her hands pressed to the stone.

I blinked at her, then said to Callum, "Tell me now. How'd you round everyone up?"

"You've been a naughty boy," Tony said, stepping in front of us.

"*Ew,*" we both said.

"You really don't have to do this, Tony," Callum said, and the other man frowned.

"My name's not Tony. It's Jim."

"Close enough," I said, and he turned the frown on me.

"I don't like cats," he said, and a load of little shocks raced up my legs, as if he'd set some supercharged fleas on me. I squawked, almost flipping over in an effort to get away from them.

"Stop it," Callum snapped, and grabbed for Tony's shoulder, but he stepped back easily.

"Naughty, naughty boys," Tony said again, and Callum yelped, slapping the back of his neck and twisting away. I couldn't do anything, as the mega-fleas were still raging on me, and Callum contorted, dancing about as if whatever I had, he had tenfold. Then a wolf came surging across the cobbles and took Tony to the ground, teeth at his throat. He screamed, and Callum shouted, "Don't kill him!"

The wolf gave him a look that very clearly said, *why not,* then leaped away, doing the same dance as we had. Tony sat up, smiling a pleased little smile, his hands raised, and the attacks on my hindquarters redoubled. Callum yelped, going back to his interpretive dance, and the wolf rolled onto her back, wriggling wildly to try and get rid of the magical fire ants or whatever he'd hit us with.

I'm not sure how long he'd have kept us there, still smiling his nasty little smile, if a cricket ball hadn't caught him smack in the back of his head. He face-planted to the ground without even a squeak, and the wolf sat up, giving us a disgusted look. I was pretty sure it was Yasmin. The look seemed very familiar. She loped off, giving voice to a howl. It was answered by more, rattling through the streets of Dimly, and Ms Jones looked toward us.

"*I need Malcolm!*" she shouted, and there was the edge of a scream to her voice, her dark hair loose and whipping around her. Sonia was helping the Old One, differences forgotten, and as we watched, the other magic-workers' fight faltered to a stop, and they turned toward the necromancers. Even Kara staggered around to face them, her face twisting with the effort of resisting, but it was no good. I could actually feel the power being drawn off them, feeding into Sonia as she faced the sorcerer. Her face was set and hard, white with effort, and Ms Jones braced herself against the combined onslaught as she turned back to face them.

"It's not about teeth, is it?" I asked.

"No," Callum said, and sprinted after Yasmin. I took a last glance at the battle on the steps, then went with him, because I wasn't losing him a second time. Patsy was right. It was starting to look careless.

THE STREETS of Dimly were a battleground. Wolves fought wolves, ghoulets scampered after the undead, Folk defended their homes and took the fight to the intruders with little apparent regard for who was on what side. Missiles were flung from windows and roofs, vegetables and bricks and charms, and still the undead came, wave upon wave. And what was clearer with every wave was that they were indiscriminate. Fauns were hauled from breweries, dwarfs from bakeries, humans from herbalists. Bodies were dropped in the street only to rise again with a golden glow and jerky, uncoordinated movements. Wolves were torn apart and abandoned. Only the ghoulets seemed impervious, and there weren't enough of them.

"How do we stop them?" I asked Callum. "How do we stop *this*?"

"We close the gate," he said grimly. "But we need the dentist. Yasmin!" he yelled. "*Yasmin!*"

A howl went up, and we struggled toward it, trying to keep out of the worst of the carnage. An undead turned eagerly toward us, and Callum belted her with a piece of pipe he'd liberated from outside a hardware store. She staggered, scowled, and started forward again.

"That did not work," I said.

"Nope," he said, and ducked through the nearest door. I scooted after him, and he slammed the door in the undead's face only to find ourselves facing a family of furious-looking elves, all of them with immaculate makeup and some very sharp knives. "Emergency?" Callum offered, and a moment later we were back out on the street. The undead lunged for us immediately, and this time Callum whacked it across the kneecaps and it went down with a horrible crunching sound.

"Sorry," he said.

"Bloody elves," I grumbled. "Could've let us stay."

"They're just scared," he said as we hurried on, the undead woman clawing after us on its broken limbs.

"So am I!"

"Yasmin!" he shouted again, and this time the howl was closer.

"So how did you get here? *With* Ms Jones and the weres and the OAP army?"

Callum fended off two undead who lunged for us in tandem, shoving one back while he kneecapped the other, then belting the second so hard that it spun away into the crowd and was set upon by two angry goblins.

"The river spirits," he said.

"The *sludge puppies?*" River spirit was a really pretty name for something that looked like nothing so much as an over-grown, multi-legged guppy.

"Well, mermaids, really."

"*What?*" I would've stopped, but that seemed inadvisable. "We're in Leeds!"

He gave me a sideways look and a grin. "All waters are connected. When Green Snake dropped the jet in the river, it ... I don't know. Sent a message or something. Murty must've been in the area, because he turned up just after you left. He roused Hayley and Dustin, and they were pretty happy to get me here and do a bit of flooding in Dimly. I don't think they've quite forgiven it for using Hayley as a figurehead mayor, or for all the magic and unicorn dust they've spilled in the river."

"*Murty,*" I growled. "Just in the area, was he?"

"That's what he said." Callum raised his pipe as a faun with a cast iron frying pan in each hand lurched in front of us, then lowered it again. "I do still owe him a favour."

I growled again, but decided we had more things to worry about than mermaids. "And Ms Jones? The OAP army?" I asked, as we stopped outside a pub where the sort of brawl legends are made of was taking place, undead being pitched out of windows and jammed into barrels, tables and chairs shattered to use as weapons, fauns and dwarfs and dryads all cheering each other on while the booze flowed indiscriminately and pixies sat in the hanging flowerpots hurling missiles at anyone who walked past below.

"No idea. I thought you'd got the sorcerer. And the OAP army probably felt they might be missing out on something."

"They're with us," someone said, and we both yelped. Yasmin grinned at us, a fluffy pink dressing gown wrapped around her and her canines still a little bloody. "We met them on the borders, and since they were obviously coming in anyway, we decided it was best to accompany them. Them and the ghoulet woman." She shuddered, and adjusted her collar. "Creepy beasts. Malcolm, then?"

"Please," Callum said. "And quickly."

"Let's go." Yasmin set off at a run, her bare feet seemingly impervious to the cold and the hard ground. We followed her, snaking and twisting through the alleys and side streets, the fight rolling and crashing around us like surf. The undead outnumbered the living painfully, and they were growing.

We stumbled to a stop at a small garage that had peeling signs advertising second-hand tyres and charmed spares, Callum trying to pretend he wasn't wheezing. Yasmin rolled the door up, and Malcolm jumped out of a folding chair, pointing a pair of chopsticks at us.

"Stop that," Yasmin said. "You singed Angie's ear the other day."

"I'm still learning."

"Well, don't practise on us," she said, and pointed at the car next to him. It was the ancient Land Rover we'd borrowed the other day, and she gave us a sharp look. "Don't use a screwdriver next time. The keys were under the seat."

"Help us next time, then," I said.

"I was unconvinced whose side you were on."

"And now?" Callum asked, swinging into the driver's seat.

"Half convinced."

"It's an improvement," he said, giving her the dimples, and the corner of her mouth twitched. She gave me a *humans* look.

We roared out into the streets, Callum laying on the horn and the accelerator in equal measure. We bowled a handful of slow-moving undead over, and as we drove Yasmin climbed half out of the window, raised her face to the low grey sky, and howled. Howls came back, shattering on the edges of buildings and bouncing off walls, and by the time Callum spun us into the plaza we had a comet trail of wolves following us, grey and black and tawny browns, running lean and muscled into the heart of Dimly, where reality shivered and the world shook and the town hall melted at the centre behind the warring magic-workers.

"Just in time," Yasmin said.

"Hopefully," Callum said, swinging out and dragging the dentist with him.

MS JONES WAS on her knees in the centre of the plaza. Not-Lewis and Sonia had come down the steps, and behind them everything of the town hall that was still standing was a seething, roiling gold. Whatever exchange of power had been going on, it had rendered the world porous. Things with too many limbs and things with too many eyes, or heads, things that oozed and things that crawled, they all poured out of the stretched portal, things so old that they'd forgotten what it ever was to be truly alive. They flooded down the steps, searching for hosts, crowding the place, and still they came, hungry for this world, hungry to touch and taste and feel and devour. Power snapped and snarled and rolled across the buildings, and the static had my fur standing out in half a dozen different directions. Gerry had Tam and Pru tucked into one big arm, and my heart did an unhappy little stutter at the sight of Tam sprawled motionless across the expanse of his grey skin. Ez had retreated as well, her face paler than ever, and when she saw Callum she took half a step toward him, then stopped.

"Ms Jones!" Callum shouted.

"Polly!" the dentist screamed, scrambling out of the car, and the sorcerer reached out to him. Callum didn't even have to push him forward. He ran directly into the vortex of power, still waving his chopsticks, and Ms Jones grabbed him, one hand on the back of his neck. The dentist's mouth became an O of surprise, but he didn't fight back. The sorcerer's power surged, and she rose to her feet, bringing Walker with her.

"The book," Claudia said, and I turned to look at her. Her blue eye was open again, but rather than the pale shade it had once been it was deeply, luminously dark, filled with strange galaxies. She limped toward me, shadowed by the kitten. "Walker absorbed some of the power of the book, and it's been building in him. He's like a battery bank for her, since you lost the actual book."

"Saved the world from pleasantness," I pointed out.

"But still lost her book."

"Is it enough of a recharge, though?" Callum asked, and the answer came back in the form of an explosion. For one moment I thought Ms Jones had sealed the portal, that it had been a collapse, but then I saw the raw, throbbing gold wound where the hall had been, and Ms Jones unconscious on the ground with the dentist next to her, patting her face anxiously.

"Oh, dude," I said.

"Is that it?" Duds asked. "Is *this* it?"

"No," Yasmin said. "It's never *it*. Not until you let it be." She spun. "Wolves!" she shouted. "This is what they bring us. Death for all. Don't be misled by promises of glory. *This is what they bring.*" And she flung an arm out to point at the undead, pouring back into the plaza, more of them than before, flocking to their leader.

Not-Lewis straightened his tie and said, "All those who serve will be saved. All those who do not"—and he looked at us—"will join the ranks."

There was a moment's silence, then Duds said, "Gives the rank and file a bad name, that."

"And we're not rank types," Yasmin said. "Are we?"

The howls that went up were deafening, not just from Yasmin's faithful, but from the wolves that had arrived with Kara too. But still, they weren't enough. I knew it, and the OAP army knew it, and the wolves knew it too. But sometimes you have to fight anyway. Even when you know there's no winning. Sometimes especially then.

"And when has a cat ever served?" I shouted.

"Unless you mean like, you got *served*," a new voice shouted, and I looked around, startled. Two kittens had appeared in the middle of the square, black and white reflections of each other, barely half grown but their eyes bright with knowledge.

"Or when *we* bring the serves," the other kitten added,

and they looked at each other quizzically. More cats were starting to step out of the Inbetween next to them, a scruffy mix of the old and the wounded, and half-grown cats with their memories still in flux. The shift locks were down, for all the good it might do. A grey cat with golden eyes appeared not far away, and looked around. I bared my teeth at him, and he tipped his head slightly. I couldn't tell if it was an apology or a *you'll keep*, but it hardly mattered right now. Cats who wanted to throw me into the Inbetween were the least of my worries.

"We'll serve *you!*" Tristan bellowed at Not-Lewis, which was probably a little optimistic, but we were all bouncing now, cats hissing, wolves snarling, the OAP army waving various makeshift weapons, their scrappy backup from the salvage yard shouting, and Sonia shook her head a little sadly, as if we were forcing her hand here.

The black kitten standing next to Claudia looked at me and said, "Go on."

"What?" I asked.

She looked up at Claudia, who didn't say anything, then back at me. "I don't know yet," she admitted. "But I think you usually do something?"

I looked at Sonia, holding the scythe she'd taken from Kara, and at Not-Lewis throwing a huge, bulky wolf that could only be Rav back into the crowd, then at the cats emerging to face the oncoming undead. There weren't a lot of us. But there were enough. We'd *make* it enough. I looked at the big grey cat again. *Boris.* And I did remember what he'd done, not just in Whitby, but in my previous death. But I remembered what he'd helped me do once, too. What I'd told him to do, because it had been my idea. My terrible, brutal justice. And Boris always followed. It was what he did.

"*Cats!*" I roared, loud enough that the word tore at my

throat. *"To me!"* And I broke into a sprint, straight at the Old One, without waiting to see if they were coming.

"The Watch!" Claudia yowled, plunging after me.

"Not bloody likely!" I shouted back, but I didn't stop. She caught up to me, and beyond her I glimpsed Boris running with us. The necromancers might be rising, but so were the cats, because we'd been here before them, before the humans, before the wars that had divided the world, and we were here still. I glimpsed Pru leap away from Gerry, and Tam, *Tam* was coming after her, and Tristan charged with them, and cats washed across the cobbles, a wave of bared teeth and furry backs and furious hearts. Because this was *our* world, *our* home in a strange and reeling universe, and we'd fight for it. No squishy old gods were just going to step in and take it.

The whole place erupted. Not-Lewis looked around in a nonplussed sort of way, and Callum yelled my name. The undead poured forward. The wolves raced to meet them. The OAP army and Gerry charged the magic-workers before they could intervene. Ez was on her phone for some reason, although the only good reason I could think of was upping her life insurance. Cold steel sang in high, fragile notes that could break the world, and as I passed Sonia I swerved away from the Old One and hit her instead, the other cats a wave that carried me forward. Carried us all forward, and into the gaping silence of the Inbetween.

24

AT THE END OF OUR ROPE

THE ENDLESS, FOAMING NOT-DARK ROSE UP AND SURROUNDED us, eager as a tar pit. Silence stuffed my ears and filled my lungs, and the utter, blank scentlessness of the place sent panic racing up my gorge. But then the void around me was rent with light as Sonia's flailing scythe hooked a corner of the world and shredded it, creating a hole in the tissue of the Inbetween. Cats flashed in and out, now one furry body against mine, then another, and I didn't let go, even as the necromancer's weight dragged us into terrible depths. I could have, could have leaped out and come back again, made sure the beasts didn't catch my scent, but what if that was the chance she needed to get free? What if it took longer if I left? *Too* long? I could feel her straining, trying to haul herself back to the world, and thought, *Come on, come on.*

More tears in the fabric of the void appeared around us, but so too did the sense of *presence*. Things pushing closer, shying away from the light but hungry and hopeful.

Come on!

Fewer and fewer cats around me now, no one wanting to hang around as things got more nippy, and still she tried to cut herself back into the world. The light that spilled from the tears lit calico fur and tatty tabby, naked cat skin and heavy ginger pelt. They were still here, and I wished they weren't.

Come on!

Sonia surged forward, half ripping her way back to the square, and I tasted her triumph, almost heard her scream of victory. And then finally, *finally* it happened. The moment was both violently sudden and painfully stretched. The necromancer was snatched away from under us, and we were left tumbling in the void as *things* flashed and snapped and tore. A whistle that echoed through dimensions marked the scythe's vanishing, and I had one moment to think, *got her*, before something wrapped me in a toothy embrace, and I was jerked away from the others.

Not entirely unexpected, no matter what anyone had said about the beasts not really having my scent, but still not ideal. I strained, trying to reach back to the world, but there was no escaping the grip of the void-monster. I just hoped taking Sonia out had been enough, that Ms Jones could deal with Not-Lewis now, and that my next life could be rather less eventful—

There was a roaring sense of impact that I felt in my bones, and the sense of teeth changed to *pressure*. I'd never wondered how far my limbs could stretch without breaking before, but apparently someone was trying to find out. I thought it was two of the beasts having a tussle over me, then the first one released me with a shudder that would definitely have been a scream if there had been any way to hear such things in here, and I came out of the Inbetween in an uncontrolled tumble. By rights I should have done a cartoon-style smash through the nearest wall, but I collided with something soft yet unyielding instead. My nose filled with the scent of musky, raw power, and Ms Jones yelled, "For the gods' *sakes*, Gobbelino, I was *busy!*"

I just stared at her, and she dropped me on the ground next to Claudia.

"Thanks," Claudia said, then tilted her head at me. "Nice move with the hair tie. Easy tracking." I shifted my stare from Ms Jones to her, not sure if all my limbs were still attached, and she added, "Alright?"

"Tam? Pru?" I managed, mostly because the answer to her question would consist of some wordless yowling and possibly a whimper, which I wasn't going to allow myself to indulge in in front of her.

"That's one down," Tam said from behind me, and I staggered around to look at her and Pru. Pru's jacket was torn, and there was blood on one ear, and she looked like she was quite prepared to eviscerate the next creature that looked twice at her.

"What?" I said, for want of anything more coherent.

Tam nodded at the steps, where Not-Lewis and Callum were staring at each other. It felt like we'd been lost in the monstrous not-dark for about three weeks at least, but Callum had got no further than the bottom step. He looked like he'd stopped mid-run with one hand out, the gold light from the hall turning the copper in his shaggy hair into soft fire.

"Hairy sushi balls," I said. "Can't a cat catch a break?" I tottered toward them.

"You," Not-Lewis said to Callum.

"Me," Callum said, warily.

"You are the North they spoke of," the creature said.

"I'm *a* North," he countered.

"Oh. Is that all?" Not-Lewis waved, and I braced myself, but Callum didn't move. I could feel the wind of the spell tearing at me, and I scooted a little closer to Callum's legs as he took his foot off the step and straightened up. "Ah. No. That is not all."

"You can't do this," Callum said. "I won't let you."

"It is done."

"It can be undone."

"Not by you. Not by *a* North." Not-Lewis flicked another spell toward us, stronger this time, and still Callum stood there, fishing his cigarettes out of the pockets of his old coat. It was split almost entirely up one side and was dripping on the cobbles, but he didn't seem to notice the cold.

"Maybe not. But it *can* be undone," he said, and looked back at the warring crowd.

"Them?" the creature asked. "Cats and humans and wolves. They're nothing."

"We're all nothing alone," Callum said, and inspected the wet cigarette packet before putting it away with a sigh. "But that's what creatures like you forget. You've been away too long. One small thing might be nothing, compared to you. But many small things are so, so much bigger."

"You are a very silly human," the Old One said severely, and he raised his hands and *shoved.* I went down, and this time Callum did too. He fell over me and we skidded away together like the cobbles were as slick as the hall tiles. He swore and slammed both hands to the ground to slow our slide, his face twisting as his skin tore.

"They were great last words," I said as we came to a stop, and he looked at me, eye-level for once.

He grinned. "I planned them."

"I thought so. Now what do we small things do? Because I'm guessing run is out of the question."

"No idea," he said. "I was hoping someone would sweep in and save us."

"That's never happened," I said.

"Right. So ... Attack?"

"Why not," I said, and we came to our feet pretty much together, although he had further to come. We charged, Callum yelling and me yowling, and Not-Lewis gave us such an astonished look that it was almost comical, except he was raising his hands to give us a blast of brutal magic at the same time. But Gerry hit him before he could let it loose, rolling the Old One across the cobbles in a charge that would've turned anything else to raspberry jam. Not-Lewis threw him back, but then Ms Jones was there, her face pale but set, setting a blast into the Old One that took both scythes out of his hands, and as the magic-workers lunged for them she flicked her hands, sending them snapping aloft then out of sight, into the Inbetween or whatever void sorcerers deal with. Callum hit Not-Lewis in a tackle and I leaped in with a couple of good bites just as Yasmin in wolf form came in from the other side. Malcolm rushed past Ms Jones to jump into the middle, all jabby-jabby with his chopsticks, and suddenly the whole place was nothing but a brawl. Not-Lewis was scrapping in a way he probably never thought he'd have to, using fists and feet instead of magic, unbalanced by the speed of our combined attack.

And, you know, it might even have worked. Maybe we could have torn old Lewis' body apart faster than he could have resisted, and then we'd have been able to do *something* with his blobby Old One form. If the sorcerer had still had her book, and we'd been able to use the magician, it would've been a real possibility. But the book was gone, and so was Ifan, and teeth and fists can only go so far against magic that's old as the earth itself.

Not-Lewis reached out, and it was Ez and Kara he dragged to him, crashing them into the crush of bodies, and Kara shrieked with fury as the magic was drawn from her. Ez snarled, her face twisting, and she shoved Callum.

"Get *out*," she hissed, but he didn't even have time to

reply. A pulse of power exploded off Not-Lewis, and everyone except Ez and Kara were thrown back in a tidal wave far fiercer than the one the sludge puppies had raised. I wound up on top of Lulu, who had been cushioned by a strategically placed wolf, and Not-Lewis roared, *"Enough! You will bow or you will perish!"*

"So dramatic," Rita said. She'd been pitched out of her wheelchair, but still had hold of a cricket bat. She pushed herself upright and looked around as if hoping for someone to kneecap.

"I vote perish!" Pru shouted. "Rather that than you lot."

"Right on, soldier!" Tristan called.

"As you wish," Not-Lewis said, and raised his arms, then paused, cocking his head like a dog hearing a whistle. "I hear …"

Kara struggled away from him. "You can't do this!" she shouted at him. "You can't use my power! It's meant to be a joint effort!"

"Quiet, human," Not-Lewis said. "I hear hooves."

"Unicorns," Ez said. She'd edged away from Kara and Not-Lewis, and now she stood slowly, grimacing.

"Unicorns?" the Old One asked, and for the first time his face looked almost natural as he smiled. "There are still unicorns?"

"One herd," Ez said, not looking at Gerry, who was on his feet already, the heavy plates of his forehead drawn down in concern.

"They were ours, you know," Not-Lewis said. "Our beautiful steeds." He turned eagerly toward the building sound of trotting hooves, ringing across the square. "My loves! Come to me!"

"He's got the hang of the humaning thing a lot better than last time," one of the black and white kittens said, poking his nose out from under a lean pale wolf that I thought might be Rav's boyfriend. "Getting all gooey over shiny horses."

"My little stabby equines," the other said, emerging next to him. "Gotta pet them all." They looked at each other approvingly.

The unicorns cruised into the plaza, knocking aside the undead that stood in their way, clearing the path for a heavy-framed mountain bike being pedalled somewhat erratically (although that could have been due to the three injured ghoulets in the basket on the handlebars) by a troll in bright pink dungarees.

"Oh, Poppy, no," Gerry said, his voice twisting at the edges, but Poppy didn't even look at him as she pedalled past. She just came to an unsteady stop and pointed at Not-Lewis.

"You is bad people," she said. "You do bad things to Gerry. And, and *everyone*. And I am no angry. But I am very, *very* disappointed."

"Yeah!" shouted the nearest unicorn. "So bloody disappointed!"

"My darlings?" Not-Lewis said, his tone a little puzzled.

"Don't you darling me, dead-lover!" another unicorn bellowed, and Poppy petted it soothingly, making it stagger.

"I knows you likes unicorns," she said, and her voice wobbled. One of the ghoulets tumbled out of the basket and bit the nearest magic-worker, who screamed.

"The unicorns are *mine*," the Old One said. "They have always been mine."

"They is their own," Poppy said severely, then took a deep breath. "But I lets them go with you if you makes promise to leave my friends alone."

"A promise?" Not-Lewis asked, and there was something in his voice that was close to laughter. "Oh, of course, of course."

"Told you we were irresistible," one of the unicorns said to the world at large, tossing her mane.

"Poppy," Gerry started, and she held her hand up sharply.

"No, Gerry, is my turn to looks after you," she said, and gave him a quick glance. Her three eyes looked damp and she sniffled. "I fixes this." She looked at Ez, then squeezed her eyes shut. "Go on, then," she said. "Go to the nasty mans."

"Yes, my darlings," the Old One said, spreading his arms wide. "Get away from the stone beast and come to your master."

They did.

It was very quick, and very messy. Unicorn horn can kill everything, after all.

OF COURSE, the Old One being down didn't mean the entire thing was over. There was still a bloody great portal to another world that had now devoured the entire town hall and appeared to be spreading, and more creepy golden beasties were still flopping and crawling and scrabbling out of it. The scythes were all gone, but the magic-workers had divided into factions that were evenly split between Kara and Tony, and they very rapidly got into a spat over who should control the Old Ones, as if anyone could. To be fair, it probably would've qualified as a magical firefight a couple of days ago, but after what had just happened, a spat seemed to cover it. It continued right up until Ms Jones walked into the middle of them, clipped both Tony and Kara around the ears and shouted, "If even *one* of you so much as boils water without using a kettle, I will throw you through the portal and leave you there. Understood?"

Tony started to say something, then sat down abruptly on

the ground, took his shoes off and started giggling at his toes. Ms Jones glared at Kara. "*Understood?*"

Kara might've still been hopped up on unicorn dust, but she was evidently smarter than Tony. She just nodded.

"Nice," Tam said, her voice rough, and I looked at her.

"Alright?" I asked.

"Could do with some custard."

"We'll see what we can do," Callum. He was surveying the undead army, who were drifting about somewhat aimlessly. Every now and then one would grab a wolf and try to nibble on it, or a human, but they didn't get very far. Unfortunately, they also weren't vacating the place. They didn't seem sure where to go, but they certainly weren't keen to go back into the portal. Every now and then a ghoulet pounced on one and dragged it off into the shadows, and I tried not to hear any crunching or dribbling.

"What do we do about this lot?" I asked Callum.

"I don't know. I had zero to do with any of this."

"Other than bringing everyone together," Claudia said, padding over to us with the black kitten still in tow.

"It was all sort of by accident," Callum said. "I didn't really *do* anything."

"You were the anchor," she said. "Sometimes it's not about leading. Sometimes it's about always showing up. Others tend to start doing the same."

He gave an uncomfortable shrug and went hunting in his pockets for his cigarettes again, although I doubted they'd dried out.

I looked at the little black kitten and said, "What about you? Any thoughts?"

She gave me a long, thoughtful look, then yawned so widely she just about fell over. I looked at Claudia.

"Yeah, she's still got a couple of weeks before we get much more out of her."

"All hail the Watch," I said, and she snorted.

"Want a job in the meantime?"

"Abso-bloody-lutely not."

"It'd be an easy one," she said. "The necromancers took out basically all the Watch cats. It'd just be making sure no one tries to take over until Anna's back on form."

"Again, no." I looked back at the kitten. "Sorry, Anna."

"I volunteer my services!" Tristan said, pushing in next to us. "Very happy to be of assistance."

"You've got enough to do calming this lot down," Claudia said, nodding at the OAP army. They were directing their backup from the storage unit to round up unconscious magic-workers, trussing them with cable ties and stacking them on the steps.

"Fair point," Tristan said, and wandered off. Ez glanced at him as she walked toward us, her feet still bare.

"Cal," she started, and he shook his head.

"No, Ez. Just no."

"Would you *stop*? What d'you think I was doing here?" She waved at her bare feet.

"Opening a portal to let monsters from another dimension through," I said. "Pretty obviously."

She scowled at me. "Really? You think Gerry *really* managed to damage the big, magical, interdimensional portal by *headbutting a wall?*"

I bared my teeth. "Well, you weren't selling bloody posies, were you?"

"I was trying to *stop* it," she snapped, and looked at Callum again. "Which I might've had a chance of doing if you'd bloody well helped."

"And I was meant to trust you?" he shot back. "Just *believe* you? After all the ..." He trailed off, waving wildly, then stalked off to where Lulu was waving a knife at a magic-worker.

We both watched as she put the knife away and got her cigarettes out, then I looked at Ez. "You were doing *something*," I said. "But I don't know what, and your track record's not great."

She gave me a half smile. "I guess I thought familial duty would win out."

"Family's what you make it. Don't think you've quite nailed it yet."

She didn't answer, and Callum looked at me as he walked back over, sucking on the donated cigarette. "We really need to sort out the dead and get these Old Ones or whatever the hell they are back into their portal."

"Sure," I said. "Let me just get my Old One herding whistle."

"It is, as you say, sorted," a resonant voice said right behind us. Callum yelped, I jumped through 180 degrees, and Ez said something impressively graphic. A robed, hooded figure stared at us. "I am sorry. Did I sneak up? Emma has said that I sneak up."

"Grim Yorkshire," Callum said, running a hand back through his hair. "Ah, hi?"

"It is sorted," he repeated, and drifted off through the crowd, his scythe swinging in smooth, easy arcs. The dead fell around him, and the golden forms didn't rise again.

Emma and Gertrude emerged from the crowd, Emma carrying two bloated ghoulets and half a dozen others trailing after them, burping loudly. Gertrude reaped a couple of the dead gently, her movements graceful, then looked at us. "Terribly sorry it took so long," she said. "We were getting the messages, but I had to impress on Grim Yorkshire how badly this could reflect on the end of year reports before he was willing to get involved."

"Are you alright?" Callum asked. "Emma said something about re-education."

Gertrude nodded, the gold light of the portal shining on the thin pale hair in the shade of her hood. "I'm not sure who was educating who by the end, really," she said, and kept moving.

Callum and I looked at each other, then at the crumbling crowd. "Can't really leave a gaping bloody portal in the middle of Dimly," I said to him. "That seems unlikely to end well."

"Probably not. But I have no idea how to shut it." He looked at Ez, and she shrugged.

"Me either."

"Great." Callum frowned suddenly. "Where's Ifan? He sent a message saying he was here with you."

"Yeah," I said, and looked at the portal. "That didn't end so well either."

"Oh," Callum said, and rubbed a hand over his face. "Right." And there was something so tired and aching in his voice that I wasn't even surprised when he got up and walked over to the portal.

I was surprised when he didn't stop, though.

I'D EXPECTED him to do some sort of sad farewell at the threshold, maybe tear his hair and wail a bit if he was really getting into it. But the magician had been as dodgy as pixie herbal tea, so we could get that over and done with nice and quick, then go and hunt out some custard. Only, instead of a decent display of mourning, the overgrown soggy parsnip just stepped straight into the wash of light coming out of whatever creepy dimension the Old Ones had been hanging out in.

"*Callum!*" I screeched, hearing Ez echoing my shout. "You fermented bloody *shark snot!*"

"What's happening?" Rita shouted. "Where's the boy gone?"

"In there!" I shouted back, sprinting for the steps. "Into the land of squishy damn gods!"

Ms Jones ran to meet me, but Ez was faster. She stuck a foot in front of me, bringing me to a stumbling halt, and looked at both of us. "I need rope."

"Seriously?" I demanded. "*You're* going after him? You'll just kick him a couple of times to make sure he stays down!"

"There's no time," she said, as Noel hurried up with a coil of rope in his hand. She snatched it off him, tying it around her waist. "Two tugs, pull us out." She stepped straight into the swirling mess of the portal without waiting for an answer.

"Got it," Noel said anyway, and Lulu pushed him out of the way to grab the rope. "Mind out, Lu."

"You're a gem, Noel, but one hand isn't going to be so speedy," she said.

"Give it here." Gerry had hurried up the stairs, and Noel, who'd opened his mouth to argue, shut it again and handed the rope to Gerry, who started paying it out steadily.

"How long can they last in there?" I asked the world in general. "What even *is* in there?"

Gerry glanced at me but didn't reply. I'd been in there, after all. It wasn't the Inbetween, but it wasn't much nicer. And it certainly wasn't made for living things.

The rope ran and ran, far further than seemed necessary, and Lulu hurried off, then came back with another. She secured the two together with a quick knot, then that was off too. How had Callum got so *far*? Were there things in there that had dragged him off? Was *Ez* dragging him off? Ifan? Both of them together? Were they fighting over which one got to kill him, and the rope was just getting tangled up in their squabbles? Was there— Ms Jones put a hand on my back and I flinched, memories of the time she'd tried to force a return to my last death still sharp in my mind. But she just rested her hand there, warm and calming, and I realised I'd been panting. I swallowed hard, and stared at the rope, willing it to stop.

"Do we have another?" Noel asked, his voice tight.

"No," Lulu said. "That's it."

"I has unicorn leash," Poppy said softly from behind us, and I turned to see sharp shiny hooves a little too close for comfort. She gave me a wide, craggy smile, but she still looked a little teary.

"Ez called you, didn't she?" I asked.

She nodded. "She tells me to bring unicorns to Dimly, then waits until she says. I is not happy, because I knows she does something not nice, but I does it. Because other things are more not nice."

"You did well," Gerry said, still paying out the rope. There were only a couple of metres left, and he let one more go, then clamped his hands down. The rope pulled taut, tight and straining, and he wrapped it around his hands for more purchase, frowning. "That's not ... they couldn't pull that hard."

No one spoke, and we were still staring at the rope as the angle rose slowly, the distant end lifting as something on the end of it took flight. It strained a little harder, then abruptly went slack. Gerry tugged it experimentally, but it didn't tighten.

"Does that mean it's broken, or something's flying toward us?" Lulu asked. She had a knife back in one hand.

"We have to close the portal," Ms Jones said, and looked around. "Whatever it is, we can't let it out."

"We can't shut it, either," I said. "Callum's still in there."

"I can go in," Gerry started, but even I joined in with the

chorus of *no*, and we stared at the slack line vanishing into the pool of gold that had been the town hall.

"How quickly can you shut it?" Noel asked Ms Jones.

"She *can't*," I said again, and no one answered. We were all wondering how fast the thing could fly, and what was going to come bursting out of the Old One's dimension. How many teeth, or claws, or mind-bending angles it might have. Time stretched long and thin, and I was painfully aware of the fragile borders of the world, drawn in morning dew and dandelion fluff. Fragile and already stretched to breaking by the day. It couldn't take much more. "Close it," I said, and the words tore my throat. "Get it closed. *Hurry!*" And as Ms Jones raised one hand, her eyes distant, power pulsing across her skin like waking dreams, I leaped for the portal.

If Callum was in there, I was going too. Because he'd only get himself eaten by something otherwise.

25

ALRIGHT IS ENOUGH

I HAD NO IDEA WHAT I WAS GOING INTO, DIVING INTO THE portal. It had been bad enough before, when it had only been slightly open, rather than this gaping wound in the world. But I wasn't staying out here while we locked Callum's only way home. We'd find another way out together. So I launched myself into a leap that should have taken me straight across the threshold, only to slam into an unyielding surface before my paws had so much as parted the boiling gold. I squawked, and instinctively hooked my claws into the barrier as it carried me out and away from the portal, and the scent of cigarette smoke and uneasy nights, damp as drenched fires, filled my nose.

Callum grabbed me with one arm before I could fall and said, "Less claws."

"Get it shut!" Ez shouted. "Quick as you bloody can." They had Ifan supported between them, and though he was conscious, his clothes were tattered and his face was scraped and bruising already.

"Put me down," he said, and Ms Jones gave him a sharp look.

"Can you help?" she asked.

"Yes, just *hurry.*" Even as he spoke a gust came out of the portal, something hot and raw and raging and filled with the sort of dust that could swallow the world. Callum turned to face the portal, still with one arm around Ifan, and the magician raised his hand to the glittering pool as it started to swell. Ms Jones stepped up next to him, and the power surged around us, the raw power of the sorcerer mixing with the sharp, inquisitive scent of the magician. The portal trembled, and Ifan said, "Cal." There was a hard, imperative note to his voice, and Callum dropped to his knees, the movement quick and urgent. He set me down and pressed one hand to the stone, the fingers of the other tangling through Ifan's.

I felt the power rise, and I wasn't the only one. Ez placed a hand on Callum's shoulder, her face pale, and behind us everyone who was able to move scuttled or shuffled or sprinted away from the hall. The cold grey of the day was for one moment blindingly bright as the portal *bulged,* outlining the shape of something that challenged the mind to make sense of it, and Ez dropped to her knees next to her brother, her free hand finding the ground between her bare feet.

Ms Jones lifted her face to the thing coming through and bared her teeth, and for one moment she towered above us, every year of her unfathomably long life etched on her skin like erosion on stone, and Ifan staggered, his mouth open as if he were crying out, but I couldn't hear over the howl of a wind that screamed through the square like it would shred reality to tatters.

"It's okay," Callum said, and his voice carried, quiet and calm. "It's okay."

There was one teetering moment when I thought the thing would tear its way through and swallow Dimly, and Leeds, and the whole damn universe, then it moved, some shifting in the bulges of its dimensions that suggested it was *looking* at us, which was in no way good.

"It's okay," Callum said again, and strangely, impossibly, he petted the stone step like it was a small, scared rabbit. "I can help."

And the grey, rainy day came back in like a hurricane moving through after the eye of the storm has passed. It swept the golden bulge of the portal back, forcing it in on itself, folding and twisting and bundling it, and everything was rain and hail and sleet and *snow*, which was excessive, and wind howled around us, strong enough that I took shelter by Callum's knees.

Which meant I heard him when he said, "I'm sorry I wasn't here. But I am now. For the north."

The portal vanished with a snap, leaving the town hall standing above us, a hollowed-out shell filled with a very localised but very violent storm. I found myself staring at Ez, who was so pale even Callum looked tanned next to her.

Then Ifan shouted, "It's coming down! *Move!*" And Callum grabbed me up just as Gerry snatched both him and Ifan by the backs of their coats and charged down the steps, everyone else scattering as the hall collapsed with the sound of worlds falling.

WILLIAM'S TEA house had been looted by anti-troll activists at some point in the last couple of weeks, but evidently the young troll still had enough contacts in town who'd talk to him now the threat of being eviscerated by necromancers was gone. He'd commandeered the sports hall that was attached to the swimming pool, a high-ceilinged, echoey place with wooden walls and a floor specially coated to handle faun hooves. We straggled in to find he'd enlisted the help of half the pubs in town, by the looks of things, and the place was crowded with trestle tables stacked with hastily assembled sandwiches and packets of crips and pork scratchings as well as mugs and urns of hot water for tea, while a truly excessive amount of beer and whisky lined one wall, guarded by a couple of grumpy-looking faeries. Against the opposite wall a large woman in a pink kimono was triaging injuries, and a dwarf was asking in an aggrieved voice why whisky wasn't classed as medicinal and available on prescription. A dryad kept trying to sprinkle witch hazel on the dwarf's injured arm, and the dwarf kept yelling they needed something stronger. Next to them, a faun with a burn dressing on their arm was sobbing about their potatoes.

After we'd slowly abandoned the wreckage of the town hall and made our way through the sodden town, Gerry had found a nice floral blouse that almost fit him and set about directing search parties to find any bodies the ghoulets hadn't eaten (there weren't many that we'd seen. Ghoulets are *hungry*), and to check for survivors from both the flooding and the fires that had been raging all through town, largely due to the OAP army's extravagant use of flammable liquids. The OAP army themselves had split up, Rita helping with first aid and Lulu directing sandwich making at a volume I could hear from clear across the hall, while Noel made tea for anyone who walked past and Duds tried to sneak whisky from the faeries, who couldn't seem to decide whether to humour him or bite him.

Callum sipped from a mug of tea and watched Ms Jones as she stalked across the hall toward us, trailed by Walker and Ifan. The sorcerer was wielding a bottle of whisky she'd snatched off a table in front of the faeries (they had very carefully not even looked at her), and Walker was telling Ifan that it had been his chopsticks that had really tipped the balance. Ifan, who had an egg sandwich in one hand, a whisky in the other, a large bandage emerging from the torn shoulder of his T-shirt, and an array of badly aligned, dinosaur-print plasters on his cheek courtesy of Poppy, just nodded and looked at me. He winked, and I narrowed my eyes at him. Just because he'd proved himself useful didn't mean I had to like him.

"Out," Ms Jones said, pointing at the doors to the swimming pool.

"I am not swimming," I said. "We've just saved the world. We should be exempt from swimming for ever after."

She just looked at me and kept walking, and we followed in her wake, because she was no less terrifying now that she was back to usual proportions and relatively human-looking.

It was quieter by the pool, just a small gathering sitting in the moulded plastic seats that ran down one edge. The double doors swung again behind us as someone else followed us through, and I looked around to see Gerry adjusting his blouse carefully.

I stopped as I saw the mermaid from Whitby sitting at the edge of the pool, one leg trailing in the water and the other pulled up to his chest. It confused the eye, like looking at two photos mushed clumsily together, a leg in what looked very like velour leisure wear matched up to half a sleek grey tail.

"What's *he* doing here?" I demanded.

"Hello to you, too," Murty said. "Is that any way to address someone who's fought the Sea Witch *and* Old Ones with you?"

I bared a tooth at him. "I didn't see you doing any fighting in there."

"Call it active support, then."

"Oh, right. Because you were just in the neighbourhood, right? What are you, our stalker?"

He gave me a wide, sharp-toothed grin, his eyes round and dark. "Hilda was worried about you, which meant Enid was worried, which meant *someone* had to make sure you didn't get eaten." He held a hand up. "I've got a friend of yours, by the way."

Green Snake coiled around the mermaid's fingers and flicked his tongue at us. He was looking smug again, but I wasn't sure he had much to boast about, calling a mermaid out on us. Even if the town flooding had been pretty handy.

Callum sat down in one of the chairs and looked at Emma and Gertrude, who were already seated. "Where are the ghoulets?"

"Sleeping it off in the back of the van," Emma said. "We're up to forty-four now, and I'm sure there were only forty-one when I arrived."

"Poppy would very much like to take some off your hands, but I'm afraid I've had to say no," Gerry said, lowering himself to the concrete floor. "It's enough worrying about the dragons eating a delivery driver or the unicorns stabbing a passer-by. She might come and visit you, though, if that's alright."

"She's very welcome," Emma said. "Maybe she can tell me why they keep multiplying."

"Well," Murty said. "When two ghoulets have been listening to Tom Jones—"

"You smell like fish," Tam said in her new, raspy voice, from very close to Murty's back. He jumped, almost slipping into the pool, and stared at her. She licked her chops.

Green Snake wriggled away from Murty and came to bump noses with me. "Sure," I said to him. "The going gets tough and you run off to join the fish-men."

"Which was very useful," Callum said, and looked at Ms Jones. "Are we okay now, do you think? Is it over?"

Ms Jones took a hefty swig of whisky and wiped her mouth with the back of her hand. "The portal's shut. I'm as sure of that as I can be. Doesn't stop anyone else trying to open another one, mind, but that Old One is very much dead."

"He is," Gerry said, his voice quiet. "I wish Poppy had never had to see any of that." He tugged at the sleeves of his blouse again, as if he were as ashamed of her seeing him in full troll mode as he was upset she'd seen her precious ponies stab someone to death. Even though the victim had been dead already, to be fair.

"It would've been worse if she'd seen what would have come after, if the Old One had survived," Claudia said. The black kitten was asleep next to her, all four paws in the air. "She did a good thing."

"It doesn't mean it was good for her," Gerry pointed out.

"That's far too often the case," Claudia replied.

"So," Ms Jones said, ignoring such concerns regarding the well-being of young trolls. She'd sat down, her elbows resting on her knees, and now she ticked things off on her fingers as she talked, the whisky sloshing in the bottle. "Old One gone. Portal shut. That bloody washing soap woman?"

"Who, sorry?" Gertrude asked, and Ms Jones waved impatiently.

"The one with the white jacket and all the curls. Necromancer."

"Sonia," I said, and the sorcerer pointed at me.

"Her. Sorry, my head's a bit scrambled still. Huge magical showdown and slamming giant portals'll do that to you. Plus I haven't had any sleep for weeks, what with all the bloody kittens. *Bottle feeding.* I'm a sorcerer, for the gods' sakes!"

"*You* didn't have to sleep with them," Claudia said. "Stopping them falling into the Inbetween every five minutes."

"I had to clean all the damn litter boxes, though. And the *mess* before they got the hang of them." Ms Jones took another large gulp of whisky and shuddered.

"I had to clean *them*," Claudia pointed out, and the sorcerer acknowledged that with a shrug.

"Fair point."

"Have a sausage sandwich," Walker said, offering her one.

"No."

"It'll help you get your energy—"

"Malcolm, I do not want a sausage sandwich. Get it away from me before I throw you in the pool."

He grinned at her, a broad goofy expression. "I missed you."

"Humans," Pru said, a note of wonder in her voice. She'd got rid of the tattered utility jacket, and was reclining on a fluffy towel someone had found her.

"Does this mean we don't have to keep him anymore?" Yasmin asked, and I jumped. I hadn't even smelled her come in over the stink of chlorine, her bare feet silent on the concrete. She crouched at the edge of the pool, trailing her fingers in the water. She'd swapped her dressing gown for a jumper and a long, soft skirt that pooled around her, and Murty examined her with interest.

"Are you sure you don't want to?" Ms Jones asked.

"I really don't."

Walker took a large bite of sausage sandwich, looked at Ms Jones and said, "You don't mean that."

"I might. Where was I?"

"Portal. Not-Lewis. Sonia," I said.

"Yes. Is she gone?"

I shivered, feeling the whip and crack of swift, hungry beasts. "She's gone."

"The scythes?" Gertrude asked. "Grim Yorkshire is rather keen for me to report back on this. He and Ethel are just checking they've caught all the souls and removed any lingering Old Ones." She frowned. "They weren't very … *impressive*, the rest of them."

"Legends are tricky things," Claudia said. "Maybe they sort of melded together when they were banished from the world. Clung to each other so tightly that they became one mind. Or maybe it was only ever one real Old One, and the rest nothing but offshoots of his power." She shifted away from the kitten, who followed her in half-asleep instinct. "Gods. Really, will *no one* take on some kitten sitting?"

Ms Jones gave a little grunt of agreement around her whisky.

"That makes sense," Gertrude said thoughtfully. "Stories are so malleable. They change in every telling, and every hearing."

"The scythes are gone, though," Ms Jones said. "One fell into the Inbetween with Sonia. The other two I threw into the void."

"Is that the same void as the Inbetween?" I asked her, and she shrugged.

"It's *my* Inbetween." She clicked her fingers. "And I'll have my hair tie back, too."

I held my paw up to her so she could pull it off, trying not to think of the sort of beasts that were loose in a sorcerer's void.

Gertrude considered it for a moment, then said, "I suppose all we can hope is that they're lost enough."

"Well, there's no getting them back," Ms Jones said. "It'd be pure bad luck if anyone stumbled on one in there."

I thought of the way Sonia's blade had rent the fabric of the Inbetween, and wondered. But not for long. I'd had enough sleepless nights. "You should have an auto-destruct function on them," I said to Gertrude. "It's very careless."

She gave me an amused look from the shadows of her hood. "One does not expect a reaper to lose their scythe."

"Well, you should *now*."

"So we're done?" Yasmin asked. "Is this what we're saying? The necromancers are all done?"

"There's a handful of magic-workers left," Gerry said. "They've been rounded up and are being held in the Blue Sprite pub."

"That doesn't sound very secure," Emma said.

"The town hall didn't have the only dungeons in Dimly," Gerry replied.

"Ez?" Callum asked, sounding tired. "And Kara?"

"Ez did what she did for the north," Gerry said. "She's out there helping with the search parties now. She wanted to stay and talk to you, but I told her she was better to make herself useful for a while first."

Callum nodded and sipped his tea.

"I think she meant well," Gerry added quietly. "I believe she really thought she could keep the north safe and handle the necromancers. And by the time she realised she couldn't, it was too late. All she could do was try and keep you out of it by claiming herself as the only North."

Callum didn't answer for a moment, then said, "I should have been here."

"You were when it mattered," Gerry said, and patted him on the shoulder as gently as a troll can, which was probably going to leave bruises.

"Is that enough?" he asked.

"It was in the end," Gerry replied, and then there was silence for a while, broken only by the hum of voices in the sports hall. It sounded like Duds was leading an off-key but very enthusiastic rendition of "Mr. Brightside".

"What about Kara?" Ifan asked, looking at Gerry with his eyebrows raised.

Gerry hesitated, then said, "We'll find her."

"You've *lost* her?" I demanded. "What about that creepy Tony?"

"Which one was that?"

"Anorak and nail file."

Gerry frowned. "I'll have to check. I don't think I've seen him."

"So not *all* of them," Claudia said, and yawned. "That's fine."

"That's *fine?*" I demanded. "What's *fine* about the strongest and the most bonkers magic-worker both still being out on the loose? What could *ever* be fine about that?"

She gave me an amused look from her mismatched eyes. "It's fine because it's alright for now. That's all anything can ever be, Gobbelino. Alright for now."

I looked at her for a long moment, then said, "Well, it's *not* alright, because I have no custard. And if there are necromancers in the world still, there also needs to be custard. Balance, you know."

"It doesn't do much for your digestive balance," Callum said, taking another sip of tea, and I glared at him.

"Fish," Tam breathed, still staring at Murty, who edged away from her along the edge of the pool. She followed, and Ifan burst out laughing, winced and touched his cheek, then started laughing again.

"What're you on, Magic Boy?" I demanded.

"Survival," he said, grinning.

"It's not humans," Yasmin said, shaking her head. "It's you lot. There's something very, very wrong with you all."

"I did wonder," Gertrude said, and Ifan just laughed harder.

THE STORM HAD DISSIPATED, spreading out into a gloriously plain grey Yorkshire sky, and the afternoon was fading into early night when Callum let us out a side door of the sports centre and onto the banks of the river. It was still drizzling, so he ambled over to a bench with a little wooden roof protecting it, which overlooked the slow green flow of the water. I followed him, the grass damp and giving under my paws, and jumped up onto the bench next to him as he lit a cigarette.

We sat in silence for a little while, watching the river flow past, holding dark secrets and helpful sludge puppies in its unseen depths. The air smelled wet and claggy and heavy with the scent of spent magic, but there was a whiff of freshly turned earth and green shoots in it too. It smelled like an early spring was on the way, which was nice, considering the world had been about to end a couple of hours ago.

"So you never learned how to tap into the power of the north, then?" I said finally, and Callum gave me a sideways look, then puffed smoke over his lower lip softly.

"I didn't. But I just … I could feel it. The pain of being torn apart, over and over, and no one doing anything to protect it, and it was just so *tired* of being used. Of everyone who swore to protect it only protecting the bits that they cared about, not the whole thing. Using it for their own ends. Never even seeing it, not really. So I … helped, I suppose." He drew on the cigarette deeply, then grimaced. "I need to stop these."

"You do," I agreed.

"You quit custard, I'll quit smoking."

"Custard's not going to kill me."

"The fumes might."

I bared my teeth at him and he grinned, and scritched the back of my neck gently. We watched the river for a little longer, then he said, "So, Watch lieutenant or something, is it?"

"I suppose." I watched a log drift past, a six-eyed, long-limbed frog-type thing with gauzy wings perched on top. It goggled at us. "Retired, though."

"Good background for a PI."

"You won't have much time for PI-ing, what with all the north protecting going on."

He ground the butt of his cigarette out and flicked it into the bin. "I think Gerry can take care of most things. He's good at it. I can just be around if needed."

I considered it, then said, "Can we agree we need to take proper cases, though? Otherwise I think we should pivot to handy person work. Much less likely to get us eaten."

"You just like the fact that it means you don't have to do anything."

"I see no problem there."

Callum snorted, and we stayed where we were, watching the deep green river, while behind us in the hall humans shared bottles with Folk, and werewolves argued with mermaids, and reapers loved the living, and trolls built bridges, and sorcerers questioned their choices of partners, and cats moved and drifted through it all, ever present and always watching.

And none of it mattered right now. Because whatever came next, wherever Kara and Tony surfaced, whatever might happen with the warring factions of weres, whatever challenges Gerry faced in Dimly, whatever side Ifan and Ez had been on or were on now, that was for the future. For now we had stood together against a threat bigger than all of us, against older and stronger things that had been one seamless whole and thought us too small and divided to be worth anything. For now we had stood together against those who believed there was only one kind worth being, only one permissible way of living, and we had won by the very fact that we were as wildly different as we were deeply connected.

And now was the slow turn of the river, and the soft whisper of the rain on the roof above us, and the chill on my whiskers that was as fresh and sharp and glorious as a promise. Now was Callum with his long legs stretched out in front of him and crossed at the ankles, and me with a few new scars for my collection, but with all limbs intact. With my *life* intact. Now was him scritching me between the ears, and me arching my neck so that he could get just the right spot, and now, right at this moment, everything was alright. And Claudia was right. That was all we could ask, and all we could hope for, and it was enough.

I looked up at Callum and he nodded at me, and Green Snake stuck his head out of Callum's sleeve, and that was alright too.

Then there was a soft splash from the river, and we all looked toward it. Murty's sleek head bobbed just off the bank, dark and big-eyed as a seal. "That's two favours you owe me," he called, and winked, then vanished beneath the opaque waters. We stared at the spot where he'd disappeared for a moment.

"Well that's just bloody fantastic," I said.

Callum shrugged and got up. "It's not the end of the world," he said, and I narrowed my eyes at him.

"Too soon," I said. "*Way* too soon."

He grinned, and led the way back to the warmth and chaos of the hall, and I trotted after him with my ears back against the rain.

It *wasn't* the end of the world, true. But one close call had to be enough for one lifetime.

Didn't it?

THANK YOU

Lovely people, thank you so much for joining me (and Leeds' best magical investigators) on this convoluted and often tentacled adventure. I never realised when I first wrote a short story about a feline PI (inspired by one of those "the name of your first pet plus the last place you went on holiday is your PI name – oh and let's see if it's your password too" social media posts) just how many of you would fall in love with an opinionated black cat with a shaky grasp of human idioms and his messy-haired partner.

And I'm so very delighted you did, because I've had the most enormous fun writing this series. Seriously, you can say *anything* when you're writing as a cat … More seriously, though, thank you. Thank you for reading, thank you for messaging and emailing and chatting with me on the social medias, thank you for helping me to name all the various books, and thank you for believing in the magic that sneaks around on the edge of our vision, as well as the magic that lurks in every one of us. I've had a fabulous time, and I hope you have too.

This may be the last Gobbelino London story (I say *may* because, as I say, I had so much fun writing it that I'm not ruling out another series in the future), but it's very much not the last weird tale of Yorkshire magic. So I hope you've got your tea handy. We're going to need it ...

As always, lovely people, if you did enjoy this final, catastrophic and somewhat chaotic instalment, I'd very much appreciate you taking the time to pop a review up at your favourite retailer, or Goodreads.

Reviews aren't just about soothing the writer's fragile ego (as much as they do work exceptionally well for that). Good reviews mean the bookshops decide we're not publishing complete rubbish, so they recommend us to more readers. More readers means more demand means more books get written, resulting in very happy writers and hopefully just as happy readers. So thank you so much for helping perpetuate what is a very lovely cycle indeed!

And if you'd like to send me a copy of your review, an adoption application for a ghoulet, cat photos, or anything else, drop me a message at kim@kmwatt.com. I'd love to hear from you!

Until next time,

Read on!

Kim

(And head over the page for some what-happened-after stories, as well as a reading suggestion regarding things happening elsewhere ...)

BEWARE THE SNAP-SNAP-SNAP ...

There may not be cats. It may not even be Yorkshire. But there are bridges, and ducks, and the *snap-snap-snap* ...

Discover the first DI Adams book today! (The series will continue in 2024.)

Baton. Light. Chocolate. Duck.

This is not DS Adams' usual kit. This is not DS Adams' usual case. She doesn't think it's *anyone's* usual case, not with the vanishing children and the looming bridge and the hungry river. Not with the *snap-snap-snap*.

But six kids are missing, and she's not going to let there be a seventh. Not on her watch. And she knows how to handle human monsters, after all. How different can this really be?

So: Baton. Light. Chocolate. And the bloody duck.

Let's be having you, then.

Scan the code to grab your copy, or head to the link to find yours: https://readerlinks.com/l/3527761/g7bm

HOW TO START AGAIN

Just because they saved the world doesn't mean they get a day off ...

Kittens still need cat-sitting.

Cats are still in search of custard.

Sorcerers are still having relationship issues.

And a certain quartet of retirement home residents have a little explaining to do ...

Discover just what did happen after The End. After all, sometimes saving the world is just where things start.

Scan the code or go to the link to grab your free story collection:
https://readerlinks.com/l/3527762/g7rm

PS if you're already subscribed to the newsletter, you won't be double-subscribed. May ghoulets nibble my toes if I lie ;)

ACKNOWLEDGMENTS

Thank you, lovely reader. Thank you for joining me on this strange and slightly toothy adventure, and sticking with me all the way to the end. It's a lot, to put your trust in some stranger hunched goblin-like over their computer half a world away, ranting on about cats and dragons and the power of tea. And I don't take that lightly. You are amazing, and it means the world that you've loved Gobbelino and Callum (and Green Snake) and all their assorted companions as much as I have. Thank you for helping me bring them into the world.

To my wonderful beta readers, especially Tina and Jon, who have never missed an instalment, and never fail to point out the gaps that live under the stairs of the story, correct me on my misapprehensions regarding animal behaviour and York-shire geography, and make me laugh while they're at it. You're the best sort of magic.

To my wonderful editor Lynda Dietz, of Easy Reader Editing, who has alerted me to the war-starting issues of hyphenation, the morphing of my Barry fixation, and the trademarking of lino. I couldn't ask for a better editor or friend. As always, all good grammar praise goes to Lynda, while all mistakes are mine. Find her at www.easyreaderedit ing.com for fantastic blogs on editing, grammar, and other writer-y stuff.

Thank you to Monika from Ampersand Cover Design, who is an author-whisperer and always creates something both hilarious and beautiful. Find her at www.ampersandbookcovers.com

And to all my wonderful, supportive, and delightfully strange friends and family, online and off, thank you. Thank you for encouraging me to be my own weird self. You're fantastic.

Now, lovely readers – on to the next adventure!

Read on!

Kim x

ABOUT THE AUTHOR

Hello, lovely person. I'm Kim, and in addition to the Gobbelino London tales I also write other funny, magical books that offer a little escape from the serious stuff in the world and hopefully leave you a wee bit happier than you were when you started. Because happiness, like friendship, matters.

I write about baking-obsessed reapers setting up baby ghoul petting cafes, and ladies of a certain age joining the Apocalypse on their Vespas. I write about friendship, and loyalty, and lifting each other up, and the importance of tea and cake.

But mostly I write about how wonderful people (of all species) can really be.

If you'd like to find out the latest on new releases, discover other books and series, plus find free reading, recipes, and more, jump on over to www.kmwatt.com and check everything out there.

Read on!

amazon.com/Kim-M-Watt/e/B07JMHRBMC

facebook.com/KimMWatt

instagram.com/kimmwatt

twitter.com/kimmwatt

youtube.com/@KimMWatt-yd1qb

bookbub.com/profile/kim-m-watt

goodreads.com/kimmwatt

ALSO BY KIM M. WATT

The Gobbelino London, PI series

"This series is a wonderful combination of humor and suspense that won't let you stop until you've finished the book. Fair warning, don't plan on doing anything else until you're done …"

– Goodreads reviewer

The Beaufort Scales Series (cozy mysteries with dragons)

"The addition of covert dragons to a cozy mystery is perfect … and the dragons are as quirky and entertaining as the rest of the slightly eccentric residents of Toot Hansell."

– Goodreads reviewer

What Happened in London (a DI Adams prequel)

"This book will grip you within its story and not let go so be prepared going in with snacks and caffeine because you won't want to put it down."

– Goodreads reviewer

Short Story Collections

Oddly Enough: Tales of the Unordinary, Volume One

"The stories are quirky, charming, hilarious, and some are all of the above without a dud amongst the bunch..."

– Goodreads reviewer

More free stories!

The Cat Did It

Of course the cat did it. Sneaky, snarky, and up to no good – that's the cats in this feline collection, which you can grab free by signing up to the newsletter. Just remember – if the cat winks, always wink back ∴.

The Tales of Beaufort Scales

A collection of dragonish tales from the world of Toot Hansell, as an extra welcome gift for joining the newsletter. Just mind the abominable snow porcupine ...